MONSTER
BLOOD TATTOO

BOOK ONE: FOUNDLING

❦ D.M.CORNISH ❦

With illustrations by the author

CORGI BOOKS

MONSTER BLOOD TATTOO
A CORGI BOOK 978 0 552 55587 6

First published in Great Britain by David Fickling Books,
a division of Random House Children's Books
A Random House Group Company

David Fickling Books edition published 2007
Corgi edition published 2008

1 3 5 7 9 10 8 6 4 2

The Random House Group Limited supports the Forest Stewardship Council (FSC),
the leading international forest certification organization. All our titles that are printed on
Greenpeace-approved FSC-certified paper carry the FSC logo. Our paper procurement
policy can be found at www.rbooks.co.uk/environment.

Corgi Books are published by Random House Children's Books,
61–63 Uxbridge Road, London W5 5SA

www.kidsatrandomhouse.co.uk
www.rbooks.co.uk

Addresses for companies within The Random House Group Limited
can be found at: www.randomhouse.co.uk/offices.htm

THE RANDOM HOUSE GROUP Limited Reg. No. 954009

A CIP catalogue record for this book is available from the British Library.

Printed and bound in Great Britain by CPI Bookmarque, Croydon, CR0 4TD

For Will and Mandii,
who were the first to believe

CONVERSION TABLE

DISTANCE
1 inch = 2.54 centimetres or 25.4 millimetres
1 foot = 30.5 centimetres or 305 millimetres
1 yard = 0.914 metre or 91.4 centimetres
1 mile = 1.61 kilometres or 1610 metres

SPEED
1 knot = 1.85 kilometres per hour

MASS
1 pound = 0.454 kilogram or 454 grams
1 ton = 1.02 tonnes or 1020 kilograms

CONTENTS

LIST OF PLATES

ACKNOWLEDGMENTS

Amazed gratitude first to God, the opener of doors; to Dyan, my lofty and passionate publisher, whose enthusiasm has fuelled this book from the start; to Celia, my ever-patient and tactfully brilliant editor, who makes me look like a better writer than I really am; to Eija, my equally patient art director, for bearing with my neurotic ways and for linguistic appreciation; to Geoff and Ricki, my loving parents, for living an example to follow and for giving me a safe place to land; to Will, faithful friend, for all those sessions in which we bounced ideas about. It is to him that I owe the term "monster-blood tattoo" – the very title of this series. Genius. To Mandii, insightful friend, for loving Europe as much as I do, and for "brown"; to Jacey, far-off encourager, for all the advice, from types of cloth to what was right and wrong; and to those who have read manuscripts or encouraged me through it all: my daring and caring sister Sheri, Phil "Mr Ip" and Em "Mrs Ip", Matty McHam, Craigus Grovus, Edwin "Man of Steele", Gary, Toom, Kirsty-Lee, Sue-Ellen, Jordan, David B, Cheryll, Ange, Maggie, Raquel, Emily, Andrew and Steph, the Cousins Lock, David K and the Once-a-Month-Wednesday Illustrators, and any others my sieve of a mind has neglected. Thank you.

D.M.C.

This is the map of the southern and central portions of the Half-Continent. The area within the small rectangle is shown in detail on the following page. There are also several pages of enlargements of this main map towards the end of the book.

a map showing the Area of

ROSSAMÜND'S
PEREGRINATIONS

- **O** MAJOR CITY
- **o** MINOR CITY OR LARGE TOWN
- ▫ LONE STRONGHOLD
- ▭ RIVERGATE
- ROAD
-  SWAMPLAND

KILOMETERS 0 100

MILES 0 100

GELDERLAND

YELLOW BILE

BLACK BILE (SCHWARTGALLIG)

AESTIVIUM
(THE SUMMER PALACE
OF THE
GIGHTLAND QUEEN)

WOORD

SOTIGHIEM

EVENGENIN

CONDUIT FELIX

HERGOATENBOSCH

ANDOVER

SEVEN PARISH

BOSCHENBERG
(THE AXLES)

CONDUCTOR CREPITUS

WURST

FIVE INCH PARISH

CONDUCTOR SECUNDA

S
U
L
K
(TRACTUS)

THE HUMUS

EINGHENIN

PROUD SULKING

CONDUIT STERCUS

HUMOUR (HUMEUR)

VESTIWEG

THE MOLD

THE IDLEWILD   WIGHTBURY

THE SPINDLE

CONDUIT VERMIS
(THE WORMWAY)

SMALLISH FELLS

WINSTERMILL

THE SPARROW DOWNS

THE MIGH

FAYELILLIAN

SILVERNOOK

HAREFOOT DIG

THE SOUGH
(BRINDLESHAWS)

HIGH VESTING

SMALL

BRANDENBRASS

ACNE

GIZZARD

BENNAT LEA

AUDAGOST

SILT MOUNDS

NEEDLE
GREENING

FISHFOLD

USELESS

USE

THE
GRUME

DOGGEN-BRASS

DOGGER STRAND

(BRANDENMEER)

N

ROSSAMÜND

IT BEGAN WITH A FIGHT

foundling (noun) also wastrel. Stray people, usually children, found without a home or shelter on the streets of cities or even, amazingly, wandering exposed in the wilds. The usual destinations for such orphaned children are workhouses, mills or the mines, although a fortunate few may find their way to a foundlingery. Such a place can care for a small number of foundlings and wastrels, fitting them for a more productive life and sparing them the agonies of harder labour.

ROSSAMÜND was a boy with a girl's name. All the other children of Madam Opera's Estimable Marine Society for Foundling Boys and Girls teased and tormented him almost daily because of his name. And this day Rossamünd would have to fight his worst tormentor, Gosling — a boy who had caused him more misery than any other, a boy he worked hard to avoid. Unfortunately, when it was time to practise harundo, there was no escaping him.

At Rossamünd's feet was the edge of a wide chalk circle drawn upon floorboards so fastidiously cleaned that the grain protruded as polished ridges. Opposite stood his enemy. Regretting the ill-fortune that had paired him with his old foe, Rossamünd frowned across the circle; sour-faced and lank-haired, Gosling stared back contemptuously. The blankness behind Gosling's eyes terrified Rossamünd; his opponent was a heartless shell. He delighted in causing pain, and Rossamünd knew that he would have to fight better today than he ever had before if he was to avoid a beating.

"I'm going to thrash you good, Rosy Posy," Gosling hissed.

"Enough of that, Young Master Gosling!" barked the portly cudgel-master, Instructor Barthomæus. "You know the Hundred Rules, boy. Silence before a fight!"

Both Rossamünd and Gosling wore padded sacks of dirty white cotton, tied with black ribbons over their day-clothes. Each boy held a stock – a straight stick about two and a half feet long. Harundo was a form of stick-fighting, and these were their weapons.

Rossamünd was never able to get a comfortable hold on a stock. With the fight about to start, he shifted his awkward grip again. He tried to remember all the names, the moves, the positions he had ever been taught. The Hundred Rules of Harundo made perfect sense, but no matter how often he had trained or fought in practice, he could never make his body obey them.

In Madam Opera's Estimable Marine Society for Foundling Boys and Girls the only room large enough for harundo was the dining hall. Trestles and benches had been dragged clear and left higgledy-piggledy against the walls. The cudgel-master raised his whistle and the two dozen other children standing around the circle fell silent. Rossamünd noticed some of them grinning knowingly. Others stared – slack-jawed and wondering – while the littlest shuddered with fear.

Gosling twirled his stock with a swagger.

Rossamünd looked to the over-cleaned floorboards and waited.

The whistle shrilled.

Gosling strutted into the ring. "Time to get your scourging, Missy," he gloated. "You've managed to dodge me all week, so you'll suffer extra today."

"That is *enough*, Gosling!" bellowed Barthomæus.

Rossamünd barely heard either of them. The Hundred Rules were racing madly about his mind as he stepped into the chalk circle. If he could just get them straight in his head, surely his limbs would follow!

With a venomous snarl, Gosling rushed him.

The tangle of Rossamünd's thoughts served only to tangle his body. *Were his hands in the right place? What about his feet? How close was he to the edge of the ring? What was Instructor Barthomæus thinking of what he was doing? What would happen if he actually did land a blow?*

Gosling swept up his stock clumsily. He was not much better at harundo than Rossamünd. Any other child, even many of the little ones, would have stepped out of the way, just as they should, and given Gosling a good crack on his back or shoulder. Instead, Gosling's vehemence forced Rossamünd to take a clumsy backward step. By a small miracle, he got his stock up in time to swat away this first strike. The sticks collided with a deeply satisfying *Chock*!

Gosling gave a furious curse as he was thrown back. He bared his teeth.

That felt right! Rossamünd thought, a tiny glow of triumph within.

"No, dear boy! No! *Left* decede, then counter-offend with a culix!" Instructor Barthomæus hollered at Rossamünd. "You've seen it done. You've practised it, lad! Just step away, then behind, then a *jab-jab-jab* with the handle! A half-hearted sustis is just not enough, boy!"

Rossamünd was deflated. Just when he thought he was getting it right, he was actually doing things worse than ever.

Gosling was on him by then, chopping at his head again and again with his stock. Rossamünd blocked one strike, swatted away another, then let one through. It smacked him crunchingly hard across his cheek and mouth. His head bursting with agony, his face stinging, Rossamünd flung his own stock out wildly, skewering Gosling right under his ribs.

With a wheeze and a gurgle, Gosling lurched backwards.

Some of the littlest children gave a tiny cheer, but quickly went silent as Gosling swung round and glared at them. Rage clearly boiled within him. He threw down his stock and leapt. Instructor Barthomæus tried to intervene, but Gosling darted beyond his grasp, tackling Rossamünd about his stomach.

"No one stops *me*!" Gosling hissed through gritted teeth

as he drove Rossamünd down to the glistening floor.

That's not true, Rossamünd thought as they tumbled. *The others beat you all the time!*

Gosling smashed at him over and over with his fists. Rossamünd saw stars as Gosling struck him once, twice, *three* more times in the head. Instructor Barthomæus blustered sharp warnings that were ignored. Finally he grabbed at Gosling and dragged him off, but not before Gosling had landed cruel blows in tender places. The boy swatted at the air as the cudgel-master heft and flung him to the other side of the ring.

"Get back, you miserable child!" roared Barthomæus.

Dazzled, his head ringing with pain, Rossamünd thought the instructor was shouting at him, and so he stayed down. Indeed, he found that he much preferred to lie still while the world swam.

Though clench-fisted and seething, Gosling did not move.

Rossamünd groaned. He felt powerful, serious pains he had never felt before.

Fransitart, the stoop-shouldered dormitory master, was called, and Verline, Madam Opera's parlour maid, too.

The telltale sound of Verline's rustling skirts arrived well before her. When she saw Rossamünd stricken within the chalk ring she gave a startled cry.

Rossamünd's senses began to fade. He was vaguely aware of voices raised in shrill anger. He dimly felt a cloth dabbing at his face. Somehow Master Fransitart was already there. The old dormitory master was growling at Gosling as the other children were shepherded out of the dining hall with a loud scuffing of boots.

Instructor Barthomæus lifted Rossamünd to his feet and wrapped him in a blanket. Verline let him lean on her all the long, crooked way to the boy's dormitory, murmuring soothing, almost wordless things as they went. The dormitory was very long and very narrow and very, very smelly. Side by side, end on end, was crammed a clutter of cots – there was never enough room in Madam Opera's. The dormitory was empty now. The other boys were still attending to classes and day-watch duties. Rossamünd's own cot was at the farthest end from the short, narrow door. With the parlour maid's help he stumbled through the inadequate gap between the beds, adding a stubbed toe to his woes. At last he could lie down, his head pounding, his cheek pounding – *throb, throb* – sharp, iron-tasting.

Verline fussed over him. "You'll need a dose of birchet to set you to mending. I will fetch some from Master Craumpalin right away! You lie still, now. I'll return as soon as I can." With that, she swished away.

Master Craumpalin was the foundlingery's dispensurist. This meant that he made most of the medicine and potives the marine society needed. From what Rossamünd could gather, Master Craumpalin had once served in the navy, just as Master Fransitart had done, though not always on the same vessels or for the same states. The old dispensurist had seen half the known world, and cured the rashes and fevers of a great many vinegaroons – as sailors were

6

called – but that was all anyone seemed to know of him. He talked even less of his past than Master Fransitart did. Nevertheless, he let Rossamünd sit with him for hours at a time while he dabbled and brewed. Most of the time Craumpalin worked in silence and the boy would just learn what he could by watching. Occasionally, however, the dispensurist became talkative and would instruct him on the uses of potives, showing him how to pour and blend and stir and store. One of the greatest thrills for Rossamünd was to watch the wonderful and often violent reactions between ingredients as Craumpalin mixed and matched them.

Red goes with green and makes purple, blue powdered in yellow makes off-white with olive spots, black boiled in white makes vermilion with orange vapours – how wonderful! These moments were so exciting, Rossamünd would hop about and usually get under the dispensurist's feet. At this Craumpalin would yell, "Pullets and cock'rels, boy! Get out of me way before I spill this on ye and melt ye to a puddle!"

Rossamünd smiled woozily at the thought. Now he wanted to sleep but his aching face would not let him. He stared dumbly at the ceiling, obscure with shadows that seemed to creep and lurch. It had been a long time since he had been in the dormitory on his own – he had forgotten just how weirdly unnerving it could be in here, alone.

Such glimpses of the oppressive dark naturally led his thinking to Gosling – Gosling Corvinius Arbour of *the* Corvinius Arbours – a powerful family with ties to some of the most ancient bloodlines of Boschenberg and

Brandenbrass, far away to the south. He was notorious at Madam Opera's for many reasons, but the chief of these was the vigour with which he strove to make everyone's life a misery. He would cut the hair of sleeping girls, glue shut the eyes of sleeping boys, put earwigs and dead things in unguarded shoes or untenanted beds, blab any secret he might discover. Punishment, no matter how severe, proved useless, for Gosling just did not care. He had been abandoned at Madam Opera's foundlingery by his family. It was said that his parents had given him up so that they might afford to keep a pair of racehorses. Such a pathetic tale of rejection had not stopped Gosling from declaring to everyone just how important he really was, that he was not some ordinary fellow with only one name, but that he had three: a firstname, a forename *and* a family-name!

This grim line of thinking led Rossamünd to brood over his own, single and unfortunate name. He had spent his entire life beneath the high peeling ceilings of Madam Opera's Estimable Marine Society for Foundling Boys and Girls. He had arrived when he was little more than a wailing pink prune, left on the doorstep with an old piece of hatbox lining pinned to his swaddling. Upon this bit of card had been written one word, scratched awkwardly in charcoal:

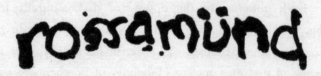

With that word he was named. The fact was officially sealed with its entry into the grand ledger that all found-lingeries possessed, and which gave all foundlings the family-name of *Bookchild*.

In the warren that was Madam Opera's, Rossamünd often hid himself away from the taunts and snickers that he still endured from the other children. He would lose himself in his favourite books and pamphlets, reading them avidly. He dared to dream that there could be a better lot for him beyond the marine society's corroding walls, and let his head fill with scenes of battles, and marauding monsters and the mighty heroes that conquered them. He might have trouble remembering the Hundred Rules of Harundo, but the things he discovered within the dog-eared pages of his precious readers would stay with him forever.

Soon enough, Verline returned. She slid discreetly along the creaking wood, her great tent of many-layered skirts making their telltale rustling. The high ceiling bounced the hissing echoes softly back till the room was filled with the gentle susurrus of her passage. He was certain she floated with her feet some inches off the floor and, to him, this added to her virtue. In his tiny world, Verline was Rossamünd's favourite. She was short and slight, her earth-dark hair hidden beneath the white cotton bonnet that female servants wore. She adored ribbons and bows, and even the plain, work-a-day clothes she wore had several knotted here and there, the biggest being a great white knot made from her apron straps, tied in the small of her back. Within the crook of her left arm, and wrapped in a cloth, she held a small porcelain crock. From it putrid, mustard-coloured fumes boiled and evaporated in the close air of the dormitory, leaving a bad stink.

Birchet!

Befuddled as he was, he still recognised the yellow steam and rank smell. Birchet was a torture masquerading as a cure.

Verline extracted a turned ladle from one of the many pockets in her white apron. She swilled about in the crock with this and brought it out filled with what he knew would be the most disgusting muck he would ever have the unhappy luck to swallow.

"Now hold your nose and open your mouth," she told him sternly.

Pinching closed his nostrils, and squeezing shut his eyes, Rossamünd opened his mouth. Verline spooned the restorative potion as best she could into the tiny hole he had reluctantly made of his lips. Rossamünd's whole head instantly flared with the fires of a thousand burning lamps. His nose was filled to bursting with the stinging stench of the mangy armpit of a dead dog, and his nostril hairs withered like straw on a fire. He was certain that cadmium-coloured steam was squirting from his ears. Just when he thought he could stand it no more, the burning-bursting subsided and left him feeling well and whole.

Better.

He burped a little yellow bubble. "Thank you, Miss Verline," he gasped.

Verline told him to rest, that she would be back with a jar of water. She left again, and before she returned Rossamünd was asleep.

MADAM OPERA'S ESTIMABLE MARINE SOCIETY FOR FOUNDLING BOYS AND GIRLS

vinegaroon (noun) also sailor, mariner, seafarer, mare man, bargeman, jack, limey (for the limes he sucks when out to sea), mire dog, old salt, salt, salt dog, scurvy-dog, sea-dog or tar: those who work the mighty cargoes and rams that tame the monster-plagued mares and ply the many-coloured waters of the vinegar seas. Such is the poisonous and caustic nature of the oceans that even the spray of the waves scars and pits a vinegaroon's skin and shortens his days under the sun.

THE great Skold Harold stood his ground. His comrades, his brothers-in-arms, had all fled in terror before the huge beast that stalked their way. This beast was enormous and covered with vicious, venomous spines. The Slothog — the slaughterer of thousands, the smiter of tens of thousands. The gore of the fallen dripped from its grasping claws as it came closer and closer. Struggling beast-handlers were dragged along as the Slothog strained against its leash.

The battle had been long and bloody. Ruined bodies lay all about in ghastly piles that stretched away as far as the eye could see. Harold had fought through it all. His once-bright armour was bruised and dented beyond repair. With great heaviness of heart he

GOSLING

checked his canisters and satchels: all his potives were spent — all, that is, but one. It would be his last throw of the dice. He fixed the potive in his sling and, taking up the Empire's glorious standard, cried, "To me, Emperor's men! To me! Stand with me now and win yourself a place in history!"

But no one listened, no one halted, no one returned to his side to defend his ancient home.

Alas, now, the Slothog was too close for escape. It paused for a brief and horrible moment. Slavering, it regarded Harold hungrily with tiny, evil eyes. Then, with a bellow it shook off its panicking handlers and charged.

With a cry of his own, lost in the din of the beast, Harold swung up his sling and leapt ...

"Young Master Rossamünd! What rot are yer readin'?"

Fransitart, the dormitory master of Madam Opera's Estimable Marine Society for Foundling Boys and Girls, stood over Rossamünd as he sat in a forlorn little huddle, tucked up in his rickety bunk. A great red welt showed on his left cheek and right down his neck. Gosling had done his work well.

The boy looked sheepishly at Master Fransitart as he pressed the thin folio of paper he had been reading against his chest, creasing pages, bending corners. He had been so taken by the tale within that he had not heard the dormitory master's deliberate step as he had approached Rossamünd's corner down the great length of the dormitory hall.

"It's one of them awful pamphlets Verline buys for yer, bain't it, me boy?" Fransitart growled.

It was the old dormitory master who had found him those years ago: found him with inadequate rags and rotting leaves for swaddling, that tattered sign affixed to his tiny, heaving chest. Rossamünd knew the dormitory master watched out for him with a care that was beyond both his duty and his typically gruff and removed nature. Rossamünd did not pause to wonder why: he simply accepted it as freely as he did Verline's tender attentions.

The foundling nodded even more sheepishly. The gaudily coloured title showed brightly on the cover:

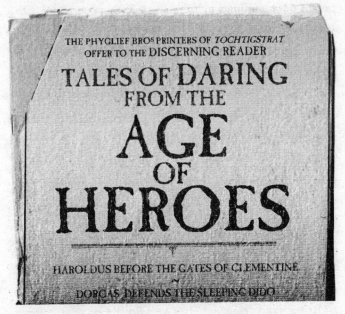

THE PHYGLIEF BROS PRINTERS OF *TOCHTIGSTRAT*
OFFER TO THE DISCERNING READER

TALES OF DARING
FROM THE
AGE
OF
HEROES

HAROLDUS BEFORE THE GATES OF CLEMENTINE

DORCAS DEFENDS THE SLEEPING DIDO

He had woken a little earlier, after recovering from his dose of birchet, to find the pamphlet sitting on the old tea chest that served as a bedside table. Every second

Domesday, when Verline was given a little time to herself, she bought them for the children from a shady little vendor on the Tochtigstrat. Today was Midwich – the day before Domesday. This particular issue must have been brought into him as a special comfort, and Rossamünd had snatched it up eagerly.

The dormitory master folded his hands behind his back. "What will Master Pinsum think of me findin' ye readin' these things again?"

Master Pinsum was one of Rossamünd's instructors. He taught the foundlings matters, letters and generalities – that is, history, writing and geography. Rossamünd found it endlessly fascinating that, whenever Master Pinsum declared this about himself, he would wave his right hand theatrically, as was done in gala-plays, and *rrrrolll* his R's with equal drama.

"I'm not much for me letters, as ye know, lad," Fransitart continued, with a cheeky twinkle in his eye, "but Master Pinsum 'as led me to thinkin' that readin' these 'ere pamphlets will shrivel yer mind. Let's just say 'tis a good thing ye're recuperatin' from th' beatin' that spineless-braggart-of-a-child Gosling gave ye – else I might 'ave to consider con-fer-scatin' that there folio." He rocked back on his heels and regarded the luminous cover. "What's this 'un about, me lad?"

Rossamünd grinned. "The Great Skold Harold, Champion of the Empire and Saviour of Clementine!"

"Ahh." Fransitart stroked his clean-shaven chin. "Ol' 'Arold, is it? Slayer of a thousand monsters in th' Battle

16

of th' Gates, Saviour of th' Imperial Capital? That were a powerful long time ago – a bit of ancient 'istory. Wonder 'ow true that version ye got there is, though?"

"Why wouldn't it be true?" Rossamünd looked horrified.

Fransitart shrugged. "Per'aps 'cause fabrications are easier to sell and more entertainin' to read." He leant in a little. "Or per'aps it's a bit o' propaganda for th' skolds, so we'll like 'em better."

"Well, I already think skolds are amazing! Would you want to be a skold, Master Fransitart? I wish that I was ... that – or a vinegaroon, of course."

For over fifteen centuries skolds had fought the monsters, so Rossamünd had been taught. Indeed, they had made it possible for civilisation to endure. They made and used all sorts of powerful, strange and deadly chemicals to slay monsters or drive them off. They also sold many of these potives and concoctions to everyday folk, allowing them to stand against the monstrous foe as well. Skolds were deeply respected, but they were also thought strange and – it was said – they usually stank of the very chemicals in which they trafficked. Though Rossamünd had seen many, he had never been close enough to confirm this reputation.

"A skold? One of those dark dabblers makin' all those dangerous smells and vile potions just waitin' to go boom in yer face? Wanderin' about, confrontin' all th' beasts and nasties out there?" The dormitory master gestured vaguely. "I be thinkin' not." He sighed. "Folks needs 'em to keep all manner of nasties away, I grant ye, but a skold will spend their days out in th' wild countryside where only their cunnin', their chem'stry and th' cut of their proofin' stand between their next meal and an 'orrible, gashin' end! I've 'ad perils enough in me life and prefer to spend what's left of it safe in these 'alls, behind th' city's many walls. And ye'll 'ave dangers a-plenty when ye go to serve on a main-ram. A-skoldin's not for me, lad, or thee either, if ye know what's right fer ye."

"Would you rather be a lahzar, then?" Rossamünd ventured, already knowing the answer.

Of strange people, lahzars were thought the strangest. Able to do wonderful, terrible things because of secret surgeries done on their bodies, they too fought monsters. Some even said they were better at this than the skolds. There were two kinds of lahzar: fulgars – who could make sparks and flashes of electricity; and wits – who could twist and squash minds, and sense where monsters and even people were hiding. No one knew exactly whence lahzars had come, but for the last two centuries they had made a profound difference to teratology – the proper term for monster-hunting. Skolds were bizarre, but lahzars could be frightening – almost as frightening as the beasts they fought.

Fransitart squinted and sucked in a breath. "Abash-me, lad, now I'm certain ye're goadin' me! To let a butcherin' surgeon go carvin' into yer rightly ordered gizzards and guts ... What's the use of it? I'm with th' skolds – they were doin' a fine job of th' killin' and th' slayin' and th' lordin' over we lesser folks for centuries afore them lahzars

18

FRANSITART

came along. Give me a skold over a lahzar on any given day, bless me eyes!"

Nickers and bogles were the names most folk gave to the monsters: nickers for the bigger ones, bogles for the smaller, though this rule wasn't fixed. Rossamünd closed his eyes as he tried to imagine a lahzar battling with some giant nicker.

The dormitory master sat down on the end of Rossamünd's sagging cot, rousing him. Fransitart gave the boy a serious look. "I 'ave 'ad to share cabin space with a few lahzars in me time, yer see: both th' lightnin'-graspin' fulgar and head-blastin' wit ..."

"You have?" Rossamünd sat up. He had heard many of the dormitory master's tales, tall and true, but Fransitart had never told him this before. "What were they like, Master Fransitart? Did you see the marks on their faces? Did they fight any monsters?"

"Aye, I 'ave, and aye, their spoors on their foreheads were clear, and aye, they did fight with as many nickers as they found and did many worse things too ... and after each meeting I was always mightily glad to be free of their comp'ny".

Fransitart looked at his feet for a moment. Rossamünd wondered what he was remembering.

"They are strange", he went on finally, "and th' unnatural organs within their bodies that make 'em so strong make 'em crotchety, feverish! Many a queer thing I 'ave seen, but nothin' quite so wretched as a lahzar made sick by 'is organs." He stared intently at Rossamünd. "My masters, lad, neither thee nor me wants to become one of them. Stick to a vinegaroon's life — 'tis a good, 'onest way to chance yer fortune."

"Well then, tell one of *your* stories," Rossamünd persisted, his pamphlet forgotten for the moment, "of when you were a sailor upon the seas. Tell me about the Battle of the Mole when you were saved by that white-haired fellow. Or when you fought against the pirate-kings of the Brigandine! Or when you captured that Lentine grand-cargo as a prize!"

"Nay, nay, me boy, ye know 'em mostly already, especially them there second two ..." The dormitory master lapsed into silence.

Rossamünd became quiet for a moment too, inspecting an illustration of Harold battling the Slothog on a page of his pamphlet. In the drawing the skold looked as if he was about to be trampled.

Fransitart stood.

The boy looked up at his dormitory master shyly. "Master Fransitart ..." he ventured. "Have *you* ever killed a monster?"

For a moment, Fransitart seemed almost angry at this question and Rossamünd immediately regretted asking it. Old salts like the dormitory master could be very touchy about their past, and it was proper never to ask but always wait to be told.

With the deepest sigh, the saddest sound Rossamünd

had ever heard Master Fransitart give, the fury passed. "Aye, lad," he said hoarsely, "I 'ave."

A thrill prickled Rossamünd's scalp.

The old man closed his eyes for a moment, and did something the boy had never seen him do before: he took off his long, wide-collared day coat and laid it neatly on the end of another cot. Fransitart rolled up the voluminous sleeve of his white muslin shirt, exposing much of his pale left arm. He bent down a little to show his gauntly knotted bicep. "Look ye there," Fransitart growled.

Wide eyes went wider as the boy saw what was shown: made from swirls and curls of red-brown lines was the small, crudely drawn face of some grinning, snarling bogle. A pointed tongue protruded obscenely from a gaping mouth, and its eyes were wide and staring horribly.

A monster-blood tattoo!

People were only ever marked with a monster-blood tattoo if they had fought and slain a nicker. The image of the fallen beast was pricked into the victor's skin with the dead monster's own blood. The stuff reacted strangely once under the skin, festered for a time and left its indelible mark. The boy looked agog at his dormitory master. He already had deep respect for the old man, but now he regarded him with an entirely new awe.

"Master Fransitart!" Rossamünd hissed. "You're a *monster-slayer*!"

Most folk would be bursting with pride to bear such a mark. Fransitart just seemed ashamed. "As things be,

Rossamünd, th' creature I killed did nought to deserve such an end and, though me shipmates boasted me an 'ero, it were a cowardly thing I did, and I am sorry for it now."

Rossamünd's astonishment grew. How could killing a monster be cowardly? How was it that Master Fransitart could be ashamed of being a *hero*?

To kill a monster was a grand thing, almost the grandest thing – everyone knew that. People were good. Monsters were bad. People had to kill monsters in order to live free and remain at peace. To feel sympathy for a bogle or to take pity on a nicker was to be labelled a sedorner – a *monster-lover!* – a shameful crime that in the least had its perpetrator shunned, or stuck in the pillory for weeks or, worst of all, executed by hanging.

How many secrets did the dormitory master have? Was he a secret sedorner? Rossamünd went pale at the notion.

The more serious Master Fransitart became the quieter his voice. He was almost whispering now. "Hearken to me, me lad! Not all monsters look like monsters, do ye get me? There are everyday folks who turn out to be th' worst monsters of 'em all! There's things I needs to tell ye, Rossamünd – strange things, things that might appear shockin' on first listenin', but ye're goin' to need to begin to git ye head about 'em …" Something caught his attention. The dormitory master shut his mouth with a sudden click and quickly pulled down his shirt sleeve.

A moment later Verline entered at the far end of the long dormitory hall.

Master Fransitart gave Rossamünd a look that said *Not a word of this to anyone*.

Surely he was about to tell him the whole shocking adventure! Now he had been interrupted, the dormitory master might never finish telling what he thought such an obviously terrible – maybe even shameful – secret. What dark mysteries could Fransitart possibly have to tell that made him so hesitant to speak them out? Rossamünd doubted he would ever have the courage to ask him to venture on the subject again. The boy had never regretted Verline's presence or thought of her as intruding – but right then, he came close to.

The parlour maid was bearing a bright-limn – a lantern holding phosphorescent algae that glowed strongly when immersed in the special liquid within – and approached with an open smile. With a sinking heart, Rossamünd discovered that she was once again carrying the crock of birchet.

"A good evening to you, Dormitory Master Fransitart," she said softly, with a dip of her comely head.

Fransitart nodded his typically grave and silent greeting, straightening the broad collar of his coat.

Verline put the bright-limn on the tea chest. She waggled the turned ladle at Rossamünd seriously. "Time for another spoon of birchet, dear heart. Master Craumpalin has kept it warmed especially for your second dose."

Rossamünd once more submitted to the cleansing fires of birchet. Once more he endured its agonies and came out the other side restored. With another belch of bubbles, he thanked Verline.

She smiled. Putting down the crock beside the bright-limn, Verline felt his forehead with a small, cool hand and peered at his bruises. "I think you are mending nicely, dear. Glory on Craumpalin's chemistry! The swelling is definitely going down. But then you have always mended quickly."

The dormitory master made an odd sound in his throat and then looked at Rossamünd gravely. "Aye, Craumpalin knows his trade. I reckon tho', that even 'e would agree with me in recommendin' that th' next time Gosling takes a shy at yer skull, Rossamünd, ye duck! Th' best salve for a wound is to avoid ever gettin' one."

The foundling looked down at the cover of his pamphlet, sheepish once more. "Aye, dormitory master," he answered softly.

Fransitart put a gentle hand on Rossamünd's bruised head. "Good lad …" he growled, with an almost tender smile. "Right, time fer supper!"

Rossamünd struggled into his evening smock, a shapeless sack with sleeves that all the children wore to dinner or supper.

"Master Fransitart, what will happen to Gosling?" he asked.

Fransitart frowned. "That li'l basket will be skippin' tonight's food and 'as been set to cleanin' out th' second salt cellar, th' buttery and th' shambles. I'm just off now to inquire as to 'is progress. Pro'bly not done 'im any sort of good! Pro'bly blamin' everyone else and excusin' hisself, as typical! A riot of ettins could do nought more than us to get th' wretched child to mend 'is errors." He shook his head. "That's enough on that. Off ye hop, Rossamünd. Say yer prayers and clean yerself afore th' meal. I will see ye in the dining hall."

Though he was sure that she had not meant it so, as he had left the hall Rossamünd overheard Verline say quietly, "What a dear, sensitive boy," and Master Fransitart rasping in reply, "Aye, *too* sensitive and *too* earnest for 'is own good. It'll be trouble and agony to 'im all 'is life if 'e don't get shrewder and tougher, just mark me. I can't watch out for 'im all th' time."

The boy brooded as he followed the narrow passages with their many doors, flaking walls and damp smells. By bewildering turns and many short flights of stairs that went down, then up, then down once more, he went first to the basins and then to the dining hall. *How might he be shrewder? How might he be tougher? How might he avoid this future of trouble and agony that Fransitart foresaw? ... And how might he get his dormitory master to finish the telling of those strange and shocking things he dared not speak in front of Verline?*

Madam Opera's Estimable Marine Society for Foundling Boys and Girls was situated on the Vlinderstrat, between a rat-infested warehouse and a stinking tannery. The building was tall and narrow, made of dark stones and dark, decaying wood, sagging under the many additions to its original structure. It had been in Madam Opera's family through a great list of generations. Rossamünd had heard this list read out once, and it went on so long he fell asleep during the telling.

Now the Vlinderstrat, or Butterfly Street, had once been a rather fashionable avenue in the rather fashionable suburb of Poéme, in the proud riverine city of Boschenberg. The ancient high-house that had become Madam Opera's found-lingery had once been one of the finest dwellings on the street, the home of her great-great spinster aunt. But Boschenberg grew and the fashionable folk had long ago moved to other parts of town. The great-great-aunt died, leaving the house locked up and decaying. Then the madam herself, rumoured to be recovering from a ruined engagement, had claimed it as her inheritance, obtained her licence, and between the rats and the stench of tanning, set up her marine society and foundlingery to begin a new, charitable life.

A hundred children who had once been unwanted or lost or both lived here to be taught a trade and skills so that they might be wanted as adults. And the organisation that wanted them most was that seemingly bottomless sink of manpower – the navy. It was the Boschenberg Navy that sponsored the running of this marine society and several others. It was the Boschenberg Navy that provided the foundlingery with its masters, men like Fransitart and Craumpalin, each one an ageing vinegaroon pensioned off to serve the few days left to him as an instructor to discarded children.

27

Every marine society boy and girl was taught to long to join the navy. It was widely known that a fellow could set himself up for good with the prize-money won when pirates or enemy vessels were captured; that you joined a family when you joined the crew of a ram (a very appealing idea to the foundlings at Madam Opera's); that every landlubber thought you were a grand chap for serving your state so honourably; and that you were better paid and better fed than most folks doing similar work on land. Rossamünd was no different: he too had learned to desperately want a life on the vinegar waves.

The vinegar waves. The thought always made him wistful.

Though he had never seen the sea, Rossamünd knew that its waters were tainted with caustic salts that gave it lurid colours and made it stink like strong vinegar. He could hardly wait till the day when he got to fill his lungs full of the sharp odour of the sea.

The navy was not the *only* employer of marine society boys and girls. Other agencies happily took on Madam Opera's children: the army, with its smart uniforms and regular meal times; the mathematicians, with their numbers and demand for genius; their rivals the concometrists, who measured the length and breadth of everything; and various miscellaneous trades and guildhalls seeking apprentices or workers. An unlucky few were chosen by people who deemed them suitable for some obscure task.

The agents arrived to make their selections at a set time in a year. The hiring season started in the early weeks of

Calor – the first month of summer, the first month of the year. It ended in the last weeks of Cachrys – the second month of autumn, before the weather became unfriendly for easy travel. This was a time of great anticipation and glee, the older children always eager to make good their escape, the middle children keen to become the top dogs of the foundlingery, and the younger ones excited simply by the atmosphere of expectation and change.

Rossamünd had watched it happen many times already over the years, but this year it was his turn to take part; yet for some inexplicable reason, each time the hiring agents had come he had been passed over. He did not know why and no one said; the agents just came, reviewed a line-up of all the older children, asked questions of the masters and Madam Opera, and read out the tally of their choices. He knew he was not very tall or impressive-looking, like others around his age. He also knew that he was clumsy, that he had trouble tying the knots Master of Ropes Heddlebulk taught, that there were times when his mind would wander and duties be left incomplete. Yet Rossamünd did know a thing or two. Not only had he learned simple dispensing from Craumpalin, but he knew a good deal of history too.

The Emperor ruled all that mattered, and the Emperor's Regents had control of the scores of ancient city-states that made up the Empire, city-states like Boschenberg, clinging to the coasts and fertile places. It was an Empire founded sixteen hundred years ago by the great hero-empress Dido, although the current dynasty – the Haacobins – were usurpers and not of Dido's line. Rossamünd had read of the many battles on land and sea. City-states warred with each other and with their Imperial master for yet more control. He knew of soldiers – musketeers, haubardiers, troubardiers and the rest, and especially about the great rams – giant ironclad vessels of war that prowled the vinegar seas, their decks congested with mighty cannon. He knew the names of famous marshals, legendary admirals. He had read of the skolds, who fought monsters with poisonous chemicals, and had even seen a few of those who had served his own city. He was fascinated by the two kinds of lahzars: the wits, who could send out an unseen shudder of energy that would return, making folk dizzy or faint, or grip a person's mind and crush it; or the fulgars, who could summon powerful electricity from within their very bodies.

But most of all he knew about monsters. He knew that there was an Everlasting Struggle, the ever-present battle between humankind and the bogles and nickers and the nadderers – the sea-monsters. Much of what he read grandly declared that humankind was winning, that the monsters were in steady retreat, that one day they would be exterminated from all the Empire. Yet occasionally Rossamünd read some article nervously suggesting that in fact the bitter fight 'twixt man and bogle was at best locked in stalemate, at worst that humankind was losing. A terrible thought – people driven into the sea by slavering, relentless terrors.

Yes, Rossamünd did know a thing or two, yet six times

now this hiring season, men from the navy board and other agencies had been around to review the hopefuls. Six times now children had been selected to go and lead adventurous lives, so many now that the eldest and most of the second-eldest were gone, never to return. Six times now Rossamünd had been passed over. One of the eldest children in the foundlingery he might now be – if still not one of the tallest – but this was little compensation for the shame of being left behind. He had been left behind by Providence-knows-who as a baby, and now, it seemed, he was being left behind again.

He was certain that he could not stand yet another year stuck in the cramped halls of mouldering wood and old, cold stone.

Gosling, too, was waiting to be chosen for work outside the foundlingery. It was his only chance to achieve all the things for which his high birth had destined him – as he often boasted. In the last five months child after child had been selected to take up his or her long awaited occupation, but not Gosling. In a raging sulk he had set about a regime of spiteful pranks, most failing owing to Fransitart's shrewd vigilance. But it was Rossamünd he specially tormented.

Two weeks after the incident at harundo practice, Gosling somehow found him reading a small book about rams. Rossamünd had hidden himself away in the tiny garret library of sagging wood precariously extended from the roof of the main building. It was all but forgotten by most. Dust was so thick on the floor that Gosling had been able to sneak up behind Rossamünd to poke him as hard as he could. Rossamünd was not startled: he could always smell Gosling well before he saw or even heard him.

"Whiling away the hours, are we?" Gosling snarled, unhappy that he had failed to spook his victim. He snatched away Rossamünd's reader and made to ruin it.

Rossamünd had played this game before. He simply folded his arms and frowned.

"Preparing to go abroad aboard your precious rams, eh? Fat lot of good reading *these* has done!" Gosling leant right into Rossamünd's face. "Don't think *you're* any better than me, m'lady. You're still here, too! No one wants *you*." Gosling stood straight, his arms folded and his nose in the air. "My family will be coming back for me soon, you'll see. Then I'll show you who's better." Gosling had been saying this ever since he had been taken into the foundlingery. His expression took on an even nastier curl. "Not even old Fransi-*fart* will make you feel better then, when you're left behind and watching me go back to the quality I was born to!"

"Do not say his name like that ..." warned Rossamünd.

"Or what? Or what?! What a fine bunch you and he would make – Rosy Posy and ol' Fransi-fart! What a stink!"

Rossamünd scowled. "He treats you as good as anyone – and better than you deserve! Call *me* what you like, but leave your betters out!" As true as it might be, this sounded lame even to Rossamünd and had no effect at all on his tormentor.

32

"He's a pock-faced old ignoramus, and when Mamma and Papa come back for me I'll get them to buy the whole stinking, tottering place and then kick him and the rest out to rot! Or ..." Gosling finished with a malicious grin, "burn this all down to the cellars!"

Rossamünd was speechless. He glared and spluttered. He failed to defend the honour of his dormitory master, or Verline or anyone else.

Gosling swaggered off sneering and making noises like a baby. "Oo, I'd better stop. Madam Rosy is going to make me eat my nasty little words. Oo ..." Just before he disappeared through the warped wooden door, he hurled Rossamünd's reader at him. Rossamünd ducked, but it still managed to glance his left cheek.

That's the last *time!* Rossamünd vowed to himself.

Days gathered into weeks. Rossamünd despaired utterly of ever receiving an offer of employment. Then, with the end of the hiring season three weeks gone, and the cold month of Lirium well under way, an official-looking stranger arrived at the foundlingery. He was shown about the institute by Madam Opera. News of the arrival and the tour flashed around the foundlingery more quickly than the burst of a skold's potive. While sitting alert in Master Pinsum's matters, letters and generalities class, Rossamünd spotted the stranger watching proceedings from the door, giving the distinct air of seeing all and missing nothing.

When gaps in his duties allowed, Rossamünd continued

to watch the stranger furtively, silently nursing his urgent, yearning hopes for a new life of adventure and advancement. He observed Gosling doing the same from a different vantage. Perhaps here was someone with an offer of employment for one of them? Perhaps for both? Perhaps, on this very ordinary mid-autumn afternoon, one of their lives was about to change forever …

But after the seventh bell of the afternoon watch, it was Rossamünd who was summoned to Madam Opera's rather large, riotously cluttered boudoir-cum-office.

Gosling would not be pleased.

THE LAMPLIGHTERS' AGENT

sthenicon (noun) a simple wooden box with leather straps and buckles that fasten it to the wearer's head, covering the mouth, nose and eyes. Inside it are various small organs – folded up nasal membranes and complicated bundles of optic nerves – that let the wearer smell tiny, hidden or far-off smells, and see into shadows, in the dark, or a great distance away. Used mostly by leers; if a sthenicon is worn for too long the organs within can grow up into the wearer's nose. If this happens, removing it can be difficult and very painful.

DOWN many well-trod flights of creaking, wobbling wood or frigid, slippery slate stairs Rossamünd went, through the all-too-familiar narrows of the foundlingery's halls and passages, all the way down to the emerald-painted door of Madam Opera's downstairs apartments. Children were normally summoned to the madam's sacred apartments only when in the worst kind of trouble.

Rossamünd's head spun. *Am I in trouble after all? Was it just chance that this stranger happened to be there?* He stood in the musty parlour before the green door, where all comers were to wait until summoned.

Tap, tap went his boyish knuckles on this hard wooden

portal. He was let in immediately by the manservant Carp. Within, the madam sat like some august queen, almost obscured by the piles of loose papers, ledgers and registers that rose in clumsy stacks upon either side of her solid blackwood desk. Her chestnut hair had been knotted high into a hive of snaking coils. She had clearly gone to some lengths with her appearance. The stranger was there, standing silently by the desk. He wore a dark coachman's cloak that hid all other attire, even his boots, and he held in his hands an excessively tall tricorner hat of fine black felt known as a thrice-high. There was something wrong with his eyes. Not wanting to be caught staring, Rossamünd flicked his attention between Madam Opera and the stranger's distracting orbs.

"You sent for me, Madam Opera?" Rossamünd croaked in a small voice, bowing uncertainly.

The Madam beamed at him. This was unnerving. She rarely beamed. "I did, my dear boy. Come closer, come closer." A hand waved at him, the handkerchief it clasped fluttering like a small white flag and filling the small office with the scent of patchouli water. "Today is a very important one for you, young Master Rossamünd." Madam Opera glanced almost coyly at the man alongside her, as though they shared a special secret.

Rossamünd felt his heart beat faster.

"Mister Sebastipole here has come as an agent all the way from High Vesting, and has declared that he would very much like to meet you." Madam Opera stood, an action which made the stranger straighten automatically. "Mister Sebastipole, I would like you to meet young Master Rossamünd. Young Master Rossamünd, Mister Sebastipole." She curtsied as she offered these greetings, her arms stretching out to encompass her two guests.

The stranger nodded, the corner of his mouth twisting slightly. "Rossamünd. What a – ah – fine name for, I am told, a fine lad."

This was an odd thing to say. Adults were often saying such things about his name, and it was by these reactions that instinctively Rossamünd would gauge a person's trustworthiness. Had he not been unsettled by the stranger's eyes he might have thought this Mister Sebastipole was subtly mocking him. Rossamünd dared one quick, determined stare. A thrill spread through his entire body: the man's eyes were completely the wrong colour! What should have been white was blood red, and his irises were the palest, most piercing blue. This man in front of him was a leer! "Mister … S-S-Sebastipole." Rossamünd bowed awkwardly. For a moment he could hardly think: everything he knew about these men was now tumbling through his brain in much the same confused way as the Hundred Rules of Harundo. Leers were trackers, trackers of men, and even more so of monsters. They drenched their eyes with forbidden chemicals to enable them to see into things, through things, to spy on hidden things, to tell even if a person was lying.

Rossamünd gulped. Unable to help himself, he looked

surreptitiously for the man's sthenicon. He was fascinated by them, and longed to try one on. It was a rare thing to meet a leer in the city, and Rossamünd had certainly never encountered one before. *What could a leer want with me?*

This fellow had come from High Vesting, Madam Opera had said. High Vesting was one of Boschenberg's colonies and the harbour of her naval fleet. Perhaps this terrible-eyed stranger worked for the navy. Rossamünd tried to quell the rising excitement that threatened to overwhelm him. Oh, to become a vinegaroon – that was his heart's desire!

Madam Opera continued gravely. "Now, Rossamünd, Mister Sebastipole is here to offer you a chance for employment – an opportunity I understand you very much desire. I want you to take his proposal seriously and consider well what a fine offer this is. Please go on, sir." She waved her hand ingratiatingly.

Mister Sebastipole cleared his throat and narrowed those intense eyes. "Well, young master Rossamünd; I have come to represent my masters in Winstermill *and* High Vesting, who in their turn represent their masters, who represent their master – that is, the Emperor himself."

Rossamünd was impressed. Somehow, he could tell that Mister Sebastipole had meant him to be.

"I am told you are quick of eye, good with letters and know a little of the chemistry," the leer continued. "Would you agree this is so?"

Rossamünd hesitated. This did not quite *sound* like the navy. "I … I suppose I would, sir."

Mister Sebastipole continued. "Very good. You see, our Imperial charge – handed even from the great Imperial Capital of Clementine itself – is the care, the maintenance and clear passage of one of our Most Imperial Master's Highroads: the Conduit Vermis, which follows its course from Winstermill through the Ichormeer – that some call the Gluepot – and on eastwards to far-famed Wörms."

Rossamünd blinked. This definitely was *not* the navy.

"I have come to offer you the employment of a life time – that is, to work the lamps with us and tread the paths of this great highway to keep it safe for all happy travellers. In short, we would like you to become a lamplighter. I am pleased to say that this good lady, Madam Opera" – he half turned his body and gave the slightest bow towards the woman – "agrees you would be excellent for the job."

Something about the way the lamplighter's agent said all this sounded very final.

Rossamünd's head was spinning once more. *A lamplighter? They wanted him to become a lamplighter? What happened to the navy?* Now he would never see the sea ...

"Um ..." Rossamünd tried his best to look grateful. "I ... ah ..." This was not the plan at all! Stuck on the same stretch of road day on day, night after night, lighting the lamps, dousing them again, lighting them again. No chance for prize-money. No chance for glory. Could it get worse? He had no choice. It was either become a lamplighter or stay at the foundlingery. A glance at Madam Opera showed her genial expression becoming stiff with impatience. He was stuck between two very unpleasant choices – the stone and the sty, as Master Fransitart might say.

"Thank you, Mister Sebastipole," he managed, giving another awkward bow.

"As you should!" Madam Opera beamed and clapped once and loudly. Nothing about Mister Sebastipole's face altered at all. He clearly had not anticipated the slightest resistance to his suggestion. Madam Opera stood and shepherded Rossamünd towards the door. "Go and ready yourself. Fransitart will know what to do ... Now, *Mister* Sebastipole," he heard her murmur as she closed the door behind him, "you will stay for a sip of tea?"

And that was that.

The necessary arrangements were made. Rossamünd was to meet Mister Sebastipole in two days' time, at the Padderbeck, one of Boschenberg's smaller piers upon the mighty Humour River. His luggage was to be limited to no more than one ox trunk and a satchel. He was to be dressed in hard-wearing clothes for a long journey, and a sturdy hat too. Unfortunately, he did not have any. Nor did he possess a suitably sturdy hat. As for the rest of his belongings, the collection of his entire life – they fitted neatly into two old hat boxes. For the rest of the day and all through the next, those interested staff of Madam Opera's Estimable Marine Society for Foundling Boys and Girls, the Vlinderstrat, Boschenberg, were a-bustle as Rossamünd was prepared for his great going forth. Even the Madam herself joined in, drawing up a list of what he needed, entitling it *Rossamünd's Necessaries*.

Masters Fransitart and Craumpalin took Rossamünd to see Gauldsman Five, the gaulder. His was the best place in this part of the city to get clothing sturdy enough for Rossamünd's journey, for Gauldsman Five made the best proofing. All proofing could turn sword strokes, and could even stop a ball fired from a musket or pistol. The simplest piece of proofing was costly, but the better the quality of protection the higher a garment's price. Proofing was, however, also absolutely necessary for folk looking to venture beyond the city walls, where monsters and brigands and other horrors waited. It was made from cloth – anything from hemp to silk – treated with a chemical potion known as gauld, which made it very hard to tear or puncture. Broad straps of gauld-hardened leather and thin padding of soft spongy pokeweed were then sewn into the lining as the unproofed cloth was turned into garments. After this the whole array was soaked in gauld, and then cooked and soaked again and so on. Each gaulder had his own methods and process, and his own secret recipes. Rossamünd thought it almost too wonderful to believe that he might be getting such amazing clothing for his very own. He was speechless with glee as he left the marine society.

Gauldsman Five's shop and fitting rooms was a whole suburb away, in the Mortar, on Tin Drum Lane, and the visit there would be a little adventure in itself. Indeed, any excursion from the foundlingery was a significant event. Rossamünd had been out from Madam Opera's only a dozen times in his whole life, usually to go down to the

Humour with the other foundlings to practise rowing and swimming. In fact, before today, his most thrilling excursion had been a trip to the house of Verline's sister Praeline in the shadows of Boschenberg's outermost curtain wall.

Fransitart, Craumpalin and Rossamünd went north along the Vlinderstrat, turned right on to the Weegbrug, and then left on to the crazily curving Pantomime Lane. They strolled past ale houses, dance halls and puppet stalls, veered right once more on to the Hurlingstrat, dodging ox wagons and omnibuses, went through the Werkersgate and there, on the left hand, was Tin Drum Lane. Gauldsman Five's establishment was about a third of the way along, tall and narrow like almost every other building in Boschenberg. Only those of quality were allowed in the front of the shop, where there were plush closets in which the wealthy and powerful could try on and admire their new proofing. Such ordinary folk as two marine society masters and a foundling had to use the poor man's closets by the great gaulding vats at the rear of the shop. As they entered this filthy place, Rossamünd watched greenish-orangey-yellow steam hiss angrily from one of the vats as an aproned man poured in a thick black liquid. A foul miasma churned in the dank air.

Fransitart spoke quietly but urgently with some grimy fellow, who spoke to another grimy fellow, who spoke to another, and before long a finely dressed man in a powdered wig appeared from a door leading to the front of the shop. Though his simply cut clothes were made of expensive materials, he had a splotched and haggard look about his face – the mark of a vinegaroon. He was one of Gauldsman Five's tailors. Fransitart must have known him and, from his look of consternation, the tailor must have known the dormitory master too.

"'Ello, Meesius," said Fransitart, a terrible light in his eye.

"Coxswain Frans?" Meesius the tailor went pale. "Is that you? And ... and with Craump'lin, too?"

Coxswain? Rossamünd had always thought Fransitart had been the gunner – in charge of all the cannon and their right firing.

"Aye," Fransitart nodded gravely, "I've come to claim me debt."

Tugging on the bristles beneath his lower lip, Craumpalin gave the tailor a knowing wink and flashed an almost threatening grin. "Lookee, Frans," he said softly, "he still knows us!"

Meesius the tailor went even paler. "A-after all these years ...?"

"Aye." Master Fransitart was as quietly menacing as Rossamünd had ever known him to be. "But I wants it in harness. Bring us yer best travellin' wear for this 'ere lad."

There was an awkward pause.

Rossamünd was bemused that his two masters could be such overbearing rogues.

With nervous sweat on his brow, the tailor hesitated.

Craumpalin folded his arms and glowered. Fransitart remained perfectly still.

43

Meesius cleared his throat. "W-well." He gestured to Rossamund impatiently. "Come over here so I can get thy measurements."

Rossamünd looked at his masters, and Fransitart gave the subtlest nod. The boy went over to the tailor, leaving Fransitart and Craumpalin by the vats.

"Lift thy arm!" Meesius growled under his breath. With a leather tape he measured Rossamünd's neck and arms and even the girth of his chest with many rough proddings.

"... I daren't keep him back any longer." Master Fransitart's voice carried softly across the vat-room floor.

"Ye dare not. And anyway, the lad is desperate to get on."

"Aye, Pin, Aye." The dormitory master sounded resigned and strangely sad. "Well at least 'e'll be stoutly protected."

At this both of the old men went quiet.

Meesius disappeared for a time then returned with a sour look, bearing two pieces of high-quality proofing. The first was a fine proofed vest with fancy silk facings and linings called a weskit. The second piece was a sturdy, well-gaulded coat – called a jackcoat – made of subtle silken threads of shifting blues. It came in at the waist and flared out to the knees. Rossamünd was stunned at its beauty.

The dormitory master told him to put on both the weskit and the jackcoat. "Ye might as well start getting accustomed to their weight," he said.

They were a little too big for Rossamünd and heavier than normal clothes, but combined with his recently washed black, long-legged shorts – or longshanks, he looked very fine indeed and could be sure he was well protected for his long journey. All he needed now was a sturdy hat.

"Yer debt is cleared, Meesius," Fransitart said, low and serious. "I 'ope we will never 'ave th' need to meet again!"

Without another word the tailor hurried off into the shadows beneath the vats. Rossamünd and his masters returned the way they had come. Fransitart looked very satisfied with himself as they wrestled and veered through the jostling throng on their way home.

"Ye've got yerself a stout set of proofing there, lad. A fine harness, indeed." The dormitory master's smug grin broadened. "Ye'll be well safe in it."

Craumpalin chuckled. "Master-fully done, Frans, master-fully done. Ol' Cap'n Slot would 'ave been impressed."

Rossamünd had no idea what just happened. He had never seen Fransitart so satisfied, so pleased – but he was too astounded at his grand new proofing to give any of it another thought.

Verline mended his two shirts and even his small clothes. She darned several pairs of especially long stockings – called trews – which he was to wear doubled back down from the knee for improved protection. Two scarves and two pairs of gloves were provided against the coming cold of winter. She also gave to him his own turnery – a fork and a spoon made of wood, a biggin – a leather-covered wooden cup with a fastening lid, a mess kid – a small wooden pail from which to eat his meals, and a flint and steel for the lighting of fires.

VERLINE

From the larder Rossamünd was allowed to put into his satchel a block of cured fungus known as dried must, a whole loaf of rye bread, a pot of gherkins that sloshed and plopped quietly when it was moved, three rectangular slats of portable soup – hard black wafers ready to be boiled down to a bland but nutritious brew, some fresh green apples, and for energy or emergencies, fortified sack cheese.

Travelling papers were arranged for him: a letter of introduction from Madam Opera recommending Rossamünd as a fine and useful boy; a waybill or certificate of travel giving him permission to move through any land or city-state of the Empire; a nativity patent to prove who he was and where he came from; and finally a work docket, upon which his conduct would be recorded in whatever job he was employed. This impressive wad of documents was put into a buff leather wallet along with (he could hardly believe his eyes!) folding money to the value of one sou – an advance of his monthly wages – and the Emperor's Billion. This was a shining gold oscadril coin given as an incentive to all those entering the service of their Imperial and Pacific Lord. Rossamünd gaped at all this money that was apparently now his.

Old Craumpalin contributed, too. The dispensurist supplied several flasks and tiny sacks, declaring them to be medicines to "invigorate both thew and wind" – by which he meant body and soul, and repellents to "fear away the bogles and nickers." Rossamünd already knew the medicines – he'd seen them before – small milky bottles holding evander water, marked with a deep blue ∃ – to show what they contained, and beneath that the tiny letters **C-R-p-N** – the dispensurist's mark. The repellents, however, were new.

"Beware the monsters, me boy! Ye've been safe in here all yer life, but out there …" Craumpalin gestured vaguely, "out *there* it ain't safe. They're everywhere, see, the nasty baskets. Big or small, they're as mean as mean can be, so just keep these potives safe and handy and ye'll go right – though I have to apologise to ye for them not being of as fine a quality as a skold brews." The dispensurist pointed to a cobalt vial. "Right! This here is tyke-oil. It don't smell like much to us, but it's good for keeping monsters away, right off. A healthy smear on yer collar and they'll stay well clear of ye. Problem is, it also lets them know ye're there, so don't go applying it willy nilly, only when ye think they've got yer scent."

Then he gingerly poked at one of the many little sacks kept within a bigger purse. Though the smell coming from them was faint, it was still unpleasantly sharp. Rossamünd hoped he never suffered a faceful of it.

"These are bothersalts. Very nasty stuff, and the sacks are fragile, so have a care. It will give any bogle – or person, for that matter – you happen on a nasty sting if you throw it at them, bag and all. Frighten them off for hours, but it also makes 'em angry, so be on yer guard for a good long while after. And *this*! This is a pretty bit of trickery!" Craumpalin unwrapped a package of oily paper to show a large lump

48

of malleable skin-coloured wax. An odour something like a very sweaty and unwashed person filled the air.

"It's called john-tallow. Smells a wee bit off to us, but it's a mile more appealing to the nose of a nicker than we are … leads them astray. Poke a little lump of this in the bole of a tree or under a rock, walk in the other direction and ye'll get yerself some space." He chuckled into his white beard. "Wonderful stuff. A warning though: always handle it by the oiled paper. If ye get the stuff on y' hands – or anywhere else come to that – then ye'll stink of it too and the ruse will be ruined. Got it?"

As the dispensurist kneaded the wax Rossamünd found that, strangely, he liked the smell. He said nothing of this and took in all he was told very carefully, very seriously, imagining a world beyond the city's many curtain walls and bastions filled with all kinds of frightful beasts.

Craumpalin lifted up a bottle of brown clay. "This here be fourth and last," he said. "It's a nullodour – I like to call it Craumpalin's Exstinker. Master Frans and me wants ye to wear a splash of it on ye all the time, no matter. Keep ye safe from sniffing noses – where ye're going there's no knowing where is safe and where ain't." The old dispensurist took up a long strip of cambric. "The best way to wear it is to liberally apply some to this here bandage, then wind it about yer chest, just under the arms like so." He wrapped the strip about himself several times in demonstration. "A good splash will do for a day and seven will last you almost a whole week. After that I recommend you wash this

and re-apply more of me Exstinker. Tomorrow mornin',
when ye be getting yerself ready, we wants ye to give this
seven splashes and put it about ye just like I've shown.
Understood?"

Rossamünd nodded sombrely. Anything to keep the
monsters away.

Craumpalin grinned. "Good lad!" He handed Rossamünd
the brown clay bottle along with a piece of paper. "There's
enough in there to last ye for a month. After that, give this
script to yer local, friendly – make sure he's friendly, mind –
skold to make ye more."

Along with all these things Rossamünd took his most
treasured possession: a lexicon of words and a simple
peregrinat – or an almanac for wayfarers – entitled *Master
Matthius' Wandering Almanac: A Wordialogue of Matter,
Generalisms & Habilistics,* that is, history, geography and
science. Cleverly, it was waterproofed, both cover and
pages, so as to be useful to any brave and literate traveller
no matter what the weather. It had been a gift one year ago,
given on Bookday, when the foundlings at Madam Opera's
remembered the entry of their name into the grand ledger – a
type of group birthday, and the only time their existence
was ever celebrated.

Fransitart appeared in the afternoon with an iron-bound
valise of shining black leather.

"Thank you." Taking hold of it, Rossamünd was at once
struck by the bizarre sense that whoever had made the case
had intended good things for its owner.

It had a lock and a key that was fixed to a strong velvet ribbon of brilliant scarlet about Rossamünd's neck.

The astounding array of Rossamünd's new equipment was then re-checked and finally packed by Master Fransitart, who stowed everything wisely so that it would not rattle or knock when moved. Remarkably, the valise did not weigh nearly as much as he expected it might when it was fully packed.

Rossamünd urgently wanted to ask Fransitart to finish the telling of the fight with the monster and the secret things, the shocking things beyond and behind this. He had the courage now that so little time was left until he departed, but Verline did not leave them alone long enough for him to venture a question.

"I know ye weren't thinking to be a lamplighter," Fransitart said unexpectedly, "but not ev'ryone who studies law becomes a lawyer, lad. Things may change for ye yet. Paths need not be as fixed or as straight fo'ward as they might first show." He looked hard into Rossamünd's eyes. "Now ye've got to be especially wary out there, me boy. Ye get me?"

Rossamünd nodded slow and sad.

"Most ev'ryone is not goin' to be as understandin' of ye as Verline here, or crusty old Craump'lin or meself," the old sea-dog continued. "Guard yeself, pick ye friends cautiously and always keep wearin' that brew ye got from Craump'lin. He knows his trade better than most — it will keep ye well protected." Fransitart sniffed. "Take me words to heart, son. It's a wild and wicked world beyond here and I'm loath to let ye out into it. But out ye must go, and ye've got to be sharp and wise and keep yeself from trouble. Aye?"

"I will, Master Fransitart, I will," Rossamünd said with all the earnestness he could muster.

The dormitory master took something out of his pocket and passed it to the boy. It was a long and thin-bladed knife in a blacked leather sheath, a tool much like the ones Rossamünd had seen fishermen use when cleaning their catch on the stone-walled banks of the river.

As he gave the knife, Fransitart fixed Rossamünd once more with a serious eye. "Out in the world a knife is an 'andy thing to 'ave. Mark me, though! If ye must use this 'ere in a tussle," he said, wagging his finger, "then make certain ye means to, or else it'll get taken from ye an' used upon yeself instead!"

Rossamünd nodded, though he did not really understand. He had no intention of using the knife for anything but the cutting of food.

To his dismay, Rossamünd was made to have another bath, though he had had one only two days earlier. "Make you nice and fresh for your great going forth, young man," Verline declared as she sent him to the tubs. Smelling like lemon grass soap, he returned to the dormitory. As all the boys were piped to bed, Weems and Gull, two of the next-oldest, who would be leaving themselves next season, and who always did things together, teased him for his flowery smell. Rossamünd just shrugged. Tonight would be the last time he would have to put up with them.

Restless with dreams and worries of what was to come and a keen suspicion that Gosling might try some horrid final prank, he slept little that night.

Finally, at the start of the morning watch, Rossamünd was roused by a silent Fransitart. He followed the dim guide of the dormitory master's shuttered bright-limn and bid goodbye, with one lingering look, to the dormitory. Snores and whimpers and sighs replied in unconscious, uninterested farewell.

So this is what it feels like to be leaving for good, he marvelled.

Master Fransitart left him at the basins to wash his face and put on all the fancy new things that were waiting there for him. He was especially careful to apply one-two-three-four-five-six-seven splashes of Craumpalin's Exstinker to the cambric bandage. Seven days' worth. He wound it tightly around his chest just as the dispensurist had shown him before donning the rest of his attire.

In the dining hall he found a breakfast of rye porridge with curds-and-whey and sweetened with honey. A lantern sat on the side to light his last meal at the foundlingery. It was as fancy a breakfast as he had ever had, and it spoke of Verline's care. He was just a little sad as he ate alone, the tap of his spoon against the bowl echoing in the lonely dark. Verline's love would be hard to live without, but at last he was getting out!

With the early glow of approaching dawn showing

through the high windows, Fransitart returned. He came into the dining hall carrying Rossamünd's satchel and valise.

"Time to be going, lad," rasped Fransitart, his voice sounding pinched and strange.

Rossamünd followed him to the vestibule by the front door where Madam Opera waited. Standing before the front doors, Rossamünd was granted his baldric. A leather-and-cloth strap that went over the right shoulder and looped by the left hip, it was given to all lads when they were declared to be passing from boyhood into manhood. Typically it was marked with the mottle – the colours – of one's native city. This one was patterned in sable and mole chequers – that is, a checkerboard of black and brown, the mottle of Boschenberg. Master Fransitart, solemn and still silent, put it on Rossamünd and, that done, plonked a handsome black thrice-high upon his head. At last he was completely equipped.

Madam Opera grimaced tightly. "You do look well set up – perhaps too well," she added with a sidelong glance at Fransitart. She gave Rossamünd a single pat on his head. "Step forward strongly, boy, like the hundreds have done before you. This world does not reward tears. Time to be on your way."

Rossamünd wrestled on the valise, fixed his new knife to his new baldric, slung the satchel containing the food, turnery, the biggin and the repellents and the rest across his other shoulder, and pocketed his purse of small coins.

Master Fransitart held Rossamünd by the shoulders.

"Goodbye, lad," he said at last.

"Goodbye, Master Fransitart," Rossamünd whispered. "Tell Miss Verline and Master Craumpalin goodbye," he added.

Madam Opera made a small disapproving noise, but Fransitart smiled and replied, "I surely will, lad. Now! Step lively, new duties await ye!"

Rossamünd took up his old stock and the peregrinat, doffed his hat as he thought a man might, and stepped reluctantly out into the foggy autumn dawn.

As he turned to go on his way, he caught a glimpse of some of the children who remained, woken early and watching from the high windows of the foundlingery. Among them was Gosling. Rossamünd was certain he would be fuming with silent jealousy.

Good riddance, he thought.

He followed the Vlinderstrat towards Hermenèguild and the river district, quickly reaching the point where tall shops and high apartments obscured Madam Opera's Estimable Marine Society from view. His heart swelling with sharp, nameless regrets, he joined the dawning hustle of Sooningstrat.

ON THE HOGSHEAD

cromster (noun) one of the smallest of the armed, ironclad river-barges, having three-inch cast-iron strakes down each side and from four to twelve 12-pounder guns upon each broadside. Generally single-masted, though the biggest may have two masts. Below the open-deck is a single lower deck called the orlop. Forward of amidships (the middle of the craft) is typically hold space for cargo. Aft of amidships the orlop is reserved for the gastrines and their crews.

MISTER Sebastipole was waiting as he said he would be, standing in the fog at the top of the Padderbeck Stair. He was wearing his telltale coachman's cloak and black thrice-high. He had his own satchel hanging across his body together with an oddly ordinary-looking box on a thick strap. Rossamünd tried not to stare at the box. Inside it would be the leer's sthenicon. He had expected it to be much more unusual, and he was just a little disappointed to see that it was so very plain and ordinary. Sebastipole had been holding a small portable clock or some other such device when Rossamünd arrived, and now secreted it away.

"You are late, young fellow," he stated flatly. "A lamps-man's life *is* punctuality – 'twould be best to start forming that habit soon, don't you think?" There was no ire in Mister Sebastipole's voice, just honest, unselfconscious reproof. Rossamünd had never encountered anything like it before.

"Uh … Aye, sir," he puffed and set the valise down.

"Well, at least you have come lightly packed. Bravo."

The lamplighter's agent pulled out an oblong of sealed paper and another of folded paper. He handed the sealed paper to Rossamünd first, saying, "This is my endorsement to our mutual masters." He gave him the folded paper, saying, "These are my instructions to you and to those who will meet you at the other end. Stow the first safely and read the second carefully." The lamplighter's agent folded his arms and stared with his disturbing eyes. "Your first destination is High Vesting and from there a fortress known as Winstermill. It is a manse, the headquarters of we lamplighters. You will be escorted thither from High Vesting. Your instructions say as much." He squinted. "Hark me, now! Do not dally on your way, but make directly to Winstermill, for my superiors are awaiting you and others like you to begin your 'prenticing. Agreed?"

"Aye, sir." Rossamünd carefully stowed the precious documents in his buff leather wallet.

Mister Sebastipole took out his little clock again, opened it and pursed his lips. With a snap of its lid, he declared, "Well, the sooner you start, the sooner away." The leer pointed Rossamünd towards steps that went down from the high wall of the canal-side street to the Padderbeck itself.

SEBASTIPOLE

The fog had become almost impossibly thick. Rossamünd could barely make out the tottering buildings festering on the other side of the narrow canal, their brooding window-lights of red and green showing only faintly.

"Down there – though you probably cannot see for all this fume," the lamplighter's agent continued with a frown at the muggy air, "down there along this very pier you will find a certain Rivermaster Vigilus waiting to take you aboard his cromster *Rupunzil*. The vessel is sound and your way is paid."

Rossamünd could see nothing but fog in that direction. "Ah … Aye …"

Mister Sebastipole gave a surprisingly warm smile and bowed. "Well, lad, the moment of departure has arrived, it seems, so I shall bid you a safe journey and leave."

Rossamünd was stunned. The lamplighter's agent might not have been the friendliest chap, but such a prodigious journey as that upon which Rossamünd was about to embark was, surely, better done with the leer's company than without.

"I … I thought you'd be coming too?" he ventured.

Mister Sebastipole smiled again. "I have other tasks to attend to here in Boschenberg. You will see me again some day not too distant, I'm sure. Just head down the stair and along five berths. A lamplighter's life is independence of thought and deed, my boy. You will need to get used to this as soon as possible. Welcome to the Lamplighters!" With that the leer bowed again and walked back up Sooningstrat.

Mister Sebastipole waved once from the top of a rise in the street and, with a turn, was gone.

Just like that, Rossamünd was on his own. Uneasy, he took up his valise and took the stairs down to the river. The fog was still too thick for him to see his destination. He passed a great post thickly painted white – a berth marker – appearing suddenly out of the gloom, then two more.

As the fourth emerged from the soupy morning vapours, he spied a vessel moored there – or the shadow of one at least. As he approached, the outlines of the craft became clearer. It was indeed a cromster, though one in very poor repair, sitting dangerously low in the water. It did not look at all steady or sound to Rossamünd, rather it looked ready to founder even in the calm of the Humour. He frowned. The foundling had not lived so closeted a life that he had not seen dozens – even hundreds – of cromsters plying the mighty river. None of them came close to luxury, but all of them were in far better repair than this tub of rivets.

Cromsters, like most other ironclad river craft, sat low in the water, with a hull and keel that did not descend too deeply into the murky wash. This was necessary since rivers, even as large a stream as this, were much shallower than any sea, but Rossamünd was sure that this one sat just a little *too* low. If the water lapped this near to the gunwale in the calm of a river, surely it would be spilling over it in great washes when the craft encountered even the smallest swells of the most sheltered ocean bays.

As he came closer Rossamünd could see that mean, sickly-looking men were wrestling great barrels aboard the craft.

"Ahoy!" came a call, and a hefty shadow of a man rolled down the sagging gangplank to the pier. "Who might ye be, lubberin' about on th' pier in th' shadowy morning mists?"

Rossamünd did not much like being told he was "lubberin'" – it was an unfriendly term seafaring folks used of those who were not. "I'm looking for Rivermaster Vigilus and the cromster *Rupunzil*!" he declared briskly.

The hefty shadow came closer and clarified itself as an unsavoury-looking fellow, tall and thickly built, with broad, round shoulders and matted eyebrows knotting over a darting, conspiratorial squint. His clothes were shabby, though they looked as if they had once been of good quality. His dark blue frock coat, probably proofed, with overly wide sleeves, was edged with even darker blue silk and lined with buff. This garment came down to his knees and covered everything but a pair of hard-worn shin-collar boots. The man emitted a powerfully foul odour, and altogether gave Rossamünd a distinctly uneasy feeling.

"And where might ye be from, young master," this fellow asked, almost sweetly, his breath proving even fouler than his general stench, "to need to see such a fellow and such a vessel?"

"I be Rossamünd Bookchild from Madam Opera's Estimable Marine Society for Foundling Boys and Girls." Rossamünd gave a nervous half-a-bow. "Rivermaster Vigilus is meant to take me to High Vesting." This stranger might have been smelly, but that did not mean Rossamünd had to be rude.

The unsavoury fellow seemed to hesitate at this, then gathered himself. "So ye're me lively cargo, lad?" he purred, giving a saucy wink. "Bit unfortunate about yer name, but there ye 'ave it. Still! Grateful to 'ave met ye all th' same." He bowed, removing his tricorn to show grey, greasy hair pulled back in a stubby baton. Patting his own chest, the captain continued. "I be Rivermaster Vigilus, yer ever so 'umble servant."

This comment on his name was certainly among the more blunt Rossamünd had yet heard. Already low in his estimation, this fellow – this Rivermaster Vigilus – sunk lower still.

Obviously unconcerned, the rivermaster ploughed on. "I'll get ye safe to yer next 'arbour. I've plied this awful river for many a long year and I knows 'er bumps and lumps like th' warts on me own rear!" He declared this so loudly that many of the crew chuckled or sneered. "Thank 'e, lads." He gave a swaggering half-bow in the direction of the crew. "This 'ere is me crew – sons of a mad woman all!" With a vague wave of his voluminously sleeved arm, he introduced the several dozen bargemen loading awkwardly large barrels marked *Swine's Lard* into the hold. These fellows looked as rough and gruesome as their captain. Rossamünd frowned at them and at the rusting vessel they worked.

What was Mister Sebastipole thinking? This lot would barely make it to the Axles, let alone all the way to High Vesting!

The rivermaster must have sensed his concerns, for he cleared his throat and said, "Aye, not th' lithest tub ye've seen, nor th' 'andsomest crew, I'll grant, but there ye 'ave it. She be me other vessel, ye see — me standby as I've 'eard it said. The poor ol' *'Punzil* (by which Rossamünd could only assume he meant the *Rupunzil*) is laid up in ordinary with a great 'ole in 'er ladeboard side. Distressin' I tells ye, and costly too. But there ye 'ave it again." The rivermaster gave a sad sigh and Rossamünd felt a certain sympathy for him. When a vessel was laid up in ordinary — that is, deliberately stranded out of the water for repairs — it was often a troublesome business. "Instead there be *this*, young master," he continued. "The six-gun cromster, *'ogshead*. She'll be our carriage to 'igh Vesting and our quarters till we get there. She's steadier than she looks and sound and able to go into all waters — fit enough to 'ave made th' voyage to 'igh Vesting and back ag'in many times, as sure as I'm standin' 'ere!"

Despite all these claims they did little to allay Rossamünd's fears. He knew too much about how a vessel should be — a benefit of being raised in a marine society. He looked the *Hogshead* up and down and spied the figurehead for the first time, protruded from the bow. It was of a snarling pig, so corroded and neglected that it looked as if it was rotting. He thought the name *Hogshead* — which he knew was also the name for a large, cumbersome barrel — profoundly fitting. A labourer rolled by them such a barrel, which emitted an odour so powerful and foul it made Rossamünd gag.

Pullets and cockerels! I hope I don't have to spend my trip next to them – whatever they are …

"I was told my fare was already paid?"

The rivermaster seemed to do a quick calculation then said, slowly, "Aye, young master, that it 'as." He gave Rossamünd a quick grin. "Welcome aboard!" He steered Rossamünd up the gangplank and on to the befouled deck of the vessel. "I'll 'ave to be about me business now. We make off shortly. Settle yerself out o' th' way. May your cruise be as pleasant as th' Spring Caravan of th' Gightland Queen."

The cromster shuddered. Its gastrines, the engines of living muscles that would quietly propel her through the water, were being limbered – stretched and warmed ready for the hard work of turning the screw that pushed the *Hogshead* along.

Rossamünd stood by the helm and waited with apprehension. He surely wished Mister Sebastipole had accompanied him. Things seemed a little too odd.

"Ready to go, Poundinch!" a sour-looking man called to the rivermaster.

"Poundinch?" Rossamünd could not help but exclaim his thoughts. "Aren't you Rivermaster Vigilus?"

"Ah, aye … well … I am one and th' same!" The unsavoury fellow rolled his eyes a little. He sucked in a breath. Then he said, "Poundinch is just another way of saying Vigilus, ye see. Different language, ye see, Tutin – like th'

Emp'rer hisself speaks: 'vigil' is th' same as 'pound'; 'ilus' is th' same as 'inch'. Ye see? Me lads prefer the more comfortable sound o' Poundinch, is all. They says it so much I gets in th' 'abit of callin' meself th' same too... and ye can calls me it as well: Rivermaster Poundinch. How'd that be?"

Rossamünd squinted. He knew almost nothing of the Imperial language – Tutin, it was called – but something sounded a little off beam.

The musty rivermaster raised an apparently conciliatory hand and gave a mildly wounded look. "It's all right, I won't be offended. I often gets people axing – 'tis almost a habit for me to 'ave to explain."

Rossamünd knew what it was to have a difficult name – to be misunderstood by it. He pressed the confusion no further.

"So, now we're all properly acquainted let's 'eave to." Rivermaster Poundinch – Vigilus – whoever he might be – smiled, then called, "Cast 'er off, Mister Pike!" to his boatswain, who relayed the order with another yell. The rivermaster took up a speaking tube and hollered within, "We'll 'ave 'er at two knots, Mister Shunt!"

The pier men threw ropes, the bargemen pushed off and with further shuddering the *Hogshead* moved slowly out and steadily down the narrow channel. Rossamünd quailed faintly with confusion, holding off an embarrassing, blubbering panic. Away from the bank wall of sandstone they went, away from the granite pier. Just like that,

Rossamünd was on his way – uncertain, and unhappily alone with this frightful crew.

The *Hogshead* slowly trod past the shadow of another cromster on its right. That it was in much better repair was obvious even in the murk. Rossamünd squinted and took a step forward to see if he might read the other vessel's nameplate, but was prevented by fog and the bustling of the bargemen. Yet, just before the other cromster disappeared into the obscurity, he thought he saw someone pacing beside it, on the pier, as if waiting for something or someone. He could not, however, be sure.

The *Hogshead* moved on.

The channel was one of the many man-made tributaries that had been dug from the main flow of the Humour many centuries ago – running into and out of the city, flowing down valleys of brickwork. Buildings often went right up to the channel's edge, making the banks an almost continuous wall of drab bricks and dark stone in which streets and sludgy drains made deeply vertical gaps. Rossamünd watched it all pass by in a silence of profound agitation. The Padderbeck Stair and its pier disappeared into the gloom.

"Now, me lad!" the rivermaster's voice boomed, offending the morning quiet, and startling Rossamünd from his unhappy funk. "Do as I tells ye, and we'll be th' best of mates, matey. So find yerself a spot on th' prow and stay outta me way."

The foundling obeyed, sitting right at the front of the *Hogshead*. The crew left him alone, free to fret on his future, as they made their way out of Boschenberg. The cromster passed beneath a heavy arch of black stone, its portcullis raised and dripping with condensed fog, and went from the dim gloom of the city-channel into the pale murk of the open waters of the Humour. In the dark sepia waters before them was a lane marked with squat quartz pillars that glowed wanly in the vaporous morning. Rossamünd had heard that these were made using an ancient and half-forgotten art, followed step-by-complex-step but little understood. The shadows of other vessels passed them by with faint thrumming hisses; ships' bells clung their warnings in the turgid damp.

In the middle of the river the *Hogshead* came about and went southwards, going downstream. The fog began to thin, showing the sun low in the east, a bulging, blood-red disc. The cromster continued south, moving past mountainous onyx palaces, past grand villas and dark stately homes, past the wooden houses and low hovels, past even the Vlinderstrat and his old abode. Before them, athwart the *Hogshead's* path, was a massive rivergate that spanned the entire width of the Humour. The Axle. Tall it was, with pale granite turrets and many high arches held up by great columns and guarded by ponderous iron grilles that descended right to the muddy bottom. Heavily fortified bastions towered by either side of each arch and strong points filled with soldiers and forty-eight pounder long guns at every mid-point between. Over five hundred years ago the Axle had been built out from the city's second curtain wall to guard it from unwanted things on and *in* the river. All the traffic of the Humour had to pass through it, and to pass through meant you paid a toll. Rossamünd had seen the rivergate several times before – though he had never passed through it – and it still amazed and daunted him. He knew very well that doing so for the first time was a deeply significant thing for a Boschenberger. It meant you were leaving the lulling, familiar security of your city, your home. It meant you were entering the broad wild places, where monsters harried and mishaps threatened. It meant your life changing forever.

Rossamünd stared at the Axle in awe.

High above, musketeers in black and brown stood upon its solid battlements, vigilant wardens who strove to keep the city safe – whether from monsters or wicked men. The scarlet gleam of this eerie morning reflected from bayonets and musket muzzles. Graceful pennants of sable and mole flicked and snapped higher still above them all. Such a mighty and well-defended wall. What Rossamünd found even more spectacular was that there was another Axle – the twin of this one – upstream, guarding Boschenberg's northern end. He felt a strange swell of pride for his city-state.

With a deep, near-silent thudding the *Hogshead* slowed, the screws pushing back against the flow of the old river. One of the many great gates in the Axle loomed. Contrary to Rossamünd's pessimism the cromster had managed to make it there without sinking. It pulled up alongside the enormous base of one of the great columns that fixed the whole rivergate to the immemorial rock petrified beneath the slime of the riverbed. Part of the column's base was fashioned into a low, grimy wharf, and by this the *Hogshead* halted to have its cargo inspected and pay the river toll. A door of pale, corroded green opened out on to the wharf, and from it marched several excise inspectors dressed in the familiar brown and black of Boschenberg.

With a grin and a wink at Rossamünd, Poundinch stepped off the *Hogshead* and held a conference with the most official-looking of all the inspectors. Rossamünd sat at the prow of the cromster pretending not to listen, and listened intently indeed to the hushed conversation. Though he did not grasp all the baffling inconsistencies of adult ways, something about their communication suggested conspiracy.

"Such a pleasure to see ye again, Clerks' Sergeant Voorwind." Poundinch touched the edge of his thrice-high. He handed over the manifest of his vessel's hold and with it a little paper package.

"And good early morning to you, Rivermaster Poundinch," the official replied with a cynical grin. "What is your cargo this time?" He took the manifest and the little paper package with it, making as if to read the first while slyly pocketing the second.

Poundinch inclined his head. "Much th' same as it always is: seventy barrels of exceptional swine's lard bound for th' soap 'ouses and wax factories of th' Considine, m'lord, and ten bushels of parsley, sage, rosemary and thyme for th' perfumeries of Ives and Chassart."

"That far south! In this old bucket?" The clerks' sergeant raised an eyebrow. "I may have to charge you an additional fee. How exceptional are we talking?"

"Full and putridly ripe. It's took a great deal of 'ard work to get it delivered and just as much to load." Poundinch smiled smugly.

"And the young master by the tiller? He's not one of your *deliveries,* is he?"

Rossamünd's spine tingled as he realised the clerks' sergeant was talking about him.

"Oh, no, no. I've taken on a cabin boy, see. Fetch and carry and such. Someone to learn th' ropes and take up th' trade, as ye like. 'E's well appraised of th' arrangements, never ye mind."

A cabin boy? Fetch and carry?

Rossamünd held his breath. What was all this double talk? Why did Rivermaster Poundinch not just speak the truth? *Does he not know that I can hear him?*

Clerks' Sergeant Voorwind frowned. "As it should be, Poundinch. We both know what happened last time you took on a cabin lad. This new fellow will most certainly incur another toll." He lowered his voice so that Rossamünd had difficulty hearing what he said next. "Be warned, the Emperor has issued an edict expanding the bans on the dark trades. We won't trouble ourselves with it now, but next time you're through be expecting to pay an even higher fine."

Now it was Poundinch's turn to frown. "As ye like it, Voorwind," he said through gritted teeth. "Don't push us too 'ard, mind, or we might 'ave to push back."

"Careful, Poundinch!" the clerks' sergeant snarled quietly. "'Twould be an easy thing for me to reverse things as they stand. If you force me, I'll push right back again, with the authority of our beloved city-state." He took a step backwards, his expression changing easily from open hostility to formal approval. "Very good, rivermaster. We'll complete our inspection, then you may go on your way."

Muttering imprecations into his creased neckerchief, Poundinch stepped back on to the *Hogshead* and waited there by the column's base for the clerks to finish their duty.

Rossamünd was certainly ignorant of much of the conversation's true meaning, but his suspicions still churned. What were the "dark trades" that Voorwind fellow had hinted at? He found it hard to understand how it was that a man like Sebastipole – punctual, officious – had, it seemed, got him a berth upon a vessel of such poor conduct.

While the rivermaster and clerks' sergeant had been in conference, sturdy men had been looking the *Hogshead* over. They had descended the waist ladder into the hold – quickly reappearing with disgusted expressions on their faces – to scrutinise the bargemen's papers. Eventually a hefty, bespectacled clerk demanded to see Rossamünd's own travelling certificates. The clerk looked very much as if he knew what to do should any document not meet his precise requirements. Rossamünd stared up at him as he handed over his papers. It was like looking up at a solid brick wall. With a cursory scan the clerk returned his papers without a comment.

Fees paid and cargo and crew declared fit, the *Hogshead* was permitted to pass. The grille before them squealed and slowly moved aside. The vessel trod through cautiously. Once clear of the mighty Axle, it gathered speed and proceeded downriver, passing the third curtain wall of Boschenberg, then the outer curtain wall and the suburbs fenced in between. Beyond the city, farmlands, immaculately tilled and primly fenced, stretched away on both sides. Gorgeously white egrets stalked and crimson-legged water-hens waddled about the banks among the sodden roots and falling russet leaves of tall sycamores, graceful elms and black, evergreen turpentines.

Rossamünd stayed at his post right at the tip of the bow, where he read his instructions and his beloved almanac, and tried his best to avoid the crew, none of whom was proving very friendly. The instructions were brief and simple: he was to remain aboard the vessel till he reached High Vesting and, once disembarked, was to meet with a certain Mister Germanicus in the offices of the Chief Harbour Governor. From there Mister Germanicus was to assist the boy to Winstermill, the Lamplighters' manse – or headquarters – where he would receive further instructions. At the bottom was a strange mark, "Seb" ending in a line with a squiggle, which he assumed was Sebastipole's mark.

That was all of it.

Rossamünd read them over and over to see if he might have missed anything, hoping fervently that this mysterious Mister Germanicus would know how to find him, for he had no idea how he could find Mister Germanicus. Gleaning little he sat back, leaning on a pile of hessian and hemp rope, fretting. From this position he could keep a close eye on the suspect crew – this Poundinch fellow most of all – and even be on the watch for monsters. Though he did not know what he would do if he found one, he still wanted to know if it was coming.

Occasionally he consulted his almanac. The maps showed that the Humour wended its way through many miles of apparently featureless regions – places the topographers had not bothered to name. They had marked instead, in the large blank areas on either side of the river, simple descriptions: "broad pastureland" on the east side, and "a great partial wilderness" on the west. They had also marked the Humour with its other names in parenthesis: "Humeur", "Swartgallig", "Sentinus" – names given by other races in other times. Only two places were noted along its course ahead of them. The first was Proud Sulking – a city like Boschenberg, of which he had some idea. The other was somewhere called the Spindle, positioned just before the Humour emptied into a large body of water to the south called the Grume. This was the enormous bay upon whose shores were noted many other cities and many other ports. He knew something of the Grume too, but what was the Spindle?

He rose and cautiously went to Rivermaster Poundinch to ask him.

"Been readin' th' charts, I see," Poundinch observed amiably. "Gets th' feelin' with all yer gawping at th' Axle, that ye tain't been out of th' city before. Am I right?"

"Only twice to visit the sister of ... of a friend. She lives in Blemish, which is a tiny village just outside the walls." These had been most magical visits to the small cottage of Verline's younger sister, and Rossamünd could not remember more wonderful times. He sighed. How he was going to miss Verline. He was determined to scratch down a letter to her when he arrived in Winstermill.

"Sounds quaint, lad. As for th' Spindle, well, it's another, further rivergate, just as menacin' as those Axles there." The rivermaster poked a thumb over his shoulder at the dark shadowy line of the rivergate they had left behind. "But it belongs to a different city, that being Brandenbrass — which is moi 'ome, by th' way. Th' Spindle is about three days from 'ere, and after that, I will takes us out on to th' Grume. We then turn left, and travel east to 'igh Vesting. All up ye'll be with us for a little under a week."

He looked sidelong at Rossamünd. "Been on a cromster before, lad? 'Cause, if ye like, when we is well clear of th' morning's fog, I can show ye about th' 'umble dimensions of me own vessel."

Despite his strong stink and his original gruffness, Rivermaster Poundinch now seemed a very friendly fellow, as pleasant as Rossamünd could have hoped for.

"Aye, a few times, sir," he answered, "though I've not actually been on many craft, sir."

Of all the fascinating things about water-going craft, Rossamünd was fascinated by gastrines. These were large boxes in the bowels of ironclads housing great muscles that turned the vessel's screw – or propeller – and their limbers, which were much smaller versions of a gastrine that were used to warm up the greater. Without limbers the muscles of a gastrine would soon tear and bruise and seize up. "Could I see the gastrines, sir? I've been told they have to be mucked out every hour or they get sick."

"An' who told ye that?"

Rossamünd's chin lifted as he answered proudly, "Dormitory Master and Ex-Gunner Fransitart, one of the masters of the marine society." Rossamünd liked to use his dormitory master's full title, but he almost never had an opportunity.

"Frans'tart, eh ...?" Poundinch frowned long and plucked at some rogue hairs on his patchily shaven chin. "I reckon I remember 'im – a terrerfyin' fellow, if me memory serves. Knew 'ow to get us to shoot straight, that's fer sure! Well, ye were told rightly, m'lad, an' I'd expect no less from Frans'tart."

"You knew Master Fransitart?" Rossamünd was agog at this. "What was he like? Did you serve at the Battle of the Mole with him?"

"Aye, aye," Poundinch chuckled. "Only briefly, not nearly so long to know 'im well, but long enough to get a feel for 'im – and th' switch of 'is rod ..." He muttered this last bit into his neckerchief, but the foundling heard it anyway.

"Didn't you like him, sir?"

"Aye! Oh, aye! Ol' Poundy likes ever-ry-one. I find it's mores a matter of who likes ol' Poundy. Frans'tart was as fine a petty officer as a navy or th' ladies could ev'r want!"

Ladies! Rossamünd had sometimes wondered if there had ever been a Goodlady Fransitart. "Was he married, sir?"

Poundinch guffawed. "Oh ho! No, there was no wife that I knew of. He weren't like th' marryin' kind to me. Now that's enough on 'im, lad. Let me con-cerntrate on th' steerin' for a bit, an' then we'll take ye to 'ave a peep at them there gastrines."

Remaining by the rivermaster, Rossamünd tried to imagine Fransitart plying his old trade with noble vigour and cavorting with the refined ladies of lofty and fashionable courts. How strange it would have been to see him pacing the decks of some great ram bawling orders stoutly amid the smoke and terror of a sea battle. The kind of sea battle Rossamünd was never to get a chance to see. He had his new trade, far inland. He thought again about Sebastipole's too-brief instructions.

"Rivermaster Poundinch?"

"Aye, lad?" Poundinch looked down at him.

"Would you know where the" – Rossamünd frowned as he read aloud from the instructions – "the 'offices of the Chief Harbour Governor' are?"

"Er ... I gather ye're meaning in 'igh Vesting?"

"Aye, sir."

"Well, most cert'nly, I do. Need to be shown to 'em, when we get there, do ye? Ol' Poundy can do that for ye in a trice!"

Gratified and relieved, Rossamünd doffed his hat and bowed to the rivermaster – as he had seen men in the streets do – and said earnestly, "I am most obliged to you, sir."

Poundinch burst with powerful laughter, sweeping off his own hat and returning the formality. "Why, 'tain't nothin', me good sir."

The *Hogshead* proved more solid than she had first appeared, pushing sturdily through many of the sub-merged snags that hindered their progress. Rossamünd was informed that the fifty-odd crew slept on the upper deck – right down the middle of the vessel, between the guns – and, as there was no room in the hold, he would be expected to do the same. He did not mind, for the hold was more cramped than the marine society and stunk horribly of pigs, sweat, and other worse unnameable things. There were no cabins upon the flat, flush upper deck except for the hold-way about halfway down the vessel, a low box-like structure with doors which opened on to the ladder that descended into the hold. There were also the twelve bull-black twelve-pounder cannon in staggered rows down either side and taking up a goodly amount of room. Six cannon were in a line on the steerboard or right side and six down the ladeboard or left side of the vessel. Rossamünd admired them.

Despite his anxieties, he found that he was actually excited to be on his first real voyage – the movement of the cromster in the water, the bustle of activity and the routine of the watches, the silent throbbing of the gastrines. The *Hogshead* was no ocean-going ironclad, yet it was much more thrilling than the small craft on which Rossamünd had made day trips in the past.

In map-reading classes back at the foundlingery, he had been taught about the oceans – the vinegar seas. He had been taught that they were a rainbow of different colours: reds, greens, azures, yellows, even black – this last one was shown on the charts as the Pontus Nubia. These lessons made him long to see the sea, and now that he was almost upon such waters he sorely regretted that an ocean-going life was not to be his.

By the third bell of the middle watch the fog had lifted sufficiently for Poundinch to trust the course of the *Hogshead* to Mister Pike and make good on his offer to show Rossamünd the gastrines. The ladder creaked frighteningly as the rivermaster led him down into the hold. It was painfully cramped below deck. Poundinch stooped low and even lower to pass beneath the beams. The stench of the place made Rossamünd's eyes water. He never thought anything could be so putrid, so foul. He was determined to make a brave showing, however, and pressed on. The rivermaster did not seem to mind, or even notice.

Poundinch waved vaguely to the forward parts, where the barrels were lashed and obscured with canvas tarpaulins.

"No need to be showin' ye that, just filthy ol' swine's lard. It's aft ye wants to be – follow me, lad, and see all th' wonder of this beauty's gastrines."

Rossamünd followed and there they were – the gastrines. His sense of disappointment was much the same as when he had spied Sebastipole's sthenicon box. As that device was just a small ordinary box, so these gastrines were just very large, ordinary wooden boxes bound with copper – but at least these were big. They almost reached the planking of the deck above. Running down either side of them were much smaller boxes of hardwood, two on each side for each gastrine. These were the limbers. From the top of each rose great cranks and several many-jointed shafts that pivoted perpendicularly and entered the side of the gastrines. They were still now, the limbers not being in use. With such a crowd of machinery there was barely enough room to press along the grimy, curving inner walls of the hold to pass. Rossamünd was amazed at the sturdy pulsating of the muscles within the gastrines; he could sense it in the air all about as they squeezed past, feel it powerfully in the planks and beams beneath his feet and at his back. What surprised him most was the warmth that came from the great brass-bound boxes, a sickly heat which made the rotten air of the hold thick and clinging. In a cramped space at the stern they met a wizened man in an apron surrounded by a compli-cated array of levers, his long, thin white hair dripping in the humidity. He looked up at the rivermaster with a silent, surly question in his eyes. Poundinch introduced him to

Rossamünd as Mister Shunt the gastrineer. It was the gastrineer's task to feed, muck out and care for the gastrines, make sure they were always limbered properly, and keep them in good health. He ranked highly in a vessel's crew.

"Hello, Mister Shunt, sir," said the foundling.

Shunt the gastrineer ignored him.

"Well, there ye are." Poundinch patted the nearest box. "These be gastrines. Not much to look at, eh? But a powerful sight more constant than a sailing vessel, and no mistake. I'll leave ye with dear ol' Shunty 'ere, so's he can talk technicalities with ye. Come straight up when ye're done, mind – no dalliancing about down 'ere."

The rivermaster retreated.

Rossamünd carefully pressed a hand against a gastrine. It was most certainly hot, like the brow of someone in a fever. The mighty throbbing of the muscles working within transmitted up his arm, and he felt his whole body *bump-thump, bump-thump* in sympathy. He admired the powerful-looking levers, many of which were half as tall as him again, each one governing certain actions of the gastrines and limbers. He looked to the gastrineer with a smile.

"Git!" cursed Shunt.

"Ah … aye! Sorry, Mister Shunt, sir, I …" Rossamünd pulled his hand away from the side of the box.

The gastrineer rolled his eyes horribly. "Git!" he grated again, stabbing a hand at the foundling.

Rossamünd blinked in surprise, then realised with horror that there was a weapon in the man's hand – a curved and

80

cruelly barbed dagger. He had never been threatened with a real weapon before. It was enough to send him stumbling back up the ladder and running back to his couch of canvas at the bow.

"I see's ye've got yerself well acquainted with our darlin' gastrineer," chuckled Poundinch as Rossamünd fled past him.

Rossamünd refused to do anything so embarrassing as cry — though he very much felt like it and might have once. At that moment, hugging his knees to his chest and scowling back any tears, he would rather have been back in the foundlingery's suffocating halls.

With the dark of his first night aboard descending, Rossamünd decided to sleep at his original station at the prow on a pile of old hessian and hemp distinct only from the other piles of old hessian and hemp as stinking less. No one objected, and so he settled in for sleep. If it rained he would rather get wet than endure the disgusting hold.

The night passed mercifully dry, yet dreams of a knife-wielding Shunt, the incessant clanging of the watch bells, and the stomping of the crew's bare feet kept Rossamünd from restful sleep. By the ringing of the morning watch at around four o'clock, he gave up on the prospect of proper rest and was rewarded eventually with a beautiful, brilliant pink sunrise.

Red dawning, traveller's warning, he thought gloomily.

The *Hogshead* was now clear of Boschenberg and its jurisdiction and roaming an ungoverned stretch of the Humour. The land on the eastern side of the river remained flat open pastureland. Upon the west it was becoming more rolling and rocky and decidedly more wild-looking. Such places were known as ditchlands, the borders between everymen's kingdoms and the dominion of the monsters. Rossamünd could well imagine bogles and nickers prowling about the stunted trees and ragged weeds, seeing who they might devour.

As the day progressed, Rivermaster Poundinch ignored everyone and contributed little to the running of the vessel. Occasionally he would growl a command, but usually he lounged silently at the tiller, his chin in his chest as if he was dozing.

Rossamünd was taken by loneliness. At that moment, alone among all these self-interested cut-throats, he would have welcomed even Mister Sebastipole's stiff manners and disturbing eyes.

Poundinch came alive suddenly at the end of the forenoon watch and the beginning of the afternoon when dinner was served by the taciturn, sour-faced cook, and again when there was gunnery practice. Early in the afternoon watch, when the river seemed clear of other craft, he roused himself and bellowed, "Right, lads! Gunnery practice! To yer pieces!"

A bosun's whistle was blown and the crew hustled to the six cannon on the ladeboard side of the *Hogshead*. Poundinch strutted at the helm post, bellowing orders, directions, abuse. "Run them out, ye mucky scoundrels! Come on, Wheezand, I've seen me grandmamma, rest her, move faster than ye, and she's been a'moulderin' in th' ground these last ten years! And I should know. I put her there meself!" At this he gave a blood-curdling chortle and many of the crew joined in.

Rossamünd chuckled nervously with them, eagerly awaiting what he hoped would be a spectacle. He had always wanted to see the cannon worked. The foundlings of Madam Opera's had never been allowed near one, regardless of their training in the naval crafts. Suddenly he realised that there *were* benefits in leaving the foundlingery and its strict policies after all.

BOOM! One after the other the pieces were fired, at a rotten stump or anything that happened to be passing by – the smaller the better, to improve the bargemen's aim.

For Rossamünd it was indeed both thrilling and deafening, and completely distracted him from his anxious woes.

BOOM! went the guns once more, the crash of their firing hitting him with a thump right in his chest, each blast filling the air with creamy, fizzy-smelling smoke that billowed and lazily drifted away. The whole vessel shuddered with each cannonade, while across the other side of the Humour great vertical splashes were thrown up, or part of a tree would collapse, sending cattle fleeing from the river bank.

After the fourth broadside, the crew were piped to cease and routine resumed. Rivermaster Poundinch went back to his languor and Rossamünd remained alone at the bow, humming within in boyish joy at what had proved a spectacle indeed.

That evening was clear and bitterly cold. A three-quarter moon was rising, swollen and yellow in the dark green sky. Muffled in his scarf, his jackcoat buckled right up, Rossamünd lay belly down on the deck of the bow and stared at the black water. For some time, he had been listening to the loud concert of a thousand frogs all singing along the banks and watching a small, pale shape dashing upon the water's surface. At first he thought it was a weak reflection of lunar light playing on the bow wave but, as two bells of the second dog watch rang, it moved oddly, darting out away from the vessel then back again. The hairs on Rossamünd's neck bristled and a shimmer of terror thrilled through his belly. He stared as the pale shape broke the surface – it was a head: a pallid lump, unclear in the jaundiced light, showing a long snout full of snaggle-jawed teeth. Its glittering black eyes rolled evilly and fixed him with a terrible gaze. His first monster …

Rossamünd had enough wit to grope for his satchel, which he never kept far from him. Perhaps now was the time to use one of his precious repellents. Just as he gripped the strap, the pale lump in the water gave a long bubbling snort and disappeared under the bow and away to the right, towards moon shadows and the root-tangled bank. Rossamünd shook with fear. He did not move for a long time but just lay staring at the right bank, trying to blink as little as possible for fear that the pale beast would spring upon him in ambush from the water. His horror was heightened when a gurgling howl rang in the dark. For Rossamünd it was pure terror. Among the crew, however, it caused but a minor stir and nothing more.

For the second night, curled up tight in pungent hessian, Rossamünd got little sleep.

... AND OFF AGAIN

rivergates (noun) great fortifications built across rivers and broader streams to protect a certain valuable place or as an outworking of a city's more terrestrial battlements. Certain riverside duchies and principalities have long used their rivergates to control trade, not just into their own domains but to those domains beyond as well.

THE next day, when Rossamünd mustered the courage to tell Poundinch of the previous night's pale monster, the rivermaster showed little alarm, or even interest in, the sighting.

"Just one of those things, me boy, and nowt to trouble yerself over." The rivermaster stroked his scabrous chin for a moment, pondering. "River's full o' strange but 'armless surprises. Be takin' my word on that 'un – ol' Poundy knows these waters."

As the day progressed they met many vessels going upriver, and were even overtaken by a faster moving cromster with a smartly dressed crew. These fine fellows hailed the bargemen of the *Hogshead*, who only sneered and returned the brisk greeting with sullen looks.

A bargeman coiling rope near Rossamünd told him off

for waving vigorously as his own reply. "Fancy-lad good-fer-nothin's," the crewman growled. "Reckons they're better than us ..."

Rossamünd could not help but wish Sebastipole had found him passage aboard the other vessel.

In the afternoon, clouds black and blue blew up from the south-east – a hint of the bitter winter to come – making the day dark and the evening even darker. Downriver a city built on the east bank of the Humour came into view, its many lights already shining in the untimely gloom. Rossamünd consulted the almanac. Proud Sulking it was called, the major river port of the vast farming region known as the Sulk and a bitter rival of Boschenberg. It had become rich from the many merchants who wished to avoid the stiff tolls of the Axles, and chose instead to pay the lesser port fees that Proud Sulking demanded. There they would unload their cargoes instead and transport them by ox-trains along the highroads and, through much danger, to their customers further upstream. In doing this Proud Sulking made a jealous and bitter enemy of Boschenberg.

Proud Sulking was not nearly as large as Boschenberg, although its bastions and keeps and curtain walls along the river bank were just as high and threatening. Its many wharves and piers were clogged and bustling with the vigorous activity of river craft, their crews and the labourers working ashore. Eager to avoid this foreign enemy city, Rossamünd was afraid that the *Hogshead* would go about and enter the river port. Instead Poundinch steered her

POUNDINCH

as far over to the opposite bank as was possible, and held his course there, with many a nervous glance over at the forbidding city. Relieved, Rossamünd watched solemnly as the *Hogshead* passed Proud Sulking by.

With night closing in, the wind diminished but the clouds remained. The *Hogshead* was now many miles south of Proud Sulking and the land on both sides of the river became boggy and threatening: holm-oak grew in squat, clotted thickets; bristling swamp oaks and sickly turpentines rose tall and stick-gaunt. This must be a monster-infested place. Here, surely, were the wilds that Fransitart and Craumpalin had spoken of with such awe and warning. Rossamünd was convinced he could feel bogles and nickers prowling and spying.

When dark finally ruled, the *Hogshead*'s stern and mast lanterns were inexplicably doused so that the cromster moved in pitch black. Even the binnacle lamp that lit the compass by the tiller was hooded to show as little glow as possible. Rossamünd knew that the lights on a vessel should never be put out: on a river or at sea, a ship without its lanterns lit in the night or a deep fog was a danger to all other river-going craft. Why would Poundinch do such a thing? Somehow Rossamünd knew better than to ask. He certainly would not consult any of the crew. In the blind night he fought against sleep.

Despite his determination he eventually succumbed and lapsed into a troubled slumber.

Sometime later he was woken by the sound of an anchor

dropping. There was some quiet cursing, and Rivermaster Poundinch's voice scolded huskily, "Keep it steady, ye slop buckets! No noise!"

The cromster had halted near the western bank at a place neither remarkable nor distinct from any other part of the river's haunted edge. All hands were pressed to duty as smaller hand lanterns were lit and the *Hogshead*'s only boat, a large jolly boat normally towed behind, was brought about to the steerboard side. The crew were nervous. They lugged up several foul-smelling kegs from below and lowered them by rope into the little craft. Bewildered, Rossamünd listened to the thumps and quiet exclamations. He sat up slowly, hoping to avoid attention, and peered over the edge of deck.

Ponderously laden with barrels, the jolly boat was being rowed slowly to the bank. Poundinch was in the bow holding high a lantern with another fellow — Sloughscab, the *Hogshead*'s own dispensurist; there were eight crew to row and two sturdy fellows sitting in the boat's stern holding primed muskets and looking alert. As it moved to shore the large rowboat became no more than the wan glow of the lantern and a silhouette of the activity within. Soon it disappeared altogether among the hanging branches and crooked, buttressed roots that knotted the river bank. Rossamünd saw, or at least thought he saw, the flicker of another lantern somewhere further in the trees. He could hear still the creaking of oars and fancied too the echoes of *hulloo*s coming back across the water. For a time everything was still, waiting – even the frogs. Light was still not permitted aboard and the limbers were even stilled. Little could be seen but a faint orange smudge striped with the indigo shadows of intervening trunks. Rossamünd imagined that he was floating in the midst of nothing, drifting in an empty universe with just his thoughts and his breath.

A flicker from the bank interrupted his wandering notions.

Then another.

A bright flash, half-hidden by the black shadows of tree trunks, was closely followed by the muffled but unmistakable popping of musket fire. The crew at once became agitated, and even more so when a loud crack snapped and echoed across the water. Quickly a dim lantern hove into view, indistinctly showing the jolly boat being rowed as rapidly as possible back to the *Hogshead*. There was a fizzing spurt and a brilliant flash, stark against the dark – another telltale eruption of a musket, fired by one of the sturdy fellows kneeling stiffly in the aft of the jolly boat.

The other sturdy fellow was missing. So was Sloughscab the dispensurist.

Rivermaster Poundinch was in the jolly boat's bow, bellowing, "Pull! Pull, ye cankerous pigs!"

Behind them whole trees shuddered and sagged. Cries rang out on board the *Hogshead*. The stern lantern flared into light and by its green glow bargemen hurried and panicked.

Rossamünd stood, transfixed by the spectacle. Through

91

parted trunks something enormous was moving. Rossamünd could barely make out what it was: long of limb it seemed, yet hunched, pushing at the trees as if they were mere shrubs. It turned its head and Rossamünd felt he caught a glimpse of tiny, angry eyes.

"Pullets and cockerels!" Rossamünd exclaimed in a horrified whisper.

There was a loud yell.

Simultaneously, one of the cromster's cannons fired, the smoke of its discharge belching obscuring blankness over the scene. The small thunder reverberated, flat and hollow, all about the land, and as its fumes cleared the giant thing was gone. Poundinch was now scrabbling back aboard his vessel spluttering foul language, crying for the anchor to be weighed and limbers turned.

Poundinch said nothing about the affair. No reasons were given for the absence of Sloughscab or the sturdy musket-wielding chap, no explanation of what the giant on the shore might have been. The contents of the jolly boat – three box-crates emitting odd and disturbing sounds – were simply hurried into the hold. Normal duties were resumed. Those on watch rapidly got the cromster moving once more. Those off watch muttered grimly for a time and went to sleep.

Rossamünd tried to sleep himself. He tossed the rest of that night over it, his head full of fear and pondering and repeating images of the nicker's angry eyes and the startling flash of cannon fire. Rising at the fourth bell of the morning watch, the foundling determined that all through the next day he would listen, as far as he possibly could, to every word spoken on board the *Hogshead*.

With the rising of the sun and the changing of watch, the crew exchanged meaningful glances with each other.

"Oi don't moind cartin' abowt bits o' bodies in them there barrels of pigs' muck," one filthy bargeman offered to another quietly at breakfast. "We're shorely paid noice for doin' it. But thowse things down thar now just bain't natural."

To this the second growled wordless agreement then waggled his finger to ward off evil. "Right you are, right you are. *Ablatum malum ex nobis*," he said, "Rid evil from among us."

Later that day, Rossamünd overheard one of the crewmen who had helped row the venture ashore the previous night say to another, "We'd made the trade fine, but that thing must have been watching for a long time, 'cause we heard nowt of it till it come out all a-quick with a roar. Scatters the corsers with a big sweep o' its terrible arm – like this." He swung his own arm wildly, thoughtlessly letting his voice become louder. "And those that it hasn't smashed are off into the trees and ol' Poundy is pushing us back on to the barge while Cloud and Blunting have a crack at it with their firelocks and poor Sloughscab hurls his potions – you know how 'e's always wantin' to give 'em a good testing – well he got 'is chance, 'cause ..."

"Gibbon!" It was the rivermaster. One eye was open as he lounged at the tiller and this single orb glared horribly at the loquacious crewman. "Don't give me a reason to remember yer name any further, me darlin' chiffer-chaffer."

At this Gibbon went pale and lapsed to silence, as did the rest of the crew. One thing that he had said kept spinning in Rossamünd's head. "... Scatters the *corsers*". He had heard of these before. Corsers were folk who robbed graves and stole from tombs to make their living. *The dark trades!*

What did such wretched people as these have to do with the crew of the *Hogshead*? Why would Poundinch stop in the middle of nowhere in the deep of night just to meet them? Was he a part of the dark trades too? After the suspicious doings with Clerks' Sergeant Voorwind at the Axle, it was becoming disconcertingly clear that this was most probably the case. And what was that gangling giant he had glimpsed? Rossamünd heard little else that day but the occasional inaudible griping, and as time went on so his anxieties increased. Surely he had to get off this unhappy vessel.

By the middle of the next day Rossamünd, huddled and unmoving at the prow in an agony of fear, spied the low wall of the Spindle as it finally appeared from around a river bend. Not nearly as tall or as grand as the Axle, the Spindle was a long, low dyke of black slate, stretching the river's mile-wide waters. Along its thick middle sections it was perforated by seven great arches and several lesser tunnels towards either bank. Each arch and tunnel was blocked by a massive portcullis of blackened iron. Great taffeta flags – one side black, the other glossy white – the colours of the city-state of Brandenbrass – were flown from the four central bastions in the middle of the river and flapped wildly in the windy morning. Rossamünd could see many great-cannon poking from hatches and strong points all along the many walls and bastions. The ends of the Spindle terminated on either bank in a strong fortress of sharply sloping walls, high, steep roofs and tall chimneys and protected by stout curtain walls of the same black slate as the gate itself. Rossamünd could even see that the ground at the foot of the curtain walls was densely prickled with a vicious-looking thicket of thorny stakes. About the eastern fortress a small wood of swamp oak and olive grew, while along both banks leafless willows wept into the black run of the Humour. The Spindle instead was squat, imposing, daunting. To Rossamünd, however, it was also the chance of escape. Hope fluttered within his ribcage and he stared at it longingly.

When Poundinch sighted the rivergate he became agitated and positively alive. He leapt to his feet and paced his station as he had done at gunnery practice, muttering and gesticulating vaguely.

"Stay easy, lads. They've not caught ol' Poundy yet," he said over and over. He called down the speaking tube to the gastrineer, as softly as he could – for sound travels too well over water. "Ease 'er down, Mister Shunt, and when she's at th' gates keep the limbers limber, ye hear. We may need

95

to make it away right quick!" Then he growled low to the boatswain, always on hand. "Secure below. No glimpses, no clues, just barrels o' fat – same ol' rigmarole … and make sure the newest acquisitions keep quiet too."

The archways of the rivergate were low, forcing the crew of the *Hogshead* to lower the mast so that it lay flat on the deck. As this was done the boatswain reappeared from below, and the rivermaster ordered him to pipe all hands on deck. Responding to such a call was instinct to Rossamünd, and he joined the end of the ragged line of crew, standing straight and as smartly as he could.

Poundinch stalked in front of them all and muttered just loud enough to be heard, "I wants us to be just likes we was an 'appy ol' crew, no secrets, no gripes, just on an 'appy jaunt down th' ol' 'umour – ye gets me?"

"Aye, Poundinch," was the common assent.

The rivermaster waggled his conspiratorial eyebrows. "No grumblin'." He glared at Gibbon. "No snarlin'." He squinted at some other bargeman Rossamünd could not see. "Now back to it!" he barked, raising his arms.

As everyone returned to his labours, so Rossamünd returned to the bow. A neat trim cromster trod proudly into the tunnel before them, its crew standing smartly in ranks on the deck. It was the same vessel that had passed the *Hogshead* two days before. Once again Rossamünd wished he was aboard her instead. As it moved away he looked longingly at the shiny nameplate on the stern. His heart froze.

The plate read *Rupunzil*.

"Rosey-me-lad! Over 'ere!" Poundinch called.

The foundling stepped over cautiously, head low, eyes wide. He could see the rivermaster staring at the other cromster's stern.

"Worked it out at last, 'ave ye?" Poundinch sneered.

Rossamünd went pale.

"Took ye a bit, didn't it?" Faster than Rossamünd could react, the rivermaster's hand shot out and grabbed him in a painful pinch by the back of the neck. "You stay right by me, lad." Poundinch bent himself and leered into Rossamünd's face. "Just remember – ye're me cabin boy, got it?"

"I – I – I – uh ... nuh ... no, sir, I mean, aye-aye, sir," was all that would come out of the foundling's mouth. He could only stand there while Poundinch's fingers pressed painfully on the tendons of his neck, and marvel at the rivermaster's sudden cruelty.

Poundinch glared up at the Spindle.

"Made by a fierce, diligent folk, this," he said in a conversational tone at odds with the grip he had on the boy's scruff. "A cause of much consternation to th' lords of yer city when it were built." He turned his glare to the boy. "Whatever 'appens from 'ere on, ye're goin' to stay right 'ere by th' tiller and ol' Uncle Poundy's side, got me?"

The *Hogshead* was passing slowly under the high, broad tunnel of a boarding pier upon which stood several stern-looking officials, each uniformed crown to boot-toe in black proofing. Bargemen at the fo'c'sle and poop fended the *Hogshead* away from the slimy walls of the arch with long, strong poles.

"Ahh ... Ahoy, clerklings!" Poundinch called in a simulation of generous affability. "Ready to pay me taxes, same as always. Where's ol' Excise Master Dogwater?" Not once, during this cheerful display, did the rivermaster let up his wicked grip on Rossamünd's scruff.

A serious-looking fellow – Rossamünd thought him even more serious than the officials serving the Axle back in Boschenberg – gave the rivermaster a long, odd look. "Excise *Sergeant* Dogwater has been re-posted to tasks more suitable," he stated flatly.

Poundinch seemed momentarily put out by this revelation, and he released his grip on Rossamünd. His face contorted frighteningly but reverted marvellously to the previous false grin. He kept his hand upon the foundling's shoulder. It must have looked friendly enough from the pier, but the rivermaster's fingers were like cunning, hidden claws.

"Very good, very good – pass on me well wishes. 'E were as fine an excise man that ever served on this river." Poundinch rocked on his heels and, after a pause in which Rossamünd swore he could see the rivermaster's thoughts turn like winch gears, added, "Present comp'ny excepted, of course ..."

"Of course." Unimpressed, the excise clerk held out an expectant hand. "Now, present your documents and your tallies and scrutineers will be aboard presently."

Poundinch did as he was bid. The papers were taken through an iron door in the arch's hefty footing. Poundinch perspired, continually pursing his lips and flexing his free hand behind his back. Under the Axle, the *Hogshead's* master had been as cool as the cold side of the pillow. Here, however, with no secretive conversations or cynical winkings with one of the clerks, he was visibly agitated.

The original excise clerk reappeared, as expressionless as before, followed by three gentlemen heftier of build and bearing heavy, long-handled cudgels – the scrutineers. With them came a quarto of musketeers, all uniformed in black with trimmings of white. In two ranks they lined up – five at the front, five at the back – on the stone pier.

The excise clerk held up his right hand and took a breath. "By the declaration of His Grace, the Archduke and Regent of Brandenbrass, and through the ratification and execution thereby of his Cabinet of the Charters set upon the sanctity of our borders, and its Ordinances concerning the same, you are presently ordered to allow to board, and then to be boarded by and searched by, Officers of the Sovereign State of Brandenbrass, and to declare upon a solemn 'aye' that you bear no contraband or other illicit articles upon or within this vessel, whether by hold or other conveyance, and that you regard inviolate the law and assertions of the State of Brandenbrass and that State's authority. How say you?"

Rossamünd had no idea what had just been said, although it sounded extremely important and gravely impressive.

It seemed that Rivermaster Poundinch had not under-stood either. His squint grew more furrowed. "I ... uh ... aye, if it's comin' aboard ye wants, then" – he bowed low with a glance to his boatswain – "by all means."

The scrutineers and the excise clerk stepped across from the pier and tapped about the upper deck for a good long while. Poundinch hovered nearby, answering the curt quizzing of the clerk with affected politeness. Rossamünd stayed by the tiller as instructed, heart knotting and unknotting alarmingly. It was a gloomy afternoon made gloomier under the shadow of this arch.

Eventually the search moved to the hatch. "What a horren-dous stench coming from below, sir!" called the clerk.

"Why aye, sir." Poundinch made to look chastened. "I intend to 'ave 'er in ordinary this winter, to give 'er a thorough swillin' in and out. Tis th' pig fat ye see – good for th' purse but 'ard on th' nose."

The clerk put a foot on the top step and the scrutineers moved to follow. He paused and half turned. "Are your limbers still turning, sir?"

"Well ..."

"Pray still them at once! You are committing a grave breach, sir!" The clerk made to mark an entry in a large ledger.

Just for a moment Poundinch looked like a cornered cat. Then, with a "We'll not be 'avin' that!" he shoved the excise clerk down the ladder and struck the nearest scruti-neer right in the jaw with one of the thick wooden pins as big as a club that were used to hold the mast.

"Let fly, Mister Shunt!" he bawled. "Let fly!"

With this the chaos began. Everyone but Shunt hesitated. The *Hogshead* lurched forward and people sprawled, Rossamünd with them. Poundinch leapt into the hold. Two scrutineers pounced after him over their fallen comrade. *Hiss — crack*. The boatswain felled one with a pistol shot to the neck as the other disappeared below.

On the pier the musketeers presented their firelocks, their officer crying over the din. "Hold fast — or be slaughtered where you stand!"

The crew of the *Hogshead* just jeered as their vessel sheered away.

"Do yar worst, ya prattling hackmillion!" cried one.

"Hold yerself, chiff-chaffing lobcock!" screeched another.

"Go lay a muck hill, Mary!" and many worse things other bargemen returned.

The quarto of musketeers fired a rattling volley that brought several to their end, while someone ashore shouted, "Grapnels! Grapnels!"

The crew returned fire with pistol and blunderbuss, their shots having little effect as the musketeers' proofing proved its quality. Only one of the soldiers fell, simply sagging where he knelt, shot through the head. Amazed at how suddenly and matter-of-factly the violence had begun, Rossamünd froze first with disbelief, which quickly dissolved into utter terror. Cold nausea griped in his guts and set his fingers tingling.

The steerboard bow struck the farther wall of the arch as the boatswain was surprised by the heavy lurch and failed briefly to keep the vessel under control. The iron-clad hull ground with loud metallic groans along the stone and the *Hogshead* lost speed. The boatswain struggled for a moment, and then reasserted his will on the vessel. Under his now sure hand, the *Hogshead* went out the other side of the arch. Grapnel hooks were thrown to ensnare the cromster but none held. The *Hogshead* was clear.

"All limbs to the screw, Shunt!" the boatswain cried into a speaking tube to the organ deck. "Git us out of 'ere!"

Below a great contest thumped and bellowed. Poundinch and whatever crew had descended to aid him tackled the excise clerk and the doughty scrutineer. The sounds they all made gave no indication of who was winning, but as the cromster gained speed it was obvious that Shunt was not involved.

Rossamünd was shocked into self-preserving action as muskets fired once more and the balls panged about them. One sent some poor chap toppling into the Humour. Another struck the balustrade near Rossamünd's head, scaring him mightily, and as he struggled to find a refuge a musket shot clouted him upon his chest.

It hit harder than the hardest thump in harundo and sat him down with a tiny, audible *huff!* For a flash his whole existence was an intense agony right next to his heart. His eyes bulged, tears streamed. It hurt too much to breathe. He shook with terror as he thought he had gasped his last.

How could they shoot at a small lad like him? What had *he* done that they should hate him so? Then breath returned. He was winded and certainly bruised, but he was not badly harmed. The proofing Fransitart had provided had done its admirable work. Wiping away the tears and mucus, Rossamünd marvelled: he had been musket-shot and had survived.

The cromster gathered more speed and made for the middle of the river, putting a hundred yards between her and the Spindle. The vessel shuddered mightily as the gastrines were strained. The crew would do all they could to make their escape: only a gallows or worse awaited otherwise.

It was then that the great-guns started.

Boom! – was the first and only warning. No range-finding splash, no whistle of a shot just missing overhead: the cannon of the Spindle were too well sighted and their gunners too well practised. The very first shot hit the stern plate, which, being the only unclad part of the hull, was one of the weakest parts of the vessel. It was a fine hit that sent wood splintering and water spraying and shook the cromster to its ribs. The next two shots struck ironclad plates along the hull, each with a dull stentorian ring. Return fire was offered by the gunners of the *Hogshead*, but what good are twelve-pounders against the Spindle's thick walls of slate and close-packed earth? The balls just bounced on the fortifications and plopped uselessly into the river. Whether it was the fourth, fifth or sixth shot of the great-guns none could tell, but one of them removed the boatswain without a trace and left the tiller as nothing more than a shattered, unusable stump. The *Hogshead* veered crazily.

A certainty took hold of Rossamünd. The time to depart had come. He was on the wrong vessel with the wrong rivermaster and probably heading for a cruel and horrible end. Equally worse, now those in the Spindle were counting him as one of the dastardly crew. He had seen hangings on Unhallows Night. He knew how criminals met their end. His chance to flee was here.

Gathering up his valise, his satchel and his hat, Rossamünd flung himself from the gory deck and into the inky chill of the mighty Humour.

MEETINGS ON THE ROAD TO HIGH VESTING

threwd (noun) threwd is the sensation of watchfulness and awareness of the land or waters about you. Though no one is certain, the most popular theory is that the land itself is strangely sentient, intelligent and aware, and resents the intrusions and misuses of humankind. Paltry threwd, the mildest kind, can make a person feel uneasy as if under unfriendly observation. The worst kind of threwd – pernicious threwd – can drive a person completely mad with unfounded terrors and dark paranoias.

THE plunge into the river was like a stinging slap in the face, and his heavy proofing tugged Rossamünd deeper. Yet the valise somehow floated and, despite the weight of its contents, prevented him from sinking altogether. He bobbed to the surface and spluttered and gasped. He could swim, though a lot of people could not – a benefit of living in a marine society in a city by a river – and swim he did, as he had never done before. The current was slow, but enough to pull him away from the Spindle and away from the fleeing *Hogshead*. He splashed and flailed for shore, terrified he might end up part of the dinner of some bottom-dwelling river bogle.

The cromster had straightened somehow and was well

distant from Rossamünd now, smoke trailing from some unseen fire, still making good its flight downstream. Shots from the vessel popped and those of the rivergate thundered. More casualties were inflicted on the *Hogshead*'s crew by accurate fire, while misses sprayed gouts of water about. With a mighty *Slap!* one of these misses struck the water off to his right. He could see it clearly, a rapid, round shadow skipping once on the surface of the river before plunging with a meaty *Chock!* into the water. With a panicked surge, he pushed for the bank.

The Humour carried him towards its eastern side. The muddy shore was almost treeless except for a thicket of tall and knotted she-oaks a little further downstream. Roots poked into the water and graceful boughs hung their long needles thickly into the same. It was an obvious landmark, and Rossamünd struggled towards the trees as hard as he could. There was no one to be seen on the bank. He prayed that those in the Spindle had not seen him leap from the *Hogshead*, and would not see him climb out of the river and into those trees. He would be associated with the bargemen of the *Hogshead* in the wrong way, he was sure, and *that* was trouble anyone would want to avoid.

His feet finally found grip on the slimy riverbed. Dragging the valise from the current's tow, he waded ashore among curtains of soughing needle-leaves. Once out of the water he staggered and lay on the grassy bank in the shadows of the copse, sobbing, shivering, thoroughly lost. For a long while he remained dazed, unwilling to move for memory of the violence just gone and the fear of violence ahead. How could he possibly survive alone out here in the wilds, where all the monsters lived? Surely he would be eaten by the next gluttonous nicker to cross his path! If not today, then tomorrow or the next day – it was just a matter of time.

The thumping of great-guns ceased. The *Hogshead* had disappeared about a bend in the river. Rossamünd watched from where he lay as two dark vessels moved out from their moorings by the Spindle and headed downriver in pursuit. They were monitors – much larger than any cromster, and more than a match for the *Hogshead*. He continued watching until they slowly disappeared around the same bend.

With a sigh he lay back, his mind blank. He had no idea what to do next.

Come on! Think! Think! Rossamünd schooled himself. *Like Master Fransitart would do!*

It occurred to him that the mysterious Mister Germanicus would still be expecting him in the fortress-city of High Vesting. Just how he was going to get there was the troublesome part. There was no going back to the Spindle to ask for another barge: he would probably be recognised and certainly prosecuted. There was no other option – he was going to have to walk.

But walk to where? Rossamünd tried to marshal his thoughts.

All about, the land was uniformly flat – mile upon mile of broad farming land. The most obvious landmark was the black threat of the Spindle to the north and the small wood growing about its eastern bastions. Rossamünd was grateful for the stand of she-oaks that sheltered him now, for he could see little other cover for miles about. He could well recall how the maps in the back of the almanac showed the region to be almost featureless.

Of course — my almanac! He took up his waterlogged satchel. Mucky water drained from a seam at the bottom. With a grimace, Rossamünd looked inside. It was a sodden mess. He gloomily took out his almanac and sat it in his lap.

Now I'll find out just how waterproof this is. He gingerly opened the cover to find that the waxy pages had survived their dunking. They were not even slightly damp. There were no illegible smears in the print — not even a smudge. What a wonderful gift! Encouraged, he looked up the map of the region among the handful of other charts at the rear of the book. A thin line of communication showed from the Spindle to High Vesting. It was evidence of a road. Winstermill showed closer, but he had been told to go to High Vesting first. So it was south to the port, some eighty miles away, in a straight line, though much longer by road. *It's a long walk, but I reckon it's what Master Fransitart would decide* ... And that settled it for him.

Rossamünd began to plan. First, he would inspect the rest of his belongings, then, when it was evening, head out first east and then south until he found the road — that spidery line on the map. Hidden among the black trunks and dense needles, Rossamünd struggled off his jackcoat and hung it over several branches to dry. Although it had saved his life, saturated it was unbearably heavy.

Freed of its constriction, he shivered with the cold and set to work. The execution of the first part of his plan was straightforward enough. Several things had been ruined by the water: most of his remaining food – the crust of rye bread was soaked and dirty; the dried must – dry no more – was still edible but would not keep for long; the slats of portable soup were sticky, as they were starting to dissolve. Happily, the gherkins and the fortified sack cheese had survived. The apples he had eaten days ago. His instructions and letters of recommendation, written in ink, were smudged beyond legibility. The bill of folding money that was his advance on wages was now a useless, sodden clump. Remarkably, the sealed paper had remained sealed. His other book, the lexicon of words, was a swollen ruin twice as thick as it used to be, its spine bulging. Much of the ink had spread, making words fuzzy, although fortunately still readable. Of the repellents only the bothersalts were affected, now doses of sludge inside their little sacks. Having never encountered bothersalts before, Rossamünd had no idea whether or not they were still useful, but decided to keep them anyway. The restoratives remained unspoiled in their tiny bottles, as did Craumpalin's Exstinker in its brown clay bottle. As for clothes – shirts and smalls and all, and for most other things in his possession – these were wet but still intact. Unfortunately though, his hat and his cudgel were gone – *and,* Rossamünd thought regretfully, *Verline once said that one should never travel abroad without a hat.*

Tipping water from the valise and the satchel, Rossamünd arranged his belongings about him so that they might dry. He would repack them before he set out – damp, ruined or otherwise, preferring them wet and wrecked to lost. Hanging his weskit next to the jackcoat, so it too might dry, he lifted up his shirt and messily splashed Exstinker on the sodden bandage. Tucking himself back in, he settled himself in the most secluded nook to wait out the rest of sunlight. After five days on the cromster, he had become accustomed to the subtle movements of the vessel in the water. His senses still pitched and swayed gently as he lay there, almost rocking him to sleep.

Some small bird squeaked three times then shot away, with a whir.

Rossamünd blinked heavily. In his hand he gripped a bottle of tyke-oil. With the bothersalts ruined, it was all he had to ward off monsters. At the first sign of one, he would splash it in its face and run. With this determination the memory of the frightening stories told by the older boys at the foundlingery came unsought. Night, they used to say, was when monsters grew bold, when the nickers roamed and the bogles haunted. He had not the slightest doubt that night was when all sorts of strife could occur, but night would also allow him to travel unnoticed by people – especially those in the Spindle. At that moment, search parties from the rivergate scared him more. Hugged in his own arms, Rossamünd managed to doze the rest of the afternoon, his chest hurting where the musket ball had struck. At one point he woke and thought he could reckon the faint pounding of guns again, carried from a long way off by gentle afternoon breezes.

The monitors must have caught the Hogshead...

When evening came, he put back on his clothes, now dry enough to wear. He gathered his near-dry gear and packed it all once more, tidy and secure, as he had watched Master Fransitart do. Reluctant to leave, he took his time, gently shaking both valise and satchel several times to test for unnecessary rattles, and repacking them again and again till there were none. All the time, a gurgling knot of fear churned in his middle. For a time he was stuck between terror of the dark and the unknown dangers ahead, and the anxiety of still being so close to the Spindle. In the end, out of sheer frustration, he set out from his hide of she-oak needles, his pulse pounding in his ears with every step.

He walked as quickly as he might across the too-soft earth of the ploughed, open field that went back from the river bank. To his left, lantern and limn-thorn lights of yellow, orange, and green twinkled in a deceptively friendly way all along walls and in the slit windows of the Spindle. Dark shadows lurked beyond its eastern end – the shapes of the trees that made the small wood there. A distant line of lamps extended east from the rivergate through and beyond this wood then turned south where flat open field and pasture spread to the horizon. This land offered easy travelling but little cover. The faintly sparkling line was evidence of the road Rossamünd had counted on to take him south to High Vesting, the lights much like those he would be employed to service on the Wormway. It was hard to see, but he went on, keeping the lantern line to his left. When it ceased he did not stop, but kept walking till the last glimmer was lost in the distance and night. He stopped then. There was no point going back, he thought, and certainly nothing to be gained from staying put. He caught his breath for a moment then sighed. Onwards, onwards he would go till the path became clear again.

The gloom of cloud was blown north-west, to reveal a high silver moon glittering coldly. Phoebë, the moon was sometimes called – Rossamünd liked that name – and her timely appearance allowed him to set his bearings. He had felt her there, hidden behind the clouds, felt her like the moving of the great ocean tides in his guts. Certain he was going in the right direction, he adjusted the valise once more and went on into the dangerous dark.

As he walked Rossamünd heard every so often odd, far-off shriekings or infrequent and muffled hoomings, and once a strange rumbling coming from the east. Refusing to be thwarted by fear, the foundling put his head down when he heard any of these, walking faster for a time, every sense tingling with terror, till eventually he tired and then slowed, sure that he could go no further.

He stopped for a moment, took a sip from his biggin and looked to the heavens to get his bearings. The great yellow-green star Maudlin had risen high and bright, proving how late it was and making him feel desperately weary.

Putting away the water, he walked on.

A black bulk appeared, silhouetted and obvious on this flat land. His heart leapt! The memory of the terrible beast he had glimpsed several nights earlier reared in his imagination. Ears ringing with tension, Rossamünd crouched low and crept in a wide arc about the shadowy bulk. Several times he was sure, with the cold grip of dread, that it had moved – yet somehow it also stayed strangely still. He was almost upon it before he realised it was a haystack, right in the middle of the field. He nearly collapsed with relief: instead of a threat, here was a place to rest. He staggered through ploughed soil so soft it almost tripped him, flopped down on the leeward side of the haystack and burrowed into the straw, dragging the valise with him. He sagged, exhausted. Sleep came quickly. Even when another shriek wailed a little too close, he slept.

A numb ache in Rossamünd's left shoulder, near where he had been shot, woke him. He rubbed his shoulder, but that only made it hurt more. He was still so very tired. He had survived his first night alone. Crawling cautiously out from his haystack burrow, he peered about. It was early morning, the sun barely over the horizon. Showing against the pale sky were giant windmills marching away to the eastern horizon in long, staggered rows. Although the very flatness of the land made him feel conspicuous, it also let him see if he was followed. As far as the eye could see in the early dawn, nothing moved on the road or the fields about except the great sails of the mills.

Yet the fear of a patrol from the Spindle still dogged him, and Rossamünd struggled through the fields for an hour. Soon it became too wearisome to tread in the soft soil and he was forced on to the road. He walked on and on but met no one else. After a while the way was intersected by a path. There was a single sign there, pointing down the main roadway. *The Vestiweg* it said – or Vesting Way, the road to High Vesting. He was on the right road and upon it he would stay.

The day became unusually warm and remained so. A south-easterly breeze came welcome and cool, as luggage and harness began to weigh on him. Eventually the valise became too hard to carry on his back and he resorted to towing it along behind him by the straps, its metal bindings dragging dustily in the sandy gravel. With stubbornness beyond his years, he walked on steadily, his thoughts completely taken with reaching High Vesting. Stops were frequent, and Rossamünd always looked furtively about as he rested. The boy found that he was not as alone as he had first felt: cows in sturdily fenced pastures lowed and chewed; birds of many kinds – warbling magpies, shrilling mud larks, tetching wagtails and silent swallows – dashed about, often calling, chasing off strangers, hunting insects that also flitted hither and thither. Of the insects the birds' favourite seemed to be the large wurtembottles. These fat black flies from warmer northern lands insisted on bumbling about Rossamünd's face, neck and especially his ears. No matter how often or how furiously he thrashed and

114

shooed them, these wurtembottles returned to their lazy harassment. There was a moment as he stepped along that he thought he spied a person – a farmer perhaps – cutting across the fields far to his left, but he could not be certain who or what it was and dared not call out. Other than this the road had been eerily empty of any other traffic. Having grown up surrounded by people, crowded with them, he had thought space and solitude a golden prize. Now isolated and far from comfort, he wished very much to be pressed by the crowd once more.

Onwards, onwards. He had to get to High Vesting.

Fortunately Rossamünd still carried enough food to keep him from desperation, including that day's main meal: a sludge that used to be the dried must and the now almost glue-like rye bread. Craumpalin had once said that hunger was the best sauce, and Rossamünd could not have agreed more as he took to the bland slop with relish. The supper was still soggy enough to even wet his thirst. This was important, for although he had enough to eat, he had little water. Rossamünd had filled his biggin with the Humour's dark waters and tried to conserve it on the way. It tasted like composting leaves, yet by the unseasonably hot day's end it was almost gone. He did not know exactly what would happen when one had no water, though he knew that it had to be bad. By sundown he could see distant trees growing in scruffy stands along the road and hoped a source of water might be among them. When he finally reached them he discovered no water, and so walked on. When, a mile later, he settled to sleep in a cave-like gap between the boughs of a huge boxthorn, he had drunk his last mouthful from the biggin.

Huddled in the shelter of the lonely tree, Rossamünd stared into the gathering dark with equally increasing disquiet. A nameless fear that something or someone dogged him made every shadow jump and loom. As the unfriendly night weighed down, punctuated as it was by distant, frightening noises, he sought to distract himself by humming happy, peaceful hymns, as he had heard Verline do for a troubled child. Still the deep dark oppressed. He hummed on softly, hoarse with thirst until somehow he coaxed himself to sleep.

A sound stirred him. It was early morning, the sky pale, the still air cold again. His throat rasped with pain, but he had survived a second night.

The sound came again, unusual and out of place.

Rossamünd quickly blinked away the sleepy grit and listened. Morning birds welcoming the rising sun with their calls – these had not woken him; the buzzing of the wurtembottles waiting for him to evacuate his thorny room – neither had these. Then it came once more, this sound, and remained, getting louder: a jangling, steady *clop-clop-clop* then the unmistakable snort of a horse.

The musketeers of the Spindle have come for me! He turned his body and craned his head as quietly as possible to see if he could catch sight of his pursuers through the spiny tangle of many intertwined boughs. Up on one elbow, neck stretched to straining, he did see something and it was not a company of musketeers, but rather a landaulet – an open four-wheeled carriage with a folding top drawn by a single, heavy-looking and mud-brown nag. It was being driven by a figure with a pronounced hunch, his face hidden behind the upturned collar of a dark maroon coachman's cloak and beneath the shadow of a thrice-high of almost matching colour. Behind the driver reclined an elegant passenger of unclear gender in clothes so fine that Rossamünd could tell the refinement of their cut from his obscure vantage point. As the carriage came near, the elegant passenger called with the clear ring of an educated woman's voice. "Well, stop here if you must! You know I have places to be and can't be troubled by every quibble or suspicion. But, stop I say, if it will cease your twittering!"

Accordingly the vehicle was pulled to a halt just before the boxthorn.

Rossamünd froze.

There was a pause, and then the woman's voice spoke clearly again. "Go on then, I shall wait!"

The driver obediently got down and began to swing his head about as if searching, revealing his face – or what should have been a face. Instead it was a rectangular wooden box pocked occasionally with small round holes on its front and two larger openings, one each on the lower end of each side. Thick leather straps held it to his head. A sthenicon! Rossamünd stared, horrified. The driver was

117

a *leer*! Rossamünd knew there was no escaping a leer: the sthenicon revealed every scent of every living thing big or small that moved within an area of a mile or more. What is more they were reported to be able to see things everyday folk could not, to peer into secrets and search in hidden regions. The box-faced driver shuffled nearer to the over-grown boxthorn bush and peered within, his head swaying and poking forward. He became still. Rossamünd sucked in a breath and lay very still, every nerve and fibre straining, waiting.

How he wished he had not lost his cudgel. How he regretted the spoiled bothersalts.

Eventually the box-faced driver stepped back to the landaulet and appeared to address the elegant passenger, as the latter leant over and both heads nodded, at times with pronounced emphasis. A conclusion seemingly reached, the woman alighted from the carriage and, straightening her fine clothes, stepped with determined poise over to where the driver had stood before the boxthorn. She wore the most luxurious and unusually cut frock coat of deep scarlet, buttoned and buckled at the side, and the shiniest, blackest equiteer boots Rossamünd had ever seen. The hem of the coat hung low and flared extravagantly, rustling as she approached.

She stopped and squinted vaguely into the little grove. "In *here*, you say?" she asked over her shoulder. Her chestnut hair was gathered up behind her crown in a bun, held with a pointed comb pinned by a hair tine ending in a clenched

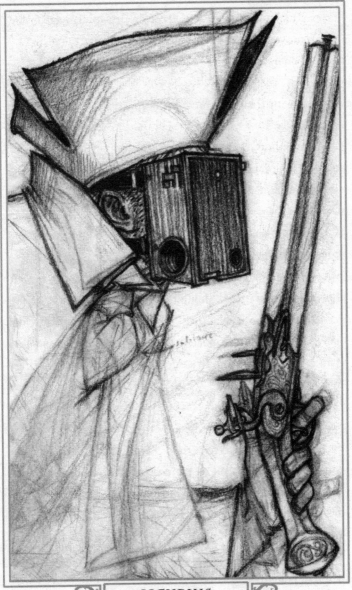

LICURIUS

crow's claw. Long wisps of fly-away fringe danced in any small movement of air.

A frown.

A sigh.

She leant forward. "You in there, little one," she called quite softly.

Rossamünd did not know what to do.

"We've certainly no intention to harm you, so you can stop pretending you're not there and come out."

Maybe she spoke the truth? Maybe she had water? Rossamünd was about to act when his leg was gripped and tugged. Involuntarily he screamed and kicked with his free foot. This, too, was grabbed and he was pulled out from his hiding-hole into the blinkingly bright morning, hanging upside down – valise and all – in the irresistible grip of the driver. Rossamünd squealed like a little piglet, struggling violently – but all his twisting and writhing did not alter his position.

"Put me down, you *looby*!" he spluttered, serving up the worst curse he knew.

The box-faced driver ignored his almost foul language and carried him round to the roadside, where he held him out in much the same way someone might have held a frantic, just-caught fish. Rossamünd continued to twist and writhe.

The elegant woman approached him as someone might approach a cornered snake.

"Now, now," she soothed, "put him down, Licurius.

We've said we'd not harm him, so we had better not now, had we?"

As soon as his ankles were released Rossamünd scissored wildly with his legs for a moment to make sure they stayed free then rolled over frantically and sprang to his feet. He looked left and right, hoping to dart away and escape. The woman regarded him closely for a long while, and he became still under her keen stare. Rossamünd was not so young as not to see that she was a great beauty, but there was a hardness to her and a *darkness*. It was then that he noticed a small blue mark above her left eye – a diamond-shaped spoor. She was a *lahzar* – one of those fabled monster-fighters who went to some far-off place to have secret surgeries done to their bodies, secret surgeries that made it possible for them to do strange and terrible deeds and fight monsters. He knew immediately by the spoor this elegant, scarlet woman wore that her special talent was to generate and manipulate electricity and lightning. Among lahzars, this group were known as fulgars.

The lady fulgar smiled. The smell of her wafted about Rossamünd, a strange scent – sweet, yet salty and sharp, too.

"Hello, little man," she offered, in what was probably her kindliest voice. "My name is Europe. *This* is my factotum," she said, indicating the box-faced driver. "His name is Licurius. What do they call you?"

Rossamünd did not answer.

Europe pursed her lips, glanced at Licurius and sighed.

"As I have said, we really have no thought of hurting you. Indeed, *little* man, you are of *little* consequence to us. I might care enough to help you, but not nearly so much as to hurt you." She gave a mirthless chuckle and then became serious. "You see, I believe you have to particularly care about somebody to put the effort into harming them. Now, tell me your name and when you've done that you can tell me what a little fellow like yourself is doing out here in the hinterlands without his hat?" She smiled in a knowing way, an expression that promised either malice or friendship, depending upon what might happen next.

For the briefest moment Rossamünd weighed his options. He relented and said, "My name is Rossamünd Bookchild and I lost my hat in the river."

"I gave you your chance, boy!" Europe was suddenly lit with a powerful yet suppressed rage. "If you're going to dash it with saucy nonsense, then this is where we part ways!" She turned on her heel as if to leave, coat hems swirling.

"I-fell-off-a-boat-bound-for-High-Vesting-and-swam-ashore!" Rossamünd yelped in one frightened breath. He continued almost as quickly. "And my name really is Rossamünd, and I know it's not the right kind of name for a lad but I was given it while I was too young to argue and now it is written in the ledger and there is no going back on that ..."

Europe stood still, cocked her head and made a wry face.

"I am a book child – a foundling – and I'm supposed to be in High Vesting so I can start my job and now I'm

probably lost and I've got no water to drink and ... and ..."
Rossamünd trembled on that awful verge where tears begin
and poise is lost. What is more, he had revealed more about
himself than he had intended. He was sure that if Fransitart
could see him now, his old dormitory master would be
shaking his head in dismay.

"I see." The fulgar pondered for a moment. "You have
very fine proofing for a foundling, little man. Did you
happen to steal it?"

"No, ma'am!" Rossamünd was simultaneously startled
and offended.

The fulgar shrugged. "Either way, maybe I can be of
help to you after all. If it is water you need there is plenty
on the carriage." She paused sagely then smiled an oddly
cheeky smile. "I could even do as much as cart you to High
Vesting, if you would like, though you will have to join me
as I work. What do you think, Licurius? Shall we aid this
poor, lost, well-dressed book child? You never know, with
your poor eyesight an extra pair of peepers could be handy
on our way."

Licurius nodded just once.

"There you go!" Europe kept grinning in mild triumph.

So they climbed into the landaulet, all three – Licurius
handing his mistress aboard – and set off down the Vestiweg
once more. Rossamünd's thoughts sang happily as he drank
his fill of water and the flat fields rocked by. Whatever
anyone else said, he thought lahzars were the finest folk he
had ever met.

SORROW AT THE
BRINDLESTOW BRIDGE

fuse (noun) six- to nine-foot pole of cane or wand-wood, tightly coiled along its entire length with copper wire and capped with copper, brass or iron fulgurite; the longer of the two fulgaris, the shorter being called the stage. A fuse extends the reach of fulgars, allowing them to deliver their deadly jolts while staying out of reach themselves.

I⊤ was supremely comfortable in the landaulet: the seats were pliant and easing, the upholstery and trimmings all wrapped in thick, glossy leather of a scarlet almost as rich as Europe's sumptuous frock coat. And there was indeed as much clean water as Rossamünd needed, stored in black lacquered panniers hanging from the back of the carriage. There were also several bottles of claret, of a rather cheap variety, so Europe informed him, mixed with apple pulp, "and not meant for small boys!" All in all, he thought it a fine way to make the rest of his way to High Vesting.

Not long into the journey, however, they crossed over a small wooden platform under which bubbled a happily babbling runnel, probably a drain for the fields. It was enough water to quench any thirst and not so far down the road that Rossamünd would have perished before he found it. This really struck him: had he pushed on, he might have been all right on his own after all. He thought life's twistings very odd.

Europe chatted gaily at first. She talked about the weather and then about the strange dress-sense of the women from the Considine, the Emperor's second capital far away south. She talked on and on about a great deal more, usually about herself: great conquests of fearsome nickers and even greater conquests of certain "stupid, wealthy dolts", as she called them – whatever that meant. Rossamünd found it all rather hard to follow, but nodded as politely and as attentively as he could. While she talked she offered him expensive foods in an elaborately offhand manner, dainty morsels the likes of which he had only ever seen in the quality street confectioners of Boschenberg. There were nibbles of many types of nut; strips of rare cured meats – gazelle, ibex, harp seal – delicately flavoured with expensive spices; and sachets of dried fruits – peaches, strange yellow triangles she called "pineapple" and which tasted so oddly and delightfully sweet he could not stop picking at them; and a small profusion little bruised things. He asked what these were.

"*Those*? Oh, they're whortleberries," she said simply, but with that one statement Rossamünd's eyes went wide. How rich could one person be! Whortleberries were the absolute king of way foods: one little dried berry, though not able to relieve the pangs of hunger, could give a full-grown man energy for almost a whole day. They grew in very remote and threwdish – haunted – places and their cultivation and trade were vigilantly guarded. All this made them astoundingly expensive, but here, now, in this luxurious landaulet, was a small fortune's worth.

"May I try one?" he asked timidly.

Europe gave him an odd look. "Certainly. They're there for the eating – though not too many, mind, or the top of your head might blow off as you run giggling down the road."

He took just one and examined it closely. It was a withered berry no bigger than the fingernail of his little finger, the colour of a plum gone bad. Very unimpressive. He plopped it quickly in his mouth. It tasted flat and disappointingly bland, but when he swallowed, a tingling started in his belly and a happy, lively warmth spread to the top of his head. Rossamünd blinked and grinned. He changed his mind and thought it the nicest thing he had ever eaten. With this new pulse of energy and surge of well-being he started to fidget and shift about in his seat.

Europe watched his antics with amusement. "Works wonderfully well, does it not?" she observed.

"Aye, ma'am! I reckon I could run all the way to High Vesting and back!" he enthused.

"Yes, well ..." Her expression became a little mocking. "Let us not go too far."

This was a little deflating, but the whortleberry made

Rossamünd's spirits so high he was not downhearted for long. Forgetting himself a little, he began to poke about the interior of the carriage, prodding at the upholstery. On the seat beside him was a plain-looking box — a case really, quite large and long and flat and lacquered a glistening black. Rossamünd went to pat its smooth surface, but pulled his hand away quickly as he felt a faint, queasy dread emanating from within it.

Europe quickly became stern. "Nothing in there, little sneak!"

She took up this box and poked it away between her and the side wall of the landaulet. "Didn't they tell you at your bookhouse that curious eyes rot in their sockets and curious fingers wither to their knuckles?"

After this the lady fulgar became quiet and ignored Rossamünd, quickly growing sullen and staring at the distant windmills and featureless land, her chin cupped in hand, elbow propped on knee. "I *hate* this place ..." she muttered. This was all she said for quite a long time.

Rossamünd had no idea what to do, and sat perplexed. Eventually he offered the lahzar one of her own whortle-berries, thinking this might cheer her, but she just looked at it blankly, frowned at him and went back to her listless maundering. Rossamünd became suddenly and painfully aware of the strangeness of his surroundings and of the two people with whom he shared the carriage. He sat very still and very, very quiet.

Later that day it rained, and this seemed to improve

Europe's mood considerably. "This is more like it," she grinned. Sitting up straighter, she called to Licurius, "Fighting weather, hey, Box-face! And let there be more of it, too!"

Once more, Rossamünd had no idea what she was talking about. Licurius ignored her as he had ignored the rain — and most everything else, it seemed.

Europe pulled the broad, bonnet-like canopy up and over them, keeping them and the plush interior dry while Licurius, at the front, was left to soak as he stoically dictated the landaulet's course. This made Rossamünd uneasy and unhappy, reminding him of the times when Madam Opera bullied and badgered dear Verline. He did not understand why one person should have all that he or she needed and dictate to others what they have or have not.

Even with the fulgar's rapid lift in spirits they continued the rest of that day's journey in silence and in the rain, Rossamünd taking the opportunity to read his already well-thumbed almanac. It said very little about the region they were in except that it was called the Sough, that it was very fertile and that it was famous for its lettuces and strawberries, though he had so far seen few of either. In the early evening, when they stopped for the night, it was still showering. Gaps in the cloud showed the glorious golden orange of the sun's late light reflected off enormous cumulous columns. In the strange yellow gloom Licurius tended to the pony, hobbling it and attaching a feed bag to its bridle. He then set small cones of repellent in a circle about their temporary camp, scratching strange marks in the soil with a stick at the intervals between each cone. He set a modest fire with wood they carried with them and when it was burning merrily put some kind of small cauldron in its midst. All this done, the leer finally prepared his bed beneath the landaulet.

From under the canopy, with the rain going *patter, patter* upon it, Europe called softly to him, "I'll be wanting the brew in about twenty minutes, I think, but be sure it has mixed well and is the right temperature."

With a quick, resentful glare at Rossamünd she took out the nondescript black box that had caused such tension earlier and handed it almost secretively to Licurius. Then she lit an oil lamp with deft strokes of a flint and steel, and, opening a compartment beneath her seat, pulled out a great clothbound book. Producing a pencil, she began to scratch and scrawl in the book, humming or *tch-tch*-ing in turn. After a while she looked up sharply and quizzed Rossamünd flatly, "You know what I am, don't you child?" She waggled the end of her pencil in the vicinity of her left brow to the small blue outline of the fulgar's diamond above it. "What *this* means?"

Rossamünd had no idea what to say. "I uh ... uh ..." He suddenly felt embarrassed to talk about her occupation, as though it was a private, even a shameful thing. In the end he nodded. Her expectant gaze was even more terrible than Madam Opera's.

"And what is that?" she persisted.

Rossamünd flushed and wished he was a thousand miles elsewhere. "You're a lahzar," he mumbled.

"I'm a what?"

Rossamünd almost rolled his eyes, but thought better of it. "A fulgar – a monster fighter. You make sparks and lightning."

Europe gave a chuckle, then sat back, her chin stuck out pompously. "I prefer the name teratologist or, if one must be vulgar, pugnator. But yes, my boy, you have it in two. No doubt you have heard of my kind – how we are spooky, how we are scary, how you common folk couldn't live without us? Hmm? Well, it's all true, and worse. Mine is a life of violence. Would you like a life of violence, little man?"

Rossamünd shook his head cautiously.

"What about a life of adventure, then? Is that where you're bound? To begin some adventurous life in High Vesting?"

The boy thought for a moment, bowing his head under her beady hazel-brown gaze, and eventually shrugged.

"Hmph!" Europe pursed her lips. "What I'd like to know is this: when does adventure stop and violence begin? Answer me that and we'll both be wiser."

Fransitart had been right after all: lahzars were strange and discomfiting folk. Rossamünd regretted accepting this one's assistance. Once more he had no real idea of what she was talking about, and certainly no idea how to reply.

At that moment Licurius stepped up holding a pewter dish full of what looked like steaming black oil, gluggy and evil-smelling. The foundling almost gagged at the stink of the stuff, but Europe put down her large book, took the dish gratefully and drank the filthy contents in a manner that Madam Opera would have declared sternly was "very unladylike!". A tingle of disgust shivered down Rossamünd's ribs as the fulgar drained the dregs and sighed a contented sigh.

"Many times better," she smiled, showing teeth scummed with black as she handed the dish back to the ever-patient Licurius. She took out her crow's claw hair tine and comb, letting silken, chestnut locks free; then she dimmed the lantern, lay back, wrapped herself in a blanket and without another word fell asleep.

It was then that another stench assaulted Rossamünd's senses: the leer had lit the cones of repellent, and their exotic fumes were now drifting over the camp. It was like nothing Rossamünd had ever encountered before and it made him feel wretched. His head began to pound and his very soul was gripped by an urgency to flee. His discomfort must have shown, for he was sure Licurius was regarding him closely beneath that blank box of a face. Wrapping his scarf about his nose and throat as if to keep out the cold, but rather to muffle the reek, Rossamünd tried to show that nothing was wrong.

Nevertheless the leer paused and leant closer.

The boy was sure he heard sniffing: the faint but definite snuffling of smells.

Then, for the first time since their meeting, the leer spoke. "Do you fare *well*, boy?" The voice came as a wheezing, hissing whisper, strangely unmuffled despite the impediment of the sthenicon. "You look like you've had a nasty turn there. All's well, is it? D'ye not like the stink of our potives?"

Feeling a greater threat under the blank gaze of this man than in the manic ways of the fulgar, Rossamünd cowered in his muffle. He did not know whether to nod or shake his head, and just wobbled it in circles vigorously.

"You smell *funny* to me. Did you know that? *Wheeze* ... you smell funny to me ..." The leer leant yet closer. "Answer, boy, or do you want of a man's courage with such a *pretty* name?"

Momentarily speechless, the foundling blinked several times, completely baffled. *What harm is there in smelling funny?* "I su ... suppose I do, sir," he started. "I haven't had a bath for well over a week now. I reckon the river has made it worse."

"*Hiss!* I know river-ssmell, upssstart!" Licurius returned, shaking with inexplicable rage. "And unwashed bodiess, too. You are neither of thesse. You ssmell wrong! *Wheeze* ..."

"I ..." When would this fellow just leave him alone? Who cared how he smelt? For the first time since he had left the foundlingery, Rossamünd thought about the knife Fransitart had given him, still in its scabbard at the end of his baldric, thought whether he might be forced to produce it as an aid to his defence. What a strange and terrible notion – cudgels was one thing, but knives and other slitting, slicing tools quite another. "Master Fransitart told me that people from different cities eat different foods, that each would make them smell *funny* to other folk."

"Of courssse." The leer stroked his throat with a hand gloved in black velvet. He sounded less than convinced.

Europe shifted restlessly, then turned to her side and intervened with a soft voice as she did so. "Leave him be, Licurius. Everyone has their secrets. Perhaps *he* should ask you, oh great leer, about a certain Frestonian girl ..."

At this Licurius stepped back and away from Rossamünd with an odd gurgle, to the boy's great relief. Shortly after, the leer doused the fire, crept to his cradle beneath the landaulet and bothered the boy no more. Even so, eyes wide in the dark, Rossamünd stayed awake for a long time, well into the small hours, feeling more unsafe than he ever had when he had bunked by himself in the haystack or the boxthorn. Not even the happy appearance of Phoebe as night-time clouds blew away east cheered him.

He felt terribly alone.

The next day, the leer paid Rossamünd no more mind than he had at any other time other than the bizarre bedtime incident last night. After another draft of that black ichor had been brewed for Europe, and the foundling had wandered briefly for a relieving stroll, they were on their way again into a frigid fog. By mid-morning the vapours cleared and the country began changing. The fields became smaller and fewer and the land rockier, sloping upwards ever more until they found themselves on the stony, uncultivated heights before a forested valley. This depression was filled with a great wood of evergreen beeches and stately pines, and into it the road now descended. Rain had washed broad ruts into the Vestiweg as it went down the flanks of the valley, creating enough of a hazard that Licurius was obliged to get down from his seat and lead the horse carefully on foot.

Europe frowned at the poor condition of the road. "Roadway gone to clay, bring two shoes and carry one away," she sighed, sipping at a glass of claret and sucking on – of all things – a chunk of rock salt. Draining the glass, she looked sidelong at her young passenger and suddenly leant across, taking his small hands in hers.

Rossamünd started and pulled back, not knowing what to expect. The lahzar stroked his knuckles absent-mindedly, and even though her touch was as soft as Verline's and her grip gentle, he was very aware that she just might shock him or worse.

She smiled. "I apologise for my factotum's behaviour last night," she offered quietly. "He's a curious fellow, and this serves me well most of the time. Unfortunately it also makes him … *twitchy*, one might say. Pay him no heed – he's harmless enough."

Rossamünd could see how, to a fulgar of such self-confessed might as Europe, Licurius might seem less than threatening. But to this boy, the leer was anything but harmless.

"Now, very shortly I am going to have some work to do."

Europe released his hands with a pat and sat back. "And you might find it scary enough, but fear not: I have been in business for a great long while now." She paused and looked heavenward, tapping her lips with a long, elegant finger. "Hmmm, too long perhaps. Nevertheless, you can be assured that you are safe."

Rossamünd looked about. "Will there be *monsters?*" he whispered.

Europe laughed – a bright, crystalline chortle – as they entered the dark gloom beneath ancient eaves. "My, my, there are *always* monsters!"

"Really? *Always?*" The foundling sat up.

Europe nodded gravely. "I am afraid so, yes. Here, there and everywhere – not that city folk would know. It's out here in the nether regions that the nickers roam and the bogles lurk. But lo! Not a fear, Europe is here!" She finished with a flourish of her hand and a grin.

Rossamünd blinked.

The light was growing dim, though the time was barely midday, as the road drove deeper and deeper into the wood – a deep green dusk full of hushed expectancy and subtle murmurings. Trunks huge and old spread out great, knobbled roots furry with moss, about which the leaf-carpeted road was forced to bend and twist. There was little undergrowth but for some scattered colonies of fungus – tall, thin, capped mushrooms, large, flat toad-stools, tiny red must, which even Rossamünd knew was good for eating and certain potions, and plump puffballs ready to pop. Bracken grew everywhere else, even upon the trees, while thin myrtle saplings sprouted here and there struggling for life.

Rossamünd had never been in such a place as this and found its appearance marvellous, more wild and beautiful than any of Boschenberg's elegant, manicured parks. Yet there was a great watchfulness here, a feeling of being observed and unwelcome. This place was threwdish: a place where monsters might like to dwell. It marred the woods' beauty and oppressed the visitor. He shivered and checked his almanac, squinting to read in the dimness. They had entered the Brindlewood, or so it said.

"What does that contain?" Europe asked a little too loudly, as she fixed her hair back into the bun-like style, just as it had been the day before.

"I was just finding out where we were," said Rossamünd.

The lahzar chuckled. "I could have told you that. This," – she waved about grandly – "is the *Grintwoode* … or the Brindleshaws, as the locals will have it. We're on the northernmost marches of the Smallish Fells, the western tip of Sulk End, having recently entered the domain and jurisdiction of High Vesting." She pointed casually to the book with her crowfoot hair tine before poking it into the bun and comb. "I think you'll find I am right."

The almanac agreed. Rossamünd was impressed.

Giving a bored look, she sighed. "I've been here before. 'Tis a troublesome place."

A short time later Licurius brought the landaulet to a

halt, stopping at a bend where the road began to descend even more steeply, falling over a series of folds in the earth before disappearing below around the flank of the hill. He alighted and went to the rear of the carriage. Rossamünd heard thumpings and scrapings. The factotum reappeared on Europe's side holding a great pole about twelve feet long, as thick as a man's thumb and tightly wrapped in copper wire. It was a fuse. Rossamünd had heard and read of them but had not seen one until now. He stared at it in open wonder.

She must be about to fight. Rossamünd's heart began to pound in anticipation.

The lahzar took the fuse from the leer with a sweet smile and lay it across both seats, one end sticking some way over the side of the landaulet. Then she retrieved something out of her precious black box and put it in her mouth, chewing slowly with a disgusted look. These apparent necessities done they were on their way again, Licurius now driving from the seat once more. The road went into a steep decline cut into the side of a hill carpeted in pine needles, bending always right and going always down. From their vantage point Rossamünd could see that they would soon come to a stone bridge a little further below, which crossed a narrow, moat-like ravine.

Europe finished her mouthful and fixed her small passenger with a serious eye. "Now, however, things shall soon proceed. You must declare to me that you will stay here within the landaulet no matter what. Do you declare it?"

Going white and wide-eyed, he nodded. "Aye, madam."

"I'm sure you do."

The roadway dipped for a moment as it crossed a creek, then passed right through and over the crown of a small knoll, either side flanked by a high earth cutting topped with sinuous pines. Beyond and below, the road widened in a clearing of grass and shattered tree stumps before constricting again at the bridge, which spanned the narrow gap in a solid, gentle curve. As they arrived on the farther edge of this clearing, Rossamünd thought he heard a rumbling, a kind of slow thudding, though he could not be sure.

Licurius halted the landaulet and climbed down once more. With a respectful bow he offered Europe his gloved hand as she alighted. The thudding was unmistakeable now, like great footsteps, and echoes among the trunks made it sound as if it was all around. While her factotum held her fuse, the fulgar straightened her frock coat, tightened buckles, and secured buttons. Suddenly the whole forest seemed to burst with a stentorian cracking.

Rossamünd leapt to his seat and looked about wildly to find the danger as Licurius lunged for the bridle of the spooked nag. There! Just before the bridge a young pine was collapsing, pushed out of the way by the tallest creature the foundling had ever seen.

It looked just like an enormous person, taller than ten tall men, except that its legs were too short, its arms too long, and its body altogether too thick, too hunched and too rectangular. It was an ettin – one of the biggest of the

THE MISBEGOTTEN
SCHREWD

land monsters – and it peered about momentarily before fixing a critical eye on the landaulet.

"Fie, fie, what do I spy? Gold-toting travellers passing us by," it boomed in a surprisingly well spoken way, forming the words with great articulations of its jaw through a mouth full of protruding, blackened and spade-like teeth. It stepped into the clearing, sending the shattered pine toppling into the gorge.

Europe gave Rossamünd a passing wink. "How so, how so, to do my work I go," she murmured, then she turned and marched directly towards the ettin, shouldering the fuse and waving to get its attention.

Rossamünd was agog: surely she did not think to challenge such a fearsome foe? It wore a large smock for modesty's sake made up of many hessian sacks stitched very roughly together. Under its left arm the ettin carried a great barrel, which had probably been a vat for ageing wine or brewing beer. The ettin waggled this distinctly, pointing within its wide gape.

"I'll not stop your chill-day stroll," the ettin hoomed, "if you'll not shrink from the bridge-crossing toll."

"Ho! ho!" Europe chortled dramatically, continuing her approach. "It's that old ruse, is it? Frighten everyday folks out of their goods?"

The ettin nodded once. From Rossamünd's vantage it seemed very proud of itself.

"What's more, you stand-and-deliver us with sweet little rhymes. What a lovely touch, don't you think, Licurius?" the lahzar continued, looking over her shoulder briefly at the leer, rolling her eyes mockingly as she did.

Licurius, as always, said nothing.

The ettin almost beamed with self-satisfaction, revealing even more crooked spade-like teeth. Rossamünd was finding it very hard to believe this creature all that terrible. In fact it seemed more like a childish prankster than a dread threat.

"And what do they call you, sir?" Europe stopped no more than ten feet away from the giant and planted her fuse firmly.

Hesitating for a moment, the ettin formed its reply with obvious effort. "I'm th' Miss-be-gotten Schr-rewd." It patted its chest.

"Well Mister Schrewd, do you know who I am?"

The ettin shook its head.

The lahzar's voice became *very* icy. "No?" She gave a cold, humourless smile. "It's a bit much, I suppose, to expect absolutely *everybody* to have heard of me. No matter."

Rossamünd was grateful she had not asked him the same question when they had first met.

"Nevertheless," she went on, "there's a problem, you see. Everyday folk don't want to pay your toll, and I for one don't believe they should have to. What say you to that?"

The ettin's face fell. It looked genuinely perplexed.

Europe pressed on. "Hmm? Well, I have an alternative for you, and it's the only one really, though I know you'll neither understand nor agree ..."

The fulgar toed the ground in a mime of unconcern.

"What's she going to do?" Rossamünd whispered to Licurius. "Will she send it on its way?" Disturbed, Rossamünd stood, causing the wagon to rock and the horse to nicker.

"Be still, toad!" *Wheeze*! Licurius hissed. "The beggar must die. That is our duty!"

This small interruption caught the schrewd's attention. It peered at them in a baffled way.

Europe took her chance and struck out with speed, jabbing ferociously into the schrewd's belly with her fuse. She spun about, as fast as the eye, with coat skirts flying, to strike again at its rump. There were no bright flashes, just a loud *Zzack!* with the first hit, and a ringing *Zzizk!* with the second.

The ettin yelped and staggered, and dropped the barrel. As this hit the ground, many apples in various states of decay and a rind of cheese bounced out. In truth the brute had not really expected much at all! It flailed its arms wildly, and whether by design or accident caught Europe up in a giant fist. This was its big mistake – the fellow had surely never encountered fulgars before. It made as if to hurl Europe into the trees, but instead, with a look of profound confusion and horror, stood suddenly transfixed. By some invisible force, and most certainly against its will, the ettin bent its arm. This unwilling action brought Europe, whose own arms were outstretched and groping, closer to its head.

All the time Rossamünd could read in its eyes *But why? But why?*

"No!" Rossamünd cried. He leapt off the landaulet, avoiding the grasp of Licurius as the leer wrestled with the near-panicked horse.

By now the schrewd held Europe up in front of its face and she quickly gripped its forehead like a snake might strike a bare ankle, sending a mighty charge of electricity straight into the monster's skull. The schrewd could not even bellow its agony as smoke began to rise from its head. It simply swayed and took one step backwards towards the ravine; then another, and another, and another.

"No ... no ... no" was all he could find to say. Tears began to flow as Rossamünd stumbled, as helpless as the schrewd, unable to do anything to intervene. The foundling dropped to his knees in horror.

Almost inevitably the ettin tottered on the brink. It paused there for one terrible moment, its usually squinty eyes almost popping out of their sockets in terror, before toppling headlong into the gorge. As it fell it released its grip on Europe, who pushed off from its hand and vaulted back nimbly to the ravine's edge. She landed lightly, ready to fight on.

In control of its voice once more, the Misbegotten Schrewd let forth a heart-wrenching wail – a cry of deep sorrow and great agony – which echoed all around the gorge, and then ended all too abruptly.

Huddled on the ground, Rossamünd wept.

He became aware through his tears that Europe was standing over him. She bent down and stroked his hair briefly, almost as Verline might have done when he had been sick or sorrowing. Then she said softly, "You broke your word, little man."

There was a sharp pain and flash of sparks in Rossamünd's head.

His body jerked violently.

Then there was nothing for the longest time.

VIGILANCE AND VIGORANTS

sedorner (noun) official name for a monster-lover, often used as an insult. To be heard even trying to understand monsters from a sympathetic point of view can bring the charge upon one. Different communities and realms deal with sedorners with their own severity, but it is not uncommon for those found guilty to be exposed on a Catherine wheel or even hanged on a gallows.

To come back to awareness after you have been unconscious, especially if you have been unconscious for a long time, is an exceedingly odd experience. The first sensations Rossamünd became aware of were his hearing and a great ache in his brain. Amid the sharp throbbing was a rushing whoosh that spun about in his head, rising till he almost understood its purpose then descending back to nothing.

Rising again.

Descending again.

After who knows how long, he came to realise it was the sighing of wind in tree tops; the voice of birds calling thin, lonely music; and the tap, tap, tap of a small scratching very close by. Smells returned: pine needles, wood-smoke and some worse stink. The sense of touch followed these other clarities as he felt his own weight pressing on something hard yet strangely yielding. He became aware that he had a hand, and that his hand was holding something that felt rough yet also soft – his scarf. He tried to move his hand and found that he could not. He was numb at every joint, frozen in every muscle. He could not even open his eyes.

It was then that memory returned. Rossamünd forgot all the sensations he had just rediscovered, and was filled instead with the recollection of all that had just passed, the destruction of the poor Misbegotten Schrewd. He should not have cared. He should have rejoiced: one more triumph of everyday folk over the ancient oppression of the monsters. Yet somehow the foundling could not see much to cheer in it. Some poor ignorant slain just for being in the way.

Instead, a great sorrow set in his heart. What would Master Fransitart think of this? Rossamünd had met his first nicker and come out of the experience a monster-lover. Unable to move or see, he lay filled with grief for some brutish giant he did not know and should not like.

A new sound broke in, right by his head. "I ... *hiss* ... hold that *something* must be done." It was the wheezing of that terrible leer Licurius. He was right by Rossamünd, far too close for the foundling's ease. The boy's stomach churned in pure fright.

"I ... I have *done* enough, don't you think? It was just a little spark to quiet him ... but look now!"

This was Europe's voice – Europe, the mighty fulgar.

Europe, the slayer of innocents.

Europe, the electrocuter of children.

How powerfully uncertain he was of her now. So *this* is what she meant by a glorious "life of violence"!

"... *Wheeze* ... What good is he? Just some squirming snot nobody wants. You spied how he cried for that beggar, shed real tears like a toddling lassss for some tottering great waste of a nicker. You did a'rightly with him, I say – we've got naught spare for a rotten little ... *hiss* ... sedorner like his-same-self there ... *hiisssss!*"

Rossamünd's soul froze. A sedorner? A monster-lover! That was one of the worst things to be called. Worse yet, they were quite clearly talking about him. What were they going to do to him?

Europe sighed a long, almost sad sigh. "Stay in the carriage and everything was good, that was all it needed ... What is it with males and listening? I wonder how this would read in the panegyric of my life, that I shock bantling brats."

"All the more reason to repair the wreckage. We should slit his belly and spill his umbles right here and leave done with it ... *gasp* ..." the leer's voice rasped right by Rossamünd's ear. "Or take his corpse and blame it on that ettin! A clear reputation is as good as a clear conscience, like you always say."

"Hush it, Box-face! You push too much! *This* circumstance does not warrant such brutal work. My word, leer! You are starting to scare me with your talk of slitting and spilling.

It has gone from worse to worse these past months — is it possible your black old heart gets blacker still?"

The leer hissed, long and cruelly. The landaulet shook for a moment, as if there was a struggle. Was Licurius daring to tangle with the fulgar?

Europe gave a yelp. "Enough, now!"

Rossamünd lay aware, terrified yet blind and paralysed. With the shaking of the carriage, this terror rose unwanted from his gut to his throat and, though he tried to suppress it, it came out as a bubbling, whimpering cough.

Everything seemed to go even more still. Then, "Aah." Europe sounded relieved. "It appears he has returned to us. Good, good."

"... *Wheeze* ... Don't be blubbering to me, then, Sparky," Licurius concluded their previous business with faintly wrathful tones, "when thisss'un places well-found blame on your pretty pate."

"Enough! *Enough!*" The lahzar's voice wavered briefly. "Cease your insolence and boil the water. You know I am sorely in need ..."

With his little outburst, Rossamünd found some capacity of movement return. He wrenched his eyes open in an instant and, as his neck still proved stubbornly immobile, rolled them round wildly, to know his fate.

He was lying under a blanket on one of the seats of the landaulet staring up at the clear sky pricked with early evening's first stars, through high, scruffy boughs — they were still in the forest. It was bitterly, breath-steamingly cold. He began to shiver. Europe was in her usual place on the opposite couch. Her hair was down and that big book she scribbled in was upon her lap. By her sat the lantern, already lit. She was looking at him with an expression he could not fathom, neither hostile nor tender. He blinked over and over at her, limbs twitching as he tried to get some use out of them.

"Good evening, little man," the lahzar said slowly, her arms folded, her right hand up and covering her mouth and chin. "Don't wriggle so. You will be able to move soon enough," she chided, as Rossamünd's wriggling turned into writhing. He did not heed her, but struggled and strained to get his body to respond. Now that they knew he was alive – that he was awake – he did not want to remain vulnerable one moment longer!

Europe leant over and placed a hand upon his shoulder. At this he yowled mightily. Europe herself shied, genuinely startled.

Licurius came over to see about the commotion. "What a noisy little toad!" he growled, gripping the foundling hard about his throat. "Hush it, basket ... *wheeze* ... or you'll die here and now!" All sound was pressed from Rossamünd as the leer clenched tighter and tighter, the boy's cry changing to a panicked gurgle.

"Let go of him, Licurius! This *instant*!" Europe glared at her factotum.

The leer ignored her completely. "Come on, little girl, squeal like you did when I had yer by the ankles ...!"

149

His arms jerking uselessly, Rossamünd tried desperately to squash the man's hand between his chin and throat.

"How dare you, leer! You serve my ends, not I yours!" The fulgar half stood, her hair beginning to bristle with static, the book sliding from her lap to the floor of the landaulet with a thump. "*Let go* your hold and step back! We have not the time for this and I have not the patience!"

For a moment longer Licurius seemed set on ignoring his mistress, then suddenly loosened his grip and turned to peer over his left shoulder. He stepped away, then hesitated, hissing, "That's not right ..." He plainly sniffed at the air, the sound of it coming clearly from the many holes in the sthenicon.

Rossamünd squirmed away as best he could, to the other side of the carriage, tears coming from eyes and nose.

"You wear thin, laggard," Europe hissed in turn. "What is it now?"

The leer did not answer but stood for many strained minutes: sniffing, listening, sniffing yet more. Europe began to growl, ever so softly, impatient with his silence.

"There's something amiss on the wind, m'lady. Somethin' unsettling ... away down there." He gestured into the trees.

The fulgar sat back rubbing her face as if she was vexed by a headache. "Well, you go and see what it might be," she sighed, "and I'll finish the treacle *myself*, shall I? Now go on with you then!"

The leer hesitated again. He gathered his cloak about

himself and stalked off, passing quickly through a black gap between rough trunks.

Rossamünd could not hear anything but the pound, pound, pound of his pulse in his ears, nor, more particularly, smell anything that he might call "amiss" or "unsettling". He was relieved beyond expression simply to be released from the murderous intentions of that wicked man. Though he breathed heavily, he became still.

In the quiet the fulgar watched the forest. "*He'll* be gone a goodly while, I'm sure, so we have some time to get you all back to how you should." Her voice was tired. "Do you have any restoratives or vigorants? I would give you some of mine, child, but that they are made particularly for my ... peculiar constitution ... and I doubt whether that crusty old leer would let you at any of *his*." She wiggled her arching eyebrows at him as if they were together in some conspiracy.

Wanting to keep her in this current friendly mood, Rossamünd managed a weak grimace and, with numbness lessening and movement returning, nodded once.

"And where might they be?"

Rossamünd grimaced as he tried for the first time to speak. "S ... S ... Saa ... Satchel ...!" With great effort he tried to sit up. Europe reached over to help him. He shrank from her touch and slid back down the slippery seat. She saw his discomfort and, taking her hands off him with a false-sounding, "There you go," took up his satchel and sat back. A powerful exhaustion settled over Rossamünd as he finally succeeded in sitting up, and he watched as the fulgar fossicked about in his belongings. After a moment she pulled something from the satchel. She held out her hand. There were the sacks of bothersalts, amazingly dry and potent again, after their dunking in the Humour had made them into pointless slop.

What remarkable things Craumpalin's chemistry can do.

"Useful." Europe cocked her head. "But not what we require."

She went back to rummaging, at one point pulling out the mash that had been his travelling papers and folding money, still damp and starting to smell. "There's a mystery," she said, placing the sodden lump on the seat beside her. A few moments more and she produced what she sought: small, familiar, milky bottles with the deep blue ∃ and Craumpalin's mark **C-R-p-N**.

"Ah-ha! I'd recognise these anywhere." She held one out. "Evander water – 'good for all'. Somebody likes you, little man, to be prescribing this. Both vigorant and restorative in one happy draught. Glorious day! Open up and don't mind the taste."

Rossamünd knew what they were and blessed the old dispensurist in his heart – as he had already, many times – for his generosity.

She broke the red wax seal and reached over to administer the restorative. If it had not come from his own belongings, had he not recognised his own bottles, he would never have let the fulgar so much as wave the stuff in his direction. Even so, he was still uneasy. As his lips came to the bottle, the smell of its contents rushed up his nose. Strong and sharp, it took away the heaviness and brightened his thoughts. Contrary to its smell, however, it tasted remarkably bland. If Rossamünd was ever to eat chalk he would have said that evander water tasted like that, a liquid with the flavour of powder. He was dosed with the whole bottle, about three swallows, and quickly began to improve – muscles loosened, vision cleared, the pain in his head lessened markedly. He arched his back and stretched his arms out and up with a groan, twisting his neck back and forth. Finding Europe watching him he ducked his head self-consciously and offered a muttered thank you to the lahzar.

The fulgar waved a hand. "Tish tosh!"

He saw the little container of whortleberries and, with a cautious eye on the fulgar, took one. She watched him impassively and did not intervene. He ate eagerly. Now he felt much better: able to move once more, though still a little stiffly; no pain; able to see, able to flee – but to where? This forest was surely just as dangerous, and the leer would find him anyway.

"Well, now." Europe seemed fidgety. "I absolutely must do the brewing. Stay! I'll be back presently. Tomorrow we'll be coming to a wayhouse, so you can have that to look forward to. You'll be much ... *happier* there, I'm sure."

Rossamünd did not doubt her.

As the fulgar climbed down from the landaulet bearing

her black occult box, a noise came, distant yet distinct, from the direction of Licurius' exploration. Looking towards the sound with a frown, Europe stepped to the ground. "That can't bode good," she observed.

The sound came again – a series of sounds really. To Rossamünd it was like someone thrashing about in the undergrowth. He opened his mouth to ask, but Europe silenced him with the palm of a hand. Though she held it there only for a moment, Rossamünd noticed five small lumps upon her bare palm, raised and discoloured like moles. He had no idea what they were.

The fulgar took something out of the black box and put it in her mouth, just as she had before the last fight. She grimaced in much the same way, too, as she chewed, putting the box back in the landaulet and adjusting the lantern, making it brighter. All the while she stared in the direction of the noises.

Was there going to be another *fight*?

Rossamünd craned his neck, wide-eyed once more at an approaching, invisible threat. They were in a clearing just off the side of a road that crested this hill. All about were closely growing pines with only the narrowest space in between each trunk. The thrashing came closer through those small gaps.

Europe stirred up the fire, put on another log: she was trying to make more light. Far from wanting to hide from any danger, unlike Rossamünd she wanted to see what was to come, confident of mastering any event. Pacing between the landaulet and the flames, she buckled up the frock coat, never taking her gaze off the wall of trunks.

There was a flash and a loud fizzing close by – some way to the right of where the leer had departed. Bright and blue, the trees obscuring it shown as black, stark poles. Rossamünd almost fell over in fright and shrank down into the seat, peering over its edge. More thrashing about, the crashing of a heavy thing pushing through thin boughs. Smaller whippings. Closer, closer. Something appeared on the edge of the light.

It was Licurius!

The leer's tricorn was gone, his cloak badly torn, ripped almost from his frame, his sthenicon half wrenched from his face, yet he still clutched a pistol. Shocked, Europe took a step towards him. Bloodied and torn, he staggered into the clearing and, with a shuddering wheeze, rasped in the loudest, hoarsest whisper he possessed, "M'lady, we are attacked!"

The dark erupted in shrieks and yells, one of them Rossamünd's own as he gave cry to his fear. The landaulet jerked violently, throwing Rossamünd from the seat to the floor as the horse started in fright at this assault and tried to bolt. Hobbled and hitched, it could not get far at all. After only a couple of yards, the carriage halted suddenly with a strangled whinny from the horse, tumbling the boy within about once more. He scrambled along the floor and peeked over the side.

Shadows dashed and darted on the fringes of the camp.

Things with big heads and little bodies were pouring out from between the trees with triumphant yammering – hard to see despite the fire and lamp light. They overwhelmed Licurius as he turned to defend himself. Down he went, firing his pistol as he fell, pressed under a multitude of gnashing, nipping bogles. Europe cried wordlessly, yet before she could intervene, she too was set upon by many small terrors. They tore at her viciously, trying to pull her down too, shrieking "Murderer! Murderer!" in shrill unison. She swatted each one as it came, throwing several off at a time with that powerful *Zzack!* that declared the fulgar was about her gruesome work. She stepped and pranced with venomous speed, spinning, striking, her eyes wide and wild, her hair standing on end, frock coat hems flying dramatically – as they were clearly meant to do – showing many-layered white petticoats beneath. It was a great spectacle of flickering sparks to see the fulgar fighting in the night. Every nasty, gripping horror that got a hold was soon sent flying, almost every strike she made giving a brisk *Crack!* and a brilliant flash like little lightning. Several times one of the beastly little things was sent hurtling to its end with a great arc of electricity strobing in blinding green between it and the fulgar. In each brief glare the whole night scene would be quickly lit like a glimpse of day. None could best her. Even if they did get a good hold, the needle-like teeth and cruel claws of these grinning fiends proved almost useless against her stout proofing.

It was not over for the leer either.

a chinless
variety

big ears for
strong hearing

no noses means
they can not smell
but they do not
produce an odour
either...

little
spines

very nasty
very quiet
very sneaky.

THE NIMBLESCHREWDS
OR GRINNLINGS

157

There was a bright, hissing flare from beneath the writhing pile of bogles that sent them reeling and filled the air with a putrid stench – surely some powerful repellent. Licurius stood among them, dark and wet with gore, smashing one a deadly blow with the handle of his pistol. The sthenicon was gone, torn off in the brutal fray. The leer glared about with his terrible eyes and struck out again, causing something to yowl piteously. Amid all the confusion and alarm, Rossamünd was, for a moment, transfixed by the leer's face! His horrible, indescribably broken face! Little wonder he wore that box! There was another fizzing, hissing flash as Licurius let off another repellent, driving a handful of the nickers back into the woods with agonised hollering. But the rest came at him, leaping up, clutching, gouging, tearing at exposed places, bearing the leer down under their ferocity. Licurius disappeared once more beneath the whelming assault.

He did not rise again.

Europe fought on and on, heedless of anything but the deadly, desperate dance she played with her many foes. Some of the grinning horrors now lay still and smouldering; many had run off in dismay. Still she faced a baker's dozen more gathering themselves after the leer's fall. She saw him then, her factotum, or what was left of him. Rossamünd had watched as the nickers wrenched and ripped at the leer until they were convinced he was destroyed – declaring their success with blood-curdling cackles and whoops of glee. Now only a dark, deformed pile remained.

The sight of it brought Europe up short. She stood now, panting, seething, almost growling. With wide, near-maniacal eyes, she stared across the fire at thirteen little grinning bogles who waited and glared back, snickering, poking and prodding each other. These grinnlings had large heads with big, square ears, no noses and lipless mouths crammed with needle teeth. And, remarkably, they wore clothes – small copies of human fashion: shirts, coats, breeches, even little buckled shoes.

For a moment it remained like this, the enemies eyeing one another. Rossamünd had expected an exchange of words, of taunts or threats, but there was just this dreadful, pregnant hesitation punctuated by the distant wailing of wounded, fleeing grinnlings. The campfire crackled, the small cauldron on it hissing quietly with boiling water.

The universe waited ...

Europe shifted her stance.

With cacophonous screeching, the thirteen grinnlings suddenly bounded over and around the fire. The fulgar kicked at the first as it vaulted the flames, sending it hurtling back the way it came with a great blinding light-ning flickering from Europe's boot sole to the bogle. She immediately sprung back, making room, and smote the next two who reached for her: right hand striking left, left hand striking right, slapping one in the face – *Zzack!* – and thumping the other square in its chest – *Zzick!*

Three down, ten to go!

Rapidly sidestepping to her left, avoiding grasping claws,

the fulgar poked the next gnashing nicker right in its eyes, sending sparks from its ears and a squeal from its throat that expired to a gurgle.

Nine!

Now the remnant grinnlings pounced as one, grappling with her together – on her back, about her legs, tugging on her arms. Rossamünd waited for them to fall to their sparking doom, but instead Europe appeared to contort violently, staggered by some dark, internal force greater than those nine grinnlings could muster. Her back arched involuntarily. Her head thrown back, she screamed. The grinnlings hesitated but remained unharmed. With cackles and evil whoopings they pressed this new advantage, biting, gouging, ripping.

Rossamünd's thoughts raced. He had to do something! He looked about wildly for a weapon – something, anything. *The bothersalts!* Snatching up the satchel he leapt from the carriage, madly digging about within the bag for the small hessian sacks. He dashed to the fight, the bothersalts still undiscovered. In the dimming light he could see Europe being pulled to the ground just as Licurius had been.

Shortly it would be over.

There they are! He grabbed at the sacks roughly, ripped them out and hurled them in one complete move – all thoughtless, terrified instinct. The repellents flew remarkably true, bursting their powder over the murderous gang just as one of the grinnlings caught sight of the foundling. There was a great chorus shriek as the bothersalts did their work. Some of the grinnlings left off their rending to paw instead at their now burning faces. Others were simply distracted by this attack from an unexpected quarter. Europe, too, was engulfed in the acrid assault, but through her pain and her dazzled senses she still had enough pith to give one final, might-be-suicidal burst of electricity. Several grinnlings fell, expiring instantly. For the rest, this was too much: wrathful sparks from one side, bitter chemistry on the other. They fled screaming, every last one, their howls diminishing as they retreated further and further as fast as their little legs could carry them.

They had done it! They had won …

On the needle-matted ground, with many dead grinnlings sprawled about and a tendril of smoke rising from her back, Europe had collapsed, dreadfully still, dreadfully silent.

9

DABBLINGS IN THE DARKNESS

factotum (noun) personal servant and clerk of a peer or other person of rank or circumstance. Whenever the master or mistress goes travelling, so the factotum must follow. Lahzars, too, have taken to employing a factotum, so as to take care of the boring day-to-day trifles: picking up contracts, collecting fees owed for services rendered, looking to food and accommodation, writing correspondence, heavy lifting and even making their draughts.

TREMBLING, and ignoring the dead bogles, Rossamünd crept closer to the fallen fulgar. His heart teetered on the brink of complete terror at the thought of being left alone in this malignant place. As he neared her, he bent lower and ever lower, trying to see her face, trying to gain some hopeful hint of her condition. She lay twisted, limbs carelessly poking every which way, long hair a wispy mess obscuring her whole head. Holding back for just a moment, he knelt beside her and gingerly poked some of her chestnut locks away from her throat, cheek and brow. She was deathly pale.

Grinnling cries in the distance.

Rossamünd scurried back to the landaulet, took the lantern and dashed back to where the fulgar lay. He knelt and looked to see if she was still alive, wanting to weep but holding it in – he had cried enough on this journey. Blood was running from Europe's nose. There were nasty bites upon her neck where the proofing did not cover. Breaths did come: short, shallow puffing. *She lived!*

Rossamünd leant closer and whispered, "Miss ...! Miss ... Miss Europe ...!"

The fulgar's lashes fluttered and slowly parted, her vision clearly swimming. They shut again and it seemed she might slip into insensibility. Rossamünd pressed twice, sharply, on her shoulder, not wanting her to pass out. She groaned and shifted, opening her eyes again to peer at him.

With a gasp, Europe pushed herself up on her arms and sat, head lolling, hair drooping. "What happened?" she panted.

Rossamünd sat back. "You won ... you beat them all."

She looked about, blinking heavily. Her eyes were streaming with ash-coloured tears.

Rossamünd winced. He had hit her with the bothersalts too.

After a long pause and a deep sigh, she whispered, "Good ... They were ... difficult." Sitting up straighter, she flexed her shoulders and rolled her head about, grunting and grimacing. "My organs have spasmed," she breathed cryptically. "Not the best time for it, at all ... I thought I was done for." Pausing for a rattling wheeze of air, she muttered, "Never advisable to ... start a fight ... when one is missing a ... a dose of treacle."

163

EUROPE

Though he did not follow what she said, Rossamünd nevertheless understood that something had gone very wrong somewhere inside her body, that her electrical organs had somehow failed her in a most terrible way. He shuddered. This must be what dear Master Fransitart had meant when he said that there was nothing more wretched than lahzars made sick by their organs.

Far away, the wailing of the grinnlings could still be heard in the cold, cold night.

Europe tried to rise but swooned frighteningly, and fell back to ground. "I ... need ... my treacle, little man," she slurred. "Take the lantern. Get the box. I'll ... I'll show you how to make it."

The foundling ran over to the landaulet and, as he did, discovered that the chestnut nag had been attacked as it attempted escape. Slain, it now lay with many nasty wounds to its neck, point and chest. How were they going to get away now?

Hold to your course. People's lives are at stake, Rossamünd coached himself. *Do as Master Fransitart would have — everything in its right order. Box first — leaving later.*

Rossamünd found her curious black case in the now jumbled contents of the landaulet's interior. As he extracted it, the feeling of sickly unease moved within once more as he gripped the smooth wood. He ignored the sensation and returned to her side with it gripped determinedly under his left arm.

The fulgar had fainted and he was forced to rouse her

once more. She came to with effort, even wiping away tears. "Good man ... N ... Now, I need you to listen ... most carefully – we have not the time for mistakes."

Rossamünd nodded once, emphatically. This was not some pamphlet story. This was a time for diligence and dependability. This was the very thing they sought to teach all the book children at Madam Opera's – the very thing expected of you when you have been given your baldric to wear.

The fulgar drooped, gathered herself and continued. "Put the box down and open it ... carefully, though. That ... that's the way."

Within the box were many compartments, each with its own hinge-and-handle lid, and lined with scarlet velvet. He peeked under one. There was a bottle of liquid within, nestled in straw.

"That's the bezoariac. There's no time to do this neatly or make it pretty." She opened another compartment and pulled forth another bottle, this one half-filled with a dark powder. She put both bottles in Rossamünd's hands and with them a pewter spoon. Then she indicated the cauldron boiling on the fire. "Take these and put two spoons of the bezoariac ... the liquid – and one of the rhatany ... the other bottle ... the powder – and stir them into the water for some minutes then ... come back to me ... Make sure there is enough water. Anything over half full will do."

He did as he was bidden. The cauldron still held enough water, so in went two spoonfuls of the bezoariac – a kind of universal antidote he had seen used in the dispensary of the marine society – and the rhatany powder – which he had not heard of before. He stirred and stirred, knowing well just how it was done because of Master Craumpalin's patience and pedantry. Figures-of-eight, making sure it did not catch and burn on the bottom of the pot. All the while his back tingled with the dread that the grinnlings might pounce once more from the shadows.

"What does it look like?" the lahzar quizzed quietly. Her voice was muffled, for she had collapsed again and was lying with her head buried in her arms.

"It was like porridge for a moment, but it has now gone thin and reddish," the foundling replied.

"Does it boil?" Europe raised her head.

"Aye, ma'am, it has just started."

She reached over without looking and took out a jar from the box.

"Quickly then, add this. Use your fingers but do not put that spoon within this jar! Understand? There needs to be the … same amount as two spoonfuls of it."

Rossamünd did as he was asked, even though the unpleasant feelings these reagents gave him were increasing with each moment as he scooped cold, foul-feeling muck from the jar. Scraping off the correct measure twice on to the spoon, he plopped it into the bubbling brew. Disgusted, he wiped his fingers on some pine needles, then stirred yet more. As he did, Europe held out another bottle two-thirds full of a black powder. The sense of terrible foreboding radiated most strongly from this little jar.

He hesitated.

"When the curd is properly mixed and thick and even and turned to honey, you must take it off the flame then sprinkle in half a spoonful of this. It's Sugar of Nnun – *don't* let it touch your skin! Mix it well in … and when that's done … bring it to me."

Sugar of Nnun! He had certainly heard of this ingredient, though he did not know what it did. Craumpalin had condemned it in no uncertain terms, stating once that only people up to no good had any business messing with it. Had their situation been any less desperate, Rossamünd might well have refused to even hold the bottle containing such stuff, so thoroughly had the old dispensurist warned him.

The brew indeed became very much like the consistency and colour of honey, even causing his stomach to rumble, deprived of dinner – and maybe some other meals – as it was. He quickly lifted the cauldron off the fire by its handle using a handy stick and placed it on the ground.

With a sharp sickliness in the back of his mouth, Rossamünd removed the stopper of the bottle holding the Sugar of Nnun. He felt sure he could see an evil puff of black dust come out from within. Squinting, he nervously tapped the right amount on to the spoon, and this he mixed into the brew. As it was stirred in, the whole lot quickly turned black, became even thicker and began to stink disgustingly.

The potion was ready.

Rossamünd took off his scarf and used this to carry the cauldron to the lahzar. "It's ready, I think, Madam Europe. I don't know if I have got it right but it seems just like it did before."

Unsteadily, Europe got to her knees and scrutinised the result of the foundling's dabblings. When she saw the brew looking very much as it should, she seemed stunned, even as ill as she was. "Well done, little man," she breathed. "Well done ... That is exactly it." She snatched the brew – the treacle, as she had called it – and, waiting only a moment for the edge to be cooler, drank greedily, taking great gulps and spilling some, surely burning herself on the hot metal. The effect of the potion was rapid. Not putting the pot down till it was empty, she had a healthy look in her eye when she did. After only a few minutes of breathing heavily and digesting, the fulgar had recovered enough to stand. She wobbled as she did, but with the foundling boy's hand to hold on to she was soon on her feet. She was still for a moment, swaying somewhat – to Rossamünd's alarm – but staying upright and staring into the dark silence of the forest.

The woods were now quiet, but for what Rossamünd hoped were the usual tree-ish creaks and whispers.

"We must be leaving," said Europe. "They will most certainly be back for another try before the night is out." She hushed as the foundling repacked the black case with its frightful chemicals. With a great sigh, she turned to gaze at the place where the ruins of what-was-once-Licurius lay.

Grief worked in her soul and showed on her face. "Oh, Box-face … Oh, Box-face …" she lamented quietly. "What have they done to you?"

With Rossamünd to help her, she staggered over to the leer's body. In the nimbus of the lantern, the grisly proof of the violence just passed showed clearly. There the bodies of two grinnlings lay where they had fallen, slain by Licurius' hand. No longer animated by foul and murderous intent they looked small, pathetic, doll-like. In their midst was the black huddle of the dead leer. Though he was mostly covered with his torn cloak, it was still obvious that he had been ripped and gouged in cruel and vile ways.

With a choking sob, Europe sagged and dropped to her knees near the corpse. She swooned for a moment, panting heavily, pushing Rossamünd weakly from her. "You must not look on this!" She stood straighter. "Go! Get your personals and ample water for one night's travel. We must be away very shortly, and not delay – those creatures have gone silent, and I like that much less than their distant jitterings. I will right myself presently. Have no concern for me: our survival is afoot now."

Nevertheless, and though she would not like it known, Rossamünd was aware that Europe wept silently as he gathered his valise and satchel, filled his biggin with water and his pockets with food. She must have cared more for the leer than the foundling ever noticed. He felt sad for her, and for the Misbegotten Schrewd. For the leer, however, he entertained no regrets – the villain had tried to strangle him! This is what Verline would have sternly called "a hard heart", but Rossamünd could not see how he might possibly feel anything at Licurius' end.

Presently Europe came over to the landaulet too, stumbling only slightly, her face dirty with tearful streaks, and hurriedly organised her own travelling goods. With the horse dead there was nothing for it – they would have to walk their way to safety.

"We must leave ... him where he lies. There's no time to bury him and no profit in bearing him away. We must go to the wayhouse. I've passed it by many times but never entered. The Harefoot Dig it is called. When we get there and settle ourselves safely we can come back here to ... to fetch him. Move on, now! We must be at the wayhouse as soon as we can!"

Gathering all which was needful that they could carry on foot, they set off by lantern light, Europe pointing the way, Rossamünd leading it. How they were to make it, the foundling had no hopeful idea. There was a sandy, be-puddled road running right by their camp – probably still part of the Vestiweg. They walked along this, the fulgar unsteady at first but soon gaining pace, though not speedily enough for him. The fulgar had to caution him to save his energy when sometimes he marched on ahead, reminding him that they had a long way yet to travel.

Soon she made Rossamünd douse the lantern. "The light will be more harmful than helpful," she whispered, "and lead the grinning baskets right to us."

He complied eagerly at this warning. What hope did an everyday boy like himself have if a lahzar was cautious and wishing to avoid any new confrontations? In the dark he vainly tried to see into the benighted forest, to see past the straight pale trunks of the pine saplings that lined the road, to find warning of any possible ambush. He could feel that Phoebë was up and shining, but deep in that narrow channel of high trees, her light helped but a little. Oh for Licurius' nose now!

After they had trod for many hours and what was surely a great distance, Rossamünd was most certainly tiring. His feet dragged, and the valise, normally so light, pulled meanly on his back and aching shoulders. His lids drooped as his thoughts lolled with warm, comfortable ideas of stillness and rest.

Europe seemed to sag as well; eventually, to his great relief, she stopped near the top of a steep hill and sat down clumsily. "Aah!" she wheezed so very quietly, "I am flagging terribly … How about you, little man? You have kept pace with me admirably till now."

He dropped next to her, dumping the valise on the verge, and took a long swig of water from his biggin. Only a few mouthfuls more remained when he was done. Taking this as a wordless but definite yes, the fulgar offered him a whortleberry procured from one of the many black leather satchels and saddlebags. Then she chewed on one herself. He took it gratefully. They sat some minutes in silence while the internal glow of the berries restored them enough to allow them to push on. Rossamünd's senses sharpened again and with them his fears of another attack by the grinnlings or, perhaps, worse things.

A firm conviction was beginning to form in his deepest thoughts: that it would be the grandest thing to return to the safety and forgetful ease of a city and leave all this threwdish wild land behind. How could anyone have ever thought it prudent to put a road through such a place as this haunted region?

The land fell away sharply from the northern edge of the road and upon its steep slope no trees grew, affording them a limited view. At last Rossamünd could see the moon, ochre-yellow and setting in the west. He turned about quietly where he was and observed the white line of the road they had already travelled as it emerged from the trees. He looked with dread at the impenetrable black of the tangle-wood valleys directly below and, beyond that, the low dark hills further north. He quaked slightly – anything could be stalking about out there. The world was so much bigger than he had ever thought: wilder, and full of threats and loneliness and dread. He hugged his knees to his chest and waited, afraid, staring at the fulgar's shadow.

As they sat, she fidgeted with the scarf about her neck and with the wound beneath. "Are you better?" she whispered.

"Aye," he whispered back. "Your neck, miss?"

"It bleeds still … and it is starting to itch awfully. I believe it may well need seeing to by a physic. That will have to wait. Let's be off again. We still have far to go and this place is starting to get me down."

The dose of whortleberry had invigorated them both heartily: they walked and walked, and walked yet more, Europe leading onwards. The road rose over hills and dropped into small valleys. The forest soon closed in again and they were surrounded now by several kinds of pine. The air was still, filled with the strong smell of sap and the hissing of breezes in the branches. Stars continued to shine brightly and shed some little light on their path from the glimpse of sky above. Of the Signal Stars, Maudlin was now absent, having passed beyond view; only orange Faustus, the "eye" of the constellation Vespasia, and the yellow planet Ormond showed, and they showed that it was very late indeed. A frightened baby owl screeched thinly, voicing Rossamünd's own lost and lonely feelings. As he read the stars, he heard the fulgar stumble heavily in front of him, and looked down to see her sink to the sandy path.

He hurried to her. "Miss Europe …?"

She was on her hands and knees, panting as she had done after her organs had spasmed. "The bite … the bite …" she rasped.

Rossamünd carefully unwound the scarf from her neck and saw, even by dim starlight, that the wound had swollen frighteningly, and even now was beginning to stink of putrefaction. He gasped. "It's going bad already, ma'am. You must surely see a physician, and soon!"

"It burns …!" She managed to sit, to lift a water skin to

her mouth and drink greedily before lying back and panting yet more. "We must go on ... you're not safe ... we ... Not long ... must ..." she rattled on, though she did not seem able nor any longer willing to move.

Rossamünd's mind whirled for a time. This panicked feeling was becoming all too familiar. He forced himself to be even-headed.

The evander water! He sat down by Europe and dug about in his satchel for the little flasks. He searched for the longest time with little satisfaction – oh no! – he must have hurled them along with the bothersalts in his hurry to help. But then he found what he wanted: just one bottle, buried right down the bottom, tangled in among the rest of the contents. He gripped it exultantly. Leaning close to the fulgar's ear he could feel heat radiating from her in a most unhealthy way. "I still have some evander water!" he whispered.

Europe revived with this intelligence and forced herself to sit up.

He gave her the little bottle but her hands shook too much now. Indeed, her whole body was beginning to shudder. He held the flask for her, removed the seal and tipped it very slowly, mindful lest it should spill and be wasted. She swallowed it all as greedily as she had the water and then lay back again. He watched her, holding his breath anxiously.

With a burst of air from her own mouth – loud enough to startle some night bird to shrill terrifyingly three times and flurry off – she sat up once more. "I can walk … We've not … not got far … to … to … go now … Help me up, Box … Box-face." Her words came in struggling breaths. "With your … help … I can … can make it."

Putting a hand on his shoulder she pushed herself up to stand. Rossamünd grimaced but did not make a sound. When she had righted herself, she murmured. "Lead … on …"

He struggled earnestly to fulfil this task, at first leading her by the hand, gripping it tightly now, completely heedless of being sparked. Then he began limping himself as she started to lean heavily or pull upon him, often stumbling, silently cursing every stone or rut that threatened to trip either one.

Interminable seemed these last few miles, though the way had, mercifully, become flatter. At one point Rossamünd thought he heard the far-off tittering of the grinnlings and urged Europe on a little faster. The further they went the more fatigued he grew and the more insensible Europe became. She muttered odd things – often in another strange, musical language, at one time saying clearly, "We've been in many scrapes, haven't we, darling …?" She actually chuckled, then became dangerously louder. "But we get away scot-free every time, hey … hey Box-face? You and me … we … making it large all over the land …" It seemed she might go quiet, but suddenly she blurted, "Oh my! What have they done to you!" and began to sob, great, deep gulps that wracked her whole body. "What have they done to you?" she hissed finally and continued to weep. She said no more that night.

Soon Europe collapsed completely, toppling Rossamünd with her in a flurry of sweat and perfume, stunning him. He lay for a moment half under the fulgar, his head full of spinning lights. He never thought a woman could weigh so much.

The soft hooting of a boobook went *hoo-hoo, hoo-hoo*. It was a peculiarly soothing sound and he focused on it to stay awake. There was nothing for it – he had to drag her. Hardly believing where he was or what he was doing, he pulled himself out from under her, fixed a saddlebag under her head, grabbed her by her booted ankles with a foot tucked under each arm, and began to walk. Pulling, pulling, finding energy he did not know he had, he dragged the fulgar. Her shoulders ground noisily and her petticoats rumpled and gathered and began to tear, but he could do nothing about either now. He must trust to her proofing, ignore her indignity and simply go on.

Despite the noise and his agony and the desperate slowness of their pace, Rossamünd pulled Europe, bags and all, along the road till his fingers clawed and the eastern horizon grew pale. The trees began to grow further apart, a fringe to the main wood, and as he gradually came about a bend in the road he thought he saw lights through the sparse trunks. He pulled on a little bit further and found that it was lights, lantern lights. He stopped to gather himself, gasping in air, and peered at this new sight.

There, in the obscure grey of a new day, he found what they sought: a long, heavy stone wall of great height on the left, protruding from the thinning trees. In a gap about two-thirds along this wall and crowned with a modest arch was a solid ironwood gate. Above it was a post fixed horizontally from the apex of the arch, a bright-limn lantern at its far end shining orange. Dependent from this post was a gaily painted sign. It showed what looked like a woman running or leaping and beneath this the barely legible letters:

... It was the wayhouse. They had arrived at last.

10

AT THE HAREFOOT DIG

wayhouse (noun) a small fortress in which travellers can find rest for their soles and safety from the monsters that threaten in the wilds about. The most basic wayhouse is just a large common room with an attached kitchen and dwelling for the owner and staff, all surrounded by a high wall. Indeed, the common room still forms the centre of a wayhouse, where the stink of dust, sweat and repellents mingles with wood-smoke and the aromas of the pot.

THE entrance of the Harefoot Dig would not open when Rossamünd pushed upon it with his shoulder. Undaunted, he carefully lay Europe's feet down. Without quibbling over whether it was polite at so early an hour, he hammered with the wrought knocker of the ironwood gate as loudly as his exhausted arms would allow. Indeed, he could only just lift them to grasp the knocker.

Eventually a round grille high in the gate emitted a gruffly quizzing voice. "Whot's this 'ere, then? Whot's yar business at this *throodish* hour?" It was a strange accent Rossamünd had never heard before — a little like Poundinch's yet different again. It was hard to understand.

"I have a ... a friend who's hurt!" Rossamünd called up

to the grille in his deepest, most certain-sounding voice. "We have escaped an attack in the Brindleshaws! We need help!"

There were slidings, there were scrapings. There was a muffled conversation.

"I see ..." the grille returned eventually. "An' whot's a scamp like yarsalf doing up so late – or so eerly, if yar'll 'ave it at that – in risky places an' with no hat on his noggin?"

Rossamünd sighed. "I lost it in the river. Please, sir, my friend is very, very ill and she needs a physician quickly!"

"A lass, yar say? We cain't have a sickly lass stuck out there. Stay yar ground."

One of the gates opened and a short man came out. He was almost as broad across the shoulders as he was tall, and wearing, of all things, a chain mail shirt over the top of longshanks and jackboots.

"Let's 'ave a look at 'er, then," this stocky gatekeeper said as he stepped on to the road. He glanced about with a quick but shrewd eye and then down at the stricken fulgar. "Blast me! That won't do at all. Pretty lass, too."

The stocky gatekeeper picked the fulgar up under her shoulders, as if her weight was of little consequence. She stirred, but little more. He directed an "Oi ..." over his shoulder. This prompted another person to move out from the shadows of the gateway. It was a woman, a dangerous-looking woman glowering into the dark spaces all about, ready for a fight. She was tall and wore a strange-looking coat-of-many-tails. She looked to the other gater, then at

Europe in his arms and, with no further prompting, stepped over with swaggering grace and took the fulgar by the ankles. As this woman obediently heft Europe by her boots, Rossamünd saw that the backs of her hands were marked in strange brown filigree. It was the quickest glimpse but it fixed his vague attentions. Monster-blood tattoos! She was a monster-slayer too. Beneath her left eye were a line of spikes, spoors of some unknown profession.

Not too gently they carried Europe through the gate, the short fellow saying over his shoulder. "'Ere, grab 'er chattels an' all, an' follow me. I'm the gater, Teagarden – I look after the gate, see – at yar service. Whot's yar name, boy'o?"

"Rossamünd," he answered simply as he gathered up Europe's fallen saddlebags. He could barely grip the straps. His hands cramped, neither shut nor open.

He was vaguely aware of a brief but pronounced pause.

"Oh. Yar pardon, lass. Mistaked yar fer a lad in this darkling hour." This Teagarden fellow actually sounded embarrassed.

Rossamünd did not quite know what to say. His exhausted mind offered no assistance. "I, ah … that's all right, I *am* a boy."

Another pause, even more uncomfortable than the first. The woman bearing Europe's legs gave Rossamünd an odd look.

Teagarden coughed in a perplexity of even greater embarrassment. "Ah yes, right you are, and I knows it too, boy'o. 'Tis the paucity of light, methinks, playing tricks.

This lass with me be Indolene – she's me fellow gater."

Rossamünd, too way-worn to care, offered only what he hoped was a smile.

Behind the gate was a dim, confined coach yard. A yardsman hurried over with a lantern, his feet crunching noisily in gravel. The light was shone in Europe's face while the two gaters took her to an entrance in the large, low house before them.

She still breathed! Rossamünd could see her cheeks puffing as he followed closely. However, her skin was a ghastly pale green, showing the deep blue spoor vividly. Great bruised rings sunk beneath each eye, while sweat ran freely from her brow and hair. She was unrecognisable. She was getting worse.

The yardsman gasped, ever so quietly. "Oi'll be! She's a *lahzar*!"

The lady gater seemed to scowl but continued in her work.

Teagarden whistled softly. "Upon me 'onour! Yar keep yar compn'y strangely, boy'o. Still, thass neither here nor there – get her inside sharply, she looks fit to expire!"

The door they approached opened, casting an oblong of light on the scene. A lanky man in a maroon powder jacket and stocking cap stood there, looking tight-faced and beady-eyed. "What is all this huff and scuffle?" he demanded tetchily.

"We've got two new arrivals, sir," Teagarden offered respectfully, "an' this lady is poorly. *Physic-needingly* so, sir.

She also be a lahzar, sir, so I'd thunk it best we come through the back ways to avoid raising an unnecessary alarum."

"Well, good-good, Teagarden, no need to wait for my permission, man, if you see a physician is needed." The lanky man, who was obviously of some importance at this establishment, seemed the type to be peeved no matter how he was answered. "Bring them in, man, bring them in. Don't wait for me to invite you. Hello there, my boy – you look most weary. Welcome to the Harefoot Dig. I am Mister Billetus, the proprietor. We will do all that we might for your mother, and for yourself, too."

Mother?

This Mister Billetus, the proprietor, took Rossamünd by the hand and gave it a stiff shake. Europe was carried on within and down a passage of white daub and many doors. It looked very much like a servants' entrance.

"Now fellows," Mister Billetus continued, "take the boy's poor mother to the Left Wing, Room Twelve." He addressed Rossamünd. "'Tis the only room we have left for persons of quality as yourselves. Quality which, if I may be so bold, I can see you have in spades. Will it do?"

Rossamünd had no idea if the room would or would *not* do. Any room was good as far as he thought. "Any room will do, sir. I just want her to be seen to by a physic ..."

"Excellent, excellent. Of course, certainly. Go on fellows," Mister Billetus said, turning to the gaters and yardsman, "the mother needs seeing to – get her to her room! Properato!"

183

Teagarden seemed reluctant, but said, "Right you are, sir. Ah ...?"

"Yes, Teagarden?"

"Like I said afore, sir, she be a lahzar."

The proprietor's eyebrows shot up. After brief reflection he recovered. "Well, I didn't make her that way, man. Money is money. Keep her hidden from my wife for now. What Madam Felicitine doesn't know won't hurt us! I'll sort the rest. Off to their room, now, *now*!"

Holding a pale bright-limn, Mister Billetus led them through a labyrinthine confusion of dark passages and darker doors.

A boy joined them and Mister Billetus said to him, "Ah-*ha*! Little Dog! There you are, you scamp! Now hurry and quick to Doctor Verhooverhoven's estates and bring the good physician back with you. No dawdling! Lives are in the balance."

Despite his fatigue, Rossamünd thought it mightily untoward to send such a little fellow out while it was still dark. Little Dog did not seem happy about it either. Nevertheless he dashed off stoutly.

"The physician should be here within the hour," Mister Billetus said with open satisfaction. "Good, good, to your room we go."

Mister Billetus stopped by a door and looked at Rossamünd just as a cat might coolly regard an agile mouse. "You, er, can afford these lodgings, can't you?"

Rossamünd's heart skipped a beat. He thought on the

184

expensive foods and fine upholstery of the landaulet – all of Europe's flaunted wealth – and declared, with a quick-witted rattle of his own purse, "Absolutely."

Billetus looked powerfully relieved. "Wonderful! So you won't object to settling a portion of your board in advance, then?"

"I, ah … no." The foundling hoped he was doing the right thing.

"Good, good. One night's billet, board and attendance for a room of such elegance – and I do believe, by the cut of your clothes, that elegance is in order – the board for such a room is six sequins, paid in advance for two nights. If you leave after the first night then we happily reimburse you. So, we should count this as your first night – since indeed it is not over yet – and say, with a carlin and a tuck, that you will be paid up to the morning of tomorrow night. Agreed?"

Rossamünd's over-taxed mind cogitated the sums: *There's twenty guise to a sequin and sixteen sequins in a sou. So – two lots of six sequins was twelve sequins. A carlin is a ten-sequin piece and a tuck a two-sequin piece. Ten and two makes twelve – twelve sequins, again. I reckon it's right – sure is a lot though* … He thought his head might burst. "Aye … I think. Uh … thank you."

Mister Billetus held out his free hand, palm uppermost.

Rossamünd looked at it dumbly for a while then realised the proprietor was wanting payment now. The foundling fingered about in his purse, finding only the gold Emperor's

185

Billion coin he had received on entering the lamplighter service, three sequins and a guise coin. He frowned, thought for a moment, and then handed the gold billion to Billetus. The proprietor looked down at his payment with astonishment.

"Does –" Rossamünd's voice caught in his throat. "Does *that* cover it?"

"Um … it's a little … irregular, but yes. It's certainly legal tender and covers the fare amply. It will even buy you breakfast for the mornings." Billetus pocketed the coin while he opened the door.

The room beyond was large and of a luxury the foundling did not think possible. There were two beds, their highly decorative heads against one wall, billowing linen and eiderdowns of the softest cotton. The floor was wooden boards polished till they were slick, the white walls and high ceiling – richly decorated with flutes and twirls – made buttery yellow in the lantern's glow. In the foundlingery a room of this size would have been used to bunk twenty, where this was meant for just two. Europe was being laid on the farther bed as Rossamünd and the proprietor entered. A worn-looking blanket – looking out of place in its fine surroundings – was stretched upon this bed to stop the coverlets from being ruined by the fulgar's travel-grimed gear.

A maid, two tubs and several pitchers of steaming water arrived.

Mister Billetus excused himself and Rossamünd bathed behind a screen while the maid attended to Europe behind another. He almost fell asleep in the tub, but the maid, finished with her attentions on the fulgar, woke him with an impatient cough. Before too long he was clean – cleaner than he had ever felt in his whole life, dressed in a nightgown and lying in a bed, the very softness of which swallowed him whole. Europe lay, much like he, bathed and in her bed, in a borrowed nightgown.

"Is she better?" Rossamünd managed, vaguely aware that the maid was hovering about doing who knows what.

"She fares as well as she may, considerin' ..." she hushed. "You can sleep, little boy – her state won't change just on your attentions."

Lamps were doused. The maid left. In the dimness of a growing dawn Rossamünd watched the feverish Europe. He could not tell when or how, but in that soft, warm bed of the smoothest cotton, sleep finally took him.

He awoke with a deep fright, released at last from churning nightmares of Licurius' bloody end. The room was too white, too bright, the ceiling too florid, and the bed too strange. Then he realised where he was. Rossamünd was beginning to tire of waking in strange places. Some comfort it was then that the bed was so soft and so warm. He stretched luxuriously, wrapped in its wholly unfamiliar feeling, then sat up and looked about. There was a tall window at the far end, its two panes flung open, letting in cold air and the bird song of late afternoon that had brought him to reality. The world beyond it, of straight trunks and bare, tangled twigs, was wintry but golden with afternoon sun. The choir of birds – the soft, insistent cooing of some type of pigeon, the twitter-twitter of many small beaks, and an unusual call going warble-warble-warble-chortle – was strangely loud and altogether foreign.

The room itself was empty, in as much as there was no one else walking about in it. However, the bed near him, on his left, before that open window, was occupied.

In it, of course, lay Europe.

He clambered out of his own and went to her side. She lay on her back, her head cushioned upon many marshmallowy pillows, the covers tucked right up under her chin. Her long hair had been gathered under a maid's cap just like one Verline would wear. Shivering as cold air blew in through the open window, bringing with it the smell of mown grass, he reached out, touching her smooth forehead with his forefinger.

The fulgar did not stir.

She felt cool now, in contrast to the feverish heat she had boiled with so recently. His curiosity mastering him, Rossamünd cautiously stroked her spoor, the small diamond drawn so neatly above her left eye. Every side was straight and of equal length, the corners clear points, its bottom just meeting the hair of the brow. He had heard – he could not remember whether it was from Fransitart or somewhere else – that these spoors were made by using some acidic substance which left a permanent, yet somehow scarless brand. Why anyone would want to do something to

DOCTOR
VERHOOVERHOVEN

themselves that sounded so painful was very puzzling: was it just vanity, or was it a warning? As far as *he* was concerned, the next time he saw a mark like this upon someone he would be *very* wary of them. He stared at her blank, sickly face, hugging himself in the insufficient warmth of the borrowed nightgown, rubbing one foot against the opposite shin, then the reverse, to relieve the chill of the floorboards.

Suddenly he decided it was time to be dressed. He found his clothes in the cupboard, cleaned and pressed. Everything was there but his shoes. Rossamünd got dressed, searching quietly all about the room as he did.

Where are those shoes?

Under his bed? *No.*

Under Europe's bed? *No.*

They were not in his closet, and so he went to the one that held Europe's effects. Her clothes had been washed, too, and the cupboard was filled with the odour of the aromatics used to clean them. With this hung a sharp, honey-like-scent he was beginning to recognise as Europe's own. He was sure he was doing something quite rude by even thinking of looking through the fulgar's belongings. He closed the closet quickly.

The door at the farther end of the room, of a wood so dark as to appear black, opened. In breezed a maid with a flurry of swishing skirts. When she saw Rossamünd standing by the fulgar's bed she seemed uncertain. She curtsied expertly, despite her burdens. "I've brought the doctor to see you, young master."

Rossamünd ducked his head shyly.

A very serious and surprisingly young man entered the room. He was richly attired in a wonderfully patterned frock coat, flat-heeled buckled shoes known as mules, and a great white wig that stuck high in the air and left a faint puff of powder behind it.

"*This* is Doctor Verhooverhoven, our physician," the maid indicated with a tray she carried, a tray holding two bowls of pumpkin soup that smelt so delicious Rossamünd was immediately distracted by it. "And this, doctor, is uh, is ..."

"Rossamünd," said the foundling matter-of-factly.

"Ah ... right you are, my ... boy," said Doctor Verhooverhoven, squinting at him. "Delighted. How are you feeling?"

"Good, thank you."

"As it should be. I want you to have some of this soup that Gretel has kindly brought you," the doctor said as the maid placed the two bowls on a small table by the fire with a simpering blush. "I have fortified it with one of my *personal* restorative draughts, so it will see you righter than ever." He half turned to the maid. "You may leave now, Gretel. If I need anything you will be the first to know."

The maid ducked her head, grinned at Rossamünd and left again.

Doctor Verhooverhoven ambled over to the sick bed, hands behind his back. He stood over the unconscious lahzar and rocked back and forth on his heels. He checked the pulse in her neck, felt the temperature of her forehead,

191

*hmm*ed a lot and scrutinised her closely through a strange-looking monocle.

Rossamünd sipped at his soup, which right then was about the sweetest thing he had ever had, and watched Doctor Verhooverhoven watching Europe.

At length the doctor turned his shrewd attention to the boy. "She is not your mother, is she, child?"

About to help himself to a mouthful of wonderful soup, Rossamünd stopped with a slight splutter and fidgeted. "I – ah … No, sir – I never actually said that she was, though, sir. Others did … How did you …?"

Doctor Verhooverhoven adjusted his monocle. "How did I know, you were about to ask? Because you've got the Branden Rose here, my boy – heroic teratologist, infamous bachelorette and terror to the male of our species! She is not, if reputation serves, the mothering type! How, by the precious here and vere, did you come by her?"

The Branden Rose? That name was familiar to Rossamünd, though he could not remember why. Perhaps he had read just such a name in one of his pamphlets? What a remarkable thing that would be to have fallen in with someone famous! He hung his head, feeling strangely uncomfortable. "She … saved me from a thirsty end – Will she get better?"

"She ought to, child, with my skilful ministrations. I have been here since early this morning. You slept, my boy, while I scraped away the necrotic tissue and stitched that nasty gash about her throat. I have also balanced her humours and bled her a little against the disease of the wound.

The only thing she needs now is that awful stuff her kind take — *plaudamentum* I believe it is called. I have sent out word for our local skold to be found, so it can be made. From my readings — which have by no means been extensive — a lahzar cannot go terribly long without it, two or three days at most ... or things begin to go sour within." The physician rolled his eyes dramatically. "But, how-now, I need not frighten you with such detail."

Unfortunately, he *had* frightened Rossamünd, though probably not in the way he had expected. Filled with urgency the boy stood. "Do you mean her treacle, sir?"

"Ah-ha! That's the one. Cathar's Treacle! Just the stuff. When did she last have any?"

"Some time last night. I don't know when exactly though, but I can brew it for her now, sir. I don't want her innards to go sour, and she's got all the makings."

The physician looked dubious.

"I made it for her the other night," Rossamünd insisted. "If I've done it before I can do it again ..." The confidence in his own voice surprised him.

"Are you her factotum? You seem to me to be a little young for it." Doctor Verhooverhoven tapped at his mouth with his forefinger, eyebrows wriggling inquisitively.

"... No — sir, I'm not." Sometimes Rossamünd almost regretted he found it so hard to lie.

"No? Ahh. We shall wait for this other to arrive then, shall we? They are a skold, and I am of the understanding that they know how to make such a concoction." The physician took a high-backed chair from a corner and sat down on it by the fire.

"But why does she need it so badly?"

"A good question, my boy! A good question. Are you sure you want the answer?" Doctor Verhooverhoven looked very much as if he wanted to give it.

Rossamünd indicated that he did want the answer.

"Of course you would. Well, you see – as I have read – when someone wants to become a lahzar, they usually take themselves off to a gloomy little city in the far south called Sinster. In that place there are butchers – 'surgeons', they insist on calling themselves – who will carve you up for a high fee. Are you following me?"

Rossamünd nodded quickly.

"As you should, as you should. So, having gone this far – so the readings report – these surgeons take *whole systems* of exotic glands, bladders, vessels and viscera and sew them right in with all the existing entrails and nerves. Some say these new glands and such are grown for just a purpose, while others hold that they are 'harvested' from other creatures – no one agrees and the surgeons of Sinster aren't telling. Either way, when it is all done, the person is stitched back up again. Now – here comes the answer to your question – all these strange and exotic glands are wrong for the body. Consequently it reacts, eventually most violently, unless something is done to stop such a thing. *That* is the job of the plaudamentum – the Cathar's Treacle. Do you understand? They have to spend the rest of their lives taking the stuff every day to stop their natural organs from revolting against these introduced ones. This morbidity – this organ decay – once it takes hold, will eventually prove fatal. If this lady doesn't get hers soon she will die. How-now, I think you'll find that covers it, anyway. Yes?"

As Rossamünd took a breath to answer, he was distracted by animated, angry-sounding conversation approaching the other side of the door then interrupted by a sharp knocking.

Doctor Verhooverhoven stood at this and called mildly, "Enter, please!"

The door was opened rapidly and a strange woman stalked in, wearing the elegant day-clothes of a refined lady, and on her face a frown of politely restrained anger.

Closely behind followed Mister Billetus, looking worried and chattering nervously even as they entered. "... Now dearest, one guest's money is as good as another's. With these nickers making the High Vesting Way impass-able, you know our visitors have been few. Every bit of custom is needful, m'dear, I ..."

"Yes, yes, Mister Bill, not in front of those who do not need to be troubled with the finer points of running such a grand establishment. Good afternoon, Doctor Verhooverhoven." The woman grimaced at the physician in a mockery of a polite smile. He in turn bowed graciously with a puff of powder from his wig. She put her attention on Rossamünd and said stiffly, "And you must be the smaller of our most recent arrivals. I am Madam Felicitine, the enrica d'ama of this humble yet *refined* wayhouse." As she said "refined" she looked sharply at Mister Billetus.

Confused, Rossamünd simply stood blinking. "Enrica d'ama" was a fancy term for the ruling lady of a household, especially of a court. It was used only by those trying to be very grand.

"It has come to my notice," the enrica d'ama continued, addressing the physician, yet pointing angrily at the inert fulgar, "that we have here, in one of our finest apartments, a pugnator, one of the fighting riff-raff. Is this true, sir?"

"Yes, gracious madam, it is – though to me her calling is of little concern. I heal all comers."

"Don't try to charm me, doctor. You share in this little sham of my husband's, though how he thought I would not know what was up soon enough is insulting at the least." She gave the harassed Billetus another quick glare. He offered an apologetic look to both Rossamünd and Doctor Verhooverhoven, but did little else.

To Rossamünd the scene was quickly becoming very strange and uncomfortable.

Doctor Verhooverhoven looked bemused. "I assure you, madam, that I am not aware of any sham so to have a part in it to play. I have come as asked, to tend to an ailing guest. This is not the first time I have done this, as you well know." He finished his statement with a gracious half-bow.

"Certainly not, but this is the first time you have invited here another almost as bad!" She turned to the door and called. "You may enter now, Gretel."

Gretel the maid came in as bidden, looking sheepishly at her mistress. Closely behind her shuffled a stranger: a short, meek-looking young woman – a girl really, younger than Verline – wearing a variation of clothing Rossamünd had seen many times before. A *skold*! Upon her head was a conical hat of black felt that bent back slightly about a third of the way up. All skolds wore some style of cylindrical or conical headwear as a sign of their trade. About her throat and shoulders was the cape of white hemp with a thick, gathered collar that skolds pulled over their faces to protect themselves from the fumes of their potives. Upon her body she wore a vest called a *quabard* – light proofing Rossamünd had seen in the uniforms of the light infantry of Boschenberg. One side was black and the other brown, the mottle of Hergoatenbosch, just like Rossamünd's baldric. About her stomach, over the top of the quabard, was wrapped a broad swathe of black satin tied at the small of her back in a great bow. About her hips hung cylinders, boxes, wallets and satchels – most certainly holding reagents and potives and everything else that skolds used in their fight against the monsters. Her sleeves were long and brown and flaring. Her wide skirt of starched, brown muslin was also long, and it dragged upon the ground, hiding her feet. Her black doeskin-gloved hands were clasping and unclasping uncertainly in front of her.

He had already seen several skolds in his life, for many served at Boschenberg's docks to ward off any nickers that might rise out of the Humour and along the city's walls.

Even so, Rossamünd knew less now about them than he did fulgars. What he *did* know was what everyone knew: that they made all kinds of potions and draughts even more powerful and fabulous than those concocted by Craumpalin and other dispensurists, who were more concerned with health and healing. The chemistry of a skold, however, was designed for harm and violence. He knew that they had served as the Empire's monster fighters – "pugnators" Europe had called them – for centuries before the advent of the lahzars. This young lady must have been the skold Doctor Verhooverhoven had mentioned, the one to make Europe's treacle for her.

For a pugnator she seemed very nervous.

With a look like triumph, Madam Felicitine returned her attention to the physician. "*Doctor* Verhooverhoven!" she demanded, "What business have you inviting such knavish individuals to my peaceful establishment? You know my delicate sensibilities won't tolerate such liberties, nor will they suffer the presence of such as these!" She pointed a bigoted finger at the skold, whose face reddened.

The physician looked very ill at ease.

"Dear wife," Billetus ventured bravely, forgetting her warning on saying *things* in front of *those who did not need to know*, "their account is well paid. They have been no real trouble, rather quiet in fact, as needs must. What possible harm is one hard-working, well-paying lahzar occupying a room she and her factotum can afford?"

The enrica d'ama's thin lie of civility failed her at last.

198

"Oh frogs and toads! Because of the principle! She cannot ...!"

"Please," the physician interjected in a low, insistent voice. "You'll wake her."

Madam Felicitine eyed him coldly but continued with deliberate calm. "*She* cannot stay here because if guests of genuine refinement were to learn that a person of violence and infamy was bunked in the suite next door, they would never return and advise others to do the same. I *will* not have this, *oh no!*" With a dark look at Doctor Verhooverhoven, she forced herself to be collected again. "No, no, the billet boxes are the place for her, though I prefer the servant stalls for the likes of these, if they must stay here at all."

She then looked gravely at Rossamünd, who was looking very grave himself. "Now it pains me child, it truly does, but things must have their right place and order, people have their rank and station; some should not assert themselves above their betters. I know you'll understand one day."

"Now, now, dear ..." Billetus tried again.

Her momentum building, the enrica d'ama went on. "That is quite enough from you, I would say! *You*, who let *her* –" That accusing finger now stabbed at Europe unconscious on the bed. " – stay *here!*" Her arms now gestured wildly at the whole room. She began to go pale. Her cheeks wobbled apoplectically. "Did you *think I* wouldn't *find out?* She simply *has to go!*"

Mister Billetus now fumbled and stumbled but offered very little else.

"*Oh my bursting knees! Keep* her in the billet-boxes if your tender heart won't allow eviction!" the enrica d'ama hissed. "*Either way, get her out of this room!*"

In the awful, echoing silence that followed came a soft, icy voice. "My money glitters as well as another's, madam, and here in *this* bed I *will* stay!"

Everyone looked in wonder to the bed where Europe had lain, apparently senseless just moments before. She was still tucked in, her head still half-buried in the midst of the many, too-soft pillows, but her eyes were open now, bloodshot and baleful – and regarding Madam Felicitine with cold disdain.

Unexpected relief burst within Rossamünd.

At last Europe had woken.

WHAT THE PHYSICIAN ORDERED

skold (noun) the term for a teratologist who does the work of fighting monsters using chemicals and potions known as potives. They throw these potives by hand, pour them from bottles, fling them with a sling or fustibal (a sling on a stick), fire them from pistols known as salinumbus ("salt-cellars"), set traps, make smoke and whatever else it takes to defeat and destroy a monster. They typically wear flowing robes and some kind of conical hat to signify their trade.

MADAM Felicitine did not appear to know how to answer such cool and obstinate certainty as she found in Europe. Suddenly rendered powerless in her own wayhouse, she quit the room with a great shower of tears and a great show of wailing.

Mumbling incoherent apologies, Billetus hurried after her, closing the dark door as he left.

Gretel and the skold looked at each other awkwardly, and then the bower maid busied herself by moving about the room lighting candles against the growing dark.

Doctor Verhooverhoven stood and stared at the floor impassively.

The skold looked from him to the bed and back, then behind her at the door. "I-I … I am s-s-sorry if I have

SALLOW

d-done s-s-something to offend, Duh-Doctor Hoo-over-hoven," she offered, appearing truly troubled.

This roused the good physician. "Not at all, not at all, girl. You were only answering to my call – and fair enough at that. Let us think no more on what has just passed – this lady needs your aid."

A look of great relief lit up her face. "A-Absolutely, yes, let's. You know I'll always he-elp as b-best I c … can."

"And a great commendation it is to you too, my dear." The physician smiled grimly.

Rossamünd was at Europe's bedside in a dash, full of hopeful concern.

She looked at him placidly, her red eyes ghastly within the oval of her sickly face. "Hello, little man … Have I been away for long?"

"Since last night … um, very early this morning." Rossamünd's voice quavered slightly in his eagerness.

The fulgar closed her eyes. "So we made it to the way-house, then? … Am I all delirium or are my senses turning hard rocks and sharp pine cones into a soft, warm bed?"

"Aye, aye, we made it here, ma'am, and the kind people helped us."

Europe chuckled weakly. "I'm sure they did – except maybe that screeching woman. Tell me now, how much has this *help* cost?"

The boy's face fell. He had not thought of it quite like that: that they were ready with assistance only as he was ready to pay. "Ah, twelve sequins for two nights."

Her chuckle grew louder, but that stopped with a soft gasp. "And you paid from my purse?"

"No, ma'am." Rossamünd puffed his chest just a little. "I paid with the Emperor's Billion, which was given me to start work as a lamplighter."

"An Emperor's man, are we? Good for you. How interesting ..." She seemed to fade for a moment, then shuddered. "I am sick, Rossamünd. I must have my treacle and very soon. You'll have to make it for me again ..."

While they had talked so, Doctor Verhooverhoven stood by, rocking on his heels once more. Now he came in quickly. "And you shall have it, madam. Here I am, the local physician, Doctor Verhooverhoven – How do you do? – and here is the delightful Miss Sallow, our own skold, who can make you your plaudamentum. Am I right, dear?" The physician turned his attention to the skold, who stepped forward, obviously in awe of the fulgar now invalid in the bed before her.

"W-why yes. I n-know all the k ... kinds of draughts n ... needed by l-lahzars. A g-good ssskold all-lways does."

The fulgar turned her mizzled attention to them both and squinted. "Ah, mister physician, you've got me a skold – how kind. Such ... tender mercies, I thank you. However, the boy could have made it for me, sir. He's much cleverer than he looks."

Ducking his head, Rossamünd did not know whether to be pleased or offended.

"I am sure he is and more, dear lady, but I would prefer

to trust to my own methods and know it's done as well as I know it can be done." Doctor Verhooverhoven nodded his head in agreement with his own statement.

"However you want it. I'll not argue with a man of physics."

"As it should be, madam," he smiled ingratiatingly. "I shall recommend a soporific be brought to you as well, to help you sleep. Take both this and the plaudamentum and then heal with that most ancient of cures – rest."

Europe closed her eyes, a knowing grin upon her lips. "And tell me, dear Doctor. At what price does your *warm* concern come?"

Rossamünd could not be certain, but it seemed that Doctor Verhooverhoven actually blushed. "You do me a disservice, madam. I seek to help you purely for the satisfaction of knowing another human creature is strolling easy once more upon the path of health."

"Certainly you do, sir," Europe softly sighed, "and what will be the account waiting for me upon my departure? We all have to put food in stomachs and clothes on our backs – I'll not begrudge you your pay."

"Two sequins pays for it all," the physician relented.

Europe raised an eyebrow.

Rossamünd thought her still very sharp and feisty for one so very ill.

Doctor Verhooverhoven quickly went on. "But enough of this unflattering talk of fiscal things – you must be easy now, and have your draught when it's done."

Rossamünd found that disturbing black-lacquer case – the treacle-box – poking from a saddlebag at the bottom of the cupboard. Once again it gave him dread chills as he fetched it out. He took it over to Europe, who roused herself and smiled weakly.

She looked to Sallow, who blushed brightly from ear to ear. "Let this little man help you, skold. I trust him."

The fulgar gave Rossamünd a strange and haunted look. "He's my new ... factotum ..." she finished almost in a whisper.

The foundling was stunned – *her new factotum?* Where did that leave him with the lamplighters?

Doctor Verhooverhoven gave a slight bow. "As it shall be, ma'am. Take your ease. Your draughts shall be ready presently." He raised his arms in a broad gesture to the skold and the foundling. "Come! Sallow. Young sir. Off to the kitchens now and do your duty. Gretel will show you the way. Tell Closet that I have sent you."

With a small bright-limn in her hand, the bower maid opened the door and curtsied to them, giving a grin. "I'll take you to the kitchens, just as the physic ordered." She stepped lightly into the hall and the skold went with her.

Rossamünd gave Europe a last look and followed, a welcome calm settling inside – things were going to turn out well. Still his thinking turned upon two questions as he followed the bower maid and the skold down the dim hall: *How am I going to be able to be Europe's factotum and lamplighter too?* and *Where are my shoes?*

206

Gretel took them through a door, down another passage, and through another door. Stepping alongside Sallow, Rossamünd became aware that she was surrounded with some very unpleasant smells and sensations. In combination with the treacle-box, these made him feel distinctly queasy.

"Hello," the skold said softly with a shy smile. "M-my name is Sssallow Meh-Meermoon. What's yours?"

"Rossamünd," he replied. *She must be kind of important, to have two names.* As always, he was half waiting for a strange reaction to his own.

"My, R-Rossamünd, it mmmust be *am-mazing* to be the f-factotum of the B-Branden Rose!"

She had not reacted. He *liked* her. *Pity she smells so badly.* "It must be amazing to be a *skold*," he returned.

"Ooh, I w-wish it were." Sallow sounded deeply troubled.

Rossamünd looked up at her sad face.

"I only j-just got back from th-the r-r-rhombus in Wörms a m-month aa-go," she went on rapidly. "Three years I was th-there, learning the E-elements and the Su-Sub-elements, the Parts, potential nostrum, all the ss-scripts, all the buh-Bases and the Combinations, the kuh-Körnchenflecter, the F-Four S-Spheres and the fuh-Four Humours, Applications of the *V-Vadè kuh-Chemica*, mmmatter and ha-abilistics. Oh m-my, what a l-lot to n-know."

Rossamünd knew from his almanac that a "rhombus" was where some skolds went to learn their craft. As to the other things she said, he had no idea what she was talking about – except that "matter" was the study of things now past, that "habilistics" the study of how things work, and that the *Vadè Chemica* was an ancient book – as Craumpalin had told him – full of the most unspeakable things. This girl seemed too polite and kind to have spent three years delving into such a grim volume.

"I have l-learnt it all, too," she carried on. "Eh-everything. Achieved hi-igh st-standards, won p-prizes. Oh, but nuh-now …"

She trailed off as they went through one last door and came into a very large room full of heat and steam and shouts. Shadows moved within this muggy air, lit glaringly from behind by a large pall of flickering orange. Delicious smells, sweet and savoury, hung thickly.

Mmm, the kitchen … Rossamünd's stomach celebrated this discovery with a gurgle.

"Bucket, you little sprig!" a refined but gravelly voice boomed. "Keep that spit turning and turning slowly, or I'll put you on it and baste you instead!"

There was a clang, then a crash, then a tinkle.

"That's it! Out! *Out!*" the voiced boomed more loudly.

A small child scurried out of the thick vapours, pushed past them roughly and out the door they had just come through. A ladle came flying after him, just missing Gretel and bouncing to the cobbled ground with a bang and a clatter that stung the ears. A very average-looking man with a red face appeared from the steam, his expression changing from a fit of fury to shamed apology and finally fixing on stiff reserve as he saw the three newcomers and at their feet the still shuddering ladle. "Gretel. Whom have you brought me? Do they not like their food? Do they want Uda to make it instead, do they?"

He was neither short nor tall, fat nor thin, handsome nor ugly, just very average. He wore an apron of the cleanest white despite all the bubblings and boilings going on around them. It was his voice that had bellowed before.

"Not at all, Mister Closet," Gretel answered merrily. "You recognise young Sallow, our skold, don't you? Little Sallow? Went off to Wörms, has come back a proper young lady and a bogle-fighter too? She needs to brew a potive here or some such, under Doctor Verhooverhoven's orders."

Mister Closet made no sign of recognition. Instead, he looked ceiling-wards impatiently. "Well ... if the good doctor has ordered it, I suppose it *must* be allowed." He frowned at Sallow and pointed to his left, his hand clutching a jagged knife. "Use the hotplate in yon corner there and stay out of the way!"

Gretel went to leave and saw that Rossamünd was padding about the place in just his trews. "I am so sorry – you haven't had your shoes returned. Sitt, the rascal, has taken his time. I will fetch them for you," she said and left them with a smile.

A silent, portly lady in an apron as filthy as Closet's was white gave the skold a small clay pot to mix in.

Rossamünd fidgeted. The uncomfortable sensations coming from the treacle-box were beginning to become unbearable. It was a great relief when Sallow took it from him. As he gave it to her he asked, "Um – Miss Skold – ah – Sallow. Doesn't it make you feel ... nervous, to hold all these reagents?"

"N-no, not r-really," she answered absently. "This is a w-well laid out b-box. Very ha-andy. Do you n-know wh-ere sh-she got it from?"

"Uh, no ..."

With great concentration Sallow busied herself in the preparation of the treacle. The skold went through all the steps just as Rossamünd had done, muttering to herself all the time. "F-first the ... bezoariac, then ... the ... r-rhatany ... then ..."

When it was finished (and Rossamünd thought it a little too lumpy) Sallow poured the treacle into a beer tankard and carried it back to the room.

Europe drank as greedily as she always did. Almost before their very eyes her face flushed with renewed vigour.

As she finished the last of the treacle Doctor Verhooverhoven turned to Sallow. "I have good tidings for you, my dear," the physician smiled to the skold. "You see, this fair fulgar has told me – while you were brewing – that she has slain those troublesome bogles in the Brindleshaws!"

Sallow looked as if she had just been freed from a terrible gaol sentence. "Really! Oh ruh-really!" She turned from the beaming doctor to the impassive fulgar.

Europe smiled in a cool, regal way, and nodded. "I hear

from the physic that you were doomed to fight them your-self, girl. I am glad to rid you of the burden. The big fellow was a doddle, but those I believe to be his little masters gave me the … hardest time. A mercantile league in High Vesting hired me to do it, so you can thank the Signal Stars the unhappy task is done. Back to brewing and books for you."

"Oh my! Oh m-my! What a r-ruh-relief," was all that the overjoyed Sallow could manage for the moment.

The offhand mention of the death of the Misbegotten Schrewd gave Rossamünd a sharp jab in his gut. The sorrow of it returned to him.

Europe lay back, closing her eyes. "I won't need your soporific, Doctor Verhooverhoven. I feel sleep coming to me anyway."

"Good to hear – just as it should be."

Taking up a candle, the physician shepherded Sallow towards the door with upraised arms. "Time for we less sleepy folk to leave. I must return to my own abode – things there also need attending to. Sallow, after you." He smiled at Rossamünd. "When you are done here, my boy, I recommend you to the common room, and get yourself a hearty meal."

The foundling nodded. "Aye, Doctor, I shall."

"Goodnight, madam!" The physician bowed gracefully to Europe. "I expect you to be in much better spirits tomorrow."

"And goodnight to you too, good Doctor," returned

Europe with equal grace. "Sleep well."

The physician and the skold left.

Feeling a little awkward at being alone with the fulgar, Rossamünd fidgeted and looked at her shyly. She still held the tankard in which her treacle had been served.

"I could take that back to the kitchens for you, Miss Europe," he offered.

She looked at him sleepily. "That's a servant's job, little man." She held it up to him anyway. "But if you must."

As he took it from her, he saw that there was a whole battery of marks running down the inside of each wrist, a tiny **X** flaring at each end. They were the same deep, dried-blood colour as the leering monster's head drawn on Master Fransitart's arm. He hesitated. "Miss Europe …?"

"Yes?"

"What are they?" he asked, looking meaningfully at her wrists.

The fulgar turned them about to show the small marks more clearly – arranged four by four in distinct sets. On the right wrist three complete sets went halfway up her arm; on the left there was only one complete set and another well on the way.

Rossamünd did a quick calculation. *There must be more than seventy!*

"These?" she queried mildly. "These are just my cruorpunxis."

"Your what, miss?"

"Cruorpunxis," she repeated, growing slightly impatient.

"Kroo-or-punk-siss. Monster-blood tattoos. Each little mark a monster I've slain."

She's killed more than seventy monsters!

"Not every one is here, though," she sighed, looking intently at her forearm. "Sometimes it is impossible to get at the beast after it's done in. Like that big brute at the bridge ..."

He was glad she would not be able to mark the Misbegotten Schrewd there. "I thought they were always drawn in the shape of those you killed?"

"Oh, well, that's the way of rude and vulgar fellows. I have preferred something a little more comely and suitable."

Rossamünd frowned. He did not like Master Fransitart being called a rude, vulgar fellow.

Europe roused herself. "Listen now," she said, heedless of his inner fuming. "While you were in the kitchens, I made an arrangement for the retrieval of ... dear Licurius ... and ... the landaulet too. I expect it to be done by tomorrow evening – please, come and tell me as soon as it is."

Yes, your blasted, wicked Licurius, went Rossamünd's thoughts.

"Aye, Miss Europe," went his mouth.

Rossamünd did not look at Europe as he walked to the door. All the bad he had witnessed her do was a heavy, black pall in his thoughts. Just inside the door he spied his shoes thoroughly clean and shining black. Over them Europe's high, violent-looking equiteer boots loomed. Rossamünd took his shoes out from under their shadow and put them on. Without a word or a backward look, he left the room.

12

A TROUBLE SHARED IS A
TROUBLE HALVED

Imperial postman (noun) A walking postman's or ambler's life is dangerous, and he is forced to be skilled at avoiding, and protecting himself against, monsters. Frequently customers of skolds, postmen invent clever and slippery ways to make sure that the post always gets through. Mortality rates are high among them, however, and the agents who employ them prefer orphans, strays and foundlings who will not be missed by fretting families.

EARLY the next morning, Rossamünd found Europe sitting quietly on a stiff chair by a newly lit fire, staring at the struggling flames. She held a soup bowl of Cathar's Treacle, meekly sipping at it rather than gulping it down. Waiting till she had finished her potive – feeling that this would be the best policy – he began.

"Miss?"

Europe turned her hazel gaze to him. "Yes, little man?"

He fidgeted. "What ... what do you think of my name?"

The fulgar looked annoyed. "How do you mean, *think*?"

"Well, it's not a name meant for a boy. Did you know that?"

Her expression relaxed. She laughed her liquid chortle.

"Oh, I seeee! So, some would have it meant for a girl? What concern is it of mine how your sires chose to label you? Things are more than their names. If you were anointed 'Dunghead', I'd still call you *that* without teasing or embarrassment. It's just a word, little man." She gave him a soft look – faint, but unusually kind.

Rossamünd's heart sang a little. The fulgar might have gone some small way to redeeming herself for the harm done at the Brindlestow Bridge.

For a time she did not speak, and Rossamünd went to leave. Europe reached over and touched him on the arm. She said, very quietly, "I understand why you asked me this, though, and I'm sure it has been a great inconvenience to you for much of your life."

He blinked at her capricious kindness. After a moment he answered, "Aye, ma'am, it has at that. They would call me 'Rosy Posy' or 'Girly-man' or 'M'lady' or … or more things besides."

The fulgar contemplated him with a serious eye. "Hardly surprising. Children begin the cruel career of the untamed tongue almost as soon as they can talk." She paused, and continued to look at him intently. He took the bowl from her to give himself something to do under that uncomfortable gaze.

"I hope you learn to master your hurts, little man."

Rossamünd kept his eyes on the black dregs in the bottom of the bowl. "Oh, I just ignored them, stayed out of the way as much as possible. Master Fransitart and Verline

216

looked after me very well, anyways, so I don't mind."

Europe shifted in her seat. "So, who are these – Master Fransitart and ... Verline?" she asked, pulling out a small, black lacquered box.

Rossamünd relaxed. "Oh, Master Fransitart is ... was my dormitory master, though not the only one: there's Craumpalin and Heddlebulk, Instructor Barthomæus and Under-master Cuspin ..."

Europe's eyes glazed and she went back to looking at the fire. It appeared that she had lost interest.

"... and Verline is Madam Opera's parlour maid, but she took special care of me," Rossamünd finished quickly, wanting at least to answer her original question.

"Madam *Opera*, now?" Europe's attention fixed on him again and she lifted one brow in her characteristic manner. "Enough names. Your first years sound almost as complicated as mine were. Go away now, little man. A woman must have her privacy. Let me know as soon as ... Licurius' body ... and the landaulet are fetched back." Her shoulders sagged and, even though she had just risen, she looked very tired.

Rossamünd nodded a little bow and, holding the soup bowl in one hand and picking up his almanac in the other, went to leave. As he opened the door Europe called, "And tell *them* not to disturb me."

"Yes, Miss Europe."

As confused as he had ever been after a conversation with the fulgar, Rossamünd went to the common room. Strangely, he also felt lighter than he had for many days.

He read his almanac and sipped on a mug of small beer. In the afternoon Gretel came to him while he still sat in the common room. Dank, the day-watch yardsman, was with her and announced to the foundling that the landaulet had been retrieved.

Rossamünd went out to the yard and found the carriage to be as much in the state they had left it as could be expected. He asked after the corpse of the leer.

"Well, ye see," said Dank, scratching his head, "there was no body, not the horse's nor this Licurius fellow's."

Rossamünd's heart sank. The growing lightness within him evaporated, without even a memory of it ever occurring at all. His face must have shown his sinking spirits, for Gretel put her hand softly on his shoulder.

"'Tis the way of things," the day-watch yardsman explained. "Monsters love their meat, and the skin and bones of people most of all. Sorry, lad. I'm sure your mistress will understand. She seems a worldly woman, if her reputation has it right."

With a heavy sigh, Rossamünd made his way to his room, Gretel and Dank — hat humbly in hand — accompanying him. When they were permitted to enter, Europe seemed in good spirits. With much "um"-ing and "ah"-ing, Rossamünd gave her the grim news.

Dank confirmed his report almost as awkwardly. "We searched as long and as far as we dared, ma'am, but turned up nought ..."

Black gloom immediately descended upon the fulgar,

and she ordered everyone from the room with a chilling whisper. As Rossamünd left she called to him. Her eyes were hard and her expression brittle. "We will need a new driver," she said.

Rossamünd hesitated, the question of *how* forming in his mind and making its way to his mouth.

The fulgar's eyes narrowed.

"Y-yes, Miss Europe," the foundling said, and left quickly.

He sought out Mister Billetus about such a task, and the proprietor told him that the town of Silvernook, a little way to the north, was the best place to find coachmen, wagoners and other drivers.

"Just go to the coachman's cottage of the Imperial Postal Office," offered Mister Billetus. "'Tis where all the drivers spend their time waiting their turn to drive the mail from town to town."

As it was deemed too late in the day for him to proceed, Rossamünd was forced to wait till the next to seek a driver in Silvernook. Instead he went to the common room to have dinner. Just as the night before, a maid served him and he chose a meal from a list upon a large oblong of card she held.

At the top it read "Bill of Fare" ... and beneath the dishes were categorised under subheadings: "Best Cuts" and "The Rakes". The difference Rossamünd could not fathom. Last night he had chosen lamprey pie from the list headed "The Rakes" because he had had it once before and did not recognise the names of any of the other meals. It did not taste very good. Tonight he picked the venison ragout, and also asked for an exotic-sounding drink listed as "Juice-of-Orange". When this beverage arrived, it had a flavour that, yet again, amazed the simple tastes of the foundling. Sharp, sweet, tangy, refreshing, the juice was like the best orange he had ever eaten. The venison ragout, on the other hand, he found a bizarre flavour in his mouth, making it tingle and smart, but he pushed it down all the same. Not even the fussiest book child ever left food on a plate.

A woman dressed in an astounding display of peacock feathers and blued fur stood at the other end of the common room and sang so sweetly Rossamünd forgot to eat for minutes at a time. Apparently her name was Hero of Clunes – so he heard people about him say – a famous actress from far away south. Rossamünd wondered what she might be doing in this remote region. Looking for "Clunes" in his almanac, Rossamünd found to his amazement that it was so far south it did not even show on any of his charts.

He finished his meal and returned to his room to slumber. Europe still lay in bed, her back to the door. Rossamünd could not tell whether she slept or simply ignored him, and cared little for the risk to find out which.

Not long after dawn he set out. Master Billetus sent Little Dog with him to show the way. Little Dog went forth barefoot, protected by proofing of much lesser quality than Rossamünd's own fine jackcoat. He proved shy at first and seemed in awe of the foundling, an attitude so new to Rossamünd that he found it unnerving.

They were let through the gates, which were firmly shut again behind them, and quickly arrived at the intersection by which the Harefoot Dig was built. A sign was there telling them that they had arrived at the Gainway. To the south, it said, was High Vesting. To the north was Silvernook, and below this Winstermill. The back of Rossamünd's head tingled as he realised how close he was to his final destination. He had just to keep going north past Silvernook and he would arrive there. If it was not for Mister Germanicus waiting for him in High Vesting he just might have. They turned left and went north up the Gainway towards Silvernook.

Little Dog walked quickly and Rossamünd strained to keep pace. It was hard work and left little breath for conversation. The pageboy kept looking about nervously, and Rossamünd joined him. Over-loud rustles made them jump and hurry on. Once a loud crack away among the trunks alarmed them so much they fled the road and hid behind a knuckle of lichen-covered rocks. It was always a relief whenever a cart or a carriage passed them by, the drivers typically offering a wave and sometimes a friendly, incoherent greeting. This traffic became more and more frequent as the day progressed.

By about the first bell of the forenoon watch – as Rossamünd reckoned it – a cart rattled by and stopped. Its rubicund driver *hoi*-ed! them cheerily, calling, "Little Dog! Ye're wanting a hitch to Silvernook?" to which the two tired walkers gave a hearty *yes*.

The driver introduced himself to Rossamünd as Farmer Rabbitt and chatted merrily about "taters" and "gorms" and how Goodwife Rabbitt was heavy with child. "Moi first, yer know," he grinned with a wink. Rossamünd thought him the happiest fellow he had ever met, and could not help but grin along with the farmer's ready joy.

The darkling forest gave way to great, high hedges of cedar trees, grown close and thick along the verges. In the midst of almost every hedge-wall there was some kind of grand and solid-looking gate. Little Dog informed him that these were the fences behind which lived the local gentry.

As they rattled on, Rossamünd thought on the perplexing choice before him: stay true to the original path – become a lamplighter and take on a boring life, or become the factotum – the servant – of a woman who did deeds with which he could never agree? It was more than he knew how to solve, and he hoped circumstances would provide a solution for him.

Soon enough they arrived at Silvernook, hidden within a high bluestone wall. The gates of the town were open, but they were watched.

The town's gaters, who wore the black uniform of Brandenbrass, eyed them sternly as Farmer Rabbitt drove through. He set Little Dog and Rossamünd down by the Imperial Postal Office, where the lads parted ways, for Little Dog had an errand to run somewhere else in the town.

"I'm sorry, Mister Rossamünd, sir," he said, "but I

probably won't be able to show you back to the Dig. You'll find yer way back a'right though, won't you?"

"I reckon so, Little Dog," answered Rossamünd, blushing at the boy's deference. "I'll have my driver by then – he'll be going back with me, I'm sure."

With a satisfied nod, Little Dog left.

The Imperial Postal Office of Silvernook was narrow and high, like every other building in the town, making the most of the limited room offered within the safety of the town's walls. And as always, its chimneys were extraordinarily tall. As far as he knew, chimneys were so lofty because it was reckoned that the higher they were, the harder it would be for some curious bogle to climb them and do mischief.

People were going into and coming out of the Imperial Postal Office steadily. Rossamünd found that he had to join a queue of high-class ladies in their voluminous skirts and festooned bonnets; guildsmen in their weathered leather aprons; and middle-class gentlemen buckled inside high collars and flaring frock coats, just so he might ask for further help. When he finally arrived at the serious woman on the other side of a perforated wall, she informed him that the coachman's cottage was beyond a certain side door, through which he proceeded directly.

The door opened on to a long drive that went between the Imperial Postal Office and another equally tall building. This drive took him to a sizeable open area at the back, large enough to turn a two-horse carriage about, surrounded on every side by high houses. In a far corner was a small dwelling with a bright red door: the coachman's cottage. A brass plaque screwed to it declared:

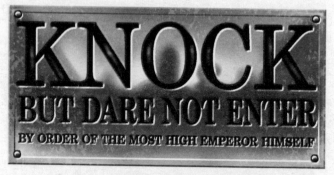

KNOCK
BUT DARE NOT ENTER
BY ORDER OF THE MOST HIGH EMPEROR HIMSELF

... and Rossamünd did just that.

There was a long pause.

He tried again, and the portal was finally opened, a thin, grudging gap.

"Hello," Rossamünd began, hands clasped meekly. "Do you have any drivers in there?"

The gap increased slightly.

"You what?" came a sour voice from within.

Rossamünd cleared his throat nervously. "I ... uh, we are needing to hire someone to drive the landaulet down to High Vesting. Um, we're at the Harefoot Dig, you see, and ..."

"You want someone to go with you down to the Dig," the sour voice demanded, "so they can drive some cart to High Vesting, aye?"

"Ah ... aye."

"And how much you got in your purse?"

FOURACRES

"I … um …" Flustered, Rossamünd counted his coins. "One sequin, a florin and eight guise."

"I seeeee." The sour voice sounded less than convinced. "Wait there."

The door closed with a bang.

Fidgeting, Rossamünd was made to wait what felt like an over-long time.

Finally the scarlet door was pulled open a crack once more. "Sorry, no drivers available," the sour voice declared, sounding almost triumphant. "Too busy! Try the Drained Mouse on Fossick's Cauld – plenty of desperate lads there. Goodbye."

"But wait, I don't …"

The door closed with an even louder, all-questions-ending bang.

Even before Rossamünd had a chance to turn and walk away in disgust the door was opened once again, wide this time. "So yer need some help with a driver, do yer?" a voice inquired.

Before him stood a cheerful-looking man with a ready, toothy smile and large ears that stuck out prominently, made more obvious by his hair, which was unfashionably short like Rossamünd's. This fellow was dressed in drab, sturdy proofing: a jackcoat strapped all the way down the front; longshanks of a thick, corded material; and white gaiters reaching as high as the knee fastened over sturdy dark brown road-shoes. Wound tightly about his waist was a broad sash, and fixed by black ribbons to both arms were broad over-sleeves of a brightly coloured taffeta of rouge and cadmium chequers.

Rossamünd instantly recognised the mottle of a postman, those faithful fellows who braved bandits and bogles and foul weather to deliver mail to and from the scattered folk of the country. The colourful cloth was set off nicely against his otherwise dull attire, and made the man look important and serious, quite at odds with his friendly expression. In his hand he held a black tricorn.

Rossamünd frowned at him, not knowing how to answer.

"Hello, lad, sorry about being so abrupt. Just had ter make sure I got t' yer in time. My name is Fouracres." The man reached out a hand for Rossamünd to shake.

The boy did just that, as Fransitart had taught him to, looking up at the man's face seriously. "Hello, Mister Fouracres. I'm Rossamünd. You're a postman, aren't you?"

The fellow nodded smartly. "Yes, lad, that I am – bit obvious ain't it? Rossamünd, yer say? Well, Mister Rossamünd, those other slothful souses in there might not want to help, but I may be of service to yer."

"How so, sir?"

"Well, I'm needed in High Vesting yer see, and I couldn't help hearing yer needed a driver to take yer ter High Vesting, so I think: two people, same problem, one solution. I'd like ter offer me services to yer as the driver yer need. I'm not as well practised as these daily-driving gentlemen – I'm a walker, yer see – but I still know how to switch a rein."

Rossamünd did not care what the man's credentials

were: he could drive, that was all he wanted to know. He accepted Fouracres' offer with glee.

The postman bowed humbly. "Just wait by the front of the office, and I will join yer as soon as I'm able," he offered with a grin.

With many an exuberant *thank you sir!* Rossamünd went back through the Imperial Postal Office and waited on the street out the front. It took a long time for the postman to emerge. As Rossamünd waited, with people and vehicles bustling by, he began fretting that he had been duped by the unwilling people inside the coachman's cottage. His fears proved unfounded, however, for Fouracres arrived soon enough, hat on head, bag full of dispatches on his back and a satchel over his shoulder – ready to leave. Before much longer they were walking back out the gates of Silvernook and returning down the road to the Harefoot Dig.

Rossamünd had found a driver!

FOURACRES

FOURACRES whistled a cheery tune as they strolled past the high hedge-walls of the gentry. He walked with an easy stride and smiled at anyone who passed. Rossamünd trotted happily beside him along the weedy strip that ran between the lanes, right down the middle of the road.

"So, Mister Rossamünd," the postman finally said, "how is it that yer could be at the Dig with a fancy carriage but no driver?"

Rossamünd thought for a moment. "There was a driver, sir, but he was killed by the grinnlings."

Fouracres looked at him. "Grinnlings?"

"Aye, sir. Those nasty little baskets that attacked us – the ones with sharp teeth and the clothes and the great big ears ..." Rossamünd stopped short and, looking quickly at the postman's own organs of hearing, hoped he had not offended him.

Fouracres seemed not to have noticed any insult. "Aaah, them! Nasty little baskets indeed! Hereabouts they call them nimbleschrewds. They've been a'murdering wayfarers here and there in the Brindleshaws for the last three months or so. I'm sorry ter hear they got yer driver, too."

"He fought hard, Mister Fouracres, killed many, but they got him in the end. I watched it happen – they just smothered him."

The postman nodded approvingly. "Well, there yer have it! To kill one or two is a doughty thing, but ter go slaying more, my word, that's a mighty feat indeed! But tell me: what was it that coaxed yer and yer driver to linger in that part of the woods – it being common knowledge they be haunted?"

The foundling did not know how to answer. He screwed up his face, scratched his head, puffed and sighed. In the end he just told the truth. Starting with Madam Opera's he told the entirety of his little adventure to the postman, who listened without interrupting once.

"So the ettin's dead, then?" was all he said when Rossamünd had finished.

"Aye, it was killed, sir, or as near enough to it, from what I saw," Rossamünd replied glumly. "I was there to watch, but I had nothing to do with it, really. It was a cruel thing, and I didn't know what to do ..."

Fouracres seemed sad to hear this himself. He sighed a heavy sigh. "Ahh, poor, foolish ettin," the postman said, distractedly – almost to himself. "He did not want to listen to me ... I warned him this would happen... There yer have it, lad: cruel things like this are done all the year long."

"Did you speak to the schrewd, Mister Fouracres?" Rossamünd was stunned.

"Hey? Oh, that I did, and often," the postman answered, after a pause. "He is – was – on my round, yer see, between Herrod's Hollow and the Eustusis' manor house. I told him no good would come of his enterprise, but he was powerfully put upon by those nasty little nickers ter keep it up. Who did the dastardly deed?"

"It was, um, Miss Europe, sir, and her factotum Licurius – but he died at the task, sir. He was the driver."

"Aah, the Branden Rose ... I had heard she might have been hired for the job, with that wicked leer as driver, you say ... a fitting end for him, perhaps?" The postman gave Rossamünd a keen look. "I've not had anything ter do with either, but I know the lahzar by her work and the leer by his blackened reputation. Is the Branden Rose as pretty as they say?"

Rossamünd shrugged but offered no more.

"What were the grinnlings doing to the schrewd?" he persisted.

"Huh?" The postman looked momentarily distracted. "Oh. Well ... if yer go by what the big schrewd said, it was the nimbleschrewds' – grinnlings, you called them? – idea to haunt the Brindlestow and stand-and-deliver travellers. I think they thought his great size would scare people more. It was inevitable really: such a scheme could never last so deep within our domain." Fouracres sucked in a breath. "I've seen the Misbegotten Schrewd about long before now. He ought'er have known better, but those grinnlings – I like that name, very fitting – those grinnlings must have come in from the Ichormeer or some other wildland up north. I say that 'cause, if it was their idea, then they can have only been ignorant of the ways of men or just plain stupid."

Rossamünd listened with rapt fascination. Here was a man who had not only seen monsters, he had talked with them! *Why couldn't they have made me a postman so I could wander around and talk to monsters too?* To Fouracres he said, "I can't believe you actually spoke with the Misbegotten Schrewd!"

"Well I did, many times. Great talks they were, very illuminating." Fouracres became sad again. "It's a great shame he had ter go the way he did – that ettin was a nice enough fellow."

Angry tears formed in Rossamünd's eyes. He kicked at a stone and sent it cracking into the trees. "I knew it! I knew it! But *she* just went and killed him anyway!"

"Now there, Rossamünd, master yerself," the postman soothed, bemused. "It's a bitter truth of our world that monsters and the vast majority of folks can't live together – certainly not happily. In everyman lands, monsters give way; in monster lands, everymen give way. It's a law o' nature."

"But you lived happily with them!"

"Some I did, that is sure, but certainly not all I met were worth stopping ter chat with. Besides which" – Fouracres leant closer – "I ain't the vast majority of folks."

Rossamünd wiped his nose. He was angry still. Things would never be as simple as they were at the foundlingery. "I would have liked to have been his friend too!" he growled.

The postman leant forward and replied quietly, almost secretively, "A noble feeling, Rossamünd. It does credit t'yer soul, and I heartily believe yer would have made an excellent chum: but I have ter warn yer not ter say as much ter many others. Such talk can get you a whole life o' trouble. Keep these things ter yerself." Fouracres thought for a moment. "I'll not trouble yer, though, nor say anything of what yer've just told me. 'Tween us alone, this ..." But suddenly he stopped – stopped talking, stopped walking, and stared rigidly at nothing.

Rossamünd had walked some way ahead before he realised. Alarmed, he turned back to the postman. "Mister Fo ..."

"Uh!" was all Fouracres said, his hand whipping up to signal silence. After only a moment more he stepped forward and whispered to the startled foundling. "We have something wicked on our path. Follow and step very lightly – yer life depends on't ..." With that the postman crept into the trees on their left.

Looking over either shoulder in awe, Rossamünd followed as quietly as he could into the wood, every snap and click underfoot a cause for chagrined wincing. He could not see anything on the road. How was it possible for this fellow to do so?

The ground all about was very flat and the trees broadly spaced. Some way in Fouracres found a modest pile of stone all about a small boulder and indicated that this was to be their hiding place.

His gizzards buzzing with fear, Rossamünd gratefully hid behind these rocks and found a gap between them through which he stared back at the road.

Fouracres put down the large bag he carried and held up a finger, whispering seriously. "No noise, no movement — ye're the very soul of stillness. Aye? The soul of stillness."

"Aye," Rossamünd replied in a nervous wheeze.

"I *will* be back."

The postman returned to the road, rapidly yet with little sound. Watching through the gap in the stones, Rossamünd saw him pick up a long stick as he went, then take out something from the satchel he carried and unwrap it. The strangely pleasant odour of john-tallow came back to him in the light early afternoon breeze. Quickly, Fouracres skewered the john-tallow on the end of the stick and began to rub it on the ground, on trunks, on leaves, creeping off the road and into the trees on the opposite side.

He's making a false trail! Rossamünd realised.

With fluid, careful speed, the postman worked deeper into the woods. Rossamünd lost sight of him and began to feel all too familiar panic.

I am the very soul of stillness! I am the very soul of stillness ... he chanted to himself.

There was a *click* close by.

With that one sound he became the very soul of dread!

There, just showing above one of the larger rocks, appeared the glaring head of a monster. Not more than five or six paces away, its long face was covered in mangy grey fur, with a pointed nose and equally pointed teeth, the top ones protruding over the bottom lip. A matted beard grew in limp strands from its chin. It had great, rabbit-like ears tipped with black fur that drooped out from behind its eyes. Large yellow eyes rolled about between slitted lids. This creature snuffled at the air as its ears twitched and swivelled.

Rossamünd had never imagined such a thing – how very happy he would have been to have Europe with him now! He clenched every muscle he knew he had, holding his wind for fear that even breathing would make him move too much. *I'm not here, don't see me ... I'm not here, don't see me ...*

However, the creature's attention was clearly absorbed by the perfume of the john-tallow. It stalked away without noticing the foundling cowering in his temporary rock shelter. Remaining frozen, Rossamünd was nevertheless able to watch it through the gap as it stepped on to the road. Hunched and gaunt and taller than a man, the nicker bent down to smell the spot where Fouracres and himself had only just been standing. Its long, furry arms ended in long furry hands from which grew long, curved claws that clicked and clacked together with every move of its fingers. Its legs bent backwards like the hind legs of a dog, and it used them to walk in an awkward, jerking way. The creature looked up the road, it looked down the road, sniffed at the ground again. Finally it started into the opposite trees.

But where was Fouracres? Daring to move a little, Rossamünd peered through his little gap in the rocks, looking for the postman out there somewhere in the trees.

Nothing.

Wanting to flee, wailing, into the woods, Rossamünd determined instead to be patient. He had survived the grinnlings – the Nimbleschrewds; he could survive this.

With a soft snort, the creature pranced further into the shadows over the other side of the road. It lingered there in the twilight under the eaves. While Rossamünd watched it, he began to get this strange niggling sensation to look to his left. He was reluctant to take his eyes from the creature, but in the end he did and looked over his shoulder. There was Fouracres sneaking back to him one slow cautious step at a time, his eyes never leaving the shadows of the opposite wood.

Relief! Sweet relief. Rossamünd could not recall ever feeling so glad, so lightened within, to see someone as he did just then. Encouraged, he returned to his vigil, in time to see the creature thread its jaunting way through the trunks and eventually disappear from sight.

Turning back to watch the postman, he found Fouracres,

THE BOGLE ON THE ROAD

his eyes still fixed on the farther trees, almost up to the rocks. He no longer had the john-tallow: that would be stuck somewhere cunning as far from them as possible on the opposite side. Rossamünd went to move, but the postman cautioned him to remain as still as he had been.

"We're not free of it yet," he hissed almost inaudibly as he crouched down beside the foundling.

Taking the postman's lead, Rossamünd stayed still and kept his watch through the gap. Muscles began to ache and an annoying hum started in his ears as he strained to hear any clue of the creature's return. This waiting was getting very hard.

Seconds slowed to minutes, minutes slowed to hours.

Rossamünd gave Fouracres a pleading look.

"Keep waiting," Fouracres insisted once more, and Rossamünd sat till he thought he could not take the buzzing of his joints or the ringing in his ears any more. He had no idea for how long they waited, just that it was so very long.

Even when a carriage went by, they waited still. But when another clattered by only a few minutes later, the postman seemed satisfied, and at last released them, saying, "It's safe enough. Let's get away from here."

Leading Rossamünd through the trees, still in silence, Fouracres allowed them to travel on the open road again only after they had put an hour's distance between themselves and their temporary refuge. Once clear of the trees, they hurried the rest of the way and arrived at the Harefoot Dig, safe at last.

It was late afternoon.

Exhausted, but promising to meet the postman in the common room, Rossamünd went to tell Europe the good news.

The reclining, recovering fulgar received the revelation with her usual, laconic grace. "You can trust this fellow?"

"He's an Imperial postman, miss. His whole life is trustworthiness!" the foundling enthused.

"Well, if a girl can't trust her *own* factotum, then who can she?" Europe closed her eyes, signalling the end of the matter.

Rossamünd rolled his eyes.

And what if a factotum can't trust his mistress?

He returned to the common room too eager to enjoy his last meal, for tomorrow they would be leaving. Fouracres was waiting for him, a pipkin of small wine and two mugs already on the table. As they sipped the small wine, Rossamünd showed the postman the cracking, illegible mass that used to be his travelling papers, letter of introduction and the rest. Rossamünd still carried them even though they were next to useless, thankful at least that Mister Sebastipole's instructions were so skeletal, for while they lacked detail they had been easy to memorise. He thought that an Imperial postman, especially one as friendly and helpful as Fouracres, would be able to help him with this problem.

Fouracres uncreased the puzzle of ruined papers carefully. He inspected the all-but-dissolved writing gravely. Soon he looked up again. "This is certainly a mess," he concluded, "but the seal is still intact on yer travelling certificate, and yer name, thank Providence. As ter the rest, well, I'll vouch for yer – what I call good, the Empire calls good. Yer mottle will help yer, too." He pointed to Rossamünd's baldric.

"Thank you so much, Mister Fouracres. I thought I was sunk."

"My pleasure, Rossamünd, though I would recommend yer got them rewritten by the Clerk or the Chief Harbour Governor as soon as yer can – and I'll help yer in that as well."

A meal of black coney pie arrived – and a jug of Juice-of-Orange with it – and they ate in silence for a time. Eventually Rossamünd mustered the courage to ask, "Mister Fouracres, what was that creature back on the road there?"

The postman stopped chewing and looked thoughtfully at the ceiling. "I don't rightly know," he answered at last. "Never seen its kind before. Bit of a conundrum – I'll have ter ask around."

Rossamünd held up his almanac. "I can't find it in here either."

"Well, that ain't surprising," Fouracres chuckled. "There's more kinds of monster than many a book could catalogue." He quickly became sad and serious. "Not that most folks think they're worth a-cataloguing anyways. Most folks would rather just see them killed and that be the end of it or at most see a list of glaring faces tattooed ter the limbs of a teratologist. Still, worth a look."

Rossamünd returned the book to his lap. "Uh ... Mister Fouracres, have you ... ever killed a monster?"

"Unfortunately, Mister Rossamünd, I have been forced ter do so, yes." The postman looked sad. "Yer see, if it's a choice 'twixt they or me, I choose me each time."

"Does that mean you have monster-blood tattoos, then?" Rossamünd could not help from asking.

Fouracres hesitated, then frowned. "Well, no, actually. I don't go a-glorying in killings my hand's been forced to do. It's just a part of getting the post ter where it needs ter be."

"Oh."

The meal finished, the Juice-of-Orange drunk, they parted ways, Fouracres promising to be ready to take the reins on the morrow morning.

They set out early, just as the sun had shown itself above the rim of the world. With Sallow detained elsewhere, Rossamünd was trusted to make Europe's treacle. He proudly handed the evenly mixed brew to the fulgar, and then left her to meet with Fouracres and help prepare the landaulet. Europe soon emerged wrapped in a thick deep magenta coat, knee-length, with its high collar and cuffs trimmed with thick, bleached fox fur. Her hair was held back in loose coils and she wore pink quartz-lensed spectacles. She appeared very differently from when Rossamünd first met her. She also still looked unwell and was, consequently, in a foul mood.

241

The night before she had settled the account with the proprietors by simply refusing to pay any extra beyond what she owed Doctor Verhooverhoven, declaring with the cold loftiness of a queen, "The boy's billion has covered expenses, as you well know. You'll not get a gander more out of him nor I."

Madam Felicitine went pale, but had said not a word.

Mister Billetus had just ducked his head and said, "Right you are, right you are. Hope your stay was as comfortable as could have been in the circumstances."

With a footman lugging out the fulgar's saddlebags and other luggage behind her, Europe stepped out into the coach yard. Rossamünd and Fouracres were already seated in the landaulet, waiting, the foundling in the passenger compartment and the postman ready to drive in the driver's box. Europe stopped by the step of the carriage and stayed there. With a quiet apology a yardsman went to hand her aboard. She shooed him away, saying, "Leave off, man, it's not your job."

Rossamünd had let his attention wander, filling his senses with the beauty of early morning. Only gradually did he become aware things were amiss. He looked dumbly at Europe, puzzled. She remained still, glaring straight ahead through those clear weird pink spectacles, her chin stuck forward arrogantly.

Rossamünd blinked. *What's wrong? What is she waiting for?*

"Miss Europe?" he asked simply.

Her eyes flicked to him. "Well ...?"

There was an uncomfortable silence. Somehow it dawned on the foundling what she wanted. *I'm supposed to help her in like Licurius did!*

He quickly jumped out of the landaulet, causing it to rock and unsettle the horse.

"Whoa! Steady lad," Fouracres warned.

Ever so subtly, Europe rolled her eyes.

With a weak smile Rossamünd handed the fulgar aboard and climbed back in once more, feeling very foolish.

"Drive on, man," Europe murmured.

Without a backward glance, Fouracres whipped the horse to a start. They went out through broad gates and turned left. Looking back Rossamünd could see further along the wall to that pedestrian portal they had been admitted through three nights earlier. In his mind he bid farewell to his first wayhouse.

Fouracres turned the landaulet right at the junction and Rossamünd was taken south this time. The Harefoot Dig disappeared behind the trees.

The Gainway took them through a woodland of younger, graceful pines, with areas of wild lawn between the slender trees. As they went on, large lichen-covered boulders now appeared here and there and the lawn became sparse and stubbly. An hour out from the wayhouse, the road began to slope gently down, and soon the trees gave way to a broad expanse of rolling downs and even larger lichen-grown stones. Every so often, thin, rutted paths would lead off from it, going to mysterious, adventurous ends. He saw one come to its conclusion at some distant dwelling. There were several of these about, he began to notice, small stone cottages built high upon lofty foundations, also of stone, with slits for windows and tall chimneys. Smoke wafted from some, that mysterious sign of homely life within.

"They're the houses of the eekers," Fouracres explained, "folk who manage to scratch out a living in the thin soil hereabouts. What they lack in material wealth they gain in liberty. The authorities don't tend to bother them much."

"But why are they so high off the ground?"

Fouracres gave a wry smile. "Ahh, to give the bogles a hard time getting them, of course."

With a slight arching of her brows, Europe looked knowingly at the postman's back. "You've dealt with some yourself, I suppose?" she said. This was the first thing she had said all morning.

The postman did not look at her. "Indeed I have, ma'am, though I am sure a near sight fewer than thee!"

"Hm." Europe lapsed into silence once more.

After two hours, with the scene changing little, they passed a milestone, a squat block of white rock upon which was carved *High Vesting*, and beneath that, *6 miles*.

Behind this milestone grew a small, scruffy olive tree. As Rossamünd looked he was sure he spied movement within, a subtle shifting within the bush. He glared into its deep shadows. There, within, he was certain there was a figure obscured by boughs, a little person with a face like an over-large sparrow and round, glittering dark eyes.

A bogle! It shrunk noiselessly into deeper shade, but its eyes remained fixed on Rossamünd, blinking occasionally with a pale flicker. The foundling stared back in breathless wonder, craning his neck as the landaulet rattled past and moved on.

"It's only a milestone, little man." Europe's curt voice intruded. "Surely you've seen one before?"

The horse whickered.

The eyes disappeared.

Rossamünd sat back quickly. Thrilled as he was by such a sight, he felt no inclination to tell Europe of it. He did not want to see this one destroyed as the Misbegotten Schrewd had been. Thinking on the encounter just past, he decided he must have seen a nuglung, one of the littler bogles, so the almanac said, often having an animal's head on a small, human-like body – what the almanac called anthropoid, or like a man. Rossamünd almost couldn't believe it: he had seen a nuglung, a real one. There were stories from ancient times that told of some of these nuglungs doing good things for people, though folk now would never believe such a notion. His almanac was typically brief on them, saying, as it always did about any kind of bogle, that avoidance was the best policy. The foundling reckoned such advice probably helped the monsters as much as people.

Opening a black lacquered box, Europe took out a soft drawstring bag with a stiffened circular bottom. It was a fiasco. Rossamünd had seen them before. In them he knew women kept their rouges, blushes and balms: the tools of beauty. He did not think a fulgar would need such things, but, when she had finished dabbing and daubing at her face with the aid of a small looking-glass, even a young lad like himself could not help but be amazed by the simple yet profound transformation. He did not think a little rosying of the cheeks and lips and whitening of the nose could be so flattering.

"A girl's got to look her best for the city," she offered simply to his gawping.

Fouracres turned in the driver's seat to say something and was visibly stunned, turning an unmanly red from ear lobe to ear lobe. He quickly resumed his original position and muttered over his shoulder awkwardly, "We'll … er … be at High Vesting in an hour or so, miss."

Europe smiled weakly. "Yes, we had deduced that for ourselves. A mere stone told us the distance about a mile back – but thank you for the thought." She hummed happily and watched the passing scene.

Recovering his composure, Fouracres once more spoke over his shoulder. "So, Rossamünd, ye're going ter be a lamplighter, are yer?"

The foundling did not know how to answer this. Was he a lamplighter or was he now Europe's factotum? He looked at her quickly. Muffled in her thick coat, she paid him no attention whatsoever, returning to her usual regal reserve.

"That's what I am supposed for, sir," he ventured, glancing at Europe once more. "Though I am not really wanting it. Do you know much about them?"

"A little," answered the postman. As he spoke he would spend some of the time looking at Rossamünd from the corner of one eye and at the road with the corner of the other, or turn his back completely and focus on the path ahead. "I was thinking of becoming one myself, yer see, when the choices were afore me. As yer can see for yerselves, it didn't take my fancy."

Here was the proof of his dull future. "Too boring, Mister Fouracres?"

The postman paused, appearing bemused. "That's not so much it … as *the reverse*."

This was not the answer Rossamünd expected. He sat up. "How do you mean?"

"I chose the quiet life of a strolling postman, for the lot of a lamplighter was a little too dangerous for mine."

Rossamünd found he was holding his breath. "Dangerous? I thought they just went out, lit the lamps and went back home."

With a chuckling snort, Fouracres looked sharply at Rossamünd. "That they do – on stretches of road travelling the fringes of civilisation, at times of the day that bogles love best ter move about in, contending with bandits, poachers, smugglers, mishaps on the road itself, living with only a handful o' others in isolated places. Then you have ter go about changing the water in the lamps themselves, regular as the seasons – that part, I'll grant yer, ain't interesting at all. Mmm, not the job for this fellow." The postman pointed to himself with his thumb as he returned

247

his attention to the road. "My hours are long and strange enough and my pay as low again as any should bear, without having cause ter make any o' this worser by joining the lamplighter service." He gave Rossamünd a cheeky, side-long smile. "Ye, however, Mister Rossamünd, seem ter be made of sterner stuff. Well, good for yer. It's a good thing yer harness is so fine, else yer might have something ter worry about. Howsoever, I'd get yerself a well-made hat afore yer venture up ter Winstermill."

Rossamünd did not answer. His thoughts were turning on all the postman had just revealed. *Bogles! Bandits!* Perhaps the life of a lamplighter might be a whole lot more worthwhile after all? This clarified his path for him: now he was actually curious, even eager, to work his official trade. *How do I tell Miss Europe this?* The fulgar had said little more on her desire for him to become her factotum since the first day at the Harefoot Dig. He looked at her once more. Though her expression was resolutely aloof, she seemed sad – not momentarily unhappy, but troubled with deep, suppressed grief. How different she was from the talkative, boastful woman he had first met on the pastures of Sulk End. A tiny ache set in Rossamünd's soul. He felt sorry for her loss of Licurius, however foul the leer had been, and he had an inkling that his devoted service might take that grief away. He was confused again.

Pondering intently on these things, he did not notice three crusty folk sitting by the side of the road with their rambling carts and rickety donkeys till the sound of their chatter caught his attention. They were sellers of vegetables of many kinds.

Fouracres hailed them as the landaulet passed. "Hoy! Gentle eekers, do yer have any letters ter send?"

All three smiled with genuine, almost bursting joy, one of them crying, "Ah, bless ye! Bless ye, Master Fourfields. No letters from us today." She marvelled at the landaulet. "What a pretty pair o' legs ye're travellin' on this ev'nin'! Much easier on the boot leather than yer usual ones!" She tossed a large pumpkin to the postman.

"And blessings ter thee, Mother Fly! Mother Mold! Farmer Math! Sorry, I can't stop, but these 'pretty legs' have places they're taking me!" he grinned back, slowing the landaulet and catching the vegetable skilfully. "I'll be back along here tomorrer. We'll have a good natter then. Thanks for the fruit, madam – t'will make for a fine soup ternight."

"Then I'll save me quizzin's fer anon," the old woman returned in a hoarse too-loud whisper, rolling her intensely curious gaze over Rossamünd and, more especially, Europe.

The fulgar did not even stir, but continued her cool stare at the country on the opposite side. The foundling, however, smiled happily at this rustic dame and her companions, who all returned his friendly expression.

"Save them all, Mother, and get yerself waddling home at the right time," Fouracres said cheekily. "Darkness comes too early this time o' year, and the chance of bogles with it."

Mother Fly laughed a dry and crackling laugh. "And ye'd

249

better pass on yerself, fancy-legs. Ye've still got a-ways to rattle before ye can make yer soup. Till tomorrer!"

"Till termorrer."

With that they passed on, Mother Fly waving cheerfully.

When they had gone a little further, Fouracres informed him quietly, "They're some of the eekers I was telling yer about. Good people, as hospitable as they get." Rossamünd wondered how it was such happy folk as these could bear to live in those tottering cottages out in this bare haunted place.

They crested a small rise in the road and before them the land spread out and down in a large basin that found its way to the sea. Rossamünd assumed it must be the mighty Grume – though he had never seen it before. So much water, and as sickly a green as Master Fransitart or Master Heddlebulk or Master Pinsum had ever described. Rossamünd marvelled and stared fixedly. *The sea! The sea!* The cloudy surface seemed to be shifting constantly, much more than the Humour ever had. Flecks of dirty white danced, reared up then disappeared – the tops of *waves* – and the smell of it blew to them from the basin below. It was like no other odour Rossamünd had ever encountered. Sharp and salty, yet somehow sweet as well, almost like a hint of orange blossoms in spring.

Europe wrinkled her nose with a look of mild distaste.

Fouracres turned to them beaming with satisfaction. He breathed in deeply. "Ahhh! The stink o' the Grume. Nothing quite like it. They say that the kelp forests just offshore improve its stink somewhat, that out in the deeper waters it does not smell so sweet. Makes me glad I'm not a sailor. Now look there, my boy. That is High Vesting."

Below and before them, on the shores of the Grume, was a cluttered knot of marble, granite and masonry that made the high protecting walls and buildings of the fortress-city of High Vesting. It was not nearly as big as Boschenberg, but somehow seemed far more threatening. Great white towers, taller than any buildings Rossamünd had known, stuck up from all the usual domes and spires. Out in the water giant blocks of stone had been laid out in a great groyne that protected the harbour. In this harbour, which the almanac had named the Mullhaven, were ships, actual ships! Even from here he could tell what kinds they were from his lessons under Master Heddlebulk. There were low, menacing rams, solid, block-like cargoes and grand-cargoes, and sleek ships still running under sail in this age of the gastrine – many being guided and poked about the harbour by small gastrine craft known as drudges. He had been told of the great size of these vessels, but was not prepared for just how big they were. He could not wait to get to High Vesting now, to go down to its docks and stand near these monstrous craft. It might well be the last time he got to see ships.

He looked back at Europe, who had been so quiet the whole way. She too was staring at the fortress-city and looked bored. She turned to the foundling and seemed to search his face, heavy thoughts stirring inexplicably in her expression. Her attention remained fixed so for only an instant; then she went back to gazing at their destination.

As they drove down the southern side of the rise and into the basin the Gainway became much broader, its paving smoother. On either side grew unbroken lanes of tall, leafless tress with smooth, silver-grey bark and high curving branches. This late in autumn, their fallen leaves were piled in great drifts along the verges. Other roads and paths joined from the surrounding farms and villages, and with them more traffic. Some of their fellow travellers gave the landaulet a curious or suspicious inspection. Soon enough they joined the queue of vehicles and pedestrians waiting to pass the scrutiny of the gate wardens – who wore a uniform similar to the soldiers of Boschenberg – and enter High Vesting by her massive iron gates. Before long they would be within the walls.

With vague apprehension Rossamünd wondered if, after all this time, Mister Germanicus would still be waiting for him.

AN OLD FRIEND RETURNS

frigate (noun) smallest of the dedicated fighting rams, usually having twenty or twenty-four guns down one broadside (guns-broad). Nimble and fast, they are considered the "eyes of the fleet", running messages, performing reconnaissance and guarding a fleet's flanks. There are oversized frigates called heavy-frigates, having up to thirty-two guns on one broadside. These are popular among pirates and privateers.

PASSAGE into the city had been easy. Fouracres had simply grinned at the gate wardens, said some pleasant words, and they had let them by with no more than a nod. Once beyond the gates Rossamünd's head was swivelling left and right as he sought to see as much of this strange new place as possible. The buildings in High Vesting were generally taller than those in Boschenberg and made of a fine white stone, often with their foundations built of granite. Windows were taller, narrower, their panes rectangular rather than small diamonds. The streets, however, were wider and in better repair than those of Rossamünd's home city.

Fouracres steered the landaulet nimbly through the throng of other vehicles: wheelbarrows, sedan chairs, carts, wagons, coaches and carriages as fine as Europe's, and some even finer. The smell of the Grume wafted up every south-facing street, brought upon breezes of frosty air. Europe covered her nose and mouth with a gloved hand.

As they went, Fouracres made arrangements. "Now what is to be yer destination here?"

Europe roused herself and spoke first. "I need to attend the offices of Messrs Ibdy & Adby on the Pontoon Wigh," she said.

"Very well," the postman replied politely. "... And, Rossamünd – yer mentioned something about Mister Germanicus at the Harbour Gov–"

"You can leave what *he* does and where *he* goes to me, postman!" Europe interrupted with a scowl. "You're my driver and you drive. *He* is my factotum, and even if only for now, he attends me! When I decide it is time, his needs shall be met. Till then, serve me!"

Rossamünd blinked.

Fouracres scowled in return. "Last I knew, madam, he and most definitely I worked for the Emperor! So till I make a declaration otherwise, yer can keep yer 'serve me's' to yerself. I'm doing yer a favour, and I'll see it through, but I ain't yer servant by any more than common decency allows!"

Europe, her eyes slitted and glaring, looked as if she could say more, much more, but then she sagged and returned to her blank stare at the passing scene. "However you want it ... Just drive, will you?" was all she said.

The postman drove on while Rossamünd intently studied the right toe of his shoe, not daring to look up.

They came to a great square: an enormous paved area cordoned off from traffic and filled with fountains and commemorative columns. At each corner was a massive statue of the *Arius Vigilans* – the Vigilant Ram – a heavily horned he-sheep in various poses of stout defiance or regal repose. These were the representative animal of Rossamünd's people the Hergotts, and seeing them so boldly displayed made him feel proud. Glamorous crowds filled the area, their energy and foreign costume a spectacle of its own.

On the opposite side of this grand square was their destination. Messrs Ibdy & Adby, Mercantile & Super Cargo was situated in a lofty building of glossy pink stone. Its front was an almost windowless mass of giant pilasters with an impressive door of dull brown bronze in their midst. Immediately above the door were two columns of windows, as narrow and tall as any other in this city. Rossamünd counted the windows by row. *Thirteen!* He had never seen such a large structure, but from what he could gather, there were several about High Vesting.

As Fouracres stopped the landaulet in the common courtyard before the office tower of Messrs Ibdy & Adby, Rossamünd, unable to contain himself any longer, asked eagerly, "May I see the rams? Miss Europe? I might never get to see them ever again."

Gulls cavorted above. To the south, out over the Grume, great bales of pale yellow cloud boiled and piled up into the sky. Their flattened undersides were a dark and ominous green-grey.

Europe looked at him, then to the postman, who shrugged and said, with a weary smile, "May I suggest this, miss, that I wait here with yer fancy carriage while you do yer dealings and Rossamünd be allowed to have a peek about. Aye?"

With a sigh, Europe pointed to a big clock upon the façade of an equally large building across the square. It was easily visible, and Rossamünd had been taught his timings at the marine society. It was a little after the half hour of two.

"Be back here in one half of an hour, not later," she allowed, sternly.

"I will! I will!" Rossamünd's heart raced as he leapt down. About to dash off, he remembered that morning and skittered back, holding out his hand to help Europe alight.

"Well done," she said, with a wry look. "You're learning."

He beamed with joy and hurried off. He had a smile for every person he passed: elegant couples out for a Domesday stroll; stevedores bearing loads; striped-shirted vinegaroons taking shore leave; flamboyantly wigged rams' captains in gorgeous frock coats doing much the same; important-looking men stuffed into stiff, ludicrously high collars talking on important things beneath feathered and furred thrice-highs. How wonderfully strange it felt to have that little time of liberty in this gorgeously foreign city!

With awe he stepped through the great iron gates that split the mighty sea wall and allowed access to the city from the piers and berths. The wall's foundations were black-ened by century-long lapping of the bitter waters of the Grume. All along its lofty summit were batteries of cannon; catapult-like devices called tormentums – for throwing great smoking bombs of the most venomous repellents; and lambasts – machines of war that flung spears dipped in various wicked poisons. As with all coastal cities, High Vesting was in deadly earnest about keeping the cunning monsters of the deep away.

Rossamünd skipped past the sea wall and down a long stone pier way. It was intersected by many long, high wooden wharves and lined with many smaller craft, some ironclad, some with hulls of wood. So many vessels were there, with their clutter of tall masts, that walking among them was like moving through a strange forest. Out beyond all this, however, out in the deeper waters of the Mullhaven, were the rams. It was these mighty vessels of war that he wanted to see. It was upon these that he had been expected to serve.

At the end of the pier, moored on a low dock that went out to the right, he discovered a frigate! These were one of the smaller ocean-going rams, with a shallow enough draught to be this close to shore. It was about the length of a monitor, but sat much higher out of the water so that it could survive the swell of the sea. Fascinated, he happily let his head swell with all the instruction he had received and reading he had done on them. He inspected the single row of ports out of which the cannon would be run, counted each one – twenty-eight in all; he admired the graceful curve of the bow, which gave these warships their name as it ran out and down to the ram; he read the brass nameplate fixed to the fo'c'sle. *Surprise*, it said. Rossamünd almost swooned. This vessel was *famous!* It was the fastest of its type in the whole navy, perhaps even the whole world. He had read of it in pamphlets and had even been taught of it at Madam Opera's. It had served faithfully for over one hundred years!

Then his gaze fixed upon an enormous, dark vessel out in the Mullhaven.

A main-sovereign!

These were the largest of all the rams and this one was absolutely gigantic, dwarfing all the vessels about. Its bow-ram did not jut nearly so far as the frigate's, for it was thought too big and too slow to successfully charge other vessels. It relied instead on its thick strakes – the iron plates that armoured the hull – and the two decks of one hundred and twenty great guns that armed either broadside. Rossamünd had always thought this an excellent number of cannon: it meant that for a main-sovereign to fight effectively, she needed a crew of at least fourteen hundred men …

"Hello, Rosy-Posy!" The cry intruded upon his technical romance.

He knew that voice.

Looking about quickly he found a face he recognised aboard the *Surprise*. It was a fellow foundling two years his

258

senior who had shipped off to serve in the navy eighteen months ago. His name was Snarl. He was taller, broader, looked stronger – but it was still Snarl. While at Madam Opera's, he had been, after Gosling, one of those most active in tormenting Rossamünd.

He looked up at his fellow foundling of old, squinting into the glare of sunlit clouds. "Oh … hello Snarl," he returned coolly. It should have been an occasion of pride to learn that one of his old bunk-mates was now serving aboard so renowned a ram, but the character of Snarl undid any feelings of such camaraderie.

"Well, well, by and by, it's ol' Missy-boots himself, come to see me sitting high on me mighty boat!" Snarl swaggered along the gangway to stand directly above Rossamünd. He called to his fellow crewmen. "Look 'ere, lads, here's a fellow I grew up with."

Some of the younger members of the crew looked down upon the foundling standing upon the pier. Some even gave him a genuine grin.

Rossamünd smiled back cautiously.

"As fine a grummet as ever there was, this one, all manners and kindness," Snarl continued in his high-handed voice. "Got a girl's name to go with it, haven't you *Rossamünd?*" Snarl had not changed.

Rossamünd turned and walked back up the pier. "Goodbye, Snarl," he muttered.

He stepped on to a wharf with the brash laughter of the fellow society boy ringing after him. Though he had only been away from his old way of life for less than a fortnight, it already felt like a long time ago. To meet another child from there, rather than bringing it all back, only made this feeling of dislocation stronger. He wondered if Snarl had leapt from the decks of a moving cromster, watched a lahzar in a fight, thrown bothersalts in the face of some grinnlings, or dragged an ailing fulgar to a wayhouse. Rossamünd marvelled that he had seen and done more in the last two weeks on his own than in two years in the foundlingery.

For a while he wandered about the many smaller craft berthed along either side, taking turns carelessly, trying hard not to brood upon this encounter. He had somehow thought that his fellow foundlings would all grow up once they had left the little world of Madam Opera's and become a little more sober, a little kinder.

He approached the end of yet another wharf. The clock over the square was still visible through all the masts. Rossamünd checked again as he had several times so far: it was time to return. He went to turn back when a powerful smell briefly overpowered the perfume of the Grume. He knew that stink ...

Swine's lard!

A firm hand cunningly pinched the back of his neck. "Well, what's this 'ere then, an' ol' chum returned to the fold?" It was Poundinch. The oily rivermaster loomed over the boy. "Miss us, did ye, Rosey-me-lad?"

Rossamünd went slack and pale with terror, a deep sinking terror that made him want to vomit.

"Ah, look – 'e's gone all emotion'l at such an 'appy reunion," purred Poundinch.

Somehow Rossamünd found his tongue. "Ah – ah – hello, Rivermaster P-Poundinch."

"Hello, Rosey-ol'-boy. I'm called Cap'n Poundinch when I'm in these parts, tho', so ye'll need to re-school yer tongue."

The pressure upon Rossamünd's neck increased subtly but so skilfully that he was compelled to step forward towards a gangplank before him. There she was, the *Hogshead*, listing slightly to the aft ladeboard quarter but still very much intact. That was where the oh-so-familiar smell had come from. It would always be the smell of dread for Rossamünd.

"Huh-how did you escape the monitors?" he somehow managed.

"Ah, Rosey-me-lad," Poundinch purred, tapping his greasy nose with the scarred and grubby forefinger of his free hand, "that's ol' Poundy's way – slipperier than swine's lard, me … Aren't ye 'appy for me?"

"… Um …" was all the foundling could offer.

Poundinch pushed him up the gangplank and followed closely behind. Rossamünd thought briefly of leaping into the water, but he had been instructed, over and over, that the caustic waters of the Grume were no place for a person to find himself bobbing about. With that escape route unavailable, he found himself where he thought he would never be again – upon the deck of the *Hogshead*. Only Gibbon was here, no other crew. He was chewing his black fingernails as he stood by the splintered stump of the tiller.

"Look 'ere, Gibbon, th' lad couldn't stay away, 'e missed us so!" Poundinch kept shoving the foundling all the way to the hatchway. Rossamünd pushed against each shove stubbornly.

Gibbon peered dumbly at the foundling for a moment, then his gaze sharpened. "Oh aye, oi rememb'r. 'Ello, boi'o."

Rossamünd kept his head down. He was too far away, he knew, for Fouracres or Europe to spy him. He reckoned also that at this less-than-salubrious end of the docks other sailors would pay little heed to the subtle struggle taking place aboard the *Hogshead*.

The hatchway was open, as it usually was, and with that cunning neck-pinch, Poundinch forced the boy to start his way down the ladder. "Just goin' to finish up an ol' con-vo-sation with this'un 'ere," he called to Gibbon as he himself started down.

Rossamünd descended slowly, his senses reacquainting themselves with the profound lack of light and the over-whelming stench. He could just make out that the hold had been cleared of all its barrels, yet the powerful odour of the swine's lard had remained, soaked into the very wood of the cromster's frames and decking – and with it the hint of some far worse foetor. Yet these smells were not all that had been left. A bright-limn hung from a central beam about halfway between the ladder and the bow. It helped little but was enough to show, to Rossamünd's horror, that the three gruesome crates bound with strong iron smuggled aboard about a week ago were still there. Two of them were side by side near the ladder and one on its own several feet away. This lonely one suddenly shook violently.

Rossamünd gave a tight yelp. He tried to scamper back up but Poundinch blocked his ascent. The captain shouted at the lonely crate and, after a few shudders more, it became still. The hold was otherwise empty but for acerbic seawater leaking in from the stern end of the hold. Rossamünd saw that it was already about an inch deep at the bottom of the steps.

"Ye knows what's in these 'ere crates, don't ye, lad?" Poundinch had stopped about halfway down and cast his hefty shadow over the foundling.

"Uh – I – n-no ..." Rossamünd spluttered and backed away from both Poundinch and the crates. The bilge water came up to his ankles now.

"Aw, come now, ye were snoopin' about, listenin' and pryin' after we took 'em aboard. Tryin' to get somethin' over ol' Poundy, were ye? A li'l morsel to sell to 'is enemies, 'ey? A li'l bit o' lev'rage to make some deals?"

The nature of this rogue's suspicions revealed, Rossamünd looked at him in disbelief.

Poundinch descended all the way to the bottom. "Those innocent rabbit eyes ye make don't work on me, mucky little mouse. I think I'll leave ye down 'ere to think again upon th' falsities of yer stubborn, lyin' tongue. We'll be back to collect them crates in a couple of 'ours, so ye'll 'ave a bit o' time to change th' tune of yer whistle." He grabbed Rossamünd by the wrist, twisting it cruelly.

Tears started in the foundling's eyes as he was compelled to squirm and bend in order to lessen the pain, movement which brought him right by two crates. "But I don't know anything! I don't know anything! I just want to work as a lamplighter!" Rossamünd howled, over and over.

Captain Poundinch ignored him and instead, quicker than a cat, gathered up Rossamünd's hands and wound cord roughly all about them, fixing it to a loop of rope that held one of the crates together in such a way that it forced him to sit.

The boy's heart froze. He had been tied right up against a crate! His mind went a white blank of panic. "But! … but! …" was all he could manage.

"Aye, 'but, but'. Ye're babblin' now, bain't ye? Got to make more sense if ye wants yer freedom, tho'." Poundinch put his greasy face next to Rossamünd's. "Ye were sooo keen to know what were in me cargo! Well now ye can 'ave a good ol' gander, as close as ye could want for," he growled. "Ye've got about three 'ours till I return – plenty of time for ye to mull, and if ye're still whole enough to speak after such a time with me prettee pieces 'ere, we'll see what we might do with ye. Ye never know, lad, if ye're lucky, ye might get to live it large on th' vinegar waves, with ol' Poundy as yer ev'r faithful, ev'r vigilant cap'n!"

With that and nothing more Poundinch left, his boots

thumping heavily, back up the way he had come. The hatch closed with a clang.

"I just want to be a lamplighter ..." the boy sobbed. The seat of his longshanks already soaked in half an inch of water, he sat with his arms on his knees and his face buried in his sleeves. Overwhelmed with bitter hopelessness, Rossamünd wept as he never had in his whole life.

Eventually calm came. He stopped crying and instead he listened. The *Hogshead* creaked in the tidal movements, the brine in the hold slopped ever so quietly, and Rossamünd's heart thumped, but that was all. He lifted his head and squinted about, his face puffy, stinging. It was very dim, but because of the bright-limn not so dark that the crates could not be distinguished clearly. Though he was overshadowed by the box he was bound to, his eyes adjusted to the weak light that also came from cracks about the hatchway. There was not even the slightest hint of movement from any of the three crates, not even the one that shook so determinedly before. Rossamünd had been making all the noise he liked but still the things they contained had remained still. They must have been empty after all. Eyeing the gaps in the crate next to him, his mind whirled.

He would be missed, surely? Not by Europe, perhaps, but certainly by Fouracres. *He'd* come to the rescue, Rossamünd was sure of it – *Wouldn't he?* ... Yet doubt took hold, and he could not be certain of anything any more. He was lost. How would they know where to find him? If Master Fransitart was aware of what had happened to him, he knew his old dormitory master would be furious and shift all obstacles to rescue him. But Master Fransitart did not know – and he was too far away to help. Rossamünd rolled his eyes in his grief and his gaze caught a glimpse of something between the slats of the crate to which he was tied.

Two eyes stared back at him, yellow and inhumanly round.

Rossamünd shrieked like a person touched with madness, and tugged and writhed wildly in his bonds. The crate jerked violently, too, and the eyes disappeared. In blind panic he wrestled for his very life to get free!

It was all in vain. The knot he was bound with was a bailiff's shank, a cunning tangle that took two hands to tie but three to undo. He barely had a whole hand of fingers available between the two of them. Surrendering to whatever grisly fate he was now to suffer – "some 'orrible, gashing end", as Master Fransitart would say – Rossamünd bowed his head and began once more to weep, waiting for some flash of pain or other rending violence.

Instead a sound came. It was a voice, small, soft, and bubbling like a happy little runnel. "Look at you," it said. "Look at you, strange little one who can cry. No need for crying now, no, no, no. Freckle is here and here he is. Lowly he might be, but not the least. A friend he is, and friendly too. So no crying now, no no, nor screaming nor throwing nor bumping of poor Freckle and his head about this little gaol."

Despite himself Rossamünd felt calmed, and reluctantly turned his head. The round, yellow eyes had returned and were looking at him again, earnestly kind.

The foundling held his breath.

The eyes seemed to hesitate, too. Then the voice that belonged to those eyes – that small, soft, babbling voice – said, "*He* is watching, too, and knows you, oh yes, hm hm. Fret not. There is always a plan. Providence provides. You'll see, you'll see."

"Who ... who are y-you?" Rossamünd managed at last. He could see little else but those big eyes – maybe a small nose ... he could not be sure.

"Why, I thought I said, or did I say I thought?" The eyes blinked a long, almost lazy blink. "Why, I am Freckle! Freckle who has been speaking all his thinking just now. I was afraid before, and I thought before that I would just think all my speaking and see what manner of strange little one you were. But I know now by your crying what you are and now I have no fear!" Though he could not see, Rossamünd could well imagine this creature smiling a rather self-satisfied smile. "Tell, little cryer, what is your name?"

"Um ... it's Rossamünd."

There was a strange, gaggling noise, and Rossamünd had the impression that this was Freckle's laugh. "I see and see I do. An obvious name. Here is a tree. I'll call it 'Tree'. Here is a dog. I'll call it 'Dog'! Very clever! What a witty fellow who gave it to you! They must be a funny fellow indeed!"

There was more of the gaggling laugh.

Rossamünd frowned. Witty and funny were not words he would have associated with Madam Opera, who had fixed his name by writing it in the ledger. "Why — why is my name so obvious?" the foundling pressed.

"Ah, your name is obvious by your weepy, weepy tears, little Rossamünd, that is all, nothing more." This little fellow was very hard to understand. "And now we're done our meetings," it concluded. "I expect you've learnt it that hands are shook together, to show a meeting met?"

A hand came out from a lower gap in the wood. This hand was about the same size as Rossamünd's, though the fingers were longer, the wrist much thinner and the skin far rougher. Rossamünd gawped at it: this was most definitely not a person's hand. He remembered himself, took it in his own grasp and politely shook. It felt warm and very much like the bark of a tree. Its grip was strong but gentle.

Looking into those bizarre yellow eyes, Rossamünd tried to show trustworthiness and friendship in his own. If he had to suffer imprisonment and oppression, then getting a chance to make friends with a kindly bogle was an odd yet amazing consolation. "Very pleased to meet you, Mister Freckle," he said solemnly. A-buzz with curiosity, he could not help but go on and ask. "Excuse me, Mister Freckle ... but are you a nuglung?"

Freckle laughed again. "They've taught you to divide and conquer too, I see — rule by division, divide by rules — the everyman creed. Ah, 'tis only fair. I named you first." The

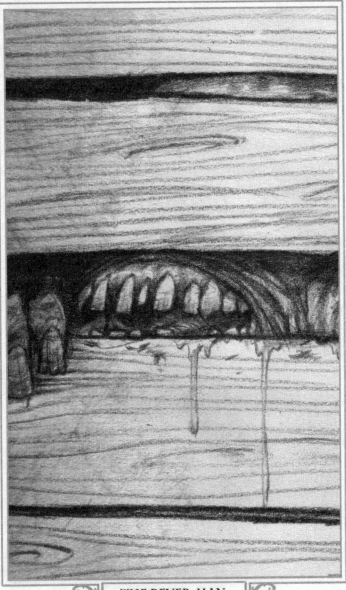

THE REVER-MAN

eyes blinked again. "As it is, you make me much bigger than my boots. No-no-no, a nuglung princeling am I not. I am just what I am, what the everyman might go calling a *glammergorn* – though really, I am just one lonely Freckle. There is no other Freckle, just this one Freckle, until he is no more." The eyes look skywards.

Rossamünd had *seen* a nuglung earlier that day, the sparrowling in the olive bush, and now he was actually *talking* with a glamgorn – which is what he understood Freckle to mean by "glammergorn". These were even smaller than a nuglung, less powerful. Again he remembered the almanac's warning, that it was best not to get too close to one.

Well, he wondered, *what would the writers of* Master Matthius' Wandering Almanac *say if they were watching me now?*

"Give it to meeee," hissed a new and broken voice.

Rossamünd started. The yellow eyes of Freckle blinked several times rapidly.

This new voice had come from the lonely crate on the steerboard side of the hold.

"Quiet, you!" Freckle warned.

"Give it to mee, toooo," the broken voice came again, full of creepy, lugubrious longings. "And to meee – we want to suck out its marrow ... ooh yes, and squish its eyeballs a'tween our rotted teeth." The crate from which it spoke rattled vigorously.

Rossamünd peered at it. A hunched darkness thrashed about spasmodically within. Fortunately its cage was chained fast to a thick oak beam. Nevertheless he shuddered and began to prise at the lashings that gripped his wrists.

Freckle's voice became commanding and hard, contrary to his normal soft sing-song. "His marrow is too well needed inside his bones, and his eyes are too busy at looking and weeping to need your gnawings!" The glamgorn's golden eyes disappeared. "Now to quiet with you!" His voice spoke from the other side of its box.

There was a *Thwip!* and a curse and an extraordinarily loud hiss from the lonely crate. "That struck us in the eye! Now we must have an eye, an eye for an eye, an eye … lov-er-ly eye …" and rotten lips smacked together.

"I know it did, and this I know, for it was sent on its mission so," Freckle said proudly. "And even less eyes will you have if you don't be leaving us be!"

There was another loud hiss. "You'd not be so brave if we weren't bound so hard, scrumptious morsel. We plan to chew on your twiggy bones, too … oh my, and me too …"

It became quiet.

Freckle's yellow eyes reappeared.

"What *is* that?" Rossamünd whispered, still picking uselessly at the rope.

"*That* is an ill-made rever-man, all bits and bobs and falling apart. Those wicked ones who made him do not know their wicked business. He's not knit too well at all, and none too sharp in the knitted noggin neither. Oh how he hates, full of grieving over half-memories and wild

271

hungers! They hate we natural ones most of all, 'cause we are made all right and they are made the everyman's way – all wrong …"

A rever-man! A revenant! Rossamünd knew of these things. They were put together by wicked people taking bits of dead bodies to make new creatures from them, all rotting limbs and ravenous. So that was Poundinch's secret trade, the reason for his suspicious conversations and the crazed flight from the Spindle. At last Rossamünd had discovered the truth. Rivermaster – or Captain, if that was how it was to be now – Poundinch was a smuggler for the dark trades, a trafficker of corpses and half-made undead. That was why he pretended to haul such odoriferous cargoes as swine's lard and pungent herbs, to hide the stink of the contraband.

The foundling shuddered once more. He had to get away!

The hold of the *Hogshead* had now taken on a greater aspect of foul wickedness. Had it not, it still held a rever-man. Rossamünd did not care how poorly made it might have been. He did not like the idea of being confined so closely with one. Its rotten reek was beginning to over-power the other rancid airs in the hold – even that of the swine's lard.

"Cut me loose!" he hissed to Freckle. "I have a knife still, hanging on my baldric. See?"

"Yes, I most definitely do see and see I do." There was a tug on Rossamünd's scabbard. "Yet my own hands are enough to do a knife's work. Hemp and wood are one thing, Rossamünd, but iron just another. I can loose your bonds but mine I cannot, unless you have learnt your strength as well?"

The foundling frowned. He was not strong enough. What was the glamgorn talking about? His hopes dimmed, and he sat for a time in a gloom. Gradually he became aware that his bottom was beginning to sting, as if he were being bitten by a thousand little ants.

"Ow! Ow!" Rossamünd realised he was experiencing the caustic nature of seawater for the first time. He had been sitting in the bilge water long enough for it to start to eat at his skin. He stood as best he could, the rope bindings preventing him from achieving more than an awkward stoop. His backside stung.

A wicked, strangled giggle came from the lone crate.

"Not good for clothes nor delicate pink skin either," observed Freckle, ignoring the rever-man's malicious glee. "That's why I like my barky hide. It hides me better from sneaky eyes and stops the stinging of the water."

"Aye, I wish I had your skin," Rossamünd agreed with a sagacious nod, "but just on my rear end." Wanting to pick up a previous thought, he continued. "Mister Freckle? Which nuglung do you serve?"

Freckle sniffed in a breath. "My, my – there's an every-man question if ever a question was one. No prying in private things! I've not asked you your private things and you shouldn't go asking upon my private things. They've taught you far too well, I can well see, too well."

Rossamünd hung his head in shame. Somehow it made sense that this glamgorn would not want to be telling an everyman child – even one as friendly and open as Rossamünd hoped he was being – much of secret bogle ways. The foundling was certain that if *he* were a bogle, he would not want to say a great deal to a person either – not unless he knew without a doubt that the person could be trusted. He apologised with a mutter, but pressed on to another mystery. "Please, at least, tell why my crying means you know my name?"

The glamgorn laughed his strange laugh. "Knowing, knowing – sometimes there has to be trusting, too …" Freckle's golden eyes frowned, then became kindly once again. "I can see you ain't ready and I know there is a time and a place, a place and a time. I might be lowly, but even I know what to say and when not to say it. Yet the time might come for knowing things, and when the need of knowing's nigh, you'll know then what I do now."

This was no help at all. Rossamünd wanted to push for more when there came the familiar thumping of boot steps on the deck above.

What now? Rossamünd quickly became quiet and the glamgorn's eyes retreated into the obscurity of his prison.

Rossamünd followed the steps as they thudded overhead and trod towards the hatch. It opened and Captain Poundinch peered down, his attention darting to each crate before stopping upon the foundling. "Well, Rosey-me-lad, I see ye're still in whole pieces." He grinned leeringly. "I've come back sooner than I said, I know, but I figured ye'll do yer thinkin' just as well upon me other tub, th' frigate *Cockeril*, as 'ere. Ye'll like 'er, she's a mite more spacious than th' poor ol' *'ogshead*."

He waggled a short-barrelled pistola hidden beneath his coat tails. Eyeing the firelock in fright, Rossamünd saw that its barrel was wider than usual – a weapon designed to knock a person down, to bludgeon him to death despite any type of proofing. "And I reckon *this* might serve as th' best gag for our little stint to the *Cockeril*. No 'ollerin's or screechin's from ye, an' there'll be no shootin's from me."

Poundinch released the knot that held Rossamünd's wrists to Freckle's crate and jerked the foundling after him and back up the ladder. "So follow me lead and a simple jaunt from 'ere to there is all for ye and me to enjoy."

Rossamünd strained his neck to try for a glimpse of Freckle. The glamgorn's now sad eyes showed briefly.

"Farewell ..." the foundling mouthed, just as he was heft clear off the ladder by the easy might of the lumbering captain. He caught one last sight of Freckle blinking a solitary sorrow-filled blink.

DECISIONS, DECISIONS

glamgorn (noun) one of the smaller kinds of monster, a true bogle. They come in all manner of shapes, pigmentation, and hairiness: big eyes, little eyes; big ears, little ears; big body, little limbs; little body, big limbs; and all the variations in between. Often feisty and jittery, certain kinds can get downright nasty, the worst of them being known as blightlings. One of the bizarre idiosyncrasies of glamgorns is that they like to wear clothes, everymen clothes stolen from washing lines and unguarded trunks. There are rumours that, dressed like this, glamgorns – and worse yet blightlings – have been able to sneak into the cities of everymen to spy and cause mischief.

THE cord that once tied his wrists now cut, Rossamünd was forced to walk before Captain Poundinch, his fear of that large pistola the only leash.

Mighty thunderclouds boiled in the west and cast High Vesting in early gloom. It was clear that Poundinch thought the hour already dim enough to move his captive. *Why else would he have returned to get me so soon?* Rossamünd reasoned.

One consolation was the fresher air, happy relief from the cloying, rotten fumes of the hold. As he was forced down the gangplank Rossamünd sucked in several headache-clearing breaths through his nose to cleanse it of the stink.

There was hardly another soul about as they went along the piers. Most of those they did pass by paid them no attention, and the few who did saw Poundinch and quickly stopped looking. Generally, the vessels berthed in this region of the docks were in bad repair, similar to the state of the *Hogshead* when Rossamünd had first gone aboard, way back in Boschenberg. There was a strong sense that the authorities did not visit this part of the harbour very often. Consequently, Rossamünd guessed that they were likely to be captained and crewed by the likes of the *Hogshead's* master, and were not places to flee to for help.

Between the stone and the sty, again! And what of poor, lonely Freckle, too ...?

The foundling walked on with his hands pushed hard into the pockets of his fine frock coat. It occurred to him once more to use his knife. Poundinch had still not taken it from him. Rossamünd could not fathom why; perhaps he figured that the pistol, his great size and greater experience would all be deterrents enough. They were, and Rossamünd let the idea go in despair.

"So ye met me cargo, then?" Captain Poundinch's rough voice intruded on the boy's calculations.

Rossamünd grunted once and nodded.

"Ye see, whether ye knew nowt afore or not," Poundinch went on, playing it as if this was just an amiable conversation between friends, "nows ye do — ye knows it all, I expect, or nears enough — and with that bein' so, I cain't afford to 'ave ye out o' me sight. Don't worry, mind, life aboard th'

Cockeril will be a might more interestin' than workin' as a lamplighter."

"*I* don't think so," Rossamünd muttered between gritted teeth. He felt cornered and cheated.

"Come, lad, that's no way t' be!" Poundinch sounded genuinely hurt. "I'll be sparin' ye all that walkin' back and forth twiddlin' with th' lamps, as th' day goes out and comes back in again, on and on. Who'd want that?"

"I would." Rossamünd had been raised to serve on a ram, but not this way and most definitely *not* with a master like Poundinch.

"What? An' waste all that wonde'ful learnin' ye got from yer society?" The captain clicked his tongue disapprovingly and shook his head. "Turn left 'ere, Rosey-boy."

They stepped on to a main dock way.

Rossamünd was getting angrier and angrier. The injustice of his own situation, and even that of Freckle, gnawed at him. *I don't want this! I have been letting other people tell me where to go, what to be,* his thoughts fumed, *I will* not *let this beggar force me to do anything more!*

With that, he sat down right in the middle of the wharf.

Poundinch almost walked right over the top of him. "What's this 'ere!" he cursed. Giving a low growl like that of a crotchety dog, the captain then said, thick and heavy, "Get up!"

Rossamünd did not stir. He refused to be forced against his will any longer. Master Fransitart, he knew with a certainty, would not have let himself be cowed in such a way. What is more, there were some people at the far end of the dock way that looked as if they might actually come to his aid.

"Geeetttt uuupp …" Poundinch seethed quietly, stepping over the foundling menacingly. "This li'l tantrum won't do ye any good, *mucky li'l snot!*" The captain leant low and Rossamünd heard the pistola being rattled near his ear as a threat. "Stand, frasart, or I'll make ye one of me *cargo* instead of me crew …!"

The boy's mind hummed now with a taut, thoughtless energy, poised at the debut of valiant effort. First leaning forward, then pushing up with hefty vigour, Rossamünd stood. His crown and the back of his head collided sharply with first the chin and then the already crooked nose of Poundinch, sending sparks through the foundling's vision. The brute captain belched a stunned curse of the filthiest language and toppled clatteringly to the wooden planks of the wharf.

Rossamünd did not wait to see what was to happen next. He just ran.

Chancing one rapid glance behind as he fled, he saw the evidence of his work: Poundinch sprawled on the dock way, fumbling between his deadly flintlock and the blood sputtering from his nostrils.

Rossamünd dashed on, bounding over and skipping about all obstacles – on towards where he had spied those better seeming people. They were no longer there! Regardless, he raced on. The sound of scuffling behind, then a steady *pound pound* told him that Poundinch was on his feet again and after him.

The chase was in earnest now.

With a stumbling skid, Rossamünd darted right, up a connecting siding that he thought he remembered joining to one of the main piers. He quickly saw that he had made a wrong turn. Without hesitation he retreated. Poundinch loomed, blood smeared over his mouth and chin – *Too close! Too close!*

"Get 'ere!" he shouted, but failed to close quickly enough on the nimble boy. Rossamünd scrambled on with a panicked yelp as the captain stumbled, his hands gripping at vacated air.

With Poundinch now so near, Rossamünd expected to hear the terrible, clapping report of the pistola and be sent to his doom with an oversized ball foiling his proofing and piercing his spine. He ducked his head without thinking, trying to make his legs move faster. He caught sight of the clock in the square, away to his left, half hidden by all those masts. Though he was moving too quickly to be able to read its time, it gave him his bearings as he sprinted to the next connecting siding. Before him two figures stepped out, two looming shadows. Rossamünd did not know whether to plead to them for help or to avoid them as best he could.

"Stop 'im! Th' thief stole me coin-bag!" bellowed the quicker witted Poundinch.

That decided it for the foundling. Well aware that most people preferred the assertions of a grown man to the excuses of a child, Rossamünd skipped desperately past one of the shadows – who seemed to ignore him, stepping past with a flash of deep magenta cloth – and nimbly into the grasping arms of the second.

He thrashed and squirmed wildly in that strong, steady grip, his panic making him deaf to the voice of his new captor. He looked back in horror to the charging captain closing in fury upon his prey.

"*Let me go! Let me go!*" Rossamünd hollered. "*He's a liar! He's a liar! Let me go!*"

"Rossamünd!" The stranger's rebuke finally penetrated. "*Rossamünd!* I know he's a liar. It's me, Fouracres!"

In an instant the foundling's whirling mind was stunned to a halt.

There was the postman, his normally grinning mouth tight with consternation, his tricorn knocked on to the wharf by the power of Rossamünd's struggle.

Utterly confused, Rossamünd looked back in the direction of Poundinch, who called to him, "Well caught, good sir! Ye 'as done me a service!"

Yet between the cruel intentions of the captain and his victim stepped that deep magenta shadow. It was Europe.

They've come – both *of them!*

On came Captain Poundinch, clearly thinking the chase concluded in his favour, his boots pounding, pounding on the wood. "Thought ye could rob a fellow of 'is rightful prize, did ye?" he gloated, with a smugly grim sneer as he hurried to claim back Rossamünd as his slave once more.

Without a word, and without hesitation, the fulgar stepped into the path of the captain. He towered over her, yet she calmly reached out her hand.

Zzzock! There was the briefest flash of green fire as she sent the suddenly amazed Poundinch, despite all his forward momentum, hurtling backwards into the oaken side of a sailing ship. He hit it hard, the wind driven from his lungs with a belching cough! His eyes fixed in shock, he dropped through the gap between the hull of the boat and the planks of the wharf. There was a muffled splash … and that was all.

Her expression masterfully serene, Europe walked back to Fouracres and the now elated foundling. Taking Rossamünd by the hand, she continued back along the wharf. "Come on, let's find this Mister Germanicus," she said quietly.

As they led him out of the docks, Rossamünd's heart was a song of freedom. *They've saved me! They've saved me! She* saved me!

While they went, he answered all their questions, giving an excited account of who Poundinch was, of why the rivermaster had been chasing him, of what had been intended for him. Then he thought of Freckle – poor Freckle – more friendly and genuine than most people the foundling had ever met. His glee at his own liberation entirely evaporated. *Perhaps Miss Europe is still in a rescuing frame of mind?*

He stopped and said, "Miss Europe? Mister Fouracres? I have a friend back on the *Hogshead* who needs saving."

Europe let go of his hand and folded her arms. Pressing her chin against her chest she looked at him shrewdly. "Really?" was all she said.

"Aye, Miss Europe, aye! I can't be free and him not!" Rossamünd implored. "I can show us the way – I remember it, it isn't far! The boat's most surely still deserted. It was when I was there, and that was but a few minutes ago."

Fouracres pursed his ample lips. "Ye're asking a lot of us, Rossamünd."

The foundling swallowed.

"And what of this Germanicus fellow?" quizzed the lahzar, with a deepening frown. "Is not your need to see him urgent?"

"But my friend *helped* me!" Rossamünd cried. "We've got to get him free!"

"You make friends too easily, little man," Europe murmured.

Fouracres sighed. "But when in straits, yer prove yer mates," he mused. "I for one will help yer. Miss Europe must shift fer herself. Lead on, let's get this done before that brute swims his way clear!"

Rossamünd did not entirely follow what Fouracres was saying, but understood his meaning. Grateful, he started back along the way he had run, looking back at Europe.

She had not moved.

"Miss Europe …?"

With a long-suffering look, the lahzar rolled her eyes. "All right, little man! I'm coming … I'm coming," she said, and mouthed a sour complaint as she followed. She showed no inclination to hurry, despite the possibility of Poundinch's emerging once more from the vinegar waters. The fulgar lagged as they hurried back to the *Hogshead*, getting tetchy when Rossamünd made a single false turn.

Yet he found the rotten, sinking cromster easily enough.

Nobody was apparent on deck.

With cunning grace, Fouracres crept aboard to check the hold below. Watching him from the berth, Rossamünd could well see how the postman had survived the dangers of his employment.

Europe sat on a bollard, crossed her legs and made as if where she was, was just where she meant to be.

The postman quickly reappeared and quietly declared the *Hogshead* un-crewed. "She's a bit of a stinker," he added, "and a sinker too, by all evidence."

Rossamünd hesitated for just a moment, overcoming his revulsion for this vessel and all the unhappy things that had happened to him aboard her.

Covering her nose with her handkerchief as she came aboard, Europe refused to go near the hold. "You were on here for *how* long?" she marvelled.

Fouracres went below again and called. "Which cage, Rossamünd?"

The foundling went to the hatchway and pointed to the prison that held Freckle, then to the third box-crate. "But watch out for that other one over there," he warned. "It's got a rever in it."

FRECKLE

The postman rapidly took a step away from the dangerous crate. "Yer what?" he barked. "I can see why yer didn't much like being on this bucket!" Several times he turned a nervous eye to it as he crouched down and tinkered with the lock of Freckle's own cage.

Rossamünd had no desire to go down into the hold while the rever-man remained, and stayed at the top of the ladder. It was only then it dawned on Rossamünd that Europe – or even Fouracres – might not appreciate rescuing a glamgorn, a monster. He almost panicked. *What will Miss Europe do?* Yet whatever might happen, he would rather chance this than knowingly leave Freckle in the certain misery of his current condition.

Though Rossamünd did not see how he had done it, Fouracres released the lock saying, "There yer are, friend o' Rossamünd, time ter be moving on."

As he swung open the top of the crate it was slammed the rest of the way as Freckle suddenly sprung from the top of his old prison, wailing delightedly, "Free! Free! Free! Poor Freckle's had enough!"

At that same moment the rever in the third box-crate shook it mightily and started up a wretched wailing. *"Let us out! Let us out! Aeeiii! We want to eat him! Let us out!"*

Not even Miss Europe, when she had fought the grinnlings, moved as quickly as Fouracres at these simultaneous eruptions from the box-crates. In a single step the postman both spun about and sprang away, a tomahawk swinging ready in hand.

Quicker than the eye, the glamgorn leapt right over Fouracres and shot up the ladder. All that Rossamünd saw of it was a small brown thing all legs and arms and those alien yellow eyes. These eyes caught Rossamünd's own as Freckle dashed past – an extremely brief yet strangely meaningful contact – before the glamgorn sprang off the deck and disappeared into the murky liquid of the Grume.

Wide-eyed with shock, "Oh ..." was all Rossamünd could think to say.

Fouracres blinked up at him in equal surprise and came quickly away from the rantings of the rever. "There yer be, yer friend is free. Let's leave this wild, broken fellow ter his raging."

At the commotion Europe had approached. "Rossamünd," she purred with icy malice, "was *that* your friend?"

The foundling turned to her and, seeing her cold expression, looked at his feet. "Ah ... a-aye."

She gave him a look of mild contempt. "You made me come down here to rescue a bogle? ... Licurius was right!" she growled quietly. "You really are a wretched little sedorner."

"Look here!" Fouracres declared, reaching the top of the ladder. "There's no need to be spitting such filthy words!"

Rossamünd's eyes narrowed obstinately and he scowled at the fulgar. "And Fransitart is right! You're the worst *monster* of all! You just go round killing no matter what! That poor schrewd did nothing to you!"

"Of all the ...!" Indignant, Europe took a step towards him.

This time he was not daunted. This time he was not going to just be meek. This time he would defend himself like a man should.

Fouracres moved as if to intervene.

Europe became still. She looked from the boy to the man, her expression twisting weirdly. She dropped her head and began to make a low, unnerving noise in her throat.

Rossamünd glanced at Fouracres, who shrugged.

The foundling took a step towards her and started as she threw her head back at last, and let out a gush of laughter. Great guffaws shook her – mighty, mirthful sobs.

Rossamünd froze in bewilderment. "Miss Europe …?"

The lahzar sank to her knees and laughed and laughed and laughed.

Going to her side, Rossamünd crouched down and tried to peer into her face. He looked to the postman again.

Shaking his head, Fouracres was just as bewildered.

Eventually Europe's violent glee ebbed. Panting, still chuckling, she looked at the foundling from the corner of her eye. "Ah, little man!" she wheezed softly. "You are about the strangest, bravest little fellow I have ever met!" Taking off her quartz glasses and dabbing tears, the lahzar got back to her feet. She perched her glasses back on her nose, put on warm doeskins against the increasing cold, and offered Rossamünd her hand, saying, "*Now* let's find this Mister Germanicus."

Rossamünd looked at the hand. He did not know what to think of her. Besides which, what was he to think of

Freckle, who had fled with no farewells? *This world is too hard*, he concluded.

Gripping the lahzar's fingers gingerly, he descended the gangplank off the *Hogshead* and wished never to see that vessel – or smell it – again. Behind them they could hear the muffled shrieking of the rever, still trapped in its tiny prison.

As they walked back through the moored vessels, Fouracres explained to him their own side of his original liberation.

It had taken Europe longer than the prescribed half-an-hour to settle up payments that were her due from her clients. By the time she had emerged from the pink building, Fouracres was already concerned whether Rossamünd was just being irresponsible, or if something was wrong.

"Without even waiting to set the landaulet some place safe, Europe was after yer," Fouracres stated matter-of-factly. "I had to catch her up and we simply walked all over the docks, asked for any sights of yer, turning up nothing for the longest time. Then some fellow with a westerner's accent and the blackest fingernails I have ever seen suggested we might try looking again in the direction where we found yer – took a few sous to wheedle even this from him.

"We had already been searching an hour or more, and had been over several parts of the docks twice over. We were in the act of following that fellow's advice, when I spied yer running yer heart out and looking as if all the utterworsts of Loquor were at yer tail. Having crossed and re-crossed that particular place several times, we simply made sure we took a way that would cut yer off ... and whoever was scaring yer," he added grimly. "The rest yer were there ter witness."

Rossamünd could almost not believe that these two had striven so hard to find him, that *Europe* had led the way in his liberation. How was he to feel about her now? If she was *this* loyal, he would happily serve as her factotum, but then ... *she hates monsters so bitterly. Oh, I don't know ...!* Rossamünd was beginning to find his lack of gumption extremely frustrating.

It was Europe who settled the question as they drove on in the landaulet. "Something is not quite right inside me, little man," she declared. "I felt it when I sent that odious bully into the harbour for a bath, and it's got a lot to do with why I let your bogle chum go. The spasm those nights ago has done more harm than I care for. I need to see my surgeon very soon."

"Are you really ill?" Rossamünd asked.

Europe smiled gravely. "I'm not dying, but I must set out on the soonest vessel for Sinster." She paused for a moment.

The foundling watched her intently.

Europe returned his stare.

"This is my aim," she continued finally. "You go to Winstermill and serve there faithfully, as you have me, as the lamplighter you are intended to be. I will go to Sinster

290

to get repaired. I have no idea how long *that* might take, but when I am back to my healthy self, I will come by your way, little man, and see how you're doing."

Rossamünd's mind boggled at the thought of what "to get repaired" actually involved. He knew better than to ask, though.

She bent down and filled his senses with her sweet perfume. "Perhaps then, you might consider again the opportunity to become my helper?"

He just smiled and nodded. He liked this and was glad it was Europe who had formulated such a plan. It gave him his task to do right now and offered him time to think further on the opportunities a factotum's life might offer rather than a lamplighter's career.

The Offices of the Chief Harbour Governor were not, a little surprisingly, near the port but in the administrative centre of High Vesting. The low marble-white building was so much like all the others in this district that Rossamünd was glad he had Fouracres with him, for he was sure he would never have been able to find it on his own.

Within they discovered that Mister Germanicus had left in a dudgeon three days before. However, he had left instructions of his own referring to the appearance of one "lazy marine society boy". These instructions were characteristically simple: he was to make his way to Winstermill forthwith, where he was expected.

With Fouracres there to smooth the way and vouch for Rossamünd whenever it was needed, the clerks and sergeants of the Harbour Governor were industrious in their help. They ratified the remains of his existing travelling certificates and identification papers, writing up new travel documents. They even wrote a covering letter, explaining – they said – the unusual state of Rossamünd's papers. What a relief it was for him – he had expected a lot of hard questions and suspicious innuendo. He was now at liberty to make his way to Winstermill.

To avoid any possibility of reprisal by Poundinch or his crew, and in keeping with Mister Germanicus' instructions, it was determined that Rossamünd should leave the very next day. They drove to a fancy hostelry known as the Fox Hole. Europe preferred it as her place of repose whenever she was in High Vesting.

Before its façade of grand marble columns, with Europe organising the footmen in the distribution of her luggage, Fouracres bid Rossamünd farewell. "Now I reckon I just might get the courts ter bring some of their burdensome interest ter bear on the *Cockeril* and her nefarious captain – that's the name of her, ain't it?"

"Aye, Mister Fouracres," Rossamünd nodded. "It was the *Cockeril* all right, and the *Hogshead*, too." He sincerely hoped that such "burdensome interest" might bring the dastardly career of Captain Poundinch to a necessary end.

The foundling stepped closer to Fouracres and whispered, "And what of the glamgorn we saved? It was a shame that he had to run off so fast. Will he be all right?"

"It's the way of those little fellows," said Fouracres, with a fatherly pat on the foundling's head. "Deep in unfriendly places yer can hardly blame the bogle for skipping away quick. As ter how he'll fare, I can't say I rightly know, though I can sure tell yer those little fellows are wily and tough. Trust it ter Providence, Mister Rossamünd – it's all yer can do."

Rossamünd's burden lightened just a little. He sighed.

Fouracres stood and smiled sadly down at him. "I will keep my eye out for yer, Mister Rossamünd. I have reason ter go Winstermill way ev'ry now and then. So ter thee I will say fer now: till next occasion. Don't trust everybody yer meet – though I reckon she might be more honourable than she seems." He indicated the imperious fulgar with a subtle look.

Seeing this, Europe approached them. "Goodbye, Postman Fouracres. Thank you for your help." She gave a very slight, almost curtsy-like bow and tried to hand something to him. A bill of folding money.

Fouracres bowed deeply, but did not take what was offered. "As I said when we were hunting fer Rossamünd, I have no need fer reward. Ter serve such a fair face and in such friendly company is reward in itself. Thank yer, but no."

With a wry look, Europe retracted her offering and entered the hostelry.

"Off I go now, Rossamünd, ter my own abode. Stay safe." The postman and the foundling shook manly hands.

Finally Rossamünd had made a friend, and now they

were to part. He began to feel as if he would never settle down, never have loved ones close by, to call his own. "I hope you can come and see me soon, Mister Fouracres. I reckon a friendly face will be really welcome where I'm going. I hope I find some more."

"Surely yer will, surely yer will," the postman answered softly. "The timing of such things is near often perfect. Take care."

With Rossamünd watching mournfully, Fouracres walked away, with a wave, into the gathering dark.

16

WITH THE LAMPLIGHTERS

lamplighter (noun) essentially a kind of specialised soldier, mostly employed by the Empire, though some states also have them. The main task of the lamplighter is to go out in the late afternoon and evening to light the bright-limn lamps that line the conduits (highways) of the Empire, and to douse them again in the early morning. They are fairly well paid as soldiers go, earning about twenty-two sous a year.

AFTER a night spent in as comfortable and as peaceful a sleep as money can buy, Rossamünd set out early by coach. The morning was of the clear, bitterly cold kind characteristic of the final month of autumn. Farewells with Europe had been strange. She had insisted on seeing him all the way into the coach and safely started on this final stretch of the journey. He would be travelling alone, trusted with carrying dispatches for the Lamplighter Marshal and his staff in Winstermill. He had wrapped the bundle of documents and letters in wax paper and hidden the parcel at the bottom of his valise.

Now he sat in the clumsy bulk of the coach, another first on this journey of firsts – leaning out of the window to bid Europe goodbye. She had been more impatient than was usual, even downright rude, that is if she said anything at all. Rossamünd was wondering why she had even bothered. As it came to the moment for him to leave she suddenly grasped his hands in hers, placing into them a small purse. Without a word, she looked deeply into his eyes, holding him like this for what seemed the longest time. He did not know what to say to her. He would help her if ever she needed it, but he had no idea how he felt about her. Yet Rossamünd wanted to say something. He had shared the most terrifying times in his life with this mercurial fulgar. Surely that rated some comment, some word of understanding between them.

Yet, before he could utter anything, there was a loud crack of the driver's whip and the coach lurched forward, tearing his hands free from Europe's firm grasp. His heart stung with a nameless regret and he poked his head quickly out of the window. "Goodbye, Miss Europe!" he called, his voice seeming small and silly. "Get well again!"

They stared at each other across the ever-growing gap. Europe's hands were pressed together before her mouth, but she did not stir. Rossamünd waved again, even more vigorously. "*Goodbye!*" he cried.

Still the fulgar continued to stare after him. Too soon he lost her in the crowd of intervening traffic. He caught a final glimpse of her, and then she was gone.

Despite his confusion, despite her brutal way of life, he felt a great weight of sadness at the parting. With a heavy heart he sat down again and looked inside the purse she had given him. A vague determination somewhere within him vowed never to part with this gift. There were coins within – gold coins! – and a fold of paper. He gave a furtive look to the other passengers. In the coach with him was a thin lady in rich satins bundled up against the cold in a dark violet cloak; sitting opposite her and to Rossamünd's right was an equally thin man in simple black proofing who made a study of completely ignoring the other two passengers. Neither of these paid him any mind, and so he counted the coins. *Ten sous!*

Uncreasing the paper he saw that it was folding money written up to the value of a further five sous. Here he held more money in his hands than he had ever even seen before! It made him feel very strange. There was another leaf of paper, a note, wrapped up with the folding money. It was written in a delicately elegant hand, the mark of a highly ranked lady, and it read:

> *For Rossamünd, to buy yourself a new hat with.*
> *A fair portion of the reward for our adventure.*
> *You have been a revelation.*
> *With more affection than I am used to,*
> *Europa, Duchess-in-waiting of Naimes.*

Rossamünd's eyes went wide. Europe – or "Europa", as he had just discovered – was a duchess-in-waiting! He had been spending his time with a peer, a highly ranked noble, and one in line to rule a whole city-state! He had rescued, and been rescued by, one who was apparently so far above him in rank, she should never have to even think on him. It was little wonder she was so confident, so self-possessed. Europe had become an even profounder mystery.

Feeling faintly uneasy about being given money earned in the slaughter of an undeserving creature, Rossamünd buried the gift-purse down at the bottom of his satchel.

North out of High Vesting went the coach, only a day after he had arrived, and back up the Gainway, whipping past the vegetable sellers. Rossamünd was on the wrong side of the vehicle to be able to wave at them. They travelled faster than the landaulet had on the contrary journey and arrived at the Harefoot Dig by midday. Here the horses were changed and his two travelling companions went into the wayhouse to buy their lunch. Rossamünd remained within the transport and dined on some of the supplies Europe had provided. These included withered ox kidney on expensive dark brown crust and a sachet of small, crescent-shaped nuts that the fulgar had called cashew stalks, with a taste wonderfully salty and exotically sweet.

Soon enough the journey was resumed. They soon made it to Silvernook, passing through with only a pause to pick up mail. Then on they went and entered country Rossamünd had not yet seen. The woodland of the Brindleshaws extended much further north, then stopped quite abruptly as the hills dropped away sharply to an expanse of cultivated flatlands. They looked familiar to the foundling and, from what he could gather of the map in the almanac, he guessed this area to be just another part of Sulk.

Twice more the coach stopped: once by a great hedge, behind which Rossamünd could spy a grand manor-house, to let off the silent woman; and a second time in the middle of what appeared to be a great expanse of swampy fields and nothing more. Here the sullen man disembarked, saying "Good afternoon," as he did, catching the foundling so unawares he was not able to respond in time. With both travelling companions gone, Rossamünd had the rare privilege of travelling in a hired coach on his own. He kicked off his shoes and lounged about on either seat, staring at great length at the passing scenes on either side. They went through several small settlements, each one guarded, fenced and gated.

As the coach continued on, the cold clear day became overcast in a thin sort of way, making the afternoon sun a dull off-yellow and turning the veil-like clouds gunmetal grey. The land was becoming wilder here, less well tended and fertile. There was something eerie about its arid breadth. Threwd brooded here, and while the day's orb was setting, it was a great relief to see the final destination come into view. There, still a few miles distant around a long bend, window lights twinkling, sat Winstermill Manse.

The name of Winstermill was – so Rossamünd's almanac read – a corruption of a more ancient title, *Winstreslewe*, given to a ruined fortress upon the high foundations of which the manse now stood. It was built right by a long line of low, yet steep-sided hills and at the beginning of a great gorge which cut through this same range. The manse looked like a country house, yet so much larger, squatter, mightier and much more solid. It had a great many more roofs of heavy lead shingles rising higher and higher as they receded from the front of the structure like a complex range of ever taller hillocks. From the midst of these, lofty chimneys even taller than those of the Harefoot Dig pointed heavenwards in baffling profusion like blunt spines. There were several round, crenellated strong points projecting out from a roof's myriad slopes, the barrels of great guns showing from some of them.

The manse's outer walls were angled inwards to help deflect the blow of a cannon shot; its lower windows narrow slits barely wide enough to admit light. The great gate was made of thick, weather-greened bronze. Lamps blazed above this threatening portal and an enormous flag, the spandarion of the Empire, a golden owl over a field of red and white, barely showing in the dark, curled and whipped above it all. This was a place made to stand against all threats, and Rossamünd admired its grim defences.

Most significantly of all, for one about to become a lamplighter, was the long line of brightly flaring lanterns that marched away from Winstermill, threading eastwards like a great, glittering necklace, disappearing into the distant dark of the gorge. It was such as these, raised high on tall posts of black iron, that he was surely expected to tend.

The coach turned off the main way, which disappeared into a tunnel made through the very foundations of the

Manse, and rattled up a steep drive to Winstermill's bronze gates. These were already opening, and the coach was admitted without having to halt. Within the curtain of the manse's outer fortifications, Rossamünd had expected to find a bustle of diligent folk marching about on serious business. Instead it was empty of any bustle, or even hustle, and no serious business seemed to be going on anywhere nearby.

A single yardsman came out to them, touching his hat as greeting. "*Winstermill!*" a coachman cried. "*Change ve-hickles if ye wish to travel further!*"

Rossamünd alighted and looked about the well-lit yard. It was wide and flat and bare but for one stunted, leafless tree growing by a farther wall. His valise was quickly retrieved for him, and the coach clattered away, together with the yardsman, retreating somewhere beyond the side of the structure. Rossamünd presumed the horses would be stabled, and the drivers rested for the return leg the following day.

The boy was left all alone now, and stood before these august headquarters uncertain of what to do next. As he waited he wrestled out the bundle of dispatches, ready to hand them to whoever should ask for them. Still no one sallied forth to greet him. In the end, if only to avoid the bitter cold, he walked to the most important-looking set of doors and, finding them unbarred, pushed his way within.

Inside was a large, blank room, square and empty. There was another door at the farther end and Rossamünd walked over to this and went through. Now he found himself at one end of a long wide hall with walls painted green like a lime in season and a single narrow rug patterned in carnelian and black running the whole length of the stone floor. A person in uniform stood about halfway down. Rossamünd strode along this lime hallway and offered up the dispatches promptly to this uniformed person — a tough-looking fellow with oddly cut hair.

As he did, Rossamünd addressed the man just as he had been trained to do, for serving upon a ram. "Rossamünd Bookchild, sir, recently arrived and ready to serve aboard — uh — to serve ... you ... here."

The rough-looking fellow looked at him, and then at the wad of paper the foundling held, without curiosity. "Not for me, son. Hand it to one of those pushers-of-pencils inside there," he said, with gruff authority, pointing to a pair of flimsy-looking, finely carved doors at the end of the lime hall.

"Oh ..." said Rossamünd.

His initial flush of courage now spent, the foundling entered those ornamented doors nervously. Beyond was an enormous, square space with a ceiling high above, and the clatter of the opening door rang and echoed within. Along the distant farther wall was a massive wooden structure of drawers, cabinets and rolling stepladders — what he would learn later was the immense and complex document cata-logue, in which all the correspondence and paperwork of the lamplighters eventually found its final burial place. To the foundling's left, and to his right, facing out from either wall, were two dark wood desks. A studious-looking man worked behind each, the one on the left looking up at him briefly as he entered, and the one on the right keeping his head down and his hand scribbling.

Between the two desks was a great blank area of cold slate, and Rossamünd, with each footstep clip-clopping too loudly, moved to stand right in the middle of this barren space. He looked to his right, then to his left. Both clerks continued their close attention to their work and offered nothing to the new arrival. With no idea of which way to go, Rossamünd ran a little rhyme in his head to solve this puzzle, thinking either left or right with each subsequent word. The rhyme itself was a short list of faraway, semi-mythical, and notoriously threwdish places, and it always fired Rossamünd's imagination:

Ichor, Liquor, Loquor, Fiel
My decision now reveal.

He finished on his right. *Right it is!* He went *clip-clop, clip-clop* and stood before that desk. Holding out the letters, he repeated himself. "Rossamünd Bookchild, sir, recently arrived and ready to serve as a lamplighter."

This clerk looked up with a scowl upon his sharp, bespectacled face. He continued to write, even though his attention was no longer on the task.

"Not me, child!" he snarled. "Him!" He put his nose back to his scribbling.

He could only have meant the other clerk, way across on the opposite side.

Right it isn't, then. Rossamünd held back a sigh.

He turned on his heel and clip-clopped-clip-clopped to the left-hand desk and its equally diligent clerk. He spoke his introduction for a third time, and this clerk stopped writing, put down his pencil and stood.

"Welcome, Rossamünd Bookchild. My name is Inkwill. I am the registry clerk. You have been expected." He took the dispatch bundle from the foundling and they shook hands. "It's a good thing you have arrived now. After today we were going to give up on you. If you had got here tomorrow, we would have turned you away, I'm afraid. In the nick of time, as they say."

As Inkwill the registry clerk sorted through the dispatches, he held up a tightly folded oblong of fine linen paper.

"This is yours, I reckon," he said, waving the article at Rossamünd.

Puzzled, Rossamünd took it slowly. It was a letter made out to him in the script of someone he knew well and loved dearly: Verline. He had been carrying it the whole length of his travel from High Vesting, and could have read and reread it at his leisure aboard the coach. He was desperate to open it, but had to wait.

Inkwill put the dispatches down and sat again. He organised a wad of papers, took up his pencil and began to quiz Rossamünd with all manner of question: age, eye colour, height, weight, origin, race; on and on they went. Often they were incomprehensible: political affinities, species bias. Whichever answer Rossamünd gave, no matter how incoherent, was filled in on the relevant forms. When each form was completed, Inkwill rewrote it twice more. Having completed this task he then looked over the foundling's newly redrafted documents and papers and read the covering letter with fixed attention.

Rossamünd's eyes nearly bugged from their sockets as he waited, breath held, to see how these temporary certificates would be received.

"I see," Inkwill said at last. "Witherscrawl won't like these; neither will the Marshal … 'tis no matter. These are perfectly legal." He gave a slight smile as his attention shifted to the boy before him. "Been through some … interesting times getting here, have we?"

Rossamünd nodded emphatically. "Aye, sir, an adventure of them."

Inkwill's smile broadened. "You'll have to tell me some time." With that he took out yet more documents and began copying pertinent details from Rossamünd's papers. When the registry clerk was done, and all the forms properly blotted and indexed, he politely told Rossamünd that he was to now make his way over to the other clerk.

"He is our indexer, and he is called Witherscrawl. He will enter you into our manning list, so that from now on you will be called on the roll, and be reckoned a lamplighter." Inkwill stood and shook Rossamünd's hand once more. "Welcome to the Emperor's Service."

"Thank you, Mister Inkwill," Rossamünd returned, somewhat bewildered. "I will try and do my very best, just as I was taught to, sir."

"Good for you. Now take this receipt and this excuse-card to Witherscrawl. I will see you tomorrow."

With that, Inkwill went on with whatever it was he went on with, and ceased paying any attention to the foundling.

Clutching a wallet of new papers and certificates, Rossamünd stepped cautiously across the gap back to the sharp-faced, sharp-mannered clerk Witherscrawl.

"Um … Mister Witherscrawl, I …" he began.

With a sour look, the clerk snatched the receipt and excuse-card from Rossamünd's hand.

"I, ah …" the boy tried.

"Shut it! I know my business!" The indexer looked down at the excuse-card with sinister deliberation and a cruel turn to his mouth. A hoarse growl wheezed in his throat. "Little weevil couldn't do a simple thing like keep his most important papers safe …!" His beady eyes shot Rossamünd an evil glare. "Makes me wonder why we are even bothering to take him in. Sit down!"

With a start, and, as there were no chairs about, Rossamünd obediently sat on the cold stone floor.

Taking a pencil in both hands, Witherscrawl proceeded to write furiously into several books and ledgers, and on to several lists. When each entry was done, he would thump it violently with a wooden handle attached to a large, flat sponge. Rossamünd winced at every blow.

WITHERSCRAWL

Witherscrawl eventually leant over his desk and looked down upon the foundling, his eyes squinting meanly behind his spectacles. "You have certainly taken your time to get here," he spat. "Gave Germanicus an awful messing around, you did. Too good for us, are you, to make your way promptly?" He poked a finger at Rossamünd's face. "A lamplighter's life is *punctuality*, boy! You had better get your habits about this, or your time with us will be brief – troubled and brief."

Those were familiar words.

"Ah – aye, Mister Witherscrawl."

The clerk leant across the desk and sneered. "Do not address me, *boy*, as anything other than 'sir'. Have you got that? You don't need to know my name, and you certainly have *not* earned the privilege to use it!"

Rossamünd felt his neck contract like a turtle's. "A-aye ... sir ..."

Finally, and with half-uttered protestations about the inconvenience, Witherscrawl led Rossamünd through a small side door and down the narrowest corridors to a small, drab cell with flaking walls. This room, furnished with only a metal stretcher – not unlike the one he had slept on for most of his time at the foundlingery, was to be his bunk for the night.

"Tomorrow," Witherscrawl informed him, "you will be woken at five of the morning, if you are not already up by then, and must move immediately to the parade yard, for the calling of the roll. Then you'll meet the

Lamplighter Marshal, our officer commanding. Then you will receive your routine and begin your instruction. Do you understand?"

"Aye, sir." Rossamünd was beginning to feel, all over again, the familiar doubts about the desirability of this occupation. Without a bath or even a wash to clean off the grime of travel, he was told that he was to have his bright-limn extinguished in no more than fifteen minutes.

Extracting another "Aye, sir!" from the new arrival, Witherscrawl left Rossamünd to prepare for sleep. The only thing on the foundling's mind, though, was the letter he held in his hand: the precious letter with dearest Verline's unmistakable writing upon it, the letter addressed to him personally. It was like a sweet song to his tired soul, an encouragement from those far off – he was still thought of, he was remembered.

He sat down on the cot, causing it to creak loudly even under his slight weight. Hands shaking a little with excitement, he prised open the seal and many securing folds to reveal the message within. The date – 23rd day of Lirium – was scrawled at the top. It had been written five days ago, the day Rossamünd had been discovered hiding in that boxthorn by Europe. Eagerly, he read on:

> My dear and most missed Rossamünd,
> How I wish I could right now see you here in front of me.
> I would hold you till you squirmed out of my grasp and
> stood there looking at me bashfully, like you used to do. As
> this cannot be, simple correspondence is all I have (– I thank
> Madam Opera for teaching me my letters!)

Yet I hug you even now, in my heart, and pray constantly too that you might be safe and thriving. It's silly of me I know but I miss you – see! My tears have smeared the ink! One day, find your way back to me, even just for a visit, so I might see you grown and well, and be filled with pride at what a fine man you are undoubtedly becoming. We could take a rest-cure to my sister, so I might show you off to her as well.

I have to tell you, too, that dear Master Fransitart is determined to come to you at Winstermill, or wherever you will be stationed on the Wormway. Though he does not show it, nor say what the cause is, I can tell that he is greatly distressed. All he will say is that there is something he should have told you long ago – though he will not speak what that is. He says that he must tell you only, in your company alone, and does not want to risk such things in letters. Oh Rossamünd, what can it be? Do you know?

Regardless, what he has to say is not so much of my worry, but rather that he is getting old, as vinegaroons go, and his pith is beginning to fail him. I don't want to worry you, Rossamünd, heart-of-my-heart, but I think you need to know, so that you might be ready to care and comfort *him* who has done as much for you for so long, when he finally arrives to you. I am frightened that this journey will be his last, my heart, so look out for him – he says he intends to leave for Winstermill as soon as winter is past its worst and the season is fit for travelling once more for one of his poor health (he listened to my pleas in this at least). Expect him within the last week of Herse, or the first week of Orio at the latest. Look out for him then, won't you?

I must end, for Madam is demanding her bath, but reply to this the instant you get it, for I – we – ache to know that you are well.

Master Fransitart sends you his blessings, or he would if he knew I was writing you. If he did know, I am sure he would tell you to stay at your task till he comes, no matter how anxious I might get.

I send you my love-filled blessings too, and over again.
Most assuredly your

PS: By the way – though this is not so important – you will
not be surprised, I am sure, to learn that the day before
yesterday, Gosling ran away from us, and cannot be
found. I am ashamed to be so uncharitable, but the mood
here has lightened considerably. Write me as soon as you
can, please! Also, Master Craumpalin wishes to know if you
have had any use for his potives.

While Rossamünd read the letter, he was first moved
with joy, but then to increasing alarm. Had Master
Fransitart, ill as he was, finally repented of letting him go
and now planned to fetch him back to the oppression of
the foundlingery? Was this the big secret? *It's the first week
of Pulchrys now ...* He counted the months on his knuckles:
*Pulchrys, Brumis, Pulvis, Heimio, Herse, Orio: that means he'll be
here in four, maybe five months!*

As to the news about Gosling: well, Verline was right –
Rossamünd was not surprised. Indeed, he was glad for
Verline and the masters' sakes, and for the littlest children
too, that his old foe had run off.

There came a heavy hammering at the door of his cell.
A discouragingly serious voice bellowed. "Douse lanterns!"

Rossamünd scrambled to unfold the blankets and pillow
supplied, and wrestled them over the unsavoury-looking
mattress.

His bright-limn still glowing, the hammering soon came again. "You don't want to start your career with us like this, son. Get your lantern out and get to bed!" That voice held promise of all manner of things terrible, unguessable.

Quickly turning the bright-limn over, so that its light would dim and gradually expire, Rossamünd completed his bed in the faint twilight of its dying glow, undressing in pitch blackness. Finally, as he lay, restlessly shifting, with many creakings and groans of the metal frame, against all the uncomfortable lumps of the mattress, his fading thoughts swam. They dwelt for a moment on Verline, and her worries, but it was Master Fransitart, his failing health and his intended visit that troubled him most. Rossamünd did not know how to feel about his old dormitory master now. He wished the old vinegaroon would just stay in Boschenberg and leave him to his new path. With a flash of guilt it occurred to Rossamünd that Fransitart might not survive the journey; though he was already regretting the intended visit, he would hate any harm to come to his old dormitory master even more.

In the orbit of his sleepy musings, he wondered, too, if Europe, the duchess lahzar, would indeed return as she had said and ask him once more to be her factotum. Worry for poor Freckle stirred him for a moment, and this became concern for where Fouracres might be that night. So spun his tired thoughts.

As sleep slowly overtook him, he marvelled that, through the many twists of what should have been a straightforward journey, he had managed to bumble, still intact, still healthy, to his destination. At last, for better or for worse, he was where he was originally destined, to finally become a lamplighter.

Tomorrow he would wake to the beginning of a whole new life.

FINIS UNILIBRIS
[END BOOK ONE]

EXPLICARIUM

BEING A GLOSSARY OF TERMS
& EXPLANATIONS INCLUDING
APPENDICES

EXPLANATION of PRONUNCIATION

ä is said as the "ar" sound in "**a**sk" or "c**ar**"

æ is said as the "ay" sound in "h**ay**" or "**ei**ght"

ë is said as the "ee" sound in "scr**ea**m" or "b**ee**p"

é is said as the "eh" sound in "sh**e**d" or "**e**veryone"

ö is said as the "er" sound in "l**ear**n" or "b**ur**n"

ü is said as the "oo" sound in "w**oo**d" or "sh**ou**ld"

~ine at the end of pronouns is said as the "een" sound in "b**ean**" or "s**een**"; the exception to this is "Clementine", which is said as the "eyn" sound in "**fine**" or "m**ine**".

Words ending in e, such as "Verline" or "Grintwoode": the e is not sounded.

EXPLANATION of ITALICS

A word set in *italics* indicates that you will find an explanation of that word also in the explicarium; the only exceptions to this are the names of *rams* and other vessels, and the titles of books, where it is simply a convention to put these names in italics.

SOURCES

In researching this document the scholars are indebted to many sources. Of them all the following proved the most consistently sourced:

The Pseudopædia
Master Matthius' Wandering Almanac: A Wordialogue of Matter, Generalisms & Habilistics
The Incomplete Book of Bogles
Weltchronic
The Book of Skolds
& extracts from the *Vadè Chemica*

A

AOWM the symbol of the *skolds*, taken from the symbols of the *Elements* in the *Körnchenflecter*. It represents the four-part systems of their discipline and learning. See the *Four Humours,* the *Four Spheres,* the *Körnchenflecter* and *skolds*.

apprentices persons working in training under the tutelage of their employer. Often abbreviated to "'prentices". A person serves and learns as an apprentice to a master for four years, after this time becoming a journeyman or companion working independently and gaining experience. When they have worked at this for no less than six years, apprentices have the right to become masters and to take on apprentices themselves.

Arius Vigilans "the vigilant ram" as seen on the endpapers of this book. The emblem or sigil representing the state of *Hergoatenbosch* and its capital *Boschenberg*, and revered for its obstinacy and hard-headedness.

army the states of the *Empire* are not allowed to have large standing armies, usually no more than 10,000 soldiers. These are considered enough for various guarding duties about the walls of cities and major rural centres. As a consequence there are many mercenary regiments (which are not illegal) roaming the lands; the states employ these to do their fighting for them. Sometimes certain states manage to gain dispensation from the *Emperor* to have a standing army of greater than 10,000 men if their lands are extensive – a nice little loophole which has allowed some to amass sizeable forces. Their neighbours, of course, do not like this. They have their ministers complain in the Imperial parliament, from which the Emperor may or may not order a reduction, and so the cycle of rivalry and envy goes on. Meanwhile the mercenaries get richer. The army referred to in the story would be Boschenberg's standing army, though mercenaries also seek recruits from such places as *Madam Opera's Estimable Marine Society for Foundling Boys and Girls*.

ashmongers dealers in corpses and products made or gained from dead bodies; the middlemen of the *dark trades*, taking the dead bodies that the *corsers* steal and the *smugglers* smuggle, and passing them on – for

317

a modest fee, of course – to their grateful, benighted customers. They also trade in *monsters*, alive or dead, and their parts. Because *skolds* and *scourges* frequently use their services they have been legitimised, but everyone knows that they are agents for those working outside the law.

Axles, the ~ the mighty rivergates that guard the northern and southern entrances of the *Humour River* as it flows past *Boschenberg*. The northern Axle is known as the Nerid Axle, and the southern the Scutid Axle. Heavily defended with great guns and soldiers, the gates prevent riverine traffic from moving through without paying tolls for cargo and/or passengers, plus a tax for the craft itself. If the master of the vessel does not get the right forms filled in when passing through both Axles he is likely to be charged twice, once for each *rivergate*. See *rivergates*.

B

baldric also called broadstraps, brightly decorated with *mottle* and sometimes even a coat of arms or sigil. Baldrics are the favourite way for most *everymen* to advertise their allegiances. Often a favourite weapon is hung from your baldric. Other similar items of clothing are sashes – made of silk; and cingulum – a more gorgeously decorated variety of baldric worn only in pageants, processions and galas (dances). See *mottle*.

bard, barding a set of *proofing* worn as armour. See *harness*.

barge any river-going *gastriner*.

bargemen workers of river-going craft as opposed to *vinegaroons*, who sail the high seas and work on *rams* and *cargoes*. *Vinegaroons* consider bargemen to be lesser creatures, not as skilled as sailors, and the bargemen resent this strongly. As far as they see it, a boat is a boat and still needs to be handled well to keep its trim in the water, wherever that water might be.

Barthomæus, Instructor ~ said "bath-o-may-uss"; one of the staff at *Madam Opera's Estimable Marine Society for Foundling Boys and Girls*.

His main responsibility is to teach the children physical skills such as *harundo* and swimming and rowing. A retired *yardsman*, he is not as old as *Fransitart* or *Craumpalin*, having arrived at the foundlingery only a couple of years ago.

Bases and Combinations the foundational chemicals from which all *scripts* (*potives* and *draughts*) are begun. Each *realm* or *script* has its selection of Bases. For example *bezoariac*, used in making *Cathar's Treacle*, is one of the Bases of the *realm* known as alembants – scripts used to alter someone's physique. The most common Base for all *realms* is water. Combinations are the ways in which both Bases and their resulting *scripts* might be combined for more potent or varied results.

baskets derogatory term meaning base and unworthy fellows, especially *monsters*.

Battle of the Gates see *Gates, Battle of the ~*.

Battle of the Mole see *Mole, Battle of the ~*.

beast-handlers or, more properly, tractors or feralados; people who feed, clean, bridle, train and control the many beasts used in warfare. They are especially used to care for and control the bolbogis, the dogs-of-war, great *gudgeon monsters* like the *Slothog*, keeping them in check with thick chains and carefully applied *potives*. Tractors lead their beasts into battle, working up their rage with the pricking of goads till they are near the enemy lines. With the enemy close, the beasts are released to storm off into the foe. Occasionally the *monsters* "malfunction" and turn on their own *army*, doing great harm till they can be subdued.

belladonna also called pratchigin in the south and sweet-lass in *Boschenberg* and its lands; a powder made from the root of the deadly nightshade bush. In small doses it is used to relieve stomach complaints. A slightly stronger dose can give a slight uplift to one's spirits. Too much belladonna, however, can put you into a coma or, even worse, kill you. It is sometimes added to *Cathar's Treacle* to help with digestion and make takers feel a bit better about themselves. It is not essential, however, and *Cathar's Treacle* works just as well without it.

bells of the watch aboard *rams* and other water-going craft, and in any naval college or school, a bell is rung on every half-hour of a watch: 8 bells are rung at the beginning of each watch, then 1 bell after the first half-hour, 2 bells after an hour, 3 bells after an hour-and-a-half and so on until 8 bells are reached again and a new watch called. Exceptions to this are the two dog-watches, where only 3 bells are rung before ringing out 8 to begin a new watch once more. See *watches*.

Best Cuts the expensive dishes on a menu; those meals said to be fashionable. The strange thing is that after a few seasons they may well find themselves listed under *the Rakes* instead, and meals once considered common and cheap make their way back into the Best Cuts. Ah, the vicissitudes of fashion. See *the Rakes*.

bezoriac, bezoariac, besorus one of the *Bases*; a thickish liquid, usually clear but sometimes straw-coloured; used in the making of *Cathar's Treacle* and many other *scripts* that change the way the body functions and also for antidotes.

biggin wooden cup or flask in an oiled leather case, with a lid of the same which fastens shut and helps hold in most of whatever the biggin is holding. For travelling, water- and wine-skins or canteens are more common, but a biggin will do over a short journey.

Bill of Fare what we would call a "menu", fare meaning "food", bill meaning "list".

billet-boxes the cheapest accommodation in a *wayhouse* or hostelry: little more than a cupboard set into a wall containing a cot and some space to store one's things. They might range as high as four billet-boxes up a wall, with a ladder to access those above the first. Cramped and uncomfortable for anyone over 6 feet tall.

Billetus, Mister owner and proprietor of the *Harefoot Dig*, along with his wife *Madam Felicitine*. He inherited *the Dig* from some distant part of the family when he was young and single after a short stint as a cooper's *apprentice,* and has run the *wayhouse* ever since.

birchet restorative *draught* used to reduce swelling and numb pain. Its powerful reaction with the body when first swallowed is thought to help against the rise of a fever as well. See *scripts*.

black coney pie a pastry made from rabbit meat stewed in a mixture of herbs that makes the flesh go dark – almost black – as it cooks.

boatswain also bosun; standing officer of a vessel, which means he stays with the craft no matter what, whether it is at sea or *laid up in* *ordinary*. With the assistance of the boatswain's mates, he is responsible for bunting (flags), rigging, blocks, cables, anchors, any other ropes or cords, a vessel's boats, the seamanship of the *vinegaroons* working the vessel including those under the *gastrineer*, turning the *watches*, and ensuring the gunwale and sides of his vessel are clean and at all times clear of clothes lines, stray ropes, caulking and any other foreign matter. One of the most learned and experienced sailors on board a vessel, he is paid anywhere from 46 to 60 sous a year.

bogle(s) the most commonly used term for *monsters* generally; it can also be used to mean the smaller varieties of *monster*, those of less than a human's height, including *nuglungs, nimbleschrewds, glamgorns* and that white creature *Rossamünd* sees in the waters of the *Humour*. Even a small *monster* is deadly dangerous and very hard to kill. Anyone wishing for a long life will treat even these with a great deal of care.

boobook, boobook owl small white and brown owl with large black eyes and a pleasant woodwind call. It is said that they are mortally afraid of *monsters,* and so to hear one is a happy sign.

book child any child raised in an orphanage, foundlingery or any other institution for the housing or care of stray or unwanted children. They are called book children because their names are always entered into some kind of book when they arrive at the institution. As a consequence it is customary for the children to take on the *family-name* of "Bookchild" when they grow up and move on, especially if they do not know their original *family-name*.

Bookday the day *Madam Opera* holds once a year to celebrate the lives of all the *foundlings* living under the roof of her *marine society*. One day does all and passes for a kind of birthday, even if the actual date of birth is known. *Madam Opera* would rather that no child get any lofty ideas about being more special than the others, though she does not enforce this policy on her staff strictly.

bookhouse another name for a foundlingery or a *marine society*. So named from the book its occupants' names are written into.

Boschenberg said "bosh-en-burg"; the great city of the people who now call themselves the *Hergotts*, and who are descended from the fierce tribes that were native to the region, the Bosch, who were eventually conquered by the *Empire*. The name means "the hill or mount of the

Bosch" where, as legend goes, the last of the Bosch made their mighty yet doomed stand before the might of a long-dead emperor's armies. See *Hergoatenbosch* and *Hergott*.

Boschenberger(s) those living in or coming from *Boschenberg*.

bosun's whistle or pipe; a whistle with a distinctive three-note call used by a vessel's *boatswain* (bosun) to order those under his authority to their respective tasks. In the *marine society* it is used in much the same way by Master *Heddlebulk*, piping the children to various tasks. The bells let them know what time it is.

bothersalts popular *potive* used to drive away *monsters*. It smells terrible, and even worse to *bogles*, affecting the mucous membranes such as inside the nose and throat, and also the eyes, stinging powerfully and even causing (temporary) blindness. There are no flashes or bangs with bothersalts, just a puff of the powder and much stumbling and screaming from the victim. One of the remarkable things about them is that even if they get wet, bothersalts will dry back into fine crystals ready for use again, unlike many other repugnants of its kind. This makes them popular among *vinegaroons* and *bargemen* and this is why *Craumpalin* knows how to make them.

bower-maid maid who looks after a bower (bedroom) and the bedding, washing and clothing needs of whoever might occupy that room. In the *Harefoot Dig*, the bower-maids simply attend to the ablutions and comforts of the guests staying in their rooms. Bower-maids can be privy to some very delicate information as they serve their masters and mistresses in the most intimate room of the house. Consequently, some bower-maids have been made betrayer by bribes, threats or pain, while certain master spies use such a disguise to do their nefarious work.

boxthorn medium to large bush with small dark hardy leaves that grows all about the *Soutlands,* especially in remoter places. It gets its name from the roughly box-like shape it gains as it matures, and for the 1–3-inch thorns sticking from trunk, branch and twig. As with all thorny plants, rural folks regard them as ill-luck, attracting and hiding *monsters*. They are thought to be a favourite hidey-hole for *bogles* and are often pruned and lopped if found growing too near civilisation.

Branden Rose, the ~ name by which *Europe* is known throughout much of the *Soutlands*, the vast southern lands of the *Empire*. She has this appellation because she has spent so much time in *Brandenbrass* that she is mistakenly believed to have originally come from that city.

Brandenbrass enormous city well to the south of *Boschenberg*, and one of its main rivals for trade and prominence. Situated on the north-western shores of the *Grume*, Brandenbrass is known for the great size of its *navy* and the adventurous roving of its sea captains and merchants. Even though it controls very little land, after centuries of strong and enterprising trade Brandenbrass has become a significant power. Its standing *army* is tiny – no more than 3,000 souls, yet such is its wealth and fame that several of the most elite mercenary regiments use Brandenbrass as their headquarters, being granted protected lands – or parks – by the city's walls to billet and train. This is a convenient and perfectly legal arrangement that gives the city first pick of many thousands of the land's best soldiers should they ever be needed. At the time of *Rossamünd*, Brandenbrass is ruled in the Emperor's name by the Archduke Narsesës and his loyal Cabinet.

Brigandine, the ~ a collection of little kingdoms far to the north-east of the *Half-Continent*, past Mandalay and Tumbalay, across the Bay of Bells (Sinus Tintinabuline). Each one is ruled by a cunning *pirate-king*, supremely successful corsairs who have amassed enough wealth and loyal following to establish themselves as minor potentates of their own realms. Some pirate-kings are secretly sponsored by certain states or kingdoms on the understanding that they will leave that state or kingdom's own vessels alone but freely harry all other shipping. In exchange the sponsoring power allows clandestine access to its own ports and markets, thus allowing a pirate-king or queen and his or her rascally hoard to flourish.

brigands also called bog-trotters, along with *smugglers*; robbers, highwaymen and ne'er-do-wells, desperate men living in the semi-wilds and rural lands, looking to waylay passers and rob them, beat them or even murder them. A brigand's life is tough and usually short, contending with both the officers of Imperial Law (such as the *lamp-lighters*) and the *monsters* that lurk all about them. The best chance a brigand has of surviving is by gathering with others of his or her kind in a violent gang or band, the bigger the better. Such a gang is ruled by the most ruthless of them, and together they can cause a lot of anguish and trouble to both man and *monster*. If a band of brigands do not have a *skold* in their midst they will commonly kidnap one and force him or her to work for them under threat of death – another risk the humble *skold* has to run. Brigands work hard to keep their dens secret, taking convoluted paths to and from their lairs. For, if a brigand's den is discovered, or even a hint of it is known to the authorities, they descend upon the murderous band with merciless alacrity. Truly, only the most destitute and desperate would ever venture on a life like this. One of the favourite weapons of brigands for hand-to-hand fights and making threats is the carnarium or "flesh-hook", such as that used by butchers. It is their distinctive item, almost a badge of the job.

bright-black   highly polished black leather; what we would call "patent" leather.

bright-limn   lantern-like device used to illuminate homes, streets and ships. Its glow comes from a certain species of phosphorescent algae known as glimbloom or just bloom, which glows very brightly when soaked in a certain soup of chemicals called seltzer. These chemicals cause the algae to glow strongly. When the algae are out of the seltzer they cease to give off light. The glass panes of a bright-limn are always arranged hexagonally and the stem of bloom hangs off-centre, which means that to "turn a bright-limn off", you simply lay it on the side opposite the stem of bloom, which leaves it out of the seltzer. Gradually it will dim down as the algae dry and become dormant. To "turn" it back on, you stand the bright-limn upright or roll it to its opposite side and very soon it will begin to glow again. The great advantage of a bright-limn is that it has no flame, and so there is no chance of an accident causing some part of the very wooden cities of the *Half-Continent* to burn down – just a puddly mess and a funny smell. They are also low maintenance, in that there is no wick to trim or oil to change. In fact a bright-limn can be left to glow continuously day and night without any ill effect. The seltzer does, however, slowly go off, changing from a pale yellow to a deep orange; when it is completely bad it becomes a dirty, toxic green and is beginning to be harmful to the algae. When the deep orange is turning filthy brown, it is time to change the seltzer.

Brindlestow Bridge, the ~ ancient bridge on the *Vestiweg*, which crosses a gorge at the bottom of which runs the Pill, a small stream that empties into the swampy lands at the mouth of the *Humour*. Originally built by the ancient *Tutins*, the Brindlestow Bridge has been refurbished several times and, as an obvious choke point, is a favourite ambush of the *monsters*, and even *brigands*. At least once a season some kind of *pugnator* has to be sent out to clear the bridge or the road of bogles.

Brindlewood, the ~ or the Brindleshaws; a broad forest of pine and *turpentine*, beech and myrtle on the hilly south-western tip of *Sulk End* (a region known as *the Sough*). The *Vestiweg* passes right through it, entering at the north-west corner and joining the *Gainway* in the forest's sparse eastern fringes. Though regarded as *ditchlands*, and largely given over to the *monsters*, the Brindlewood is tame as *ditchlands* go and several brave folk still make homes there. These Shawsmen live in lonely manors or dwell in towns such as Herrod's Hollow – a logging town – to work the nearby sawmill, or *Silvernook*, and are frequent patrons of the *Harefoot Dig*.

broadside side of a *ram* or other vessel of war; also the name for the simultaneous firing of the guns on one side of a *ram*.

Bucket kitchen boy employed at the *Harefoot Dig*. Whenever he has a free moment he likes to play at cards with the other boys working at *the Dig*.

buff, buff-leather soft, untanned leather, still strong and durable; the type of leather favoured by *gaulders*, making very tough *proofing* indeed.

"by the precious here and vere" exclamation of surprise, wonder, amazement or exasperation, meaning "by the precious west (here) and east (vere)". In the *Half-Continent*, although the usual north, south, east and west are more common terms, directions of the compass are given classical names used by great peoples of the past:

- north = nere, said "near"; also nout, said "nowt"
- south = sere, said "seer"; also scut, said "scoot" or sout, said "sowt"
- east = vere, said "veer"; also est
- west = here, said "heer".

C

cannon   muzzle-loading guns charged with black powder wrapped in cloth or paper canisters and usually solid iron round-shot, fired by a match through a primed touch hole or by use of a flintlock mechanism. They come in a range of weights: the small-guns – 3, 4, 6 and 9 pounders; the long-guns – 12 and 18 pounders; the *great-guns* – 24, 32, 42 pounders; and the siege-guns or cannon-royal – 50 and 68 pounders. The numbers denote the approximate weight of the shot fired from the cannon. The guns themselves are much heavier (for example, a 32 pounder weighs between 2 tons and 2¾ tons and is roughly 9 feet 8 inches long. A typical cannon is also called a culverin, long-barrelled with a decent range. There is also a stocky short-barrelled cannon known as a lombarin or lombard, named after the Lombards of the island of Lombardy who invented it. Though their shorter barrels mean a significant reduction in accuracy, it means that they can fire a much bigger shot of metal than a culverin of the same weight. So, a lombard weighing about 2.8 tons, roughly the same weight of that 32 pounder culverin mentioned earlier, would be a 50 pounder, firing 50 pounder shot. Lombards are more popular on the cruiser class of *ram* – the frigates and the drag-maulers – where they allow these smaller vessels to blast out a considerably higher "weight of shot" as it is called, than if they were armed with just culverins. The loss of range is compensated for by the superior agility of these lighter ironclads.

cargo(es)   box-like *gastrine* vessels that carry goods and even passengers all about the *vinegar seas*. Cargoes sit much higher out of the water than the low and menacing *rams*, having two more decks above the water than a *ram*. All decks are used as hold space, although cargoes do carry a small battery of *cannon* on the topmost deck. Cargoes move appreciably slower than *rams* of the same tread of *gastrines*, which makes them easy prey for pirates and privateers. Consequently they usually travel in convoys with an escort of two or three *rams* – typically dragmaulers or heavy frigates. The largest cargo, the grand-cargo, is as big as the biggest *ram*, the *main-sovereign*, and dwarfs most other vessels, yet it is slow and will not leave a port without a strong escort. These vessels are costly to build in both money and time, and their owners are loath to lose them. Cargoes require about one-tenth of the manpower required to work a *ram*. See *gastrines*.

carlin coin *money*; a silver ten *sequin* piece or five-eighths of a *sou*. See *money*.

Cathar's Treacle or *plaudamentum*; *draught* drunk by *lahzars*; its main function is to stop all the surgically introduced organs (mimetic organs) and connective tissues within a lahzar's body from rejecting their host. The nature of the ingredients and the way in which they react means that Cathar's Treacle does not keep for very long at all, a few hours at best, and has to be made afresh each time. It must be taken twice a day, or the *lahzar* risks *spasming*. If *lahzars* go more than a few days without the treacle their organs start to rot within them, and after a week without it the lahzar's doom is certain. The *parts,* or ingredients, for Cathar's Treacle are as follows:

   10 of water
   1 of *bezoariac*
   ½ of *rhatany*
   ¼ of *Sugar of Nnun*
   1 of *xthylistic curd*
   ½ of *belladonna* (optional)

There are other *draughts* that a *lahzar* must take periodically, but Cathar's Treacle is the most important. For *fulgars* the next most important is a daily dose of fulgura sagrada or saltegrade. For *wits* it is a daily drink of iambic ichor; Friscan's wead every two days; and two tots of cordial of Sammany three times a week plus other traces throughout their lives. Such dependency is a tradeoff for the immense power they possess. A *physician* would also recommend a dose of *evander* every so often to lift the *wind* and fortify the *pith*.

chain mail despite the advent of *proofing*, chain mail is still made and worn. It might not be bullet-proof like *gaulded* clothes, but is effective against the raking claws and snapping teeth of *bogles*, and if some kind of *proofing* is worn beneath, then the protection is excellent – a kind of troubarding. See *harness*.

Chassart also Chastony or Chassault; one of the southernmost *city-states* of the Frestonian League, famous for its soaps and perfumes.

chemicals the main way people have used to confront the threat of *monsters* of the millenia. These chemicals come in all manner of exotic concoctions and brews. See *scripts*, *potives* and *draughts*.

327

Chief Harbour Governor the most senior pilot of a port and harbour, in charge of all the other pilots and of the movements of shipping into and out of his jurisdiction; they have a universal reputation for being irascible and rude, which probably comes from dealing with egocentric captains and masters all day.

"chiff-chaffing lobcock" talkative fool, someone who says or talks too much, a "flabbermouth".

city-state(s) the lands of the *Empire* are divided into distinct domains, each dominated by a city and ruled by a regent in the Emperor*'s* stead. These regents are all dukes, duchesses or earls, as the *Empire* will not allow anyone to hold the title of "king" or "queen" and so get lofty ideas (the only exception to this is the *Gightland Queen*).

claret a usually cheap red wine mixed with apple or pear pulp. It has become fashionable for the more jauntily rich to drink it, part of a whole adventure of slumming it with the lesser folk.

Clementine capital city of the whole *Empire*, where the *Emperor* has his three palaces, each housing one of the Three Seats (Imperial thrones). Situated in an ancient region called Benevenetium, upon the edge of the *Marrow* – a great gorge-like trench or drain dug a millennium ago from the capital to the sea, 2,300 miles to the east. A massive city, it is home to 2 million souls and the Imperial Parliament, where representatives of all the member states and realms and conclaves bicker for a bigger share. It was built aeons ago on an even more ancient granite plateau; a massive citadel of marble and granite with ponderous fortifications and fourteen huge gates and equally huge drawbridges, famous and named with appropriately lofty names: the Immutable Port, the Port Aeternus, the Immortal Gate, the Undying Door, the Sempiternal Gates, the Amaranthine Gate, the Port of the Elect, the Perdurable Door, the Doors Inviolable, the Stout Gate (Door), the Port Indomitable, the Impenetrable Gates, the Doors of the Potential, the Sthenic Gate. It has been described as "... a heap; a rambling urban palace of tall marble and spired granite, its towers sharing spaces with the clouds. It has become a place of corrupt opulence and epitomises all that is broken in its far-spread kingdom ..."

clerk's sergeant non-commissioned officer in charge of military clerks; a common rank among *revenue officers*, where they are often far more active than their title of "clerk" might suggest.

Closet head cook of the *Harefoot Dig,* with only a modicum of ability as a cook. If he was not an old chum of *Billetus,* he would probably have been replaced by *Uda* a long time ago. As one of the live-in staff, part of his pay is given as accommodation in the staff quarters.

Clunes one of the southernmost realms of the *Empire,* famous for the skill and sweetness of its singers; they are said to have gained such talent from their contact with the reclusive and musical folk of Hamlin and Cloudeslee.

Cockeril, **the ~** privately owned 32-*guns-broad heavy-frigate* in harbour at *High Vesting.*

concometrist also metrician; one of a highly trained group of fastidious researchers and soldier-scholars whose sworn charter is to measure and record the length and breadth of all things. Trained for five years in colleges known as athenaeums, they are released on the world bearing two precious gifts awarded to them upon graduation. The first is a calibrator, a yard-long ruler of hardened wood marked with feet and inches, either end being capped with brass ferules. The calibrator is both a tool of the trade and a trusty weapon. Concometrists can be recognised by the calibrators they carry. The second award is the mysterious numrelogue, a large book 2–3 inches thick, to be filled with the cryptic formula and strings of ciphers that only their kind know, recordings of all a concometrist has seen, investigated and measured. When a numrelogue is full it is handed back to the concometrist's governing athenaeum and he or she is handed a new one to fill. Navigators, surveyors and metricians (measurers) are all types of concometrist. They also make good clerks because of their attention to written detail. See Appendix 4.

conductors also trunk roads; major roads between cities maintained at the expense and energy of the local rulers; these were originally made to allow easier marching for armies but are now just as busy as routes of trade. See *highroads.*

conduit(s) major roads between cities maintained at the expense and energy of the Emperor, originally built by the soldiers of *Empire* as they forged their way into new lands. See Imperial *Conductors* and *high roads.*

Conduit Vermis the *Wormway,* running from *Winstermill* to *Wörms* and passing through the *Ichormeer.* Once the Conduit Vermis enters that swamp it quickly becomes one of the most dangerous roads to travel, oppressed by powerful *threwd* and *haunted* by a great variety of *monsters*. All attempts to civilise that stretch of the *Wormway* have failed, often disastrously.

corsers grave robbers, tomb raiders and suppliers to the *dark trade*s. They provide corpses and body parts for the growing demand of benighted laboratories all about the land. It is dangerous, putrid work: corsers run a continual risk of falling foul with the authorities and *monsters* (those *bogles* who creep about in cemeteries and tombs are among the most vicious and violent), yet the money earned in this line of work makes the risks worth the while taking.

Corvinius Arbour one of the more powerful family houses in *Boschenberg*, connected with the mighty Saakrahennemus clan of *Brandenbrass*, whose ancient lineage has sprouted many of history's prominent figures.

counter-offend counter-strike move in *harundo*; one of the many moves that are part of the *Hundred Rules of Harundo*.

coxswain petty officer in charge of the small boats aboard a *ram* or *cargo* such as the jolly boats and the captain's launch; paid about 36 *sous* a year.

Craumpalin, Master ~ said "krorm-pah-linn"; *dispensurist* working at *Madam Opera's Estimable Marine Society for Foundling Boys and Girls*, attending to the medicinal needs of children, other staff, *Madam Opera* herself and even many folks who live and work in the neighbourhood of the *marine society*. Trained as a *dispensurist* by the *navy*, he served with his old friend and messmate Master *Fransitart*. When *Fransitart* was pressed into service as a boy, it was a young Craumpalin who befriended him first and has stayed true to him since. If you ask him, Craumpalin will tell you he was born in the Patricine *city-state* of Lousaine.

Craumpalin's Exstinker a *potive Craumpalin* makes for *Rossamünd*, to hide his smell from noses that do not need to know. See *nullodours*.

cromster(s) one of the smallest of the armed, *ironclad* river-barges, having 3-inch cast-iron strakes down each side and from four to twelve 12-pounder guns (see *cannon*) upon each *broadside*. Generally single-masted, though the biggest may have two masts. Below the open-deck is a single lower deck called the orlop. Forward of amidships (the middle of the craft) is typically hold space for cargo. Aft of amidships the orlop is reserved for the *gastrines* and their crews. Cromsters sit low in the water and are generally suitable only for rivers and the inshore currents of sheltered bays. You might find cromsters much further up a river than any *gastrine* craft, yet only the most foolhardy or brave (between which there is seldom any difference) will take them out into the deeps of the *vinegar seas*. Their short keels make them ideal for shallow waters; however, large swells can wash over the deck dangerously and capsize them. Though not as fast as other *gastrine* vessels (6 knots at best), cromsters are small, sturdy and manoeuvrable and one will find them the most commonly used of all river-going craft. The crew of a cromster, as with all other riverine craft, are known as *bargemen*. See Appendix 7.

cruorpunxis spilt-blood punctures, said "kroo-or-punks-sis"; the proper name for a *monster-blood tattoo*.

cudgel or fustis; any wooden stick, heavy, sometimes bound or studded with iron or another metal and usually of no more than 4 feet in length; usually fashioned straight from the branch of a tree and used in the martial training of *harundo* and other stick-fighting disciplines. Types of cudgel range from the smooth and straight *stock* to the knot-and-knuckle-headed knout; they include the excessively knobbly *knupel*, the gabelüng ("fork in the road") with its two-pronged head, the stang (or quarterstaff), and the over-long prugel-staff. Cudgels are normally preferred over swords because heavy, blunt blows do more harm through *proofing* than the cut or stab of a blade. They also serve well as walking sticks.

cudgel-master person who has won the right to bear a *knupel*, and so is deemed skilled enough to teach others.

culix said "cyoo-licks"; blow with the butt end of a *cudgel* or stick: one of the many moves that are a part of the *Hundred Rules of Harundo*.

curtain wall surrounding walls of a city, so called because they go straight up and down like a curtain. This makes them vulnerable to cannon-fire but provides an impenetrable barrier to adventurous bogles. Curtain walls built in the last few hundred years, however, may have a sloping outer face called a scarp, to help deflect shot from *cannon*. Each city will have several rings of curtain walls, a new line built as the population expands beyond the previous ring. The older the city the more encircling curtain walls it will possess.

D

Dank day-watchman of the *Harefoot Dig*, having charge over protecting the *wayhouse*, its guests, owners and employees against attack from *brigands* and highwaymen and, most importantly, *monsters*. He hands over his responsibility to *Teagarden* when the evening watch begins.

dark trades, the ~ clandestine trafficking of illegal goods, but most particularly corpses of people, body parts of man and *monster* and whole *monsters*, dead or alive. It is exceedingly dangerous for those involved, from the *corsers* and trappers, the *ashmongers* in the middle to the various secret clients, yet the demand for the products of the dark trades is the highest it has ever been and the money to be had makes the dangers endured entirely worthwhile.

day-clothes also schmutter; any garment not proofed.

days of the week the first is Newich – the "new watch", then Loonday – the "moon's day", Mareday – the "sea's day", Midwich – the "middle watch", Domesday – the "family's day", which is a day of rest, followed by Calumday – the "sky's day", and finally Solemnday – the last day of the week, when people stop work two hours earlier to go home and celebrate the closing of another successful seven days. See *months of the year* and Appendix 1.

Dido ancient Empress and founder of the *Empire* of the *Half-Continent*, from whose line was reckoned the Emperors until the Haacobins usurped the Three Thrones. Great-granddaughter of the legendary Idaho of the Attics, she was betrayed by her ministers and fled to save her life, gathering about her other remnant races from the fall of the Phlegms to begin the *Empire* in which this book takes place. The Didodumese are her scattered descendants, and most *peers* – especially the Antique Sanguines (see *social status*) – claim some link to her and so to her glorious great-grandmother.

Dig, the ~ nickname used by locals for the *Harefoot Dig*.

dispensurist(s) said "diss-pens-yoo-rist"; "lesser" kind of *skold*, concerned only with *potives* and *draughts* that help and heal. Six months at a *rhombus* and two years as an *apprentice* dispenser under a fully qualified dispensurist will get you your licence to practise. Dispensurists are liked and trusted, even more than *skolds*. They are also considered to be *habilists*.

ditchlands as far as men reckon it, the world is divided into five distinct regions or *marches*. Ditchlands are "frontier territory", the fourth-most region or *march* and the outermost domain of man, just before the *wilds* (where everymen seldom go and never dwell). Ditchlands are the "front line" of humankind's push to civilise the whole world. In ditchlands populations are small and live very close for mutual strength, always behind walls, with windows permanently barred and doors kept locked even at the height of day. Chimneys here are built highest of all. No one goes anywhere without wearing *proofing*, even indoors during the day. Everyone keeps stores of *potives* supplied by *skolds* and carry some on all excursions out of doors. Many ditchland communities are supported by a sturdy military presence of either *pediteers* (soldiers) or *lamplighters* or both. Small fortresses built along the main road in the region typically form the hub of a settlement and are the last places of refuge in event of some major attack by *monsters*. See *marches*.

dolatramentist(um) said "doll-la-truh-men-tiss(tum)"; any mark made on the skin to show one's skills and heroic feats, either *spoors* or *monster-blood tattoos*.

Domesday said "doams-day"; fifth day of the week and typically a day of rest. See *days of the week*.

draught(s) • any concoction meant to be taken and have effect by swallowing, as opposed to *potives*, which work externally. See *scripts*. • the depth to which the hull and keel of a boat or ship descends into the water. A vessel with a shallow draught can negotiate shallow waters.

drudge the smallest of the ocean-going *gastriners*, employed to tug and tow other larger vessels about the crowd of a harbour. Some are armed with *cannon* and work to guard their port. These are called *gun-drudges*. See *rams*.

E

eekers folk who, because of poverty or persecution or in protest, live in wild or marginal places, often alone and scrounging what life they can from the surrounding land. Many eekers are political exiles, sent away from, or choosing to leave, their home city because of some conflict with a personage of power. It is often marvelled upon by other folk just how it is that eekers survive in the *haunted* places where they are forced to live. It is commonly held that most have sedorned themselves, that is, become despicable *sedorners,* so that the *monsters* will leave them be. They are already mistrusted and despised for their eccentric ways, and such a suspicion only makes them doubly so.

Elements, the ~ the basis of the four-part system of understanding used by *skolds, physicians* and other *habilists*. Simply put, the elements are earth, air, fire and water and have many accompanying corollaries. See the *Four Humours*, the *Four Spheres,* the *Körnchenflecter*.

Emperor the supreme ruler of an Empire, in this context the *Empire* of the *Half-Continent*; the original line of Emperors was descended from Dido, the founder of the *Empire* and great-granddaughter of Idaho, the mythic hero-queen of the Attics. The current Emperor is Scepticus XLV Haacobin Menangës, who is working to reconcile the Didodumese and their supporters to his dynasty's claim.

Emperor's Billion, the ~ name given to the shiny gold *oscadril* coin given to any person as an incentive to enter the Emperor's Service and become an *Emperor's Man*. This type of payment is called "coat and conduct" money, promised to anyone who wishes to join up, whether to serve the Emperor, or some realm's *navy*, or even a mercenary regiment. From this coat and conduct money new recruits are meant to pay for their travel to their new job and for parts of their kit when they get there. A billion is any coin that is the largest denomination of a realm's currency (for example, the *sou* is the billion of *Soutland* money). See *money*.

Emperor's Highroads, the ~ see *conduits*.

Emperor's Man, an ~ any person working for the *Empire* and therefore the *Emperor*. *Lamplighters* are Emperor's men because they are employed by the *Empire* to watch the *Emperor's Highroads*.

Empire, the ~ also called the *Haacobin* Empire, the Old Empire, the Benevenetian Empire, or the Empire of the City-states. When the Sceptic Dynasty (said "sep-tik") ruled, it had been called the Sceptic Empire. The imperial domains of the current *Haacobin Dynasty* are divided into three parts (pars regia magna). In the north is the Seat, where *Clementine* the Imperial Capital is, and includes the western lands of the Stipula, the agricultural lands of the Leven, and the Table, which extends right along the southern wall of the *Marrow*. In the east is the Verid Litus made of the old inheritance of the Orprimine on the coast, and the mining lands of the Sink beneath. In the south is the *Soutlands* extending from Catalain and the western edge of the *Ichormeer*, across to *Hergoatenbosch* and Thisterland, and down along *the Grume*, the Patricine and the Lent, reaching as far inland as Maine and ending at the northern edge of the wildlands known as Dusthumlinde (the Dusthumës). These lands are divided up into *city-states*, the boundaries of each being fixed in the Henoticon – the Formula of the Division of the Land drawn up in *HIR* 1011 by Empress Quintinia Excrutia Scepticus. Heavily amended, the document still stands as the legal blueprint of borders and border rights and is constantly invoked as states wrestle with each other for mutually coveted lands and their resources. The original Henoticon is kept in the subterranean vaults of the Quintessentum (the Imperial Archive in *Clementine*). Control is maintained through its sprawling conquests with the aid of the sub-capitals: cities of grandeur built by the *Haacobins* to keep an eye on their restive subjects so far from the friendly gaze of *Clementine* itself. In the Soutlands are the sub-capitals of the Considine and the Serenine. On the Verid Litus is the Campaline. They are gorgeous places and an essential part of the "Grand Tour", attracting tourists from all the lands.

enrica d'ama   said "enn-ree-kah dar-mah" or "enn-ree-ka deh-arm-ah", lady of the house; chatelaine, woman in charge of the running of a home, *wayhouse*, hostelry or even a palace, with authority over all the servants and even any guards; not necessarily the owner of the home, *wayhouse*, hostelry or palace.

equiteer   said "eh-kwit-tear"; another name for a cavalryman. Horses are not used in great numbers outside of cities because *monsters* tend to find them the most tasty of the beast of burden. Consequently the use of cavalry is limited. If one is to move a squadron of equiteers about the country one has to be prepared to defend them against curiously hungry *monsters* thinking with their bellies.

equiteer boots   footwear typically worn by equiteers, made of *bright-blacked* leather and reaching to the knees. At the top of the boot, coming from the outer side, is a flaring panel of *proofed* leather called a shin-collar. This protects the knee, especially when bent as the *equiteer* sits in the saddle. Equiteer boots also have raised heels anywhere from 1 inch to 2½ inches high, which hook on to the stirrup and so provide a better seat in the saddle.

ettin among the largest of the land-living *monsters*, looking like enormous deformed men (as much as 50 feet tall); strong of limb but not hard to hurt or even slay despite their size. They are not very bright; indeed, many are quite simple to outwit. When they are in a rage, however, they can do great harm, and gangs of them marauding for food in the winter months can be terrible.

Europe, Miss ~ experienced and well-known *fulgar*, who encountered *lahzars* in her childhood and was instantly fascinated. This fascination turned to obsession and she ran away from home, travelling secretly to *Sinster* to be transmogrified by the best *surgeon* available. Since then she has been all over the world, conquering *monsters* and men's hearts wherever she landed. As *Rossamünd* noticed, the inside of her forearms are lined with tiny X's, *cruorpunxis* showing her many-score kills. They are dainty little marks, showing Europe's distaste for the vulgar, leering faces that are by far more common, their "prettiness" belying the violence and mayhem done to earn them. See *fulgar, lahzar,* the *Branden Rose*.

evander, evander water *restorative* draught that fortifies the body's capacity to fight disease, infection or poisoning while also giving a lift in spirits.

everymen everyday people; not *monsters*, which are called üntermen. This includes *skolds*, *sagaars*, *leers* but excludes those who have tampered with their biology in any way, that is *lahzars,* who are known as ubelmen.

excise master, excise sergeant those working to collect the tolls and taxes lawfully demanded by their lord. See *revenue officers*.

explicarium spurious list of invented or obscure words drafted to apparently make some fabulous, fabricated tale more palatable.

F

factotum personal servant and clerk of a *peer* or other person of rank or circumstance. *Lahzars* have taken to employing a factotum to take care of the boring day-to-day trifles: picking up contracts, collecting fees for services rendered, looking to food and accommodation, writing correspondence, heavy lifting and even making their draughts. When on the road and looking for a place to kip for the night, a master/mistress and his or her factotum may find that restrictions of accommodation or finances mean that only one gets a room (and, consequently, a bed). The factotum must make do, and will usually share floor and bench space with other servants next to a kitchen or common room stove. Such arrangements are typical for most servants.

false-gods mighty *monsters* standing several hundred feet high who appear only every thousand years or more and are meant to live deep, deep down at the bottom of the *vinegar seas*. They are reputed to be able to control people's minds, and each one has secret septs and cabals among *everymen*, who worship and revere them and seek with ancient sciences to raise them up from the deeps. The *Emperor* and his regents have special agents whose sole task is to root out and destroy these septs and cabals, for whenever a false-god has risen from the depths it has meant doom for civilisation, and history has taught that only the *urchins* and their kind can drive them back into the sea ... and it has been a long time since anyone had anything to do with an *urchin*.

falseman, falsemen also called liedermen; *leers* who can tell a person's true emotional state, and so, most usefully, can determine whether or not that person is being truthful. The washes they use to change their eyes make the whites turn bloody red and the irises go a bright pale blue. See *leer*.

family-name also famillinom; the name of your sires that you are born into, the name of your whole family. Among *peers* this is the most important name, for it declares one's pedigree. "*Bookchild*" is often given to orphans and foundlings as a kind of surrogate family-name, but really it is a *forename*.

Farmer Rabbitt happy tiller of the soil and herder of cows who has a smallholding on the edge of the *Brindleshaw* folklands (land set aside for common use) near *Silvernook*. He often goes into that town to trade and re-supply his rather remote farm. His wife Judy is even merrier than he, and they make a jolly couple indeed.

Faustus   the red-star and actually a distant planet that nightly moves through the constellation of Vespasio and follows green *Maudlin* across the sky – who, as legend has it, is his lover – forever chasing and never catching. Faustus is regarded as the *Signal Star* of frustrated or jilted lovers and of lost causes.

Felicitine, Madam   one of the region's minor gentry, and wife to Mister *Billetus*, proprietor of the *Harefoot Dig*. She married young and below her station, and is well aware of it. Painfully alert to the commonness of her surroundings, she works hard against *Billetus'* more relaxed attitude to keep the tone of *the Dig* one befitting a lady. She seldom enters the common room, allowing it to remain as a concession to "Mister Bill's worldly ways". Despite all this snobbery and friction, and after over twenty years of marriage, she and Mister *Billetus* are still very much in love.

fiasco   small case or box or compartmental bag in which a woman might keep her cosmetic unctions, beautifying creams and other such applications; sometimes also called a clutch bag.

Fiel, Fiele   said "feel" or "fee-ell"; a land so far over the oceans from the *Half-Continent* it is considered a myth. The few reports that exist of it say it is filled with even more fabulous and terrifying creatures than dwell in the *Half-Continent*.

firelock   any flintlock small arm, such as a musket or pistol. See *flintlock musket* and *flintlock pistol*.

firstname   the very first name a person is given, nominated at birth, the name by which a person is most commonly known and called.

flintlock musket   or just musket or *firelock*; a long-barrelled muzzle-loading firearm that fires a round bullet of lead about ¾ inch in diameter called a ball. You can hit what you are aiming at with a musket as long as it is no more than 150 yards from you, though the ball will still travel with ever-diminishing force for about 600 yards. After every shot the musket must be reloaded. The flintlock mechanism that makes this and other such weapons work is a hammer held by a spring, holding a piece of flint. When the hammer is released by pulling the trigger, it flies forward and the flint strikes an upright piece of steel known as the frizzen, which is thrown back exposing the pan full of fine-grained priming powder beneath it. The flint causes sparks to fly off the steel frizzen and into the pan, catching the powder alight and sending the flash through a small hole in the side of the barrel called a touch-hole. This flash ignites the gunpowder packed in the barrel itself, which blasts out the ball. When a flintlock is fired, there is a distinctive two-part flash as first the pan flares and then the barrel itself. The very quick have a chance to dodge the shot when they first see the flash in the pan. If the tales are to be believed, some *monsters* have also realised this.

flintlock pistol a small arm with the same flintlock mechanism as the *flintlock musket*; often lavishly crafted, with the butt of the handle typically formed into a club so that, after the weapon has been fired, it can be gripped by the barrel (reinforced for such use) and swung about like a truncheon. An innovation for both the pistol and the musket has been the "*skold*-shot": ball treated in certain deadly *scripts* that make them far more harmful to a *monster* than a normal bullet, which rarely does any real or permanent harm. The only problem with *skold*-shot is that its chemicals slowly react with the inside of the weapon's barrel, wearing it out far more quickly than conventional ammunition. This increases the chance of the weapon bursting, or blowing a hole in its side just when you least expect. The pistoleer is a type of adventurer who specialises in using flintlock pistols; these are dashing fellows with a taste for glamour and high excitement. Armed with *skold*-shot they even have some effect as *monster-hunters*, although they have to earn well, as they need frequently to buy new pistols, worth about 21 *sequins* each.

florin coin money; a 10 *guise* piece or ½ *sequin*.

fo'c'sle or forecastle; forwardmost section of the upper deck of a *ram*, between the fore mast and the bow. Given that the decks of a *ram* are flush (that is, flat) the correct term for this part of the vessel is the forward deck. In the vernacular of the *vinegaroon,* however, the old term remains.

folding money bills of paper obtained from a bank or local ruler, where the equivalent value is purchased in coin and written upon the bill; lighter and more convenient than coins, they are also a whole lot more fragile.

forename name a person takes on or is given or granted in later life. Nobility and the pretentious will give their children a forename as well as a *firstname* when they are born, to show how special and important they are.

foundling(s) also wastrel; stray people, usually children, found without a home or shelter on the streets of cities or even, amazingly, wandering exposed in *the wilds*. The usual destinations for such foundling children are workhouses, mills or the mines, although a fortunate few may find their way to a foundlingery. Such a place can care for a small number of foundlings and wastrels, fitting them for a more productive life and sparing them the agonies of hard labour.

Fouracres hardy Imperial postman who has been on many adventures while delivering the mail and survived many an encounter with a *monster*. Sometimes called Fourfields, as a play on the word "acres", he has also given the name "Quarterfields" as an alias when this has been necessary. Fouracres has worked in the Empire's service as an ambler (a walking postman) for 16 years. See *Imperial Post Office*.

Four Humours, the ~ these are considered the basic parts of a properly functioning *pith* (metabolism). Each is also paired with a season of the year and corresponds to the other four-part systems of understanding the universe. There is blood, of course, also called sange and represented by the letter A and paired with summer; then phlegm, represented by the letter W and paired with winter; followed by yellow bile, also called choler and represented by the letter M and paired with spring; and finally black bile, also called melanchole, represented by the letter O and paired with autumn.

Four Spheres, the ~ the first and innermost sphere is a person's soul, his or her internal being. The second sphere is a person's body. The third sphere is the world. The fourth sphere is the cosmos. Teaching on the Four Spheres also coincides with the *Four Humours* and the elements as shown in the *Körnchenflecter*:

♦ soul = phlegm = water (W)

♦ body = melanchole (black bile) = earth (O)

♦ the world = choler (yellow bile) = air (M)

♦ the cosmos = sange (blood) = fire (A).

Skolds learn these along with all the other four-parts, so as to gain insight into the functioning of the systems about them and how to interact and alter them through their chemistry.

Fox Hole, the ~ also Voxholte, *Hergott* for "foxhole", said "voks-halt"; elegant and refined hostelry in *High Vesting* famous for its height (7 floors!) and the size and opulence of its rooms. The exceedingly wealthy or famous like to stay there.

Fransitart, Dormitory Master ~ born of unknown parents, Fransitart lived with his little brother as a wastrel on the streets of *Ives*. The day after his brother died in his arms, Fransitart was hunted and taken by a press gang, and put aboard the main-ram *Adroit* as a ship's boy. There he met *Craumpalin*, who defended and befriended him, and they have remained true friends and brothers-in-arms since. How it is that Fransitart and *Craumpalin* have come to be serving in a state entirely different from the ones in which they were born is a story entirely all its own. Fransitart's affection for *Rossamünd* has a lot to do with his grief over his younger brother.

Freckle *glamgorn bogle*; small, tough and friendly-seeming.

Frestonia a small collection of *Soutland* states, the chief among these being the *city-state* of Frestony. They have formed their loose confederation in answer to the rising power of the inland states of Castoria, Pollux, Maine, Axis, Isidore and Haquetaine.

frigate smallest of the dedicated fighting rams and the middle of the three rates of cruisers, usually of 20 or 24 *guns-broad*, with only *gun-drudges* being smaller. Nimble and fast, they are considered the "eyes of the fleet", running messages and performing reconnaissance. Despite being the smallest *rams*, the largest frigate can be almost as long as a *drag-mauler*. These oversized frigates are called heavy-frigates, having up to 32 guns on one broadside. They are popular among pirates and privateers. See Appendix 6.

frock coat coat normally worn by men with a long hem reaching the knees and often flaring out jauntily. With more and more women seeking adventure it has become fashionable for them to wear frock coats too, often more gorgeously decorated and trimmed, the hems flaring even more extravagantly than the male version. Frock coats for either sex are almost always *proofed*.

fulgar(s) said "fool-garr", also astrapecrith ("lightning-holder"); a *lahzar* whose surgically inserted organs (known as the systemis astraphecum) allow him or her to make, store and release immense charges of electricity. Fulgars have several tricks up their sleeves, which together are known as eclatics. These include:

♦ arcing – the most basic skill: simply generating a charge of electricity and releasing it by touching the target. Indeed, a fulgar has to make physical contact to have any effect, for the electricity must be earthed to do its work.

♦ resisting – which can be used in combination with arcing, where a fulgar makes little charges between thumb and forefinger, or hand on thigh, or hand to hand, storing the arcs for a bigger "zap". In this way the fulgar's whole body can become charged with electricity, and anyone grabbing it would get the full force of the shock.

♦ impelling – a bizarre potency that requires experience and talent to master, whereby fulgars take hold of people and make them move or not move as the fulgar sees fit. It is done by subtle manipulations of a continuous charge running through the victim and requires a lot of energy to perform. The best results are achieved when the fulgar has a firm grip on his or her foe.

♦ *thermistoring* – another potency requiring skill and wisdom, it involves bringing lightning bolts down from the sky. This is the only potency that does not need touch to have effect, for the fulgar acts as a channel for the bolt, directing its blast to targets even 100 yards away. The better a fulgar gets at *thermistoring* the greater control he or she has over the bolt's final direction. Along with this is also a little trick called terading or "grounding", where they let some of the charge of the lightning earth itself through one arm while letting the rest of the charge out or storing it in the organs. Grounding greatly reduces the chance of a thermistoring fulgar being blown asunder by the bolt.

♦ vacillating – a nifty little eclatic whereby fulgars send a mild arc through themselves to protect from the potencies of a *wit*. It is a variation on resisting but without storing the charge. The harder a *wit* tries, the stronger the fulgar needs to make the arc. Vacillating also helps fend off some of the terrors of *threwd*, although its efficacy is limited and diminishes as *threwd* becomes stronger.

Fulgars get their name from the artificial organ known as the Column of Fulgis, a jelly-like muscle that produces the electrical charges they wield. Most fulgars mark themselves with the *spoor* of a diamond, which is the universally recognised sign of their kind. See *fuse* and related topics, *lahzar* and *thermistoring*.

fulgaris said "fool-gar-riss"; two poles of differing lengths used by *fulgars* to extend their reach and give a *thermistor* control over bolts of lightning. The longer pole is the *fuse*, the shorter being the *stage*. Both fulgaris are wound tightly with copper or iron fulgurite wire and capped at each end with ferrules of the same metals.

Fundarum non Obliviscum motto of *Madam Opera's Estimable Marine Society for Foundling Boys and Girls,* writ large across the top of the main entrance; a *Tutin* phrase which means "found [but] not forgotten". Very touching.

fuse 6- to 9-foot pole of cane or wand-wood, tightly coiled along its entire length with copper wire and capped with copper, brass or iron fulgurite; the longer of the two *fulgaris*, the shorter being called the *stage*. A fuse extends the reach of fulgars, allowing them to deliver their deadly jolts while staying out of reach themselves. The second, and more bizarre, use for them is an aid in *thermistoring* – the calling down of lightning bolts from on high. This can normally be done only on overcast days, as clear weather does not provide the necessary conditions for the generation of lightning. The *fulgar* sets an arc in the fuse to "call down a bolt from the grey", that is, to encourage a lightning strike. When the bolt hits it travels down the fuse and into the *fulgar* and is either stored within (but only very temporarily, for risk of bursting asunder) or redirected through the hand or the *stage*, which gives greater control in determining the final direction of the *levin-bolt*. Fulgars who *thermistor* often do it at great risk to themselves, and are often called *thermistors* or thunderers. See *fulgar, fulgaris, lahzar, stage, thermistor.*

G

Gainway, the ~ very old road and the main way between *Winstermill* and *High Vesting*. It continues further north beyond *Winstermill*, heading far into *Sulk* and eventually finding its way to *Proud Sulking*. These days the southern stretch of the Gainway is often considered a part of the *Wormway*. As the Gainway approaches *High Vesting* it becomes a beautiful broad avenue lined with tall ancient oaks and a marvel of the region in autumn, when people might travel just to see the red and golden glory.

Gallows Night traditional night for many executions by hanging, prisoners being kept specially for then. A great public spectacle, it is not to the taste of some.

gander term for a *guise*, the smallest denomination of money in the *Soutlands*, and used mostly in *Brandenbrass* and its neighbouring areas. A play on words: *guise* sounds just like "geese": gander is a male goose.

gastrine(s) engines that turn the *screws* (propellers) of *rams* and other vessels. A gastrine is a big box of wood bound with metal, inside of which great muscle-like organs (called gastorids) have been grown about a metal section of treadle-shaft (what we would call a "camshaft") or shaft-section within the box. On the organ deck of a vessel these boxes are put in a row, their shaft-sections connected by great pins, making a whole treadle-shaft that runs the length of the vessel. Each line of gastrines (know as a "gastrine pull" or just a "pull", which includes its accompanying *limbers*) is attached to a set of gears and great levers called a dog-box, which allows the *gastrineer* to determine the level of power of each pull and where it is used: all on one *screw* or two screws, or even three for the biggest *rams* and *cargoes*. The muscles of a gastrine are made by learned people known as viscautorists ("gut-growers") especially for this purpose. They are raised inside each gastrine box from basic living matter, like a kind of senseless animal. Inside the box are many wooden protrusions called bones, on to which the muscles fix as anchor- and leverage-points. Once a gastrine is "fully grown" the muscles inside and the whole box itself are one complete organ. To open the box is tantamount to surgery. In this fully grown state the gastrine is taken from the test-mills ("laboratory-factories") to the dockyards to be lowered into the bowels of the receiving vessel. There its shaft-section is fixed to those of the gastrines on either side as each is integrated into the pull. When stimulated by their *limbers* the gastrines' muscles begin to move, gaining momentum until they work on their own to push and pull at the treadle-shaft, which turns the gears, which turn the screw and so moves the ship. Like ships themselves gastrines are often referred to as "her" and "she". Through special chutes and hatches a gastrine is fed a series of "meals" each day, comprising a nutritious, lumpy soup called pabulum. Beneath the pull is a sluice-way that allows the waste expelled from the gastrines by discrete pipes to wash down the middle of the vessel into the bilge to be pumped out into the sea. With all this pabulum soup and waste sloshing about, the organ deck can smell almost like a butcher's shop. Nadderers (sea-monsters) love the taste of gastrines and are attracted by the slick of grime and effluent that trails in the wake of a gastrine-run vessel. A large part of a vessel's crew is devoted to the care of the gastrines, their *limbers* and the pull they are a part of. In fact gastrines and the rest have precedence over the men serving them, being fed first and cared for first; without your gastrines the crew quickly becomes irrelevant. In the course of its working life a gastrine might die from disease, old age or from damage sustained in a fight or a storm. Sometimes when this happens, the gastrine seizes up, interfering or even stopping the movement of the *screw*. This is known as clearing, and when it occurs the *gastrineer's* mates grab great axes hanging from the walls, chop into the side or top of the gastrine box and, up to their armpits in *ichor*, hack the stiffened muscles away from their part of the treadle-shaft to allow free movement of the *screw* again. As you would expect, this is to the ruin of the gastrine itself, which must be replaced as soon as possible. It is best to replace all the gastrines of a pull at once, but this is expensive both in money and time; it is far more usual for single gastrines to be replaced as needed. When this happens the remaining gastrines behave sluggishly for a while. Some say it is because they are mourning the loss of a fellow. Others say this is daft. The longest a gastrine will live is about twenty years, if its life is easy and its work even and steady – like a *cromster* on the river *Humour*. A gastrine working in the pull of a vessel like a drag-mauler – speeding up, slowing down, stopping abruptly as something is rammed, enduring mountainous seas, taking shocks as the vessel is hit by *cannon* balls or assaulted by sea-monster*s* – such a gas-trine will survive only about five years before needing to be replaced. There is almost no sound made by a working gastrine, more a silent *pound-pound-pound* that throbs right through a person's body. When a gastrine vessel such as a *ram* passes you by, all you will hear is the hiss of the water parted by the bow and running down either broadside, and feel a faint throbbing in the air about. Just as a vessel under the power of sails is said to be "sailing", so a vessel under the power of gastrines is said to be "treading", the past tense being "trod". When a vessel is at anchor it will usually have its gastrines treading over slowly without the *screw* being engaged, keeping them ready for a quick start if a threat or startling news makes it necessary. See *gastrineer* and *limbers*.

gastrineer petty officer on a vessel, of the same rank as a *boatswain* and in charge of the healthy running of the *gastrines* and *limbers*. On large vessels the gastrineer will have a sizeable crew under his command, the most senior of these being the gastrineer's mates, all working to make sure the *gastrines* are fed, healthy and working well. Even a half decent gastrineer will be well aware of the strange quirks of his *gastrines*, even naming them, knowing for example that No 3 is sluggish on extremely cold days, that "Lillith" (No 6) is inclined to work too hard, making Nos 5 and 7 lazy, and so on. He passes this knowledge on to his mates so that they might learn the ways of a *gastrine* pull and go on to serve their own vessels. A gastrineer earns about 50 to 70 sous a year, not including *prize-money*.

gastriner any vessel powered by *gastrines*.

gater or gatekeeper; person who guards and watches a gate, allowing or refusing people thoroughfare.

Gates, Battle of the ~ considered the great battle of the current age, fought in *HIR*1395 (the last year of the Sceptic Dynasty) between the armies of the *Empire*, the Soutland City-states and the *Turkemen*. The battle forms part of a time known as the Dissolutia, where one dynasty fell and another rose to take its place. At the time the southern city-states, known as the *Soutlands*, had gained such power and relative independence that they formed a league, the Stately League, to petition the *Emperor*, Moribund Scepticus III, for greater say in the running of the *Empire*. This petition was denied and consequently the Stately

League or Leaguesmen determined to gather a grande *army*, march the dangerous miles north and force a "yes" from the old stinker. Moribund Scepticus III caught wind of this and knew his own *army* of 80,000, though tough and experienced, was no match for the League's *army* of several hundred thousand citizen-soldiers and mercenaries. So, as the *peers* and marshals and soldiers of the Stately League started on their great enterprise, the Sceptic *Emperor* called for help from the only source of sufficient strength, his great rival the Püshtän, the Lord of the Omdür and *Emperor* of the *Turkemen*. The *Turkeman Emperor* eagerly took the chance to aid his anxious cousin and rapidly mobilised a grande *army* of his own, conveniently camped on the northern border of the wildlands dividing the two powers. This duly arrived, ahead of the Leaguesarmy – as the Stately League forces were being called. With gratitude and rejoicing the terrified people of *Clementine* lowered the gates of the great bridges that guard the crossings of the *Marrow*, the mighty drain that protects the northern borders of the *Empire*, and let the *Turkemen* across. It was a great day for the Püshtän, for no Turkeman *army* had ever won across the *Marrow*, and now they were being invited like so many guests. No sooner had his soldiers completed the day-long crossing of the bridges (such was the size of his *army*) than they immediately stormed the outer walls and districts of *Clementine* and put the middle and inner city under siege. The battle raged all night in the suburbs and along the walls as *Turkemen* infantry and their horrifying bolbogis, giant monsters bred for war, wrestled from street to desperate street with the Empire's elite regiments. Moribund Scepticus III had been betrayed. Heralds were sent by the dozen to the approaching Leaguesarmy, though only three made it through alive to tell them of the Emperor's distress and the threat of defeat by the hated *Turkemen*. What had begun as an expedition of conquest had now become a quest of salvation, not just of the *Imperial Capital* but of all the Stately League held to be distinctly their own. Without rest the Leaguesarmy night-marched the final miles. By the dour, grey afternoon of the next day they were deploying their first battalions for assault upon the rear of the *Turkemen* force. With *Clementine* skilfully invested, the confident marshals of the Püshtän turned their attention to defending themselves against the arrival of the Leaguesarmy. Moribund Scepticus III, his family and attendants watched from the highest minarets as the two

347

great armies faced each other across the field before Clementine's famous gates. Both he and the *Turkemen* marshals below were amazed at the size of the Leaguesarmy. Almost half a million soldiers of the proud *Soutlands* had arrived, and before their trailing columns had even arrived upon the field, the Leaguesman marshals began the attack. The massive artillery parks of the *Turkemen* roared, sending hundreds of Leaguesmen to an immediate end. The terrible bolbogis were sent forth bellowing, barely restrained by their panicking beast-handlers, musket ball and *cannon* shot of the Leaguesarmy stopping only a meagre few. Strutting proudly behind these *gudgeon* beasts came the *Turkeman* infantry – the heavy-armoured ghirkis and musket-wielding infantis. To meet them strode 200,000 *haubardiers* and *troubardiers*, hundreds of *skolds* and *scourges* and with them a company of lahzars, only recently arrived in society and used for the first time in war. Wherever the *Turkemen* bolbogis were left unchallenged by *scourge* or *lahzar* they prevailed, destroying whole battalions of their enemy. But where they met a knot of *scourges* or a lone *lahzar*, there they ultimately met their end. The *Emperor* watched in horrified wonder as the first deadly bolts of lightning stuck down, summoned by the *fulgars*, startling everyone but the *fulgars* themselves. And though the *scourge Haroldus* is credited as the great hero of the day, it was these newcomers, the *fulgars,* who most quickly bested the bolbogis, while the *wits* dismayed whole companies of *Turkemen* under the agony of their frission. When the two armies were fully engaged, the Emperor's survivors, who had remained quiet till then, stormed from sally ports with *Haroldus* at their head, besetting the besiegers and attacking the right flank of the Turkeman *army*. Surrounded, the hard-pressed *Turkemen* fought valiantly on. Their most mighty bolbogis, the *Slothog*, still stood and shattered 100 men with every blow. The Leaguesarmy line began to falter where the *Slothog* raged. The few lahzars that remained were not near enough to help, the rest all gone to their dooms and with them all the *scourges* and any *skold* who could make a stand. Even as the right and centre of the Leaguesarmy began to crush their enemy, the left was on the verge of crumbling. In the nick of time *Haroldus* and the *Clementine* elites struck home, rolling up the *Turkeman* right flank and driving them in on the centre in a rout. Though the legend has it that the "great *skold*" challenged the *Slothog* alone, he was in fact supported by the doughty battalions of both *Clementine* and the Stately League. There, after a grisly struggle, *Haroldus* sent the Slothog to its doom, losing his own life in the process. But the deed was done and with the death of the *Slothog,* the Leaguesmen pushed forward and the *Turkemen*, their last gambit played and ruined, ran headlong into the ravine of the *Marrow* or fled into the wildlands that surround the capital, and few ever made it back to their homes or the smiles of loved ones. The *Empire* had won – or had it? The original order of business had not been settled, the League had not had its demands heard. Their marshals conferred with their ministers and their peers and offered parley to the *Emperor* if he would just hear them out. Here now was an opportunity for Moribund Scepticus III to save himself and his own dynasty, to share some of his power and remain on the three thrones. For no matter what reformations the Stately League would force, the *Empire* would survive. But, with his remnant *army* looking to him to be still strong in the flush of first victory, while the Leaguesarmy seemed exhausted, at an end, Moribund became obstinate. He was not going to be some lapdog to the states, bending and twisting to their whims: he was the *Emperor* Supreme, as his sires had been before him. He ordered his troops to the attack, shut the gates and went to the baths in a glow of false security. With surprise in their favour the Emperor*'s army* prevailed for a time, but as they pushed the Leaguesmen back so they encountered a third of the Leaguesarmy's strength including 20 battalions of *troubardiers*, held in reserve. With a rataplan of drums and the cry of war these reserves pressed into the fight, the Imperial Army breaking against them like so many waves. With their force on the brink of annihilation, the Imperial marshals quickly capitulated and their entire weary *army* still 40,000 strong were taken captive. They did not stay captive for very long. The next day, and unknown to the *Emperor,* a delegation did arrive at the tents of the lords and marshals of the Stately League. In its number were many disaffected and jealous ministers and *peers* who, either fed up with the flaccid corruption of their incumbent master or wishing to rule for power's sake alone, had formed an uneasy alliance against their Imperial master. They received the complaints of their southern brothers and a compact was quickly made: if the Leaguesmen backed their cause and their candidate for a new dynasty, then their new *Emperor*, once safely installed, would make sure their needs were answered. Till all this was accomplished the southerners would remain as Clementine's and the new Emperor's guard. Thinking he was loved by all his subjects, convinced of the unfailing loyalty of his ministers, Moribund Scepticus III sat secure in his inner palace, confident of the impregnability of Clementine's ancient walls. Yet that very night, as the Leaguesmen upstarts were let tamely into the city, he was violently slain by agents of the new compact, and their chosen replacement, the conniving Menangës of the family *Haacobin*, thrust into his place. Moribund Scepticus III's sons and daughters, granddaughters and grandsons, brothers, sisters, nieces and nephews and distant cousins too were arrested, to be either slaughtered, imprisoned in the deepest dungeons and so forgotten, or sent into distant exile. Over 200 people suffered or died that night, each one of them of the same family line. So began the reign of the *Haacobin* Dynasty. So ended the line of the Sceptics.

gauld, gaulding chemicals and processes that make many different kinds of cloth and other organic materials highly resistant to tearing, cutting or puncturing – "bullet-proof" if you wish, yet not much heavier than the original fibre and still almost as flexible. Any garment like this is called *proofing* or, less commonly, gaulding or gauld-cloth. Each *gaulder* has his own secret recipe, inherited and vigilantly guarded, and, though some recipes are more effective than others, the end result is much the same: cloth, leather and such once soaked, boiled, baked, dried, re-soaked and so on in a series of solutions will by the end of the process be extraordinarily toughened. Combined with panels of multi-layered gauld-leather or plates of steel, and backed with *pokeweed* padding, *proofing* can keep the wearer very safe indeed. Another of the advantages of *gaulded* clothing is that it is incredibly hardwearing – even the cheaper kinds. Consequently, the uniforms of soldiers on campaign and *wayfarers* out on the road typically last for years rather than months. In fact it has become more common for those who can afford it to wear *proofing* more than *day-clothes*. While *proofing* will stop a sword thrust or a musket ball, it cannot, unfortunately, stop bruising or bones being broken beneath it as they take the shock of a blow, or internal ruptures from heavy hits to the chest or abdomen. This is why blunt and heavy weapons like cudgels are so popular. And all *gaulded* cloth will eventually wear out. Fibres being struck repeatedly begin to crush and tear till the *proofing* is useless. Damage like this appears

350

slightly darker and scuffed, and the cheaper the gaulding is, the quicker this "wearing out" in battle occurs. Small areas of light scuffing can be re-treated and "healed" by a *gaulder* who knows his business, but once the damage to your *proofing* goes beyond this, you know it will soon be time to replace your *harness*. *Gaulded* clothing that is new and in good repair is said to be "bright", a term left over from the days when metal armour was the norm.

gaulded   treated with the *gaulding* process.

gaulder   craftsperson who makes *gauld* and uses it to make *proofing*.

Gauldsman Five   one of the best *gaulders* in *Boschenberg*; he has been supplying high-quality *proofing* to most of the city's wealthiest *peers* and magnates for over four decades. With a good reputation comes high prices, though even Gauldsman Five's cheapest garments offer excellent protection for the *money*.

generalities   geography, general knowledge and common sense.

Germanicus, Mister   agent of *Winstermill Manse*, who is waiting for *Rossamünd* in *High Vesting* to take the boy on to his new masters. Mister Germanicus is a patient man, but even he has his limits.

Gibbon   *boatswain's* mate and *bargeman* aboard the *cromster Hogshead*; his big hope is to one day own his own vessel and press his crew to do his dastardly doings.

Gightland Queen, the ~   common name given to the Queen of Catalain, because much of that realm's lands are taken over by the swamp known as the Gight. She is the only "king" or "queen" allowed within the political structure of the *Empire*. No one remembers how this liberty was secured, and the records of it are kept utterly secret, yet every Emperor or Empress has allowed the title to remain while the best a regent of any other state can hope for is grand- or arch-duke or duchess. It is boasted that traditions maintained in the Gightland Queen's courts are a faithful continuation of the ancient rites of the Attics, the long-gone ancestors of the *Empire*.

glamgorn   or glammergorn; one of the smaller kind of *monster*, a true *bogle*; they come in all manner of shapes, pigmentation, hairiness; big eyes, little eyes; big ears, little ears; big body, little limbs; little body, big limbs; and all the variations in between. Often feisty and jittery, certain kinds can get downright nasty, the worst of them being known as blightlings. One of the bizarre idiosyncrasies of glamgorns is that they like to wear clothes, *everymen* clothes pinched from washing lines and unguarded trunks. There are rumours that, dressed like this, glamgorns – and worse yet blightlings – have been able to sneak into the cities of everymen to spy and cause mischief.

Gluepot, the ~ another name for the *Ichormeer*, an enormous swamp and fen on the western borders of *Wörms*, through which the *Conduit Vermis* runs – a very dangerous and *threwdish* place.

Gosling (Gosling Corvinius Arbour) *foundling* at *Madam Opera's Estimable Marine Society for Foundling Boys and Girls*. Being born of nobility, he truly thinks he is better than the common "plugs" he is forced to bunk with at the foundlingery. He is just biding his time until he is allowed to leave – not long now – and then he will show us all just how superior he is. Then we will all be sorry we ever thought we were even worthy of breathing the same air as he.

great-guns another name for *cannon*, especially those firing 24 pound shot and heavier. See *cannons*.

green-fire name for the electrical sparks and arcs made by a *fulgar*.

Gretel *bower-maid* at the *Harefoot Dig*, born in *Boschenberg* but now one of the live-in staff at *the Dig*. She is cheerful and chatty and has a "thing" for *Doctor Verhooverhoven*.

Grinnlings, the ~ name *Rossamünd* gives to the *nimbleschrewds* because of their broad, apparently wickedly grinning mouths. See *nimbleschrewds*.

Grintwoode, the ~ *Hergott* name for the *Brindlewood*.

Grume, the ~ said "groom"; the bay of milky olive water on which *High Vesting* and *Brandenbrass* have their ports and harbours.

grummet least skilled and lowest ranked ship's boy aboard a vessel; an offensive term when used against anyone of higher rank or standing. Because of their special instruction, children from a *marine society* are automatically of a higher rank than these when they arrive to serve on a vessel. To use this term of them is very insulting.

gudgeon said "gudd-je-onn" or "gud-jin", also made-monsters; any *monster* that has been made by men, by necrologists, black *habilists* and taxidermists out of parts of real *monsters*, people, inanimate objects and animals. Usually the most vicious of any creature. *Rever-men* are a type of gudgeon, as are bolbogis like the *Slothog*; it is also argued that *lahzars* are gudgeons too.

guildhalls   headquarters of the local arm of a guild. Guilds are tradesmen of a particular trade who once, many centuries ago, got together to make sure that the quality of their work was uniformly high, and that prices were always fair. They have grown to have significant monopolies, wrestling with mercantile corporations over markets, with *peers* over self-governance, and even with the *Emperor* over the running of the *Empire*. At their worst they fix prices, hold suppliers to ransom and in some cities force non-members out of their trade. At the same time they do well at protecting their own from exploitation.

guise   said "geez" or "gees"; coin of smallest value of the *Soutlands*, made of bronze. Worth one-three hundred and twentieth of a *sou* or one-twentieth of a *guise* or one-four hundred and eightieth of an *oscadril*. It is represented by the letter "**g**". See *money*.

Gull   friend and gormless stooge of *Weems*; foundling at *Madam Opera's Estimable Marine Society for Foundling Boys and Girls*.

gun-broad, guns-broad   a description of the number of cannon down just one *broadside* of a vessel of war.

gun-drudge   *drudge* fitted with a small battery of *cannon*. See *drudge*.

guns   the measure of a vessel's strength in *cannon*; the entire battery of *cannon* carried by a vessel.

H

Haacobin, Haacobin Dynasty   said "har-koh-bin"; the current family and court ruling the *Empire*. They overthrew the old Sceptic *Emperor* immediately after the *Battle of the Gates* and have ruled ever since.

Haacobin Empire   another name for the *Empire* in which *Rossamünd* is a citizen; so named for the current ruling dynasty, the Haacobins, who seized power in *Clementine* two centuries ago. Before them was the Sceptic (said "septic") Dynasty, which held power for half a millennium.

habilist(s) "clever people"; what the citizens of the *Half-Continent* think of as a "scientists", who study and are involved in one, some, or all of the pursuits of *habilistics*. Includes *dispensurists*, *skolds*, *scourges*, *physicians*, *surgeons*, viscautorists ("gut-growers", those who grow organs such as are required in *sthenicons* and *gastrines*, a process known as viscautory), even taxidermists. The darker students of *habilistics* are the black habilists or morbidists: the necrologists (those who raise corpses to life); the cadavarists (those who make monsters from parts, an illegal discipline called fabercadavery); the therospeusists (who grow *monsters* from living matter, an illegal art known as therospeusia (said "ther-ros-spew-zee-ah"); or the transmogrifers (*surgeons* who operate on people to make *lahzars*, a process known as transmogrification or clysmosurgia). Though these dark philosophies are illegal throughout the *Empire*, they are welcomed in other realms, such as *Wörms* or *Sinster* (yet their secret work continues unabated). Habilists are sometimes derogatively called cankourmen, for all their dabbling about with chemicals, and this term is often used to especially mean a black habilist.

habilistics or natural philosophy; "science" as the people of the *Half-Continent* understand it, involving the studies of how things work and perhaps even why they work. Mostly it involves lots of reading of ancient or even secret texts, dissections of corpses of men and *monsters*, making lots of potions (*scripts*), watching the stars wheel about the heavens, and searching for the most powerful chemical in the cosmos. Each domain of study is called a philosophy.

hair-tine ornamented "needle" of wood or cane used to hold hair in place; often lacquered and richly decorated at one end.

Half-Continent, the ~ also called the Haufarium, Sundergird or Westelünd; broad over-sized peninsula where, in one small part, this story takes place.

hanger or sometime sea-hanger; slightly curved military sword with a narrow yet heavy blade favoured by the navies of the *Half-Continent*; not to be confused with the infantry hanger, which is more typically called a *jacksword* and has a straight blade.

Harefoot Dig, the ~ "rabbit-footed" (as in "fast-footed") girl; *way-houses* such as this are typically given names taken from a locally famous event or person or object.

harness also called *barding*; another term for a set of *proofed* garments. The most basic is a *proofed weskit* and *jackcoat* or *frock* or platoon-coat, and as a set is called half-harness. After that comes threegauld or trebant, comprising a more solid, close-fitting garment called a haubardine that reaches the top of the thighs, from which hangs tassets or plates of proof-steel that cover the upper leg, over which is worn a well-*proofed* jackcoat or *frock coat*. The most complete harness is known as true or full harness or troubarding, and usually incorporates a haubardine with tassets and metal chest and even arm armour as well. Anything less than half-harness is known as dog-, jack-, or parlour-harness, a make-do of bits and strips of *gaulded* cloths, and is considered as useless as not wearing any *proofing* at all. See *proofing* and *gauld*.

Harold (Haroldus, the Great Skold) ~ actually a *scourge*, he is lauded as the hero of the *Battle of the Gates*, even though he died in that fight and was on the losing side. In the unsettled times that followed the battle, the new *Emperor* needed a hero to focus attention on positive things, and the greatest advantage that Harold presented was that he was not alive to argue or disappoint. Ah, such is propaganda. See the *Battle of the Gates*.

harundo a form of bastinado (or bastinade art) or fustigating, that is, stick-fighting or *cudgel*-play. There are other types of bastinado including a wild version called gyre and a graceful form from Tuscanin called fustigio. Harundo is popular because of its elementary yet effective moves. It is capable of taking on most other forms but lacks their distinctive or flamboyant strikes.

haubardier(s) said "haw-bard-ear"; foot-soldier or *pediteer* wearing threegauld *harness* of a haubardine with platoon-coat and tassets. On their heads they wear their telltale mitre, a tall tapering hat with a flat crown. Their main weapons are the musket with bayonet and a *jacksword*. Designated heavy infantry. See *pediteer* and *harness* and Appendix 2.

haunted frequented by *monsters*, home to nameless fears; infected with *threwd*.

Heddlebulk, Master of Ropes master and teacher at *Madam Opera's Estimable Marine Society for Foundling Boys and Girls*. As his title suggests, his main responsibility is to teach the knots, splices and rope-work required of little *vinegaroons* ready for service to their regent. He is an old *bargeman* who used to work the *Humour* aboard *cromsters* and *monitors* and on the piers.

Hergoatenbosch said "herr-goh-ten-bosh"; the vast protectorate lands of grain fields and pastures stretching west from the shores of the *Humour* and *Boschenberg*, and under the control of that city.

Hergott(s) race of people who live in *Boschenberg* and *Hergoatenbosch*. It is also another name for Bosch, the language they speak; though, as true children of the *Empire* they more commonly use Brandenard, the language of trade throughout the *Soutlands*.

Hermenèguild canal-side suburb of *Boschenberg*, crowded with merchants and their shops.

Hero of Clunes famous actress and singer who comes from *Clunes*, and whose reputation for beauty of face and voice are well deserved.

High Vesting originally a harbour guarded by a fortress with a score of *eekers* as neighbours. In the 150 years since its founding it has grown into a city of 100,000 souls. It was sited and built by *Brandenbrass* as a harbour exclusively for an expanding *navy*. After the *Battle of the Mole* the *rams* were moved closer to home, while many Boschenbergers began to settle behind its walls, using it as a welcome port of trade free from the strictures of the *Axles*. A power shift inside the city gave the more numerous Boschenbergers control of the city and immediately placed it under the protection of their old home. The Dukes of *Boschenberg* were only too happy to oblige. Though perfectly legal, this understandably infuriated the regent of *Brandenbrass* and his subjects, who built the *Spindle* in retaliation.

highroads also called *conductors*; major ways of traffic between cities. Imperial Highroads, or *conduits*, are those sponsored and maintained by the *Empire*, while ordinary highroads are tended by the states they travel through. Any one highroad will be in various states of repair along its path: anything from paved to bare earth that becomes a quagmire in the wet. The further a highroad travels from civilisation the worse its condition becomes. Some, like the Felicitine Way connecting *Clementine* with the *Soutlands*, almost disappear, becoming little more than a rutted footpath as it goes through the Grassmeer before emerging again in friendlier lands. See *conduits* and *conductors*.

HIR stands for "*Horno Imperia Regnum*" (this year of Imperial Sovereignty) and is a designation of years of the current age reckoned from around the time of the Empire's first establishment.

Hogshead, **the** ~ slow, run-down *cromster* of 6 *guns-broad*. See Appendix 7.

hogshead large barrel holding about 54 gallons. A normal barrel holds about 36 gallons.

Humour, the River ~ ancient waterway draining out of the swamps of the Gight in Catalain and running south to empty into *the Grume*. It is the main line of communication for great cities such as Catalain, Andover, *Boschenberg* and *Proud Sulking,* as well as many smaller towns and fishing villages. Once *threwdish* and *haunted* by all kinds of *monsters*, the Humour has been tamed by centuries of use by *everymen*, making it safer, although not *monster*-free. Sometimes also called the Humourous.

Hundred Rules (of Harundo), the ~ rules encompassing the movements and counter-movements of the bastinade (stick-fighting) art of *harundo*, as learnt by *Rossamünd* at the *marine society*. As a part of these Hundred Rules are the names given to each of the moves or positions. These include:
dexter – the right-hand side
sinister – the left-hand side
decede – step aside
regrade – step back
procede – step forward
pugnate – charge or rush
offend – strike out
counter-offend – counter strike
absist – defend to attack again
sustis – pure determined defence
machina – unbalancing strike to torso
turbus – high to low overhead strike
falacia or faust – a feint

iterictus – low, tripping strike
frausiter – leg strike
torque – "round-house" strike
ban – disarming strike
titubarus – unbalancing hip strike
capat – strike at the head
internunt – strike at the body
bracchiatus – strike at the arm
lacert – upper arm or shoulder strike
obtrector – quick follow-up attack
spinat – back or upper spine strike
posticum –buttocks or lower spine hit
radix – (illegal) strike to the groin
culix – hit with the handle-end
ventus – spinning strikes
intrudus – poking strikes
versus – flat strike, side to side
orto or ortus – upper cut, low to high

These can be employed in combinations including the obturamentum, a defensive routine with counter-strikes, or the flagellum, a series of quick strikes, and many others. To have even a basic facility with *harundo* you are expected to know every one of these names.

Hurlingstrat *Hergott* for "hireling street", where those looking to 'prentice themselves out to a master or those seeking an *apprentice* can go at certain times of the year to a public market held for the purpose. Found in the suburb of Bleekhall.

I

ichor any fluid of the consistency or colour of blood such as monster blood, or like a discharge of pus.

Ichor shortened, poetic form of *Ichormeer*.

Ichormeer, the ~ proper name for the vast swamp also known as the *Gluepot* or Sanguis Defluxia, taken from the vile, dark blood-like colour of the waters and bogs. It is said that parts of the Ichormeer are so *threwdish* that they can drive a person mad. With a great loss of life, the *Wormway* was cut through its southern reaches and the Ichorway joined to it in the hope of taming the swamp. These roads have done little, however, to curb the *threwd* or cow the *monsters* that make the Ichormeer their home. Full of festering bogs and farting ponds it is shunned now by men, and any who travel through it along the *Wormway* do so seldom, very quickly and under heavy escort.

Imperial Capital capital city of the whole *Empire*. See *Clementine*.

Imperial Post Office a rather excellent service provided by the *Emperor* and his bureaucracies; a mail-delivery service mostly done by coaches along *highroads* between cities and major rural centres. For places off the *highroads*, the *Emperor* kindly provides amblers – walking postmen who get into all the nooks where people sequester themselves. An ambler's life is dangerous; they are typically skilled at avoiding or protecting themselves against *monsters*. Frequent customers of *skolds*, amblers invent clever and slippery ways to make sure the post always gets through. Mortality rates are high among them, however, and the agents who employ them prefer orphans, strays and *foundlings* who will not be missed by fretting families. Your lowest ranked ambler can earn about 27 to 30 *sous* a year.

indexer mathematicians trained to keep large lists of numbers in their heads, and to have sharp memories that can be accessed in much the same way you or I might go through a filing cabinet.

Indolene said "inn-doh-leen"; fellow *gater* with *Teagarden*, guarding the *Harefoot Dig* during the bitter night. She is actually a *sagaar*, a combative dancer who has slain more than a handful of *monsters* in her time, several of them in the act of assaulting the *Dig*, as is proved by the *cruorpunxis* marked upon her arms. Indolene hails from a large *Soutland* state called Isidore.

Inkwill, Mister one of the registry clerks at *Winstermill*, recording in triplicate all documents and forms received by or sent from the *manse*. Inkwill is actually a *concometrist* who did his five years' training at the Pike Athenaeum in *Brandenbrass*. As concometrists and mathematicians are old rivals, Inkwill and *Witherscrawl* do not get on very well at all.

Instructor Barthomæus see *Barthomæus, Instructor*.

ironclad • *(adj.)* to be covered in riveted strakes (sheets) of cast iron thick enough to stop a *cannon* ball. A strake will stop any *cannon* shot, though it might buckle some under the blow of a 68 pounder. Repeated hammering from many hits can, however, weaken the great rivets holding the plates to the side to the vessel, eventually causing them to come away. The exposed wooden planks beneath, while sturdy enough to repel a few shots, become a weak point and a target. For *ram* captains who prefer a straight shootout, this is the goal of their tactics, to pound off an opponent's strakes and leave him vulnerable and ready to "strike his colours" (lower his flag and given in). • *(n.)* another name for *rams* or any other craft covered in iron sheet armour. These iron sheets are coated in a protective chemical known as braice, which makes the metal turn dark brown and stops the caustic waters of the *vinegar seas* from corroding it.

Ives one of the larger *city-states* of Frestonia and Fransitart's place of birth.

J

jackboot high boot reaching over the knee and having a flaring "collar" about the top, but being open behind the knee. They are usually made of *bright-black* leather.

jackcoat differs from a *frock coat* in that its frock is not as long and does not flare out as far. The materials used to make a jackcoat are cheaper or less fine. It is more a commoner's item of clothing.

jacksword or infantry *hanger*; straight single-edged sword with a short, heavy blade and heavy handle; as much good as a club or a sword, and favoured by soldiers.

jakes, the ~ latrine, loo or water-closet.

john-tallow repugnant *potive* kneaded into an oily clay whose main purpose is to smell so good to a *monster* that it draws it more than the scent of a person. Given that smell is one of the subtler senses of a *monster*, that they can tell the difference between *everymen* and their own kinds by smell, deluding them in this way is very effective but also very difficult. Used in conjunction with other odour-alterants, it can make for some powerful effects. See *scripts*.

Juice-of-Orange though we might take orange juice for granted, for the poor and rustic of the *Half-Continent* it is typically unheard of and a rare treat indeed. The growing of particular fruits can be a mildly difficult task, as orchards attract certain *monsters*. As such it makes the price of these fruits prohibitive for the less well-to-do.

K

knupel said "noo-pull", also called a virga; the most rough and knobbly of all the cudgels, it is often awarded to those who gain mastery of a bastinade (stick-fighting) art such as *harundo*. A knupel is about 4½ feet to 5 feet long, thick at the hitting end and thinner at the strap-bound handle. Regarded as a "battlefield" weapon, a knupel can cause horrendous injuries.

Körnchenflecter, the ~ said "kern-chen-flek-tr"; also called the Parts-wheel or Principia Circum: a table showing how the *Four Elements* react to or retard each other. From this is made a complex set of tables known simply as the Reactive Index, where all the *Sub-Elements* are shown in their reactions to each other. With it a *habilist* will plan combinations and experiments accordingly. The Körnchenflecter is valued not so much for the information it displays but as part of a skold's history, a treasured symbol of the trade. See Appendix 3.

kraulschwimmen said "krowl-shwim-men"; some of the biggest and most cantankerous of the nadderers (sea-monsters), usually resembling enormous, grotesquely deformed fish. Intelligent and cunning, they spend most of their time warring with the *false-gods* over control of the Deeps. Many also have a sweet tooth for *vinegaroons* and the muscles inside *gastrines* and will come to the surface to hunt for these along the cargo lanes of the world's oceans.

L

ladeboard left side of a ship if you are facing the front or bow, the side of a vessel usually put against a wharf or pier; corresponds to our "port".

laggard a *leer* who can see through things, into dark and hidden places, and look at things far off. The name comes from the word "lag", which means to scour or scrub something. The washes they use to change their eyes make the whites turn olive-brown while the irises become a deep yellow. See *leer*.

lahzar(s) sometimes spelled in old texts as "lazhar", said "luh-zar"; also called catharcriths, thanatocates ("death-bearers"), orgulars ("haughty ones" – the name once given to the heroes of old), spooks-and-pukes or just spooks. Though no one knows for sure, it is commonly held that lahzars first appeared in the *Empire* around *HIR* 1263, over a century before *the Battle of the Gates*. They were said to be among the survivors of a race of previously unknown peoples from far north-west beyond the *Half-Continent* who called themselves the Cathars. It was rumoured that these Cathars were fleeing the destruction of their realm by the rise of one or many *false-gods*. Settling in the far west beyond Hamlin and Pechenneg, and in the once small stronghold of *Sinster* in the east, these Cathar refugees brought with them their ancient surgical knowledge, techniques unknown in the *Half-Continent* except to a learned few. These techniques were called clysmosurgia and involved grafting into a person's body special organs – called mimetic organs – harvested from beasts, altered and grown in vats. Once put inside a person's body these mimetic organs could give the subject unheard-of abilities; the power to generate deadly arcs of electricity inside the body (the *fulgar*), or send forth brain-frying waves of invisible energy (the *wit*). Clysmosurgia was quickly rejected by the conservative as a form of "dark" or "black" *habilistics* (also called morbidology) and it was declared illegal throughout the *Empire*. Yet since their refuges were, and still are, beyond the Imperial jurisdiction, the Cathar *surgeons* continued their work. To put a person through clysmosurgia is called transmogrifica-tion, and a person so transmogrified is called a "lahzar", a Cathar word meaning "those who have returned (from the grave)", called so because of the long period they are under the surgeon's knife. One side-effect of having these imposter organs within them is a constant dull ache, occasionally sharp. For *wits* it manifests itself behind the eyes and in their skulls; for *fulgars* it hurts in their arms and shoulders and down in their guts. Even a lahzar's scars might ache on cold days. Another problem is gauntness caused by the overworking of their *pith* – what we would call "the metabolism" and "immune system", as their bodies strive to accommodate the intruding flesh; this can bring on mood swings and even psychotic episodes. Lahzars might be powerful, but they are far from happy folk. It took almost three-quarters of a century before people began to catch on to just how much more effective these new lahzars were against *monsters*. During that period lahzars were outlawed in Imperial lands. Their success at the *Battle of the Gates*, employed in disobedience to Imperial law, won them a grudging acceptance in society. Since then, while clysmosurgia remains an illegal realm of *habilistics*, lahzars themselves have been legitimised, their labours rivalling and even eclipsing the work of the traditional *skolds*. Because, however, lahzars have so many alien organs stuck into them it is still a topical parlour-room debate as to whether or not lahzars are actually a kind of *gudgeon*. This is an idea that lahzars find completely offensive and refute utterly. As a consequence of this question, their foul moods and strange draughts, lahzars are still considered pariahs, a necessary evil. Even with an expensive set of *proofing*, non-lahzars would find them extremely difficult to beat in a fight, and this has granted them a status that is not low but simply outside the existing social ranks. This unique status has made becoming a lahzar popular with the fashionably bored young sets of the gentry and the *peers*, and they spend large chests of their mama's and papa's *sous* to make the trip to *Sinster* and seek out the best transmogrifer they can afford. A *surgeon* of average skill will perform clysmosurgia for about 1,200 *sous*; the best will do it for about 3,000 *sous*. Payment can be made in advance, or over a period of time from the lahzar's earnings as a monster-slayer, soldier or bodyguard. After an initial period of interviews and testing a subject is either refused or allowed to proceed. A refused subject is free to seek another *surgeon*. If accepted it takes several days to complete the operations to make a person into a lahzar (transmogrify them). The whole time the subject is kept drugged and strapped to the cutting table. Once the transmogrification has been done, and the lahzar has been "made", it can take anywhere from one month to half a year for a person to recover. During this recovery they receive training from the surgeon's aides (called articles) in the ways of a *wit* or a *fulgar*. From time to time it is common for lahzars to return to their *surgeon* for observation and "repairs" – operations to mend damage caused by illness, organ rot, *spasming* or violent injury. These repairs require only a day or so under the knife and a fortnight at the most for healing afterwards. The "skills" or "abilities" or "powers" their organs give to a lahzar are called potencies (*sing.* potency). It is these potencies that make a lahzar so effective against *monsters* (and people, too, for that matter). The arcs and lightnings of a *fulgar* and the mental and sensory assaults of a *wit* are much more consistent in their deadly power and easier to deliver than a skold's or scourge's *potives*. Despite this lahzars are regarded less as civilisation's heroes and more as a distasteful new "fad". Obviously lahzars will charge for their services, commanding high prices for the efficacy of their labours:

> ... when a spook does set their hand to job,
> ye'll knows ye nickers be gone for good.

In a quiet year they can earn around 200 *sous*; in bumper years when *monsters* are overactive this can rise to 500 *sous*. See *fulgar*, *wit*, *Sinster* and *surgeon*.

lahzarine said "lazz-er-reen" also orgulous; of or pertaining to a *lahzar*; concerning all things to do with *lahzars*.

laid up in ordinary vessel that has been emptied of most of its crew and its stores, taken up out of the water on to a dry dock to be careened (have its hulled cleaned), thoroughly repaired, overhauled, refitted and made ready for another lengthy service on the *vinegar waves*.

lambast(s) great rope-and-steel sprung engines of war used to hurl large harpoon-like projectiles known as bastis. The blade-like tips of these bastis are typically treated with toxic *scripts* designed to especially harm monsters. A thick chain attached to powerful steel arms is wound back with a large winch that takes several men to operate. When the chain is wound right back it is locked with a trigger and the bastis is laid into a special groove or track. When all is ready, the trigger is tripped and the bastis is flung out as far as 300 yards.

Lambasts are most usually found on rams, where their main job is for use against *kraulschwimmen* and other nadderers (sea-monsters), but they are also used to throw harpagons, great grappling-hooks made to ensnare other vessels, or as a last resort when the shot lockers are empty and the powder all used.

lamplighter(s) essentially a kind of specialised soldier, mostly employed by the *Empire*, though some states also have them. Their main task is to go out in the late afternoon and evening to light the *bright-limn* lamps that line the *conduits* and *conductors* (highways) of the *Empire*, and to douse them again in the early morning. They are fairly well paid for soldiers, earning about 22 *sous* a year.

Lamplighter-Marshal most superior officer of the *lamplighters*; the one that Rossamund is going to serve under is in charge of the whole of the *Wormway* from *Winstermill* to *Wörms* and the *lamplighters* who work along it.

lamplighter's agent clerks and the like seeing to the business of the *manse* and the *Lamplighter-Marshal* in far-off cities and other lands. Their main tasks include visiting and delivering dispatches to other *manses* and Lamplighter-Marshals, organising supplies and suppliers from the suppliers' end, seeking new recruits, hunting down leads on smuggling rings, appealing to the *Emperor* in *Clementine* itself for more pay or resources and so on.

landaulet said "land-or-let"; open topped, four-wheeled carriage usually drawn by a single horse and having two seats within that face each other. A folding top divided into two parts may be drawn completely over to protect from inclement weather. Used in the cities where horses are safer; only the foolish or those capable and willing to defend their trusty nag dare take a landaulet out beyond.

leer(s) also called perspiriths ("sense-holders"), cognisters or vati-seers; a creepy lot trained in seeing small and otherwise missed detail, remembering faces, following scents and trails, spying, shadowing and all such prying arts and the use of the *sthenicon* and *olfactologue*. They soak their eyes over a period of months in special potives collectively called washes or opthasaums, which irreparably change the colours of the eyes and permanently alter the abilities of their sight. The first of these opthasaums prepares the eye for transformation and is called

Saum of Adparat or adparatic syrup. After a month of soaking in this wash, one hour each day, the leer spends another month soaking his or her eyes in either of two washes: Bile of Vatës will make the more common leer known as a *laggard* with brown and yellow eyes, and cognistercus or Swill of Cognit the less common *falsemen,* with red and pale blue eyes. The whole process of changing a person's eyes is called adparation, and one can tell a leer by these weirdly coloured orbs. Each also takes particular kinds of *draughts* to enhance his or her capacities in day-to-day duties. Leers are highly sought after: *laggards* in the wild places to warn against *monsters* and other lurking dangers and to track *brigands*, *smugglers* and escaped prisoners; and *falsemen* in the cities to work for the wealthy and for government, wheedling out the dishonest and sycophantic and interrogating the suspicious. Though they alter their biology in a chemical way they are not regarded with nearly as much suspicion or loathing as *lahzars* and are not questioned as potential *gudgeons*. See *falsemen* and *laggards*.

left-decede   to decede is to step aside quickly, 90° to the line of attack, while turning to face your attacker as, it is to be hoped, he or she stumbles past you. A left-decede is a rapid sidestep to the left with a half-turn to the right – a defensive move that is part of the *Hundred Rules of Harundo*.

Lentine grand-cargo   massive cargo vessel that comes from the ports of a distant southern coastal region known as the Lent.

letter of introduction   letter written for you by a significant person of rank and merit, saying who you are and your qualities (and flaws), recommending you to whomsoever should read it. It is often sealed with a wax seal, to add a sense of veracity. An excellent letter of introduction can open many doors.

letters, to have your ~   to be able to read and to write competently – neatly and with correct spelling – more than a few words or simple scrawled sentences. Those who can read but have never been taught to write are called partly lettered. ("I can read me letters, sir, but a cain't make 'em.")

levin-bolt   another term for lightning.

Liberum Infantis   *Tutin* for *book child*.

Licurius said "ly-kyew-re-us"; a *leer* and *factotum* for *Europe*. Originally one of the lifeguard of the Duchess of Naimes, he has served *Europe* for over ten years. Licurius has left his *sthenicon* on too long, letting the organs within grow up into his nose and face. *Leers* who let this happen are known variously as breach-faced *leers*, aspexitors or leerbrechts; and any biologue that is allowed to grow unchecked like this is said to be exitious (said "eck-zi-shoos") or ruinous. During his time with *Europe*, Licurius' thoughts have become darker, more suspicious and bitter, and his hatred for *monsters* has grown. More recently the two of them have begun doing wicked and infamous things, things they will not talk about, and somehow it has been Licurius who has led in them.

limbers small versions of a *gastrine*, metal-bound boxes of wood in groups of twos of threes down either side of each *gastrine*. They are used to warm up and loosen the muscles of the much bigger counterpart to make them ready for operation. If a *gastrine* is not massaged by a limber first, it could tear, become swollen and infected, thereby reducing its performance and even occasioning its death. The limbers themselves are warmed up by the gastrineer's mates, who crank long handles in the limber-box that turn a much smaller version of a treadle-shaft within called a maiden. Once the revolutions of the maiden have reached a certain rate, the muscles of the limber, having been nicely massaged by this turning, will take over and by a series of jointed levers, repeat this process on a greater scale with the *gastrines*. If a vessel needs more speed it may put some or all of its limbers to work, helping the *gastrines* to turn the main treadle-shaft. There is a risk of permanent harm being done to the limber, but because they are much easier and cheaper to replace, this risk is often taken. The best a captain could hope to get by putting "all limbers to the *screw*" – as it is called – is an extra knot or, at best, two. This may not seem like much, but at the relatively slow speeds of all water-going craft of the *Half-Continent*, 1–2 knots can equal the difference between success or doom. See *rams*, *gastrines* and *gastrineer*.

limn-thorn *bright-limn* fixed to a pole, or hanging from the same.

Liquor common collective name for the vast expanse of deep ocean or gurgës to the east of the Half-Continent, beyond all the smaller pontis (seas) and mares (oceans).

Little Dog quiet pageboy in service to the *Harefoot Dig*. He is the bottom of the rung and it is his job to fetch and carry and run messages to wherever he is sent, even the dangerous countryside. Although Little Dog is well aware of the risks he endures and lives in constant dread of being sent out on wild nights, no one else seems to consider this, and he finds himself dashing about in the unfriendly dark bearing little more than an rsvp to a dinner. Poor little fellow – he has faced many terrors for a boy so young, and has survived each one so far …

long-johns outer underwear made from wool; leggings for warmth and protection, with reinforced knees. Some have socks sewn on to the ends and are referred to as sock-johns or smockjacks.

longshanks shorts with legs reaching to the knees, often *proofed* and very hardwearing. Typically worn with *long-johns* as is the fashion, long-shanks are preferred to breeches, and are certainly more fashionable.

looby fool, idiot, stupid person, ignoramus. A *lubber*.

Loquor said "loh-kor"; a distant land far to the east, beyond *Wörms* and the mountains of the Tausengramdornin ("thorns of a thousand tears"). It is said to be deadly *threwdish* and filled with the most fearsome *utterworsts*.

lubber or landlubber; a derogatory name given by *vinegaroons* to any landsman, or anyone clumsy or dangerously awkward.

M

Madam Felicitine see *Felicitine, Madam*.

Madam Opera see *Opera, Madam*.

Madam Opera's Estimable Marine Society for Foundling Boys and Girls *marine society* run by *Madam Opera*. See *marine society*.

main-sovereign largest of all the *rams*, with a minimum of 100 *great-guns* running down one *broadside* (not including *lambasts* or *tormentums*); enormous and slow and needing drudges to help them manoeuvre. See *rams* and Appendix 6.

manifest list of the cargoes carried by a vessel.

manse fortress or large fortress-like house that serves as the headquarters for *lamplighters*, and a place of final refuge should it be needed.

marches also called bounds, extents or parts (partitions), or the precincts of man. The division men have given to their domains, calling them rather grandly the Exculta Hominum Vita Partitio or "divisions of civilisation". They are based on the perceived safety of each region from *monsters* and the effects of *threwd*. There are five marches starting with the safest or "quietest", as it is commonly referred to:

urbis (city) > paris (parish, canton or pagis) > scutis (soke or fenceland) > fossis (*ditchland*) > horridas terrestrum (the wilds).

The first four marches, from the city to the *ditchlands*, are known as the termina hominis, "the precincts of man" and are seen as radiating out from each city in a series of expanding rings. *The wilds* remain the horridas terrestrum, "the rough (or frightening) lands" and are all the wide, shapeless places beyond the four rings of the precincts, uncharted and untamed. Of them it can easily be said "here be *monsters*".

marine society institution established to teach children the rudiments of naval life and so prepare them for the ever-needful *navy*. In a typical marine society, life is divided up into *watches*, just as it is on a *ram* or *cargo*, and for several years, until they reach the age of work, each child is taught ropes and knots; *watches* and routines; signal sending and reading; hoisting flags; scrubbing, swabbing, holy-stoning and mucking (that is, cleaning); climbing ratlines; recognising ranks, types of vessels and their descriptions (tabulation); *letters* (making a marine society child highly prized); simple cosmology (the positions of stars); and reading charts. Extra subjects peculiar to different marine societies might include bastinade (stick-fighting, of which *harundo* is a part); stowing and setting hammocks; rowing; *matter* (history); and generalities (geography). Marine societies are run by an owner, or someone appointed by the naval board of that *realm*. Typically they are staffed with semi-retired *vinegaroons* seeing out the last of their days in continued service to their regent. It is one of the few pension options offered to sailors past their prime, and to get a position at a marine society is considered a great stroke of fortune or Providence.

Marrow, the ~ also called the Würtem-way, among many other names. Just above *Clementine* is a massive man-made gorge, a huge moat to keep all the terrors of the foul lands beyond from invading *Clementine* land. It represents the northernmost extent of the *Empire*, and was started in a time before it even existed. In its early days the *Empire* took up the work of finishing the Marrow, taking another 200 years to do so. This required vaults of money and several thousand lives, with labourers lost to accidents, brutal punishments and attacks from the ever-present *monsters*. The Marrow runs west to east for 1,200 miles from the Foeder Cidës to the Pontus Cadmia ("yellow sea"). At the bottom of this gorge is a clogged, trickling stream that started in a swamp and flowed to nowhere, cutting a groove in the granite plateau. It was along this eroded waterway that the moat was begun, and now the waters of that stream flow from the swamp to the Spout, a collection of pipes protruding from the cliffs along the Pontus Cadmia far away to the east. All along the Marrow are giant fortresses known together as the Ortygometra ("land-rail") linked by a *conduit* called the Geometra. These fortresses keep watch on the Empire's northernmost border, while its *pediteers* march patrols along the Geometra. Though not very beautiful, the Marrow is recognised as one of civilisation's great wonders, a testament to man's determination against the *monsters*, and seeing it is a part of the Grand Tour.

matter the subject in school we would call "history".

Maudlin said "moord-lin"; a planet and one of the brightest lights in the night sky, having a distinct greenish tinge. The largest planet, it can be seen as a tiny yet definite disc. Away from city lights, you might also spot Maudlin's largest moon, Jekyll, circling the planet in retrograde orbit (opposite to the direction of orbit of almost all the other planets and moons). Maudlin rises late and so is a mark of the passing of midnight and the approach of morning. She is said to be fleeing *Faustus*, who chases her each night across the cosmic dome, and so is held as the Signal Star of the suffering, the desired and the desirable.

Meesius said "mee-see-us"; one of *Gauldsman Five*'s many fitters and a retired *vinegaroon* who once fell foul of *Fransitart* and *Craumpalin*, in the solution of which he found himself owing them a great debt they have never previously claimed.

mess-kid small wooden pail with high sides for eating food out of.

Messrs Idby & Adby, Mercantile & Supercargo mercantile company which, having lost one too many ox-carts of goods on the *Vestiweg*, hired *Europe* to do her deadly work for it in the *Brindleshaws*.

370

Midwich the "middle watch". See *days of the week*.

milt the depth of one's self; the core of one's soul and convictions, deeper even than the heart.

Misbegotten Schrewd, the ~ average-sized *ettin* said to *haunt* the *Brindleshaws*.

Mole, Battle of the ~ great naval battle near a small navigation island call the Mole. It was fought over 30 years ago between a collection of states including *Brandenbrass* called the Solemn League set against the islands of the Wretchwater and their supporters the mercenary state of Lombardy and a third mysterious ally. The conflict was one of many over the long contested rights of use and passage of two bodies of water: the Gullet, the narrow strait between Coursing and the mainland; and the Quimpermeer, that part of *the Grume* north-east of the Gullet. Strangely, Quimperpund, the state these rights worked against most, though part of the Solemn League, did not send *rams* to the conflict. This was a profound betrayal, and though the Solemn League won the battle it resented Quimperpund's treachery and, so many years later, still do. *Fransitart* and *Craumpalin* were both present at the battle, serving on board the 88 *guns-broad* main-ram, the NB ("Naufustica Branden") *Venerable*, with *Fransitart* directing the fire from the first gun deck, while *Craumpalin* served at one of the guns and handed out *restoratives* when there was a lull or a desperate need. That was back in the time before they joined the *Boschenberg navy*. See the *Surprise*.

money most currencies of the *Empire* have three denominations: the billion – the biggest coin representing the most amount of money; the dollion or dollar – the middle or secondary coin; and finally the common or comma, which is the smallest coin in size and worth. For example, the most used currency is that of the *Soutlands*, used in almost all inter-realm and international transactions. It is divided into:

> *sous* (billion) > *sequins* (dollar) > *guise* (comma)
> = 16 *sequins*   = 20 *guise*

With the Imperial *oscadril* it works like this:

> *oscadril* (billion) > *special* (dollar) > *commial* (comma)
> = 14 *specials*   = 18 *commials*

There are many, many more currencies around the *Half-Continent*, some left over from pre-Imperial times and still used among locals, especially in more remote or rustic places. It can very complicated, and money changers have made a *very* profitable industry out of unravelling the mysteries of currency exchange.

monitor(s) 24 to 32 *guns-broad* river-going vessels of war, similar to *rams* in that they have an enclosed gun deck, yet sitting lower in the water. They are *ironclad* and powered by *gastrines*. The heavy keel is much reduced in size and the vessels have a much shallower *draft* to allow for the shallower depth of rivers and shoreline waters. They handle poorly in stormy seas, although this does not prevent them being taken on patrols close inshore. With their shallow *draught* they can bring their guns to bear alarmingly close to land.

monster(s) also called üntermen, *nickers*, bogles, beasties, bugaboos, *baskets*, *sprigs*, *kraulschwimmen*, nadderers, nasties and many other names; any creature not considered human or a dumb animal. The most basic division is into two:

◆ Incolids: the natural, native monsters, which are thought of as forces of nature, a physical expression of nature defending itself

◆ Homonculids: the man-made monsters (*gudgeons*), which are considered perversions of nature, certainly by monsters themselves and by most people as well.

What distinguishes a monster from a person is that it is often more grotesque, bent, disproportioned (this is a human perspective, of course), possessing claws and fangs and spines and a murderous intent to kill people. What makes monsters different from the dumb animals that walk the earth is harder to define, although it is agreed by most scholars of the *Half-Continent* that clear rational intelligence and the capacity to speak (even the rudimentary gruntings of the dumbest *ettin*) are the most important difference. For *nickers* (land monsters) it is also agreed that a common difference is that many *nickers* walk about on two legs and have two (or more) arms. This is not absolute, however. For nadderers (or sea-monsters) it is generally their cleverness and cunning and their enormous size that distinguish them from the fishes, the sharks and the whales. No one knows where the monsters came from, but for as long as history records, humankind has been locked in a war with them – the Hyadthningarvig or Luctamens Immensum or the Immerwar – the Everlasting Struggle, not just in the *Half-Continent* but all the world over. As humans seek to expand their empire, their grip and control of the land, so the monsters resist them, plaguing and spoiling. Yet monsters find it hard to live where men have gained control, and the more people living in one place the fewer monsters there will be, although there are always some. This makes the cities the safest places for people to dwell, and from them *everymen* wage their side of the war. There are rumours of some *realms* that live in understanding or even cooperation with the monsters, but this is unthinkable for those dwelling in the *Half-Continent*; such a thing would be the act of vile *sedorners* (monster-lovers) and a crime against humankind. No one knows absolutely where monsters come from. Old histories say that there have been many – *urchins*, the *false-gods*, many *nuglungs* and *kraulschwimmen* – who have been in existence since before humankind. These they call the primmlings ("the first"). However, it is known too that new monsters keep appearing, made after this prehistoric time. Theories abound as to where they come from. Probably the most unusual is found in the *Vadè Chemica*, which suggests that they are knit together in mud and slime made fertile by *threwd* and the sun's warmth. *Habilists* name this hot *threwdish* mud "gravidia lutumi" ("pregnant slime") and theorise that the stronger the *threwd* is in a place and the muddier it is, the more likely that place is to spawn monsters. This whole process is known as spontaneous self-generation, and monsters who are born in such a way are called sprosslings ("born ones"). See *nuglung, glamgorn, nicker, kraulschwimmen, bogle* and *gudgeon*.

monster-blood tattoo also *cruorpunxis*; tattoos given to someone who has just slain a *monster*, and made with some of the siphoned blood of that same *monster*. Once pricked into the skin, the monster's blood reacts strangely with *everyman* blood, causing a quickly festering, throbbing sore that eventually sloughs off its scab to reveal permanently port-red to blood-brown marks beneath. These tattoos are usually a highly stylised face based on the *bogle* the person slew. Those who make a profession of marking tattoos in *monster* blood and making *spoors* are called punctographists. The best punctographists – those who make the most impressive images and do it with the least pain – earn themselves a comfortable living. A decent *cruorpunxis*, say about 2 inches by

2 inches, will set you back about 2 *sous*. Punctographists are most likely to be found in busy rural centres where *monsters* haunt the lands about, and in cities where wealth and fashion keep them in demand. Saved monster blood (called cruor or sometimes *ichor*) will remain useable for a little over a day before congealing. Kept cool and hidden it can last for almost three days. This gives the victorious *pugnator* a little time after slaying the *nicker* to bottle its blood and make for the nearest major town to get a tattoo.

monster-hunters those whose work it is to defend the realm of humans against the realm of *monsters*. See *teratologists*.

monster-lover being of such a disposition is a terrible crime. See *sedorner*.

months of the year there are 16 months in the *Half-Continent* year, most of 23 days, with three having 22 days. This means that there are 4 months in each season. For summer there is Calor (22 days), Estor (23 days), Prior (23) and Lux (23). For autumn there is Pilium (23), Cachrys (23), Lirium (23) and Pulchrys (23). For winter there is Brumis (22), Pulvis (23), Heimio (23) and Herse (23). For spring there is Orio (23), Unxis (23), Icteris (23) and Narcis (22). The year always ends with a day to spare, Lestwich, the last day of the year. This means that the new year always starts on a Newich, and therefore the dates of the year always fall on the same days year in, year out. Farmers, fishermen and other folk working by the seasons and the evolutions of the moon like this calendar a lot: its predictability makes their lives that little bit simpler. See *days of the week* and Appendix 1.

morbidity putrefaction or bacterial breakdown and decay.

Mortar, the ~ suburb in *Boschenberg* famous for its *proofing*.

mottle patterns and colours of allegiance shown on clothes, *harness*, flags, *baldrics* and other sashes and ribbons. Every state, *realm* or organisation has its own mottle, a distinctive combination of two or more colours (or tinctures) arranged in immediately recognisable patterns. Tinctures have definite meanings and are used accordingly. For example, the colours of the *Empire* are rouge and cadmia with leuc (red and yellow with white) meaning "justice, honour, wisdom"; the mottle of *Boschenberg* ochre and sable (brown and black) meaning "hardiness and wisdom (shrewdness)"; *Brandenbrass* sable and leuc (black and white) meaning "wisdom and integrity". The following list shows the colours used in mottle, their proper or technical name, positive meaning, and negative meaning:

♦ white: leuc, argent – wisdom, integrity, chastity, joy – death, fear

♦ yellow: cadmia, or – understanding, honour – cowardice, mendacity

♦ orange: orot, orange – courage, determination – betrayal, perfidy

♦ red: rouge; gules – eagerness, justice – blood, destruction

♦ pink: geranium, carman – merriness, humanity, ruth – fainthearted-ness, gluttony

♦ purple: orient, brawn – majesty, fortitude, discretion – false hope, madness

♦ deep blue: prüs, cobalt – steadfastness, constancy – oblivion, frustration

♦ light blue: celest, azure– peace, prudence – poison, confusion

♦ green: chloris; vert – freedom, hope, health – disease, jealousy

♦ brown: ochre, tann – nature, hardiness – excrement, dimwittedness

♦ deep brown: mole, sepia – honesty, antiquity – irascibility, decay

♦ black: sable, nycht – mourning, wisdom, shrewdness – cunning, death.

When flying flags negative meanings are shown by hoisting a pure black strip (the black rider) beneath them. For example, a fortress succumbing to the effects of *threwd* might fly an orient (purple) flag with a "black rider" to show that the place is overcome with madness. By using the same device one could pass insults to an enemy across the field of war. You can say a lot with colours.

muck hill pile of poo.

mules square-heeled slipper with no heel piece or quarters; any flat-heeled, soft shoe that is fastened to the foot and leg with ribbons.

Mullhaven, the ~ harbour and roads (safe anchorage) before *High Vesting*. Its name is *Hergott* for "sandy harbour".

musket see *flintlock musket*.

musketeer foot-soldier or *pediteer* wearing half-*harness* of a *weskit* with platoon-coat and a *thrice-high*; his main weapon is the musket fixed with bayonet. Designated medium infantry. See *pediteer* and *harness*.

N

Naimes said "naymz"; moderately large *Soutland city-state* found in the south-western corner of a fertile farming region known as the Villene (said "vill-enn"), a region inland of Frestonia. Naimes has grown rich on the trade of timber, meat and certain semi-precious metals and gems. Being pinched, however, between the great powers of Haquetaine, Maine, Westoverin and Castoria has limited its growth. Its regent, the Duchess of Naimes, has suffered no little embarrassment at the way-ward behaviour of her daughter, her only child and heiress.

nasties one of the many euphemisms for *monsters*.

nativity patent official document that declares the place and time of birth and bears an official seal and signatures. The record of all the places a person might live and any citizenship he or she might be granted is also recorded on a nativity patent. Without one, it is hard for a person to establish his or her identity and almost impossible to get decent work or even be allowed into most cities.

navy unlike standing armies, the states of the *Empire* are allowed to have navies as big as they can afford them to be, and so the states do just that. These standing navies are known as fleets-in-being and serving in them is the single most common occupation, with only the merchant marine coming anywhere near as close (after this comes serving the bureaucracies of the *Empire*). Navies are mostly made up of *rams*, those massive *ironclad* vessels of war, and employ them in various integral tasks:

♦ landguarde = coastal patrols and guarding the integrity of maritime boundaries.

♦ ward-marchant = protection of *cargoes* and the like, often in convoy.

♦ marquelin = privateering and execution of letters of marque (government granted right to do the work of a pirate).

♦ line-of-fleet = operating in battle fleets and squadrons.

♦ kraultrekker = on the prowl for *kraulschwimmen* and other sea-monsters to drive them away from ports and cargo lanes.

♦ main-surveyor = exploration, charting and reconnaissance: spying, basically.

- courser = (not to be confused with *corsers*) commissioned with the sole task of hunting down and sinking or capturing pirates.
- register-ship = responsible for carrying currency, precious metals and other goods valuable to state or *Empire*.

Universally calling themselves the *Senior Service*, the navies of the states are always looking for new recruits. They put up posters promising great rewards, fete famous or valorous captains to keep their popularity high, press vagrants, foundlings and merchant vinegars (men serving on merchant vessels) into service, offer convicted criminals a berth in place of serving in the notoriously foul prisons, pinch or entice the crew from the *rams* of other states; in short, do whatever it takes to keep their ships fully manned. Life in the navy is tough, and *vinegaroons* often die younger than landlubbers (or just "lubbers" as *vinegaroons* will say), affected by the caustic sprays that wash over their *rams* and pit and scar their skin. Yet the pay is higher for equivalent work on land and the chance of *prize-money* very real. Though *vinegaroons* do not wear uniforms, their *rams* have distinct collections of flags, unique for each state or realm, called bunting. The biggest piece of bunting is the enormous rectangular flag known as the spandarion, showing the *mottle* and sigil of the state to which the *ram* belongs. A fleet decked out in full bunting flapping proudly in the breeze is a most beautiful sight. There are also cypher flags or burges – used to communicate from vessel to vessel – run up on lines between the masts. By these a commodore or admiral can give orders to his squadron or fleet, and vessels can relay simple information. A typical navy consists of 20 to 30 capital *rams* including 3 to 5 *main-sovereigns*, 60 odd cruisers (see Appendix 6), and many schooners and other small *sailers* for observation and running messages (advice boats). It is usual for a *city-state* to support more *rams* than it could ever shelter in its harbours because such a thing is not intended or ever likely to happen. This is because about two-thirds of any navy is at sea at any one time. Maintaining even a half-decent navy costs mind-bogglingly immense amounts of *money*, *money* that a state may not always have in its coffers. Consequently, navies will be involved in their own private enterprises, or invest in companies and seek investors from among those who benefit most from their labours. Naval agents are responsible for all this wheeling and dealing, and great clouds of them bustle about the *Half-Continent* in pursuit of funding for their masters. See *rams* and *vinegaroons*.

377

nicker(s) general name for all *monsters* that live on land (sea-*monsters* generally being called nadderers) and also used more specifically of those *monsters* who are the size of a person or larger. See *monsters*.

nimbleschrewd(s) type of blightling (the worst sort of *glamgorn*) who gets about in gangs. As with many other *glamgorns* they like to dress in human clothes and adore making mischief wherever and however they can. A nimbleschrewd's idea of mischief goes far beyond just simple pranks (these they will do); what they like best is making *everymen* miserable and wretched and even killing them. See *glamgorns*.

nostrum *scripts* that are not part of the common lexicon (popular and well-known *scripts*). Instead they are the unique or rare concoctions of a specific *skold* or school of *skolds*.

nuglung(s) small but very powerful kind of *bogle*, often having a head like a twisted version of an animal's. It is said that nuglungs serve the *urchins*, the lords of the *monsters*, as messengers and spies, and are often found sneaking and prying into the deeds of men. They are notoriously tough to kill, although most *potives* work just as well on them as on any other *monster*. The worst, most violent and cruel of the nuglungs are called pernixis. See *monsters*.

nullodour a collection of *potives* designed to hide or confuse or fake certain smells. Their most common use is to mask the distinctive odour of a person so that he or she remains unnoticed by *monsters*. Used in conjunction with *john-tallow*, it offers you an excellent chance to throw off pursuit and escape with your life.

O

old salt one of the many names for a sailor of the high seas. See *vinegaroon*.

olfactologue "smell-machine"; a biologue (biological device) used to make smells profoundly more noticeable while also increasing the wearer's ability to discern subtle differences in odours otherwise impossible to sense. Made of a simple wooden box strapped over the nose and mouth but leaving the eyes unobstructed. See *sthenicon* for a detailed description of the parts that make up an olfactologue. As with a *sthenicon*, if you wear an olfactologue for too long the organs inside will start to grow up your nose and into your face. After about a week, the box could still be taken off, though you would find tendrils up your nose that would tear out painfully. After a month of wearing an olfactologue (or a *sthenicon*) it could not be removed without surgery and the loss of the front of your face. Used most by *leers*, who swallow special *draughts* beforehand to help make their senses sharper and sniff exotic powders to retard the invasion of the biologue's organs.

Opera, Madam third daughter of middling gentry. In her twenties, Madam Opera Gelderwine found true love with a daring *equiteer* officer of superior breeding and charm only to have a scandal (so serious that few still know anything about it and of which Madam Opera will never tell) dissolve the engagement and leave the young agonised Opera forever unwilling to try at love again. Taking on the title "madam" anyway, to put off any more suitors, of which there were several, she set off on the Grand Tour and travelled the known world for several years seeking solace in glamorous cities. Running out of money she finally returned to *Boschenberg,* the city of her birth, to find all that remained to her was an old mansion in a rundown part of the city. With no income and no prospects she took up one of many *navy* contracts being offered at the time to run a *marine society*, the first unmarried woman to have ever done so. Hiring pensioned *vinegaroons* as her staff (who received their pay from the *navy* rather than from the Madam, and included *Fransitart* and a year later *Craumpalin*), she began her Estimable Marine Society for Foundling Boys and Girls. She is a lonely, middle-aged lady who spends most of her days stalking about the *marine society* seeing who she might catch at "knavery and misdeeds!" as she calls it, or sitting in her private rooms receiving guests and dictating letters for *Verline* to take down. To the children Madam Opera seems grand, calculating and sour. To any of the young men who act as agents for the various services seeking to hire *marine society* children, she seems an obvious flirt.

operasigis pain-marks or grief-signs, said "oh-por-ah-sij-jiss"; another name for *spoors*.

Ormond one of the *Signal Stars*; the fourth-brightest light in the night sky, preceded by the white planet Penelopë and followed by purple Hadës. Ormond rises even later than *Maudlin*, and its appearance shows that the night is old and dawn approaching.

oscadril also oscar or owl; the largest coin of the *Empire*, made partly with gold and worth 1½ sous. On one side is a relief of the Sagacious Owl (the symbol of Clementine's mint) and on the other a Pillar or two Pillars entwined with a sash (a symbol of the *Empire* itself). If you were to toss a coin for a test of luck you would say, "We'll flip for it! You tell me – the Pillar or the Owl?" Various Emperors have tried over the centuries to make the oscar the standard currency throughout their domain. Yet somehow it has never worked and the *sou* remains the merchant, and therefore most common, coin.

P

Padderbeck, the ~ one of the many quays in *Boschenberg*, situated along the banks of the *Humour*; small quay built along a narrow canal called the Stoorn, coming off the main flow of the river to increase the access of trade. Other similar canals include the Humrig, Glastornis and Glachtig.

Padderbeck Stair, the ~ walkway about and steps leading down to the *Padderbeck* itself, though the two names are often used interchangeably.

pamphlets large many-paged periodicals, a cross between what we would call "newspaper" and "magazine", often filled with scandalous and fabulous stories of current politics and past events. The pamphlets that *Verline* kindly buys for the *marine society* are paid for by her sister the Lady *Praeline*, who has the money to afford them.

panniers baskets or boxes with fastenable lids that are borne by animals or fixed to carriages for carrying stores and goods.

parlour maid usually a maid-servant who waits at the meal table. In Verline's case, however, though she is called a parlour maid, her responsibilities and chores involve much more than just serving *Madam Opera* meals.

Parts, the ~ or just lower case: parts; all the *Elements*, *Sub-Elements*, chemicals and minerals and other ingredients that are used to make *scripts*.

patchouli water water in which the petals of the patchouli flower have been soaked. The water is then strained to leave a pleasantly scented liquid for dabbing about oneself or dripped into a kerchief to be wafted about the room.

pediteer said "ped-it-ear"; the common name for a foot-soldier, as opposed to an *equiteer* or cavalryman. *Musketeers*, *haubardiers*, and *troubardiers* are the three most common pediteers. Along with them are the ambuscadiers, frankarms, and other light infantry.

peer(s) the nobility, those considered or considering themselves to be of high-born blood: ancient kings and queens, dukes, duchesses and the rest. All of the regents of the states of the *Empire* are peers; indeed, you can never be a regent unless you are a peer. There are certain bloodlines within the peerage that are considered superior to others such as the *Corvinius Arbours* of *Boschenberg* or the Saakrahennemus of *Brandenbrass*. Probably the most superior is a broadly scattered bloodline: those of a group called the Didodumese (said "dy-dod-dyoo-meez"), a lineage not reckoned in the person's name but by their birth and nativity patent. The Didodumese are all those descended from *Dido*, the founding Queen of the *Empire* who ruled 1,600 years ago. There are even some without a peerage who belong to this illustrious set, scattered and squabbling across the whole *Half-Continent* and beyond. The current *Haacobin Emperor* is not one of the Didodumese, who hold that the supreme leader of Dido's realm must be one of her descendants. He often contends with their political arm in the Imperial parliament and their spies and assassins in the palaces.

peregrinat almanac made hard-wearing and even waterproof for use by *wayfarers* and other travellers.

Phoebë the most common name for the moon, the governing orb of the night sky.

physic, physician well liked and well respected, physicians train for four to six years at physacteries, spending a further year or two in a sanatorium (hospital) before being granted their full degree. With this they are allowed to be called "Doctor" and are free to practise their trade in the wide world. There they tend to all the aches and sprains of the ailing public, bleeding, balancing the humours, diagnosing and recommending *draughts* to be sought from *dispensurists* or procedures needed from *surgeons*. Physicians will even attempt a little surgery, which they are qualified to do, and folks are much happier to be under a physic's knife than those butchers the *surgeons*. Physicians charge for each attendance and can earn about 300 sous a year.

381

physics the study and practice of caring for the sick and injured; what we would call "medicine".

Pike, Mister *boatswain* of the *Hogshead*; a very quiet and obedient man who yet manages to control the crew set under him.

Pinsum, Master ~ the most bookishly learned of *Madam Opera's* employees and master of *matter*, *habilistics* and *generalities* at the *foundlingery*. He has never been a sailor nor even seen the *vinegar seas*, but rather was a small-time actor before serious lumbago (chronic muscular pain in the legs) made it impossible for him to continue in a job that required so much standing up. Answering a petition of employment put out by *Madam Opera,* he began work at the foundlingery while *Rossamünd* was still a baby. He also teaches *letters*.

piped to bed one of the many signals given by the masters of the foundlingery upon the *bosun's whistle* to tell the children to go to bed. Once it is blown the foundlings have 15 minutes to be beneath their blankets. See *bosun's whistle*.

Pirate-kings of the Brigandine, the ~ pirate-kings associated with the Brigandine Coast, north-east of the *Half-Continent*, beyond the *Liquor*. There are other pirate-kings sitting in their strongholds in other lands, but those of the Brigandine are the most infamous.

pith also pluck or constitution; what we would call "metabolism". It also means intestinal fortitude or "guts".

plaudamentum see *Cathar's Treacle*.

Poéme once-fashionable suburb in *Boschenberg*, now given over to factories and warehouses; where *Madam Opera's Estimable Marine Society for Foundling Boys and Girls* is also found; now famous for not much at all.

pokeweed or pockweed; a reedy plant that grows in swamps, and best in *threwdish* swamps, from whose stems is made a tough, durable fibre of the same name. It takes well to *gauld* and is prized as padding in *proofing*.

Pontoon Wigh, the ~ a main street in *High Vesting* that runs parallel to the coast. Clean and possessing a glorious square, it is an address much sought after by the best corporations and mercantiles.

Pontus Nubia the "black sea" whose acrid waters are quite literally black like ink.

poop or poop deck; rearmost section of the upper deck of a *ram*, between the aft mast and the stern. Given that the decks of a *ram* are flush (that is, flat) the correct term for this part of the vessel is the aft deck. In the vernacular of the *vinegaroon,* however, the old term remains.

portable soup flat, unappetising-looking oblong slats of black material about the size of a man's hand. They are made from a broth-like soup of beans that is strained, mixed with powdered bone and dried till it is hard. It is then etched with the manufacturer's mark, wrapped in greased paper and shipped off to sell. Soaking one slat in hot water for about half an hour (or three hours for cold water) will cause it to dissolve into the black goop it was to begin with. Not very tasty, but light, nutritious and it takes up little room, making it an ideal *wayfood*. It can even be eaten as it is, though you would have to bite and chew very carefully or risk cutting up your mouth and tongue.

potive(s) any concoction meant to have an effect externally, that is, not by swallowing or some other introduction into the body, as opposed to *draughts*, which need to be swallowed to work. Some potives still have to touch exposed skin to have an effect. See *scripts*.

Poundinch, Rivermaster master of the *Hogshead*, also going by the name of *Rivermaster Vigilus*; he has served on many vessels on the *vinegar seas* and gained a lot of experience on the behaviour and temperaments of both people and ships.

Praeline or properly the Lady Praeline, said "pray-leen"; younger sister of *Verline*. Her locally famed beauty allowed her to marry well above her station, much to the shame of both families. His parents see her as a grasping upstart; her parents (now passed away) saw her as getting "hoity" and too big for her own boots. Her sister is just happy her husband treats her fairly.

prattling hackmillion person who talks big but cannot back it up with action; "hackmillion" is a term used of someone who makes many swings and showy stabs at an opponent with a sword or other weapon but to little or no effect: all show and no results.

precincts of man, the ~ see *marches*.

prize(s), prize-money prizes are what we might think of as "performance indicators". Typically they are the capture of another *ram* or a *cargo*, or even a seaside town or city; the taking of some significant person worth ransoming; or the proven slaying of a sea-monster (the bigger it is the better the reward). Prize-money is paid as an incentive to heroic endeavours and is distributed to the whole crew of a *ram* by their government in amounts deemed appropriate for the deed accomplished. This distribution, however, is very uneven, with the captain of the vessel getting far and away the largest share, the rest trickling down till the lowest yonker (cabin boy) or *grummet* might receive barely more than an extra day's pay. It really does depend on the quality of the prize taken. There have been occasions where the capture has been such a haul, like a fleet of treasure ships bound for Turkmantine, that the prize-money earned by the entire crew is enough to set each one up for life. The smaller *rams* – the *frigates* and drag-maulers (see Appendix 6) – are more active, and on average their crews can expect to double their year's pay with prize-money. The *vinegaroons* of the larger *rams* – iron-doughts, main-rams and *main-sovereigns* (see Appendix 6) – will normally earn about half their annual pay extra as prize-money. For a fee, naval or prize agents will take care of the tiresome and punctilious work involved in securing a crew's prize-money, and naval offices are bustling with them all year round. Prize-money is also offered to landed folk for the killing of *monsters* or capture of criminals.

proofed treated with *gauld* to turn into *proofing*. See *gauld, gaulder*.

proofing any garment *proofed*, or treated with *gauld*, so that it has become sturdy cloth armour as good as, if not better than, any ancient metal suit. See *gauld, gaulder*.

Proud Sulking also called Schmollenstolz; the major city of the farming region known as *Sulk* situated on the east banks of the river *Humour*. A quiet rival of *Boschenberg*, it offers access to its ports and cheap land transport so that *barges* might discharge their cargoes and avoid the high tolls of the *Axles*. It is also becoming the preferred river-port for the taking in of produce from *Sulk* – grains, vegetables, cotton, flax, limestone – for export to the rest of the world. This was once Boschenberg's monopoly.

prow front, pointed part of a vessel forming part of the bow. On a *ram* the prow curves down and forward into a beak called a *ram*, from which these vessels take their name.

pugnator said "pug-nay-tor"; a common, some consider vulgar, term for *monster-hunter*. See *teratologist*.

"Pullets and cockerels!" exclamation of disgust or surprise or astonishment; it means, quite literally, "hens and roosters!".

Q

quabard said "kwe-bard" or "kay-bard"; a shorter version of a haubard; like a *weskit* only lined with *gaulded*-leather plates and fitting more tightly, fastened with buckles at the side or back rather than buttons. See *harness*.

quarto also quarter; any body of soldiers significantly smaller than a platoon, which is roughly 30 men. Typically a quarto is around 10 souls.

'quins slang for *sequins*.

R

Rabbitt, Farmer ~ see *Farmer Rabbitt*.

Rakes, the ~ items on a menu considered to be common and unfashionable; food for rough and rustic folk to eat; the cheap part of the menu. See *Best Cuts*.

ram(s) also rams-of-the-main, men-of-war and sometimes grandly called naufustica; the *ironclad, gastrine*-powered ships of war used by most of the navies of the *Half-Continent*. The forwardmost tip of the prow is pushed forward in a great iron "beak" called the ram, giving these vessels their name. With their iron hulls blackened or browned with special chemicals to stop corrosion (called braice) and sitting low in the water, rams look sinister and powerfully threatening. Yet though the outside might be dark iron, within a ram is a world of wood: beams, posts, planks, bulkheads, smelling strongly of creosote, gunpowder and sweat. Rams are generally divided into two types: the smaller, lighter, faster, less heavily armed called cruisers; and the big, heavily gunned and armoured and slower kind known as capitals, rams-of-the-main or just rams. Cruisers have only one gun deck and no more than three masts. They are the workhorses of a *navy*, used most in escort, reconnaissance and running messages. They are the eyes and ears of the fleet, roving out from the main battle (fleet) to find the enemy's position. The lightest cruiser is the *gun-drudge*, followed by the *frigate*, the largest being the drag-mauler. This cruiser has the largest ram of all, and is built to charge monsters and other vessels and survive the impact. Drag-maulers are the fastest rams at about 14–16 knots. The quickest ever, *Scythe* 36, achieved an unheard of 18½ knots in a fair wind with all *limbers* to the *screw*. *Frigates* are only a little slower at about 13–14 knots. *Gun-drudges* can manage only about 11 knots. Capitals or rams have two gun decks, with the heaviest *cannon* arranged on the second or lower gun deck. Essentially floating batteries, capitals line up stem to stern one after the other in a fight. This is called the line-of-battle, and in this formation enemy fleets will pound away at each other for hours until a decision is reached. Cruisers are considered too small to take a place in the line-of-battle and patrol behind their own line to protect its flanks. The lightest capital is the iron-dought, whose upper gun deck extends only two-thirds the length of the vessel and travels as fast as 11½-12 knots. The next is the main-ram. Achieving no more than 11 knots, they are still by far the most common of the capitals, forming the backbone of all serious navies. The largest of all rams are the *main-sovereigns*, which are so large they can do little better than 8 knots and often require *gun-drudges* to help them manoeuvre. Different captains will employ their rams in different ways, concentrating one or a combination of the three basic tactics:

♦ gunnery – simply standing off another vessel and blasting at it with your *cannon* till it submits. Rams rarely sink under a barrage of shot but their masts and upper works are typically smashed and their strakes (iron plates) always in need of serious repair.

♦ ramming – where the ram is moved into a favourable position to gain momentum and strike another vessel with its beak. Ramming is most likely to sink a vessel.

♦ boarding – involving getting in close, launching harpagons (see *lambasts*) and drawing alongside the enemy so that your crew armed with pikes, axes, hangers, blunderbuss, *bothersalts*, grenadoes and pistols can drop gangplanks and leap the gap between. Boarding is the best way to keep a ram intact for recommissioning into your own navy.

Though a captain may train his crew as he wishes there will be a preferred method for the whole fleet as set by the lords of that particular *navy*. Commonly, states who build their own rams are more inclined to board or shoot, for they know how much it takes to make one. States that buy rams from others and from private manufacturers will as happily sink a vessel by ramming it as blast away at it with guns. It is interesting to note that the larger a ram is, the more its captain will be paid to work her. When a ram is commissioned (officially named and launched), it is quickly crewed and sent to sea. There it will spend the rest of its days, returning to its home port only occasionally and rarely staying for long. See *frigate, navy* and Appendix 6.

reagents any of the ingredients used for *potives* and *draughts*; also called *parts* or *the Parts*.

realm • a specific group of *scripts* all with similar effects. See *scripts*. • in the politics of the *Empire* and its neighbours, a realm is any region controlled by a king or queen.

red must edible fungus from the must family. Not all musts are toothsome, and some are downright poisonous. One of the great advantages of red must is that it keeps a very long time, squashes without bruising, is very light and very good for you. This makes it ideal *wayfood*.

repellents typically a combination of the realms of *scripts* (repugnants, fulminants, and discutants) incorporating all chemistry designed to dissuade and drive *monsters* (and people) off. *Bothersalts* is one of the more popular repellents, though not the most powerful. Others include Salt-of-Asper, Frazzard's powder, glitter-dust, trisulxis, bombast's ash, boglebane and green-flash or gegenshein.

restorative *scripts* concerned with reviving and healing. See *scripts*.

revenant, rever-man, rever what we would call "zombies", "the walking dead"; some are whole re-animated corpses, others are made from bits and pieces of different corpses and even animal parts. They take a lot of learning and skill to make properly. If not well preserved their stink gives them away. If their brains are not reconstituted correctly they are wild and unmanageable. The best quality revers are used as assassins, often dissolving to puddles of untraceable filth when the dastardly deed is done. Occasionally one breaks free of its *everyman* masters and terrorises a community for a while or escapes into *the wilds*, where it gets short shrift from the local *monsters,* who hate such abominations and are hated by them in return. See *gudgeons*.

revenue officers employed by almost every state or realm, they are used to gather the duties and taxes of imported and even exported goods. Revenue officers have a mandate for search and seizure, and go on patrols and raids. Usually efficient and zealous, they have the power of state and *Empire* behind them and the fear of the gallows or Catherine wheel at their employ. They are the harriers of *smugglers*, *corsers*, *ashmongers* and all those involved in the *dark trades*. Such as these guard both the *Axles* and the *Spindle*, and work closely with *lamplighters* to catch the crooks.

rhatany one of the ingredients in *Cathar's Treacle*, made from the poisonous black rhatan bloom, which is native to many of the most *threwdish* and *haunted* swamps and bogs, particularly the *Ichormeer*. The whole flower is dried and crushed very finely to make the powder. On its own it is very poisonous.

rhombus as the story says, a place where *skolds* go to learn their craft. In their two years there the student *skold*, called a rhubus, learns the basic *scripts* and from these how to prepare his or her own *nostrum* and vulgum. In this they are taught the *Elements* and *Sub-Elements*, the *Bases* and their *Combinations*, *Körnchenflecter*, the *Four Spheres* and the *Four Humours*. They also study the *Vadè Chemica* and many other forbidden books on *habilistics*, ancient and new, as well as *matter* (history). People are not allowed to attend a rhombus unless already have their *letters*, that is, they can read and write.

rivergates great fortifications built across rivers and broader streams to protect a certain valuable place or as an outworking of a city's more terrestrial embattlements. Certain riverside duchies and principalities have long used their rivergates to control trade, not just into their own domains but to domains beyond as well. Though the cause of wars and great resentment, ancient Imperial Concessions that allowed these states to legally inspect and tax riverine trade under Imperial observation were kept when the *Haacobin Dynasty* seized the Imperial Seats. This has been much to the disgust of other states who have suffered the toll ways for centuries – and a bitter disappointment, too: it had been hoped that the *Haacobin* Emperors would bring a new kind of justice to the *Empire*. Since then, a handful of more aggressive states have successfully lobbied the *Emperor* for the right to build their own rivergates, and so to have their share in the great profits. This has meant that some rivers have two or three or even four such structures choking them, as their owners rant and politick and threaten the others – for example the troubles on the *River Humour* between *Boschenberg* and its ancient *Axles*, and *Brandenbrass* with its smart new *Spindle*. Many of the less honest have devised ways to get by rivergates, especially those engaged in the *dark trades* or others wanting to avoid the taxes and tolls they charge.

rivermaster the most senior officer aboard a *barge* or any other river-going craft; not always the owner of the vessel; lower in rank than a captain. You have to serve on the *vinegar waves* to be allowed that rank.

rock salt salt mined like a rock from the earth. *Fulgars* suck or chew on lumps of the stuff to keep the concentration of salt in the blood high, thus making them better conductors of electricity.

Rossamünd said "ross-uh-moond"; awkward boy-hero and under-grown *foundling* of *Madam Opera's Estimable Marine Society for Foundling Boys and Girls*.

Rupunzil, the ~ fine cromster of 16 guns, owned by *Rivermaster Vigilus*.

S

sagaar(s) dancers and fighters whose skills and art came originally from lands far to the north beyond the *Marrow* – Samaarkhand, Mansuûng and Ghadamése – and were first encountered by the *Empire* as it came into conflict with the kingdom of Wenceslaus. There are many forms and styles of sagaris (the skill of the sagaar), more complex and varied than *harundo* and the other bastinade arts. Sagaars live to dance, to attain a state known as "the Perpetual Dance", where every action, every tiny lift or twitch, is all part of one unbroken, lifelong dance. In the lands of their origin they are court-entertainers and the prime *teratologists* (*monster-hunters*), employing their extreme flexibility, nimbleness and speed with varieties of *potives* even older then the *skolds'*. In the *Empire*, sagaars are thought of only as *teratologists* and find many opportunities to hunt and drive off *monsters*. Yet all sagaars would just prefer to dance. Sagaars usually wear tight-fitting clothes to allow unhindered movement of limb and those of the *Empire* also mark themselves with *spoors* in the form of spikes radiating down and around one cheekbone, just under the eye (usually the left). It is well known that sagaars and *lahzars* do not like each other very much.

sailer vessel under the power of sails rather than *gastrines*; not to be confused with a sail*or*, a fellow who works on a ship at sea.

Sallow Meermoon reluctant fugelman *skold* of the communities about the *Brindleshaws*. Being forced by her parents and fellow citizens to train as a *skold* at the *rhombus* in *Wörms*, she has recently returned and is very unhappy with her lot in life. Despite this she has still been very thorough about being a *skold*, even down to getting the vertical-stripe *spoors* that are a mark of her trade. A fugelman is a *teratologist* employed by a community to be available to defend it from *monsters*. Candidates for this task are usually local, and most are proud to serve their homeland in such a way. Fugelmen are traditionally *skolds*, but wealthy communities have taken to sending their candidates off to be transmogrified into *lahzars*.

scourge also exitumath or orgulars ("haughty ones" – the name once given to the heroes of old; this is a title also given to *lahzars*); a *skold* who specialises in monster-hunting exclusively, making and using the most powerful, dangerous and deadly *potives*: *potives* that melt things on the spot, or cause them to almost instantly rot or turn to carbon or even petrify living things to stone. Scourges are typically covered from head to toe in special bandages and wear quartz-lensed spectacles to protect them from their own chemicals. Though they are preferred to a *lahzar*, scourges are still regarded as a bit unhinged and unmanageable, and live a life of violence much the same as their *lahzarine* rivals.

screw(s) what we would call a propeller; a method of propulsion used by *gastrine* vessels. *Gastrines* turn the shaft which drives the screw that in turn pushes the ship forward.

script(s) also called thaumacrum; the name for all the chemical concoctions made by *dispensurists*, *skolds* and *scourges*. They are divided into basic "types" or *realms*:

♦ restoratives or vigorants – healing and well-being, such as *birchet* or *evander water*

♦ fulminants – explosions and flashes and makers of fire, such as *Licurius* uses

♦ discutants – concusives, closely related to fulminants, though not causing fire

♦ pestilants or venificants – poisons

♦ mordants – corrosives such as special kinds of acid used by *scourges*

♦ abruptives – preventative measures such as *nullodours*

♦ repugnants – scripts that repel like *bothersalts* and those that attract, like *john-tallow*

♦ alembants – scripts that alter the biology, such as the washes that transform the vision of a *leer's* eyes. *Cathar's Treacle* comes under this heading too

♦ expunctants or obliterants – scripts that utterly destroy or slay instantly, many of which are theoretical "super-weapons".

There are four recognised physical states these *realms* can come in:

♦ fumes – smokes and gases

♦ pomanders or ashes – powders

♦ liquors or waters – liquids

♦ sugars or salts – crystallised versions of the above three.

scrutineers another name for *revenue officers*, sometimes used to especially mean those who have the power of search and seizure.

Sebastipole, Mister ~ *leer* and agent for the *Lamplighter-Marshal* of *Winstermill*; has served there for over half of his life. His mother coming from Pollux and his father from Sebastian, Sebastipole was raised in the small south-eastern kingdom of Burgundia. He is sharp-minded, efficient and fiercely loyal to the *Lamplighter-Marshal*. About ten years ago, Sebastipole became a *leer* at the request of his superiors. He appreciates the power of his augmented sight but finds the wearing of a *sthenicon* repulsive. Therefore, although he possesses one, he uses it only seldom, when duty calls for it. His eyes give him away as a *falseman*. See *leers*.

sedonition the state of being a *sedorner*; loving *monsters*, or at least not hating them, as most folks do.

sedorner official and most insulting and incriminating name for a *monster-lover*. Anyone having any sense of friendship or understanding with *monsters* is said to be under the influence of outramour – the "dark love". Those worse affected by this outramour are apparently meant to run off into the wilds to spend the rest of their short lives with the *bogles* they so admire. To be heard even trying to understand *monsters* from a sympathetic point of view can bring the charge upon you. Different communities and realms deal with *sedonition* to different degrees of severity, but it is not uncommon for those found guilty to be exposed on a Catherine wheel or even hanged on a gallows.

Senior Service, the ~ the name the *navy* gives itself; service in the *navy* is considered superior to service in the *army*, as a *lamplighter*, in an Imperial post or anything else. See *navy*.

sequin second-highest value coin of the *Soutlands*, made of a silver alloy. Worth one-sixteenth of a *sou* or 20 *guise* or one-twenty-fourth of an *oscadril*, it is represented by the letter "**q**". See *money*.

she-oak medium to tall tree with a single straight trunk and possessing long needles instead of leaves that droop to the ground and hiss musically in even the lightest breeze; tough trees that grow in almost any environment.

Shunt, Mister *gastrineer* of the *Hogshead* and probably one of the nastiest fellows you are ever likely to meet. He speaks little and uses his knife a lot.

Signal Stars, the ~ also called the Superlatives. The nightly glowing orbs that are said to show one's way through life and the land. They include the Signals of Paths (also known as the Atrapës) which aid navigation (probably the most important and genuinely useful); the Signals of Ardence, meant to aid those in love; the Signals of Lots, apparently watching over those making important choices or testing their fate, and so on. The stars that do not have these mystic or informative qualities are called the Luminaries.

Silvernook large town between *High Vesting* and *Winstermill* made rich and bustling by the silver mine nearby opened over a century before and still proving to be a plentiful source of the precious metal.

Sinster city where *lahzars* are made; remote, built on the fork of two *threwdish* rivers in the region known as Burgundis. It is divided into two parts: Sinster Major and Later Sinster. Sinster Major is the original city founded before the beginnings of the *Empire* by a community of Burgundians. When, centuries later, the survivors of the fall of Caathis (the Cathars) arrived, they were welcomed, and expanded the city, building Later Sinster. It is from here that they perform their blasphemous surgeries to turn people into *lahzars*. Ironically, the notorious surgeons of Sinster are also the best, and despite their reputation as black *habilists*, have secretly saved the life of many of the *Empire's* loftiest *peers*.

Sitt footman and boot-black – or shoe polisher – working at the *Harefoot Dig*. As it was once so excellently said, "A scuff, madam, is a terrible thing!".

skold(s) also *habilist* or zaumabalist ("soup-thrower") or fumomath, the term for a *teratologist* who does the work of fighting *monsters* using chemicals and potions known as *potives*. They throw these *potives* by hand, pour them from bottles, fling them with a sling or fustibal (a sling on a stick), fire them from pistols know as salinumbus ("salt-cellars"), set traps, make smoke and whatever else it takes to defeat and destroy a *monster*. We might call them "combat chemists". They typically wear flowing robes and some kind of conical hat to signify their trade. The most common hat is the overtap, which folds back slightly over the wearer's head (see page 229). More serious and aggressive skolds will mark themselves with distinctive *spoors*, a vertical bar running over the eye (or both eyes) and down the face from hairline to the jaw; or a horizontal bar from one earlobe across the mouth to the other earlobe. Skolds learn their arcarnum ("secret knowledge") and the skills peculiar to their trade at one of many organised "colleges" about the *Empire* called a *rhombus*. It takes at least two years to properly prepare a person as a skold, and any more years spent after that hone their knowledge and some skills still further. Entry into a *rhombus* is expensive and difficult, and places are limited. The best have waiting lists over 20 years long. The forerunners of the skolds were the self-taught rhubezhals (said "roo-beh-zaal"), the *monster-hunters* of the ancient people know as the Skylds. In fact the word "skold" is a corruption of "Skyld", a name given to those rhubezhals who ventured beyond their lands to serve ancient foreign kings. These expatriate rhubezhals learnt new skills and *scripts* in the new lands, and began formalising their knowledge, writing it in books. Finally they formed guilds with each other – the rhombuses – and began to train new hopefuls. And so the skolds as they are recognised today were founded. Skolds earn a good portion of their living also making *potives* to sell to everyday folk, so that they might also protect themselves from and even fight the *monsters*. *Scripts* made for this common use are called vulgum; *scripts* that skolds keep secret to themselves are known as *nostrum*. Your basic vulgum *potive* like *bothersalts* sells for about 1 *guise* for one dose. The average skold will earn about 180 sous a year in *prize-money*, *monster*-ridding contract fees and sales of their vulgum. Used broadly the name skold can mean one of five different trades:

♦ skolds – sometimes called high skolds, formally trained at a *rhombus*, your standard "combat chemist";

♦ *scourges* – also formally trained, usually the most talented *script* makers, employing the most deadly and powerful *potives* to do their work and often excessively violent;

♦ *dispensurists* – formally trained, makers of healing brews;

♦ rhubezhals – still existing in the eastern lands of *Wörms*, Skald and Gothia, they are healer and *monster-hunter* in one, taking on *apprentices* to pass on their knowledge. Rhubezhals possess secrets now lost to the skolds, who regard them as backward;

♦ ledgermains – self-taught "skolds" making *potives* from books with often wildly varying results. They are scorned by the others as dangerous, unlearned, irresponsible and dishonest.

Small groups of skolds might gather themselves into a tight group known as a school, sharing recipes and developing their own special *nostrum*.

Slothog, the ~ a famous bolbogis or dog-of-war used by the *Turkemen*; it was one of the largest ever made and met its end at *the Battle of the Gates*. Its back and shoulders were covered in 4 to 6 foot spines which it could burst out just once in a battle to do terrible execution. Like most of the best quality made-*monsters*, when it died it dissolved into a useless puddle, preventing the enemy from learning the secrets of its creation. Most bolbogis live for only a dozen years or more. The Slothog, at the time of its demise, had been alive for an unprecedented 43 years, causing misery and destruction for 41 of them. Bolbogis are more common north of the *Marrow*, that is, outside of the *Empire*, especially ones of the Slothog's size. In the *Empire* smaller kinds like *rever-men* and the schtackleschwien ("shta-kell-shween") can be found, usually employed as "guard dogs" or for hunting criminals. In the *Empire*, making such creatures is illegal but owning them is not. Other general names for bolbogis include bollumbogs, teratobellum and carnivolpës. See *gudgeon* and *monsters*.

smugglers also called bog-trotters, along with *brigands*. Many goods are illegal in one *city-state* or another, banned in the *Empire* or some other *realm*, and the smugglers see it as their task to provide relief from the tyrannies of such policies. There is nothing a half-decent smuggler will not secret across borders, carry from one city to the next. They lubricate the *dark trades*, trafficking all those blasphemous bits about. A smuggler may even turn to piracy if the rewards are high enough. Their main foes are weather, *monsters* and *revenue officers,* whose major task is to catch them. Even *lamplighters* play their part in bringing smugglers to justice. As with most things illegal, the promise of a lot of money makes the danger well worth it.

Snarl once one of Rossamünd's fellow *foundlings*, Snarl was employed a year ago by the *Boschenberg navy* and considers himself to have reached the acme of all that there is to wish for as a once-rejected *foundling*. His time at *Madam Opera's* was spent bullying and teasing those smaller than himself (almost every other child), but not with anywhere near the vigour or cruelty of *Gosling*.

social status comprising ten recognised positions or "situations", the first two being known as the *Peers*, the next two the Quality, then the Lectry, the Commonality and lowest of all the Varletry.

♦ First: Lords and Nobles [*Peers*] — those of highest inherited or granted rank within the *Empire*, holding the most important tasks, such as regents of the different states, Imperial magistrates or ministers in the Imperial parliament. Highest ranked for the first and second situations are Princes (rare), then Duke, then Marquis, Earl (or Count), Baron, Viscount and, least of these, Baronet.

♦ Second: Antique Sanguines [*Peers*] — the "Old Blood", the old families whose rank and line can be traced back to before the beginnings of the *Empire*. They may not occupy many of the best jobs but know full well that there is a big difference between "old" nobility and "new" nobility. There are more princes and princesses among the Antique Sanguines.

♦ Third: Magnates [Quality] — those who have come from lower ranks to acquired enormous wealth and with it bought great power. Such are the greatness of their riches that the *Peers* and even the Emperor will go to them for financial backing. The highest ranked magnate is an Elephantine, followed by a Vulgarine (or Vulgard), and least a Niggard. The most senior are called Lords.

♦ Fourth: Gentry [Quality] — the landed class, owning vast acreage and living in comfort, burdened by neither the responsibilities of higher rank nor the lack of anything their hearts desire. Although most own land in the country they prefer to live in the cities. Country gentry are considered a little backward by their city "cousins". The Gentry imitate those of better situation in manner and fashion. Highest rank is Companion, then Esquire and finally Gentleman.

♦ Fifth: Bureaucrats [Lectry] — managers, lawyers, physicians, chief clerks, naval officers, administrators, scholars, teachers, guild-masters and other self-made folk. These all work and live in good comfort and are never in want.

♦ Sixth: Merchants [Lectry] — as their title suggests these are the exporters and importers, the shop and factory owners, the sellers, the traders. It is from this situation that many Magnates rise, having found a niche market or secured a monopoly and exploited it to the utmost. This class also includes farmers who own their own holdings and guild-affiliated craftsmen. *Surgeons* are considered among this class, as well as most *skolds* (except those born into a better situation). They live in moderate comfort with long hours of work.

◆ Seventh: Peons [Commonality] – the unskilled or un-guilded craftsmen, skilled farmhands, foremen, *vinegaroons*, soldiers, *dispensurists*, *leers*, *lamplighters*, *gaiters* and *yardsmen*, *sagaars*, miners, factory-hands, stevedores, *apprentices*, chief servants and such as these. They live tolerably well and work very hard.

◆ Eighth: Servants [Commonality] – maids, valets, kitchen-hands, page-boys, stable-hands, and all others such as these who live hard and work even harder, often earning not much over 10 *sous* a year.

◆ Ninth: Rustics [Varletry] – unskilled labourers, lower class farm-hands, tinkers, hawkers, woodcutters, peltrymen (trappers), rhubezhals (see *skolds*), living tough, hard working lives.

◆ Tenth: Destitutes [Varletry] – those with few prospects living wretched, desperate lives, often driven to desperate acts (such as *brigands*). Many of the criminal types are lumped into this class, regardless of how successful they might be.

Those of a higher situation have the power to influence the lives of those below them. *Lahzars* occupy a strange place in society, and no one is at all sure where to put them. High-born *lahzars* rely on their inherited situation, yet those of lower status at birth seem to be accorded a grudging respect similar to their noble fellows. It is all very perplexing and forms a common topic of many a parlour-room gathering.

Sooning Street street in *Boschenberg* that leads out of the suburb *Poéme* and down to the canal-side suburbs and the *Padderbeck*.

soporific any *potive* or *draught* designed to make people become woozy or sleepy, or put them to sleep.

sou(s) said "soo"; the highest-value coin of the *Soutlands*, made of a gold alloy; worth 16 *sequins* or 320 *guise* or two-thirds of an *oscadril* – the *Emperor's Billion*. It is represented by the letter "**S**". See *money*.

Sough, the ~ said "sow"; the hills and more particularly the fenlands right at the south-western tip of *Sulk End* and forming the eastern flank of the mouth of the *River Humour*. The fenlands of the Sough are untamed, despite the presence of the Arxis Sublicum or Pollburg in its midst, a fortress established by the *Empire* under the pretext of providing protection, but there really to watch over trade coming in and out of the *Humour*.

Soutlands, the ~ also the Soutland City-states, said "sowt-lands" or "sutt-lands" depending on what part of the *Empire* you are from; all the southern conquests of the *Empire* situated south of the great *threwdish* plains of the Grassmeer. They were systematically subdued by the Imperial armies over 1,000 years ago and are now home to the racially mixed descendants of the old combatants, many of whom still claim racial distinction from their neighbours.

spasm, spasming wretched condition where a *lahzar's* body rebels for a moment against the foreign organs squeezed within it and the organs fight back. This happens when the mimetic (introduced) organs are being used and is usually as a result of not taking one's *Cathar's Treacle* and the rest. It is, however, a risk (very slight) that *lahzars* run all the time, whether they have taken their concoctions or not. The results of spasming can be various, from a slight strain within that goes away after a few hours to severe internal haemorrhaging and serious organ damage. After spasming a *lahzar* often needs to return to his or her transmogrifier (*lahzar*-making *surgeon*) for observation and even further operations. See *lahzar* and *Cathar's Treacle*.

Spindle, the ~ *rivergate* built by the *city-state* of *Brandenbrass* as a rival to the *Axles*. Sanctioned by the *Emperor*, its presence has added another half to the cost of doing trade on the *Humour*, making life difficult for all those cities further upriver including (and most importantly) *Boschenberg*. Petitioning and debate rage among the two cities' Imperial ministers and their regents and for a student of history it all sounds like the rumblings of yet another war.

spoors marks worn by *teratologists* and other folk of violence as signs of their trade, made using a milky liquid known as rue-of-asper, or just rue (not to be confused with the repellent "Salt-of-Asper") carefully painted on to the skin in whatever shape is desired. Apparently, it stings like lemon-juice in a paper cut. Left for about an hour, and stinging the whole time, the rue-of-asper is then washed off with a solution of vinegar and cloves to leave a deep blue mark. Alternatively, the rue can be washed off with a solution of dilute aqua regia, when it will leave a white mark.

sprig(s) type of *monster*, small and nasty and often plaguing homes and homemakers, and so its use as an insult is obvious.

Spring Caravan of the Gightland Queen, the ~ seasonal peregrinations of the *Gightland Queen*, forced to move from one of her six palaces to another as the stench of the piles of rotting food scraps and backed-up excrement from overused sewers becomes too much to bear or mask. She and all her possessions, family, servants, retainers, ministers, clerks, house guards and spurns (bodyguards) take to the road in a long, gorgeous procession, making their way to the next palace and leaving behind an *army* of servants to clean the previous one. The comfort and opulence of these caravans are seen as the epitome of all things comfortable and luxurious, as is everything the *Gightland Queen* is supposed to do. See *Gightland Queen*.

stage shorter of the two *fulgaris* at 3 feet to 4 feet long and used by *fulgars* to help in directing a lightning bolt in the right direction once it has been "*thermistored*" from the clouds. It is also a convenient baton to extend a *fulgar's* reach and parry blows from opponents' weapons. It is not considered politic to "come to hand strokes" (enter into a hand-to-hand fight) with *fulgars*, for any metal weapon that touches them will carry a deadly charge back to the wielder, and although wooden weapons do not conduct an arc so easily, they can be burst to bits instead. A better way to fight *fulgars* is to hit them with the long reach of a *flintlock musket* or pistol. Indeed, the best way, it is said, to fight a *fulgar* – or a *wit* for that matter – is to be on the other side of the *Empire* and have someone else do it for you.

steerboard right-hand side of a vessel if you are facing the bow; corresponds to our "starboard".

sthenicon said "s-then-i-kon"; a biologue – a biological machine; device used to seek out tiny or hidden smells and to show things difficult to see – whether hidden or far-off – more clearly. Usually a simple, dark wooden box, with leather straps and buckles. The back, which goes against the face, is hollowed out and sealed within with a doeskin-like material. On each side of this protrude stubby brass horns. Air and the attendant odours enter through these hornlets and, by the organics inside, are rendered more odoriferous. If the compactly folded membrane inside that enhances smells so effectively was spread out, it would stretch around 120 squares of feet. At the middle of the top of the box is a modest lens, through which vision is received. Upon the sides of the sthenicon, at the same height as the lens, are three slots, which the user can push in and out in various ways to alter the nature of how he sees. A small hole in one of the lower corners is bored into the front of the box, apparently to render the user more audible when talking so that the device need not be removed to allow the wearer to speak. Another slot in the bottom of the box allows soups, thin stews and special *draughts* that augment the use of this tool to be slurped with only minor inconvenience. The whole kit is fastened to the head – over nose and mouth – with the straps and buckles mentioned earlier. If a sthenicon is worn for too long the organ within can begin to grow into the user's own nasal membrane and even into the face. Used mostly by *leers*.

stock • or calmus; the straight stick used by beginners in *harundo* and other stick-fighting arts. • an elaborately high neckerchief, wrapping about the whole neck and throat.

strake(s) large cast-iron sheets riveted to the wooden sides of an *ironclad* vessel. One sheet of a uniform length is one strake, so that someone spotting a *ram* at sea could count the number of strakes down one *broadside* and, with a little arithmetic, have a good idea just how big she is.

stramineous the colour of straw.

"stuck between the stone and the sty" to be faced with two equally unpleasant choices or situations.

Sub-Elements, the ~ all the metals, earths, liquids and gases that make up the *Four Elements*. It is the Sub-Elements that form the cosmos, the earth and all that is in it. Some of the many Sub-Elements include fire-flash (hydrogen), fire-damp (methane), small-air (helium), aeris regia (oxygen) and so on.

Sugar of Nnun one of the more notorious ingredients, it is in its own right a deadly poison whose constituents only "those wicked men of *Sinster*" know anything about. It is rumoured that one is corpse liquor, a filthy deep-brown *ichor* that comes from the rotting of bodies and is highly illegal within the *Empire*. Sugar of Nnun is used for many of the more dangerous or powerful scripts, particularly those used by *scourges*. It is Sugar of Nnun that makes *Cathar's Treacle* go oily and black, and its combination with the other ingredients that renders it helpful rather than harmful.

Sulk, the ~ broad flat lands all along eastern banks of the *River Humour* and south of Gightland (Catalain) extensively farmed by a cooperation of many states and also dug with several quarries providing many building materials and minerals for much of the *Half-Continent*.

Sulk End south-western tip of the vast bread-basket of *the Sulk*; probably the least populated part of that region, although the land is well tamed, becoming only middlingly *threwdish* as it nears the Smallish Fells in the east and the *Sough* in the south-west. Sulk End is famous for its lettuces and strawberries and the giant windmills that grind most of the region's grain and much of its powdered earths as well.

surgeon(s) sometimes called butchers, because they poke and dig and carve into people, or sectifactors (coming from sectification "to operate on a living creature"). Surgeons are seen as the dark cousin to the *physicians*. Most surgeons train at the same institutions as *physicians*, but concentrate more on the autopsy and workings of human and *monster* than theories and cures and higher knowledge. A surgeon's main tasks involve amputation of gangrenous or ruined limbs; simple surgeries like appendectomies; the removal of bullets and splinters or teeth and spines from *monsters*. If anyone in the *Half-Continent* were bothered to view the statistics they would find that more people survive the ministrations of a surgeon than of a *physician*. Yet despite all the seemingly miraculous work surgeons might do, they are still mistrusted; and this is primarily for their connection with *lahzars*, and with fabercadavery and therospeusia (the making of *monsters*) and all the worst excesses of black *habilistics*. Because of this surgeons are far less common than *physicians* or *dispensurists*. People prefer, if they must deal with a surgeon, to have a *physician* or even a *dispensurist* act as a go-between. Indeed, in many realms it is illegal for a surgeon to practise without the presence of a *physician*. It is rumoured that the current *Emperor* will not even let a surgeon touch him. As with many other professions there are various grades of surgeon:

- articled surgeons – gain their training through apprenticeship only, usually working as aides to more skilled surgeons. Articled surgeons may, through an intensive interview at a physactery (see *physician*), be granted higher status if they have served 10 years or more. Also simply called "articles".

- house surgeons – train for a year, gaining a diploma and with it the mandate to perform the simpler operations: extracting foreign matter from the body and amputating limbs.

- Imperial or senior surgeons – having completed the full examination of 3 to 4 years are granted a degree, which warrants these surgeons to perform all and any kind of "butchery" they deem necessary.

- carvers – self-taught, book-learned individuals, often serving because there is no qualified surgeon available. They will normally do only amputations and bullet extractions and are most common in armies and navies.

A strange little twist that goes some small way to salvaging the surgeons' generally bad reputation is that they are prepared to attend duels and there tend wounds, while any self-respecting *physician* would never be party to such knavery.

Surprise, the ~ 28 *guns-broad frigate* of the *Boschenberg navy*, which has been in service for a century. Formerly part of *Brandenbrass navy*, it was captured by *Boschenberg* shortly after the *Battle of the Mole*. It has a glorious history, taking many prizes of pirates and sea-monsters, making successive generations of crews wealthy. At the *Battle of the Mole*, while still serving *Brandenbrass*, it played a significant role in the fighting. For much of the battle the *frigate* had served as all smaller *rams* do, trawling behind the main line of battle in support, picking up survivors, towing larger vessels that had been immobilised, watching exposed flanks. For several hours its captain, a certain Mister Codmoss, had been watching his confederates in the Solemn League's combined *navy* being ground to a stalemate by the Wretcherman fleet: an immovable line of the 23 main-rams centred on the cumbersome *Sucathia*, an enormous *main-sovereign* of 156 *guns-broad*. For the Solemn League a stalemate was a loss: Wretch could still dictate the terms of its waterways and hold the Grumid states to ransom. At a critical moment Captain Codmoss spied a break in the Wretcherman line as a rising swell shifted the well-founded positions of the enemy *rams*. Though it was not its role, the courageous Captain Codmoss could see that there were no capital *rams* available to seize this opportunity. Signalling another *frigate* to follow his lead, Codmoss sent the nimble *Surprise* dashing through the fortuitous gap into the waters beyond the enemy line. As it passed the stern of the main-ram *Caldbink* 74, it sent a volley of raking fire from its 32 pounder *lombarins,* crashing through the main-ram's vulnerable stern windows. The crew of the *Surprise* who survived would recall the horrid sound of their shots smashing down the length of the *Caldbink*'s gun decks, causing great execution to her startled gun crews. Once clear on the other side, the quick-thinking Codmoss spied the *Sucathia* and came about in a wide arc, avoiding the determined attentions of enemy *frigates* and *gun-drudges* as he did. Putting all *limbers* to the *screw*, the *Surprise* gained all possible speed and rammed the mighty *main-sovereign* just slightly forward of amidships. The clamour of the impact – of rending, tortured metal and splintering beams – was said to be heard over the muffled din of battle by those watching the distant battle through spyglasses from the Foulmouth on the northernmost tip of Wretch. Indeed, the force of the impact was enough to tip the *Sucathia* sharply to its left, listing dangerously to the *ladeboard* side, pointing the guns on that *broadside* uselessly into the water, while the unengaged guns of the *steerboard* poked into the sky. The valiant *Surprise* was even worse off; now taking on water, its ram and bow were staved almost completely in and stuck fast in the shattered side of the *main-sovereign*. With half its crew sustaining serious injury in the collision, worse was yet to come. As the gun-crews of the *Sucathia* recovered, they quickly learnt their predicament and turned their attention and their guns to the diminutive upstart protruding from the ram's *steerboard* side. *Cannon*-muzzles were traversed as low as possible and soon enough a murderous fire was pummelled down on to the exposed wooden decks of the *Surprise*. In less than one quarter of an hour the valiant *frigate* was smashed to a useless hulk. But this was all the *Sucathia* could do, for even in such a ruinous condition the *Surprise* could not be prised free, and the *main-sovereign* was unable to contribute any more to the fight. With the *Sucathia* neutralised by a vessel almost one-sixteenth its size, the main-rams fighting against her were released to bring pressure to other points along the enemy line. After only another hour the *Battle of the Mole* was over with the Solemn League the winner. With this victory the easy passage of their *cargoes* was secured. As for the heroic, hapless *Surprise*, with three-quarters of her crew dead or dying (including Captain Codmoss) and nothing more than a *ironclad* shell of splinters and blood, she was towed back to *Brandenbrass* by the 80-gun main-ram *Director*. There she was left for several years, rusting in the shallows off the Silt Mounds, before a private contractor, in a fit of patriotism, took her into dry-dock and remade her anew to be employed as a marquelin (a privateer vessel – see *navy*). It was in this capacity that she was captured by the *Boschenberg navy*, which quickly took her into its service, proud to have won such a noble vessel for its fleet.

sustis pure determined defence, with *cudgel* held up; one of the many moves that are part of the *Hundred Rules of Harundo*.

swamp oak dark, scruffy tree that grows tall in bogs and fens; the presence of swamp oaks is said to indicate the presence of *monsters*, and so they are chopped down when found in the *precincts of man*.

swine's lard oily fat of dead pigs, boiled, and used for cosmetics and *scripts* alike.

T

Teagarden *gater,* head of the night-watch and chief *yardsman* at the *Harefoot Dig*. The *chain mail* he wears, though a little old-fashioned, is an heirloom that has passed through 12 generations to make it to him. He wears it with pride, but is a practical man and so has a stout haubardine beneath (see *harness*).

teratologist(s) also *pugnator*, *monster-hunter*, theroscaturgis ("beast-destroyer") or catagist(~is) ("destroyer"). Strictly speaking, a teratologist is one who studies *monsters*. The term is used, however, to mean anyone with a professional interest in *monsters*, especially those who simply want to destroy them. Teratologists include: *lahzars* – both *fulgar* and *wit*; *skolds* and *scourges*; *sagaars* (the dancers); and filibusters or venators, everyday folks with no particularly unusual skill, just a bunch of *potives* bought from a *skold*, a sturdy brace of weapons, a keen eye and a cunning mind.

Different teratologists have different reputations:

- A *skold* or filibuster walking into the common room of a *wayhouse* will typically find himself or herself being greeted warmly and invited to join a table of regulars in a drink.

- If a *fulgar* or a *scourge* walks into the common room of a *wayhouse*, he or she might be greeted by a wary nod, a brief word of welcome, or general wariness.

- The arrival of a *wit* is met with suspicious silence, with people staring, or turning away embarrassedly if the *wit* looks their way; no hearty welcomes, no free drinks, just barely concealed fear and loathing.

- *Sagaars* are too new to the culture of the *Empire* for folks to generally know what to do with them. Usually they are regarded a strange curiosities or otherwise ignored.

teratology technically it is the study of *monsters* and anything to do with them (such as *threwd*); more broadly it also means the study and practice of theroscaturgy ("beast-destroying"); that is, *monster*-hunting.

test shortened from testle ("appliance, apparatus"); the place where a *skold* or *scourge* or any other *habilist* makes *potives* and *draughts*; what we would call a "laboratory". Confusingly, it can be anything from a building to a cart or portable box.

thermistor • act of *thermistoring*. • the name for a *fulgar* who thermistors – that is, causes lightning to strike from an overcast sky. They do it at great risk to themselves, and because *thermistoring* can only be done on cloudy, rainy days, thermistors have a reputation for being gloomy and dour – which, as it happens, is often true. Sometimes also called thunderers. See *fulgar*, *fulguris*, *lahzar*, *stage*.

thermistoring the action of using a *fuse* to make lightning strike from the sky. See *fuse* for a more detailed description of how this is done. See *fulgar* and *thermistor*.

thew the body; one's strength of limb and health, including *pith*, one's metabolism.

threwd also called the Horrors; threwd is the sensation of watchfulness and awareness of the land or waters about you. Although no one is certain, the most popular theory is that the land itself is strangely sentient, intelligent and aware, and resents the intrusions and misuses of humankind. Paltry threwd, the mildest kind, can make a person feel uneasy as if under unfriendly observation. The worst kind of threwd – called pernicious threwd – can drive a person completely mad with unfounded terrors and dark paranoias. Many expeditions of several thousand sent to tame certain regions of terrible threwd have disappeared without a trace. Once or twice a survivor or two has returned, ravening and broken. Not even a lahzar's potencies can protect from the most pernicious threwd. It is well known that wherever threwd occurs, there *monsters* are too. Some *teratologist* scholars go so far as to suggest a mutually beneficial relationship between all *monsters* and the threwd. It has even been posited by the more eccentric natural philosophers that threwd is not just strong and weak, but also good and bad. Such an idea borders on *sedonition* and is not taken seriously. Several old books have said that there are those *monsters* powerful enough to have their own threwd, the power to terrify, drive mad or control weak minds at will, and that the worst of them can project such threwd far beyond themselves to take a whole place under their control – a forest for example. In fact the mind-control exercised by the *false-gods* is thought to be a kind of threwd.

threwdish possessing or radiating *threwd*; haunted; frightening or terrifying, especially because of the threat of *monsters*.

thrice-high taller variation of a tricorner hat, with its three angled brim-panels protruding straight rather than curving in towards the crown.

Tin Drum Lane main thoroughfare of the *Mortar* in *Boschenberg*, where some of the city's, even the region's, best *gaulders* can be found. The stink of boiling *gauld* in all its varieties hangs over the street like a cloud.

Tochtigstrat Hergott for "windy or breezy street".

tomahawk small-headed axe with a hollowed blade on one side and a broad spike on the other; the handle is often entirely bound with leather or sergreen (shark-skin); light, effective in a fight and good for throwing, too.

tormentum(s) essentially large catapults used to throw great hollow metal shells called censers at any threatening *monsters*, especially the bigger kinds. These 4-foot-diameter censers are filled with prodigious amounts of fizzing, smoking *potives*, and are flung in fuming arcs at any oncoming *nicker*. They are especially popular in harbour defences, for gigantic nadderers (sea-monsters) have the nasty habit of rising out the depths at certain times each year.

treacle shortened form of *Cathar's Treacle*.

trews either long, thick woollen stockings or tight-fitting leggings of the same material, worn as an undergarment.

troubardier said "troo-bard-ear"; foot-soldier or *pediteer* wearing full-*harness* of a haubardine with tassets, a testudo (metal back-and-breastplate) and sometimes pauldrons (metal shoulder armour). They protect their heads in distinctive full-faced metal helmets such as bascinets, sallets, or the odd-looking hundshugel. Main weapons are the poleaxe (actually a hammer and a bec-de-corbin on a pole), langrass (huge two-handed sword) or clauf (long metal-studded club). Designated assault infantry. See *pediteer* and *harness*.

tuck • or tuckin; small tin-silver coin worth 2 *sequins* or one-eighth of a *sou*. • name given to a small foldable knife.

Turkemen, the ~ said "tur-keh-men"; not in this current story. The Turkemen, their ruling caste the Omdür, and their Emperor the Püshtän rule a vast empire to the north of *Clementine* and the rest of the *Haacobin Empire*. For many centuries they have had their thoughts bent on conquering the Haacobins. The threat of the Turkemen is the main reason the various rivalling parts of the *Empire* remain in uneasy unity.

turnery eating utensils made of wood instead of cuttle, that is, pewter.

turpentine tall, broad-spreading evergreen tree with a rough dark grey trunk and small dark leaves, associated with *threwd* and *monsters*. Its sap and wood are strongly resistant to the caustic waters of the *vinegar seas*, making it favoured for the construction of wharves and other harbour structures. Great forests of turpentine are grown to meet the demand for lumber, and these plantations attract all sorts of skulking *bogles* and *nickers*.

Tutin said "tyoo-tin"; a race of people who conquered the *Soutlands* and beyond, the most senior being the *Emperor,* who rules from *Clementine.* Also the language spoken by them, which is very close to Latin in our own world (to the purists I give my deepest apologies).

tyke another name for *urchin*.

tyke-oil *potive* that works in the opposite way to a *nullodour*, in that it intensifies your smell while making it as foul to a *monster* as possible. The idea is to make you repulsive and seemingly inedible. It is a last measure when you know there is no getting away from a *monster*.

U

Uda said "yoo-dah"; second cook of the *Harefoot Dig*, serving under *Closet.* Most people would say that Uda is a better cook, that you can tell when she has made a dish and when she has not; so much so that some regulars ask for her to cook their meal, which she hates because *Closet* find it so offensive. Once or twice *Closet* has ignored these requests and has been caught out each time. Uda has even been employed by local nobles to cook for their grand dinners.

umbles one's gizzards and guts.

Unhallows Night another name for *Gallows Night*.

urchin(s) also *tyke*; among the most powerful of *monsters*, having human-like bodies but heads like different kinds of animal. Very rarely seen by people, if at all in modern times, they are said to be almost indestructible. Ancient texts suggest that the lords of the *monsters* are among their number and that there was once, many thousands of years ago, free communication between everymen and urchins. Probably the best known is one called the Duke of Crows, an urchin-lord or nimuine, ruling an enormous *threwdish* forest called the Autumn of Sleep.

utterworsts • the wildest, most black-hearted of monsters; • anything considered the worst kind of evil.

V

Vadè Chemica said "vay-dah kem-i-kah"; ancient book on *habilistics*, particularly the making of *scripts* (called scryptia or scryptics). Said to contain destructive, forbidden information, it was apparently written by a group of unknown authors from a now-lost race who were so far in advance of current "technologies" that it is still an authority today. Indeed, most have trouble fathoming exactly what large parts of it mean. In the *Empire* it is illegal to have a copy of the *Vadè Chemica*, though many people have secret copies of excerpts from it, including a small 7-volume series called the *Seven Nephthandous Tomes*. Outside of the *Empire* it is held in higher regard. The *rhombus* in *Wörms*, for example, has well over a dozen copies and its *apprentices* study it closely the entire duration of their training. The *skolds* from *Wörms* are thought to be the best in *the Half-Continent*.

venison ragout spicy dish made of cubes of deer-meat and various vegetables, cooked in a thick, rich sauce till they are so tender they almost fall apart.

Verhooverhoven, Doctor local *physician* of the *Brindleshaws*, a fellow in his early thirties who enjoys the good favour of the *peers* and gentry of that region. Born in *High Vesting* of poor parents, he scraped together enough to pay for his own training in the physic arts, working for four years as a surgeon's assistant onboard various *rams* of the *Boschenberg* navy.

Verline said "verr-leen"; parlour-maid to *Madam Opera* and the eldest daughter of a proud serving-family, who see service as an honour and a dignity. Tender and caring of almost all of the children of the Madam's *Marine Society*, Verline has a soft spot for *Rossamünd*: something in his awkwardness reminds her of herself as a child. Her role is to tend to the needs of *Madam Opera*, though she is often caught up in some mission of tenderness for some child or other. Almost as beautiful as her younger sister *Praeline*, Verline is the darling of the all-male staff at *Madam Opera's*, who often leave her little gifts and do whatever she asks. Verline herself would never dream of abusing such affection, and returns it whole-heartedly to the men she calls "those dear old salts". *Praeline* (or more properly the Lady *Praeline*, for she has married well above her station) provides the money to her older sister to buy such small luxuries as *pamphlets*.

Vespasia   also Vespasio; constellation sitting high in the night sky. At certain times the red planet *Faustus* will appear like an eye in the midst of Vespasia. This is regarded by the superstitious as a sign of ill fortune.

Vestiweg, the ~   or Vesting Way; road running from *Proud Sulking* parallel with the *River Humour*, meeting with the eastern bastion of the *Spindle* before going through the *Brindleshaws* to a junction with the *Gainway*.

Vigilus, Rivermaster ~   master and owner of the fine *cromster Rupunzil* of 16 guns.

vigorant(s)   *scripts* concerned with reviving and healing. See *scripts*.

vinegaroon(s)   common term for a sailor at sea but not on a river (*bargemen*), whether working a *ram* or a *cargo*, and of any rank. Two things that make a vinegaroon stand out in a crowd is the clumsy, rolling walk that comes from moving around decks constantly rolling with the sea; and red, pitted and blotchy skin, especially on the face, damaged by the caustic sprays and spindrift of crashing waves and wind-whipped waters. The life of a vinegaroon is hard and they often die young; for one to live into his sixties is a remarkable feat.

vinegar seas, vinegar waves   also the acerbic seas, the lurid seas, the soda-seas, or the Main; sometimes also called simply "the vinegar", "the deeps" or even just "the sea" or "the ocean", of course; named for the sharp, sour-wine smell of their waters, caused by the exotic salts that dissolve up from the ocean floor. Although these salts smell similar, they make the seas and oceans distinctly different colours: bright yellow, orange, red, violent blues, murky greens, white and even black. The acrid nature of the sea water is inhospitable to people. After half an hour in the water, your skin will become red-raw and sting sharply. After about three-quarters of an hour, painful blisters will form and even pop. After an hour and a half in the vinegar, the salts in the water will have leeched into your body, retarding and even stopping the precise chemical reactions in your cells that keep you alive. Shock sets in, and soon after this your end will come. The creatures that make the vinegar seas their home, including the nadderers (sea-monsters), are made to live in it and thrive. Anything caught from the oceans for eating has to be soaked in brews known as dulcifiers (said "dool-sih-fy-ers"), which neutralise the poisonous salts and (apparently) improve the flavour of the meat. This process is known as "soaking", and can take a long time to do properly. Fortunately, there are several types of fish that do this naturally within their own bodies and can be caught, cooked and eaten straightaway. Most of these, however, do not taste nice.

Vlinderstrat Hergott for "butterfly street"; *Madam Opera's Estimable Marine Society for Foundling Boys and Girls* is an address upon its crumbling walks.

Voorwind, Clerk's Sergeant *revenue officer* in charge of one of the many gates of the *Axle*. His pay does not stretch far enough to properly provide for the needs of his 12 children (aged between 4 months and 8 years old – one set of triplets and two sets of twins), and so he has taken to receiving bribes as additional income.

W

watches there are 7 watches in a day, the day starting at 12 noon. Each watch is 4 hours long, except the two Dog Watches, which are only 2 hours each and were devised to make sure that people working by the watches do not have to do the same ones over and over. A bell is often rung or a drum beaten or a bugle sounded every half-hour of a watch; 1 bell (or rataplans or blasts) for the first half-hour, 2 bells for the second half-hour, 3 bells for the third and so on; 8 bells signals the beginning of the next watch, even for the Dog Watches.

- Afternoon Watch from 12 noon till 4 pm
- First Dog Watch from 4 pm till 6 pm
- Second Dog Watch from 6 pm till 8 pm
- First (Night) Watch from 8 pm till midnight
- Middle (Night) Watch from midnight till 4 am
- Morning Watch from 4 am till 8 am
- Forenoon Watch from 8 am till midday.

See *bells of the watch*.

411

Way, the ~ a rather poetic term for roads and a life lived wandering them.

waybill piece of paper granting the bearer access to any of the states or cities marked on it. You are allowed to enter a state not marked on it provided your other documents are in order and you get permission from the appropriate bureaucracy of the new state and the correct entry on your waybill as soon as possible. The best kind is an Imperial waybill, which declares you a "Citizen of the *Empire*", and gives the right to cross from one state to another within the *Empire*, without needing particular permission from that state's regents or representatives.

wayfarers also hucilluctors (said "hyoo-sil-luk-tor", meaning "one that goes hither and thither"); frequent travellers of *highroads* and byroads. A rugged and tough lot, hardy and knowledgeable in outdoor survival and thrival; usually good at running away – from the authorities and *monsters*. Too much skulking about can become irksome, and many a wayfarer, in country that impresses constant tiresome wariness, longs to be able to stroll down the road in the broad day with happy pace and an easy whistle. The term can also mean any traveller on the road. See Appendix 5.

wayfoods foods prized for their lightness, nutrition and long life, and therefore by *wayfarers* (travellers), *vinegaroons* (sailors) and *pediteers* (soldiers). Fortified sack cheese, *portable soup* and *red must* are all common wayfoods; the *whortleberry* is among the most expensive and the most remarkable.

wayhouse what we might call an "inn", a small fortress in which travellers can find rest for their soles and safety from the *monsters* that threaten in the *wilds* about. The most basic wayhouse is just a large common room with an attached kitchen and dwelling for the owner and staff, all surrounded by a high wall. Indeed, the common room still forms the centre of a wayhouse, where the stink of dust, sweat and *repellents* mingles with wood-smoke and the aromas of the pot. The *Harefoot Dig* is large as wayhouses go, with stables and carriage sheds, a carvery as well as a common room, a reading room, many different kinds of bedroom to suit different purses, a large staff and full-time guards.

Weegbrug *Hergott* for "weighbridge"; a busy street in *Boschenberg*, being the address of many warehouse and store yards.

Weems fellow *foundling* living at Madam Opera's. Taller than *Rossamünd* even though he is younger, and apt to pick on our boy.

weskit *proofed* vest. See *harness*.

whortleberry one of the best and most expensive of *wayfoods*. They are prized because one small berry can give an adult enough energy to last much of a day and even revive the spirits like a good *restorative*. Whortleberries come from (not surprisingly) the whortleberry bush, small with dark thorny leaves; it is found only on the western side of the *Half-Continent*. The semi-independent farming region of the Patter Moil has grown wealthy and powerful cultivating them, as have the kingdoms of Wenceslaus and Stanislaus (the Lausid states). Yet these "cultivated" plants do not produce nearly as powerful fruit as those found in wild and *threwdish* places. Brave pickers still venture into the *wilds* to collect this better harvest. Those who survive can make twice as much for the same amount as the orchard-grown variety. They are best picked when pink and fresh; typically they are dried to increase their keeping. Another method of preserving them is to make whortleberry jam, carried in clay jars and eaten with one of the many hard-breads available as *wayfood*. Their amazing properties work just as well in any preparation of the berry and all keep for a very long time. They apparently work for *monsters* just as well, and the orchards in Patter Moil and the Lausids are heavily guarded.

wilds, the ~ places beyond the civilising influence of humankind; places where *monsters* abound and *threwd* is strong, and plants grow fecund and free. People do not live in the wilds, and pass along quickly if travelling through them, normally in groups with a solid guard or powerful *potives*. Acquisitive *everymen* ogle the wilds greedily, desiring more land, more room, more wealth, and so they periodically send expeditions to tame some part of it, fighting with *monsters*, building fortresses and outposts. If all this goes well they then invite settlers to make a home, the desperate seeking a better life, to try to make the wilds into a *ditchland*. These expeditions fail as much as they succeed. See *ditchlands* and *marches*.

413

wind the soul or spirit of a person; feelings of well-being and other emotional states, the psyche; associated with one's *milt*.

Winstermill modern fortress built shortly after the *Battle of the Gates* to declare the new Emperor's firm grip on things. It now serves as the *manse* (headquarters) of the battalion of *lamplighters* serving on the *Wormway*.

Winstreslewe ancient name of a fortress built by the *Tutins* to guard what were once the southeastern borders of their realm. *Winstermill* was erected upon its foundations, which already included the tunnel through which the *Gainway* and the *Conduit Vermis* pass and meet.

wit also called neuroticrith ("holder of a distorted mind") or strivener; a kind of *lahzar*, a wit's potencies (skills or powers) cannot be seen like the sparks and flashes of a *fulgar*, but are rather felt. Collectively called antics, these potencies are subtle and more sinister, affecting the victim's mind, brain and nervous system. They are all variations on an invisible bio-electrical field, a "pulse" of energy called frission that wits make with their surgically introduced organs. The use of frission is called witting or strivening:

◆ sending or witting – the most basic and best known antic, involving a "sending" and a "returning" of frission all about the wit. With the returning a wit can get an internal, mental idea or feeling of where all sources of electricity are about them, whether an animal or a person or a *monster* or even a biologue ("living machine") like a *gastrine*. It takes practice for wits to understand and interpret the returning. With experience they can actually recognise the distinct electrical flutterings of a particular person, and so sending is often used to track people down. Beyond the cities this antic is used to warn early of a *monster's* approach, well before even a *leer* can tell. As a side-effect of this, any living creature caught in the frission will feel sick or dizzy and even faint for a moment, throwing off concentration or causing a mis-step or fumble. Those who might suffer from travel sickness will be worse affected, vomiting and staggering. The very best wits can send with only the slightest disturbance to those around them.

◆ scathing or striving – probably the most notorious of the antics, scathing is a raw pouring forth of power that twists and agonises the mind. With it an experienced wit can lay flat a whole room of foes, while the most skilled can use it to permanently break or even kill with frightening accuracy. Sometimes referred to as "the eye (or glare) of death".

♦ writhing – with this antic a neuroticrith can cause aches and pains in victims' limbs, causing them to twitch with the ache of it; conversely, it can be used to temporarily paralyse people and leave them without feeling. Worse yet, writhing is used to momentarily blind, or stop ears or render a person mute. It requires a goodly amount of experience and a modicum of talent to use this potency with any use or effect.

♦ faking – this is a very difficult potency, with the wit requiring a view of his or her victim. With delicate, subtle and precisely "aimed" probings of their frission, the wit can make a person think that he or she has heard or felt something, when in reality there is nothing. The best wits can even make people believe they have seen something that is not there. People can be driven barmy with such unseen pestering, or have their attention diverted at just the wrong moment.

A wit who is "green" has little control over the direction of the frission and it tends to radiate all about. With practice wits gain control over the area and direction of their frission till they can send it to a particular point. Most wits need to see what they are aiming at, but the most talented need only gently send (wit), find the target and afflict it from afar. Wits must be careful with all their potencies; if they overreach themselves and push too hard they risk a violent bout of *spasming*. Excessive use of any of the antics will leave them exhausted and prone to illness. Along with this, after only a few months' strivening, wits will begin to lose their hair until they become completely bald. Some then show their baldness with pride; others cover it with often brightly coloured and jauntily styled wigs. Either is a telltale mark of a wit. They also mark themselves with the *spoor* of an arrow on the arch of an eyebrow, between the eyes or the corner or lower lid of one or both eyes; this is the universally recognised sign of their kind. Wits are trusted even less than *fulgars*, and their surly demeanour (due in some part to the constant pain they suffer) does little to help their grim reputation. See *lahzars*.

Witherscrawl, Mister sour *indexer* of *Winstermill*; punctilious, fastidious, intelligent and rude to those he deems of less worth than himself. Clever enough to write with both hands without having to look.

wordialogue collection of words; a lexicon, normally upon a particular subject or set of subjects.

work docket small cardboard book marked with the Empire's or your own city-state's seal, in which your work history is recorded: the date you started your job, the date you left it, and any outstanding points good or bad your employer feels beholden to mention. A "good" work docket can get you almost any job you wish; a "bad" one relegates you to the meanest of labours. The seal they bear makes them hard to forge.

Wörms ancient city in the east, beyond the *Ichormeer*, situated on the western flanks of the mighty Wormwood forest; made mostly of black stone, with its walls topped with spikes and gallows, and built right in the midst of land that is still *threwdish* even after centuries of effort, Wörms is a grim place full of serious, intense people and renowned for the quality of its *skolds*, especially its *scourges*, and for the *proofing* made there. It was the second city founded by the Skylds – an ancient people who fled over the Mare Periculum to the *Half-Continent* (which they call Westelünd) many thousand years ago. The people of Wörms still proudly call themselves Skylds and their oldest and most powerful houses reckon their descent from those early times.

Wormway, the ~ the *Conduit Vermis*, the Imperial *highroad* that runs from *High Vesting* to *Wörms*; it runs through the Smallish Fells, along the top of Hurdling Migh and right into the red horror of the *Ichormeer*. The region immediately surrounding the Wormway is a *ditchland* known as the Idlewilds: a collection of colony towns, fortresses and cothouses (the homes of the *lamplighters*) each founded and sponsored by different powers, including the *Empire*, *Boschenberg* and *Brandenbrass*.

wurtembottles lazy, fat black flies living as maggots in the putrid bogs of the Wurtemburg Foulness beyond the Imperial boundaries and flying south when transformed from a pupa. Some see them as carriers of foul diseases.

X

xthylistic curd said "zy-lihss-tik" curd; one of the ingredients for *Cathar's Treacle*, being made from the glandular secretions of certain sea-monsters combined with the dried marrow and a powder of well-seasoned bones. See *Cathar's Treacle*.

Y

yardsman one of a number of people responsible for the protection and order of a driveway and accompanying yard outside a *wayhouse* or manor-house or palace or any other such place. Your average yardsman earns from between 25 to 35 sous a year depending on his or her abilities.

Z

Oh, my bursting knees! There is no entry for "z" at all.

APPENDIX 1(A)

THE 16-MONTH CALENDAR OF THE HALF-CONTINENT

Season	Month	1	2	3	4	5	6	7	8	9	10	11	12	13	14	15	16	17	18	19	20	21	22	23	NUMBER OF DAYS
SUMMER ~A~# (THERISTRUM) (JUVINAL) (SANG – BLOOD)	(S) CALOR (CALORIS)	N	L	M	M	D	C	S	N	L	M	M	D	C	S	N	L	M	M	D	C	S (S)	N (S)		22
	ESTOR (ESTORIS)	L	M	M	D	C	S	N	L	M	M	D	C	S	N	L	M	M	D	C	S	N	L	M	23
	PRIOR (PRIORIS)	M	D	C	S	N	L	M	M	D	C [3]	S	N	L	M	M	D	C	S	N	L	M	M	D	23
	LUX% (LEUC)	C [2]	S	N	L	M	M	D	C	S	N	L	M	M	D	C	S	N	L	M	M	D	C	S [5]	23
AUTUMN ~O~ (PETILIUM) (SENTIMUR) (MELANCHOLE – BLACK BILE)	● PILIUM (LIDE)	N	L	M	M	D	C	S	N	L	M	M	D	C	S	N	L	M	M	D	C	S	N ●	L ●	23
	CACHRYS+	M	M	D	C	S	N	L	M	M	D	C	S	N	L	M	M	D	C	S	N	L	M	M	23
	LIRIUM‡ (LIRIO)	D [4]	C	S	N	L	M	M	D	C	S	N	L	M	M	D	C	S	N	L	M	M	D	C	23
	PULCHRYS*	S	N	L	M	M	D	C	S	N	L	M	M	D	C	S	N	L	M	M	D [11]	C	S	N [8]	23
WINTER ~W~ (DIVORTIUM) (BLINDUR) (PHLEGMS – PHLEGM)	(S) BRUMIS* (THE BRUME) (MIDDLEMONTH)	L [12]	M	M	D	C	S	N	L	M	M	D	C	S	N	L	M	M	D	C	S	N (S)	L [6] (S)		22
	PULVIS*	M	M	D	C	S	N	L	M	M	D	C	S	N	L	M	M	D	C	S	N	L	M	M	23
	HEIMIO*	D	C	S	N	L	M	M	D	C	S	N	L	M	M	D	C	S	N	L	M	M	D	C	23
	HERSE	S	N [10]	L	M	M	D	C	S	N	L	M	M	D	C	S	N	L	M	M	D	C	S	N [1]	23
SPRING ~M~ (ARBUSTRUM) (CALIBUR) (CHOLER – YELLOW B????)	● ORIO (ORIS)	L	M	M	D [9]	C	S	N	L [7]	M	M	D	C	S	N	L	M	M	D	C	S	N	L	M ●	23
	UNXIS (JUDE)	M ●	D	C	S	N	L	M	M	D	C	S	N	L	M	M	D	C	S	N	L	M	M	D	23
	ICTERIS	C	S	N	L	M	M	D	C	S	N	L	M	M	D	C	S	N	L	M	M	D	C	S	23
	NARCIS	N	L	M	M	D	C	S	N	L	M	M	D	C	S	N	L	M	M	D	C	S	–		22
		–																							(1)

THE NEW YEAR ALWAYS STARTS ON NEWICH

MIDDLE-MONTH EVE

FOUR-YEAR'S EVE (ONCE EVERY 4 YEARS)

LESTWICH (YEARS END)

APPENDIX 1(B)

DAYS OF THE WEEK (7)

N - **NEWICH** first day of the week
L - **LOONDAY**
M - **MEERDAY**
M - **MIDWICH**
D - **DOMESDAY** a day of rest
C - **CALUMNDAY**
S - **SOLEMNDAY**

VIGILS - DAYS OF OBSERVANCE
(THESE NUMBERS CAN BE FOUND IN THE CALENDAR)

1 - DIRGETIDE
2 - HALFMERRY DAY
3 - MALBELLTIDE
4 - MANNER
5 - MELLOWTIDE
6 - NYCHTHOLD

7 - PLOUGHMONDAY
8 - EIGHT-MONTH'S EVE (CLERK'S VIGIL)
9 - THISGIVINGDAY
10 - GALLOWS NIGHT
11 - VERTUMNUS
12 - MIDTIDE

(S) = SOLSTICE

(E) = EQUINOX

THE DATE UPON WHICH
THE SOLSTICE & EQUINOX
OCCUR IS VARIABLE, HENCE
THE TWO POSSIBLE TIMES
SHOWN FOR EACH EVENT.

* SAID TO BE THE COLDEST MONTHS,
UNFRIENDLY TO TRAVELERS.

% IN THE OLD CALENDARS THIS WAS
ONCE THE FIRST MONTH OF THE YEAR

\+ THESE TWO MONTHS WERE ONCE IN
THE REVERSE ORDER. THEY CAME TO
BE SWAPPED WHEN THE EXCEEDINGLY
TALL AND EXCESSIVELY SPOILED
DAUGHTER OF MORIBUND SCEPTIC III
COMPLAINED SO BITTERLY THAT SHE
SHOULD HAVE BEEN BORN IN THE
BEAUTIFUL-SOUNDING MONTH OF
LIRIUM RATHER THAN THE UGLY-
SOUNDING (AS SHE THOUGHT IT)
MONTH OF CACHRYS. SHE MADE
COURT LIFE IMPOSSIBLE UNTIL HER
MUCH-HARASSED FATHER DECREED
THE SWAP BY IMPERIAL EDICT. THE
CHANGE HAS REMAINED EVER SINCE,
EVEN AFTER A WAR WAS FOUGHT
OVER IT.

APPENDIX 2

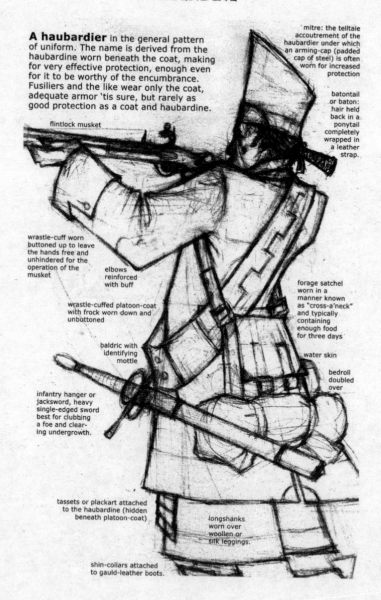

A haubardier in the general pattern of uniform. The name is derived from the haubardine worn beneath the coat, making for very effective protection, enough even for it to be worthy of the encumbrance. Fusiliers and the like wear only the coat, adequate armor 'tis sure, but rarely as good protection as a coat and haubardine.

mitre: the telltale accoutrement of the haubardier under which an arming-cap (padded cap of steel) is often worn for increased protection

batontail or baton: hair held back in a ponytail completely wrapped in a leather strap.

flintlock musket

wrastle-cuff worn buttoned up to leave the hands free and unhindered for the operation of the musket

elbows reinforced with buff

wrastle-cuffed platoon-coat with frock worn down and unbuttoned

baldric with identifying mottle

forage satchel worn in a manner known as "cross-a'neck" and typically containing enough food for three days

water skin

bedroll doubled over

infantry hanger or jacksword, heavy single-edged sword best for clubbing a foe and clearing undergrowth.

tassets or plackart attached to the haubardine (hidden beneath platoon-coat)

longshanks worn over woollen or silk leggings.

shin-collars attached to gauld-leather boots.

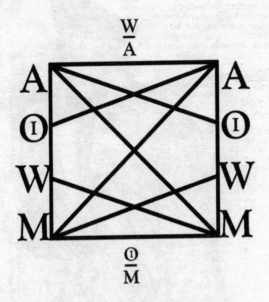

THE KÖRNCHENFLECTER
OR PARTS-WHEEL OR PRINCIPIA CIRCUM

A DIAGRAM OF THE REACTIONS
BETWEEN THE FOUR ELEMENTS WHERE
A= FIRE; ⓪ = EARTH; W = WATER; M = AIR
Fire reacts with earth, earth reacts with fire.
Earth reacts with water, water reacts with earth.
Water reacts with air, air reacts with water.
Water retards fire.
Earth retards air.

APPENDIX 4

A navigator

The black-and-white chequers upon his baldric (the mottle of the concometrists) can just be seen through the open part of the maincoat. By the maincoat and the shaved hair, it is clear this fellow works as a consultant for the Empire's navies.

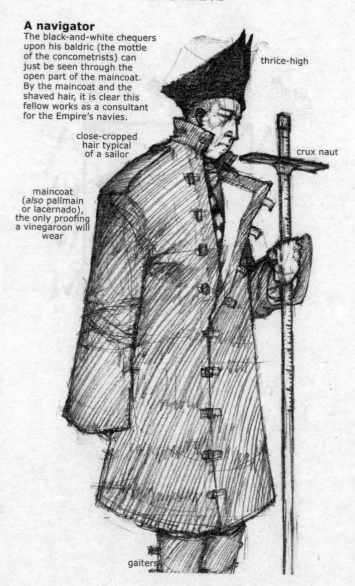

thrice-high

crux naut

close-cropped hair typical of a sailor

maincoat (*also* pallmain or lacernado), the only proofing a vinegaroon will wear

gaiters

A wayfarer of the Soutlands

heavily armed and well provisioned, this individual is equipped for existence in the ditchlands and even the wilds. His clothing provides fine protection from harm and foul weather. Under the jackcoat (which, of course, is gaulded) would be some kind of proofed vest, and longshanks have gaulded "plates" sewn into their lining.

This person is so accoutred that he could easily be employed as an ambuscadier (light infantry skirmisher) should there be an opportunity. Indeed, the fellow may well have been occupied in such manner at one time or another.

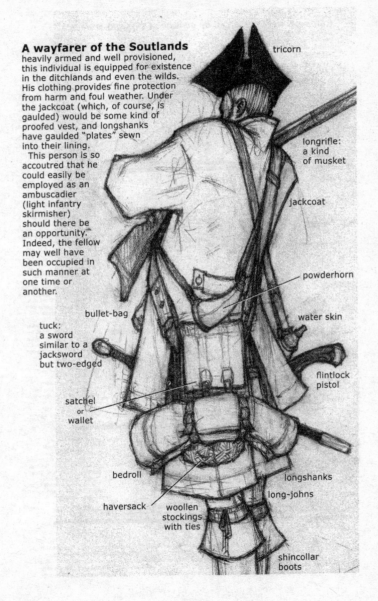

tricorn

longrifle: a kind of musket

jackcoat

powderhorn

bullet-bag

water skin

tuck: a sword similar to a jacksword but two-edged

flintlock pistol

satchel or wallet

bedroll

longshanks

long-johns

haversack

woollen stockings with ties

shincollar boots

APPENDIX 6

Rams-of-war: *presented by division of size and armament*

gun^b=gun-broad:
the number of artillery
pieces running down
one broadside.

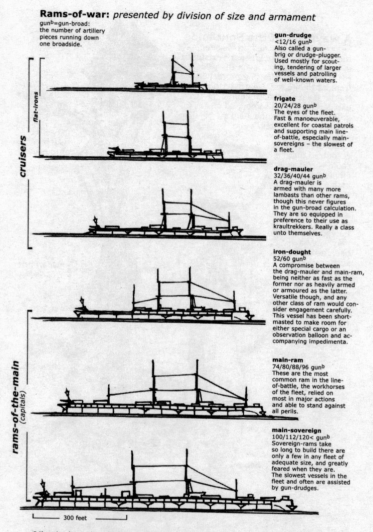

gun-drudge
<12/16 gun^b
Also called a gun-
brig or drudge-plugger.
Used mostly for scout-
ing, tendering of larger
vessels and patrolling
of well-known waters.

frigate
20/24/28 gun^b
The eyes of the fleet.
Fast & manoeuverable,
excellent for coastal patrols
and supporting main line-
of-battle, especially main-
sovereigns – the slowest of
a fleet.

drag-mauler
32/36/40/44 gun^b
A drag-mauler is
armed with many more
lambasts than other rams,
though this never figures
in the gun-broad calculation.
They are so equipped in
preference to their use as
kraultrekkers. Really a class
unto themselves.

iron-dought
52/60 gun^b
A compromise between
the drag-mauler and main-ram,
being neither as fast as the
former nor as heavily armed
or armoured as the latter.
Versatile though, and any
other class of ram would consider engagement carefully.
This vessel has been short-
masted to make room for
either special cargo or an
observation balloon and accompanying impedimenta.

main-ram
74/80/88/96 gun^b
These are the most
common ram in the line-
of-battle, the workhorses
of the fleet, relied on
most in major actions
and able to stand against
all perils.

main-sovereign
100/112/120< gun^b
Sovereign-rams take
so long to build there are
only a few in any fleet of
adequate size, and greatly
feared when they are.
The slowest vessels in the
fleet and often are assisted
by gun-drudges.

flat-irons

cruisers

rams-of-the-main
(capitals)

|— 300 feet —|

** there is a lesser class of vessel: **sloops**, small wooden sailing vessels, inexpensive when compared to
the exorbitance of even a small ironclad gastriner, used by less powerful states as advice boats, spies,
and for post runs. A gaggle of these little wooden sailers can still be a significant annoyance to a ram and
their command is often given to the most reckless, daring and foolhardy of the lieutenants. Sloops rate
guns-broad from 2 to 9 guns, though even the largest ship-brig is still much smaller than a gun-drudge.*

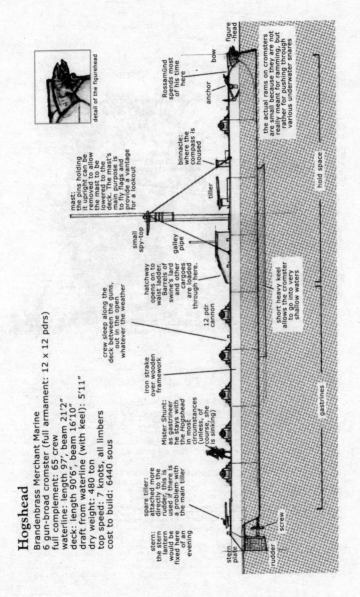

detail of the figurehead

Hogshead

Brandenbrass Merchant Marine
6 gun-broad cromster (full armament: 12 x 12 pdrs)
full complement: 65 crew
waterline: length 97', beam 21'2"
deck: length 90'6", beam 16'10"
draft from waterline (with keel): 5'11"
dry weight: 480 ton
top speed: 7 knots, all limbers
cost to build: 6440 sous

figure
-head

bow

Rossamünd
spends most
of his time
here

anchor

the actual rams on cromsters
are small because they are not
really meant for ramming, but
rather for pushing through
various underwater snares

mast:
the pins holding
it upright can be
removed to allow
the mast to be
lowered to the
deck. The mast's
main purpose is
to fly flags and
provide a vantage
for a lookout

binnacle:
where the
compass is
housed

hold space

tiller

small
spy-top

galley
pipe

crew sleep along the
deck between the guns,
out in the open
whatever the weather

hatchway
opens on to
waist ladder.
Barrels of
swine's lard
and other
cargoes are
loaded
through here.

short heavy keel
allows the cromster
to go into very
shallow waters

12 pdr
cannon

Iron strake
over wooden
framework

Mister Shunt:
as gastrineer
he stays with
the Hogshead
in most
circumstances
(unless, of
course, she
is sinking)

gastrines

spare tiller:
attached more
directly to the
rudder; this is
used if there is
a problem with
the main tiller

stern:
the stern
lantern
would be
fixed here
of an
evening

screw

stern
plate

rudder

APPENDIX 8

HAROLD FACES THE SLOTHOG
ALONE BEFORE THE GATES OF CLEMENTINE

This is the engraving found in the pamphlet Rossamünd reads after
his beating from Gosling; the one he stares at for a moment when he
is talking to Fransitart. You can just make out the cylinders and
satchels – so famously empty – hanging about Harold's waist, while
the "beast-handlers" struggle to keep the Slothog under control.
The picture is a romantic view of the event. In truth, Harold was one
of over a hundred who tackled the Slothog, though he was certainly
the only teratologist among them. Still, propagandists tell of him as
standing alone, and that is how popular history chooses to
remember him.

THE
HALF-CONTINENT
~ AN EXPLODED VIEW ~

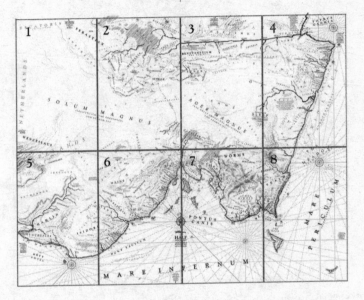

On the following pages will appear eight enlargements of the map of the Half-Continent, roughly following the divisions shown above. Numbers in the grid correspond to the number at the bottom of each enlargement.

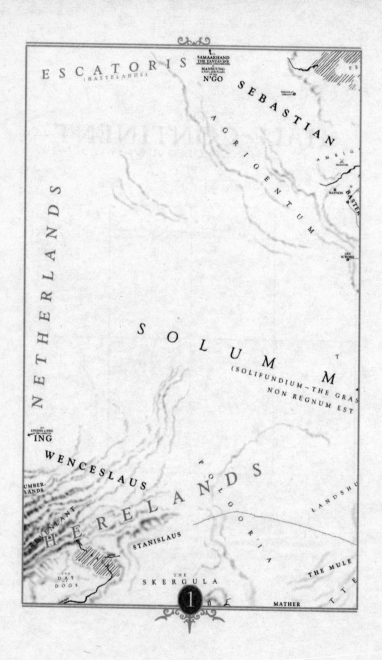

ESCATORIS
(BASTELANDS)

THE
SAMAAKHAND
THE TANTAVINE
MANKUUNG
& TOFL-AND PLAINS
OF THE
N'GO

SEBASTIAN

FE

A
G
R
I
G
E
N
T
U
M

SEBASTIAN
ORGANO

AMBIG

BASTION

BAST

GRE
SCROBE

N
E
T
H
E
R
L
A
N
D
S

S   O   L   U   M   M

(SOLIFUNDIUM – THE GRAS
NON REGNUM EST

T

TO
CHANG-LYNG
AND THE LANDS OF
ING

WENCESLAUS

UMBER-
LANDS

P
O
L
O
O
R
I
A

LANDSHU

REVENENT

H E R E L A N D S

STANISLAUS

THE
DAY
DOGS

THE
SKERGULA

THE MULE

TTE

MATHER

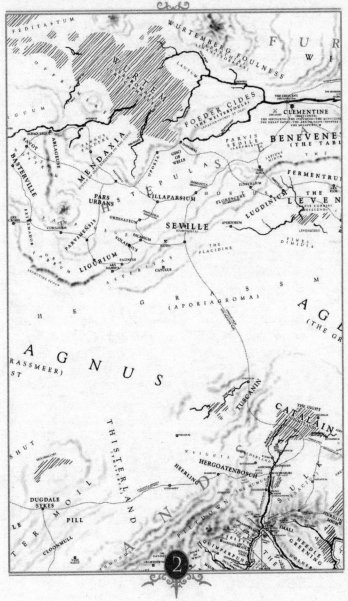

FEDITASTUM

WURTEMBERG FOULNESS
(BLANKENHALL)

F U R
W I

OPPRIUM

WURTEX
(REMPRONIAL)

LAUTUM

THE CRESCENT
(ORTHODOXA)

FOEDER CIDES
(THE WATERVOLKS)

✕ CLEMENTINE
THE LORES · THE EVENTURES
THE ORTICUME · THE INQUIRIUM · THE QUINTETTE
THE GREAT DAYS · THE ARK · THE SOON · EPISTRES
THE MAXIPINUM

BENEVENE
(THE TABLE

PARVIS
SEDILE
(SEPTIMINI)

SAVOY

ABLAEGUS

THE
LEPIDO MINOR

LUNA

THE

FERMENTRUM

ABRAQUEACE

TARNUE
DERE

GISO
OF WELLS

BASTERVILLE

MENDAXIA

OPORIA

THE
LEVEN

HIS CURRENT
NEGLIGUND

PULAS

HORTUS
DAMANCY

LUNSTHLUM

LUGDINIUM

PARS
URBANS

VILLAPARSIUM

FLORESCERE

TABU

EXTERMINADOR
LABRUM

COMUGURIS

ORDINATEUM

SEVILLE
(CORONILIA)

AVERPORUM

FINES
DIMIDIA

ARX
CROWN

TARVMESSIS

ESCARIUM

PATEO

THE
PLACIDINE

LEVENWISES

LIGURIUM

VOLABRIUS

PAGINFUR

ARX
MANUL

CATULUS

M
S

ASPERITAS SCOUR

ASPERITAS

G

R

A

S

S

AGD
(THE G

H

E

G

(APORIAGROMA)

RASSMEER)
ST

A G N U S

SHUT

MOORHOUND

THISTERLAND

PURIOUN

TUSCANIN

THE GIGHT

CATALAIN

WEIGHTS

SIDEBLAW

S

DUGDALE
SYKES

PILL

MOIL

HEERLING

HERGOATENBOSCH

PISTOWN

PIETOWN

U

L

L

BRACELAN

NEEDLE
MIGHT

LE

CLOONMULL

ELSE

SMALL

NEEDLE
GREENING

HOLDER

A

D

THE

QUIMPERPUM
PORT OF
DEAD LUCK

429

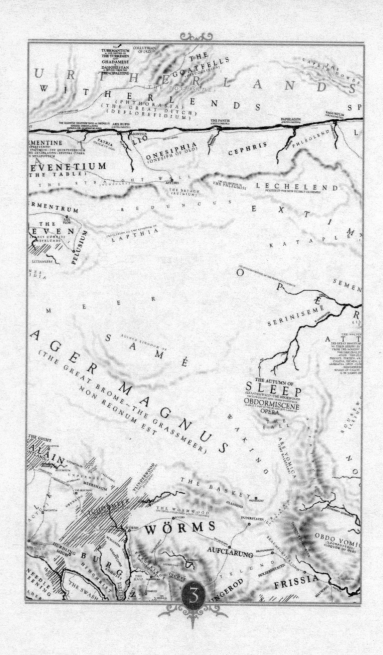

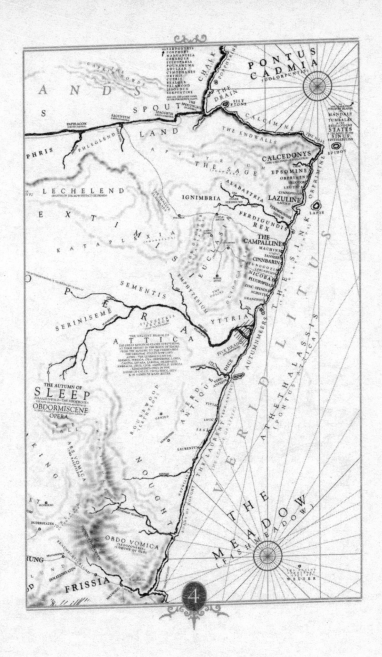

431

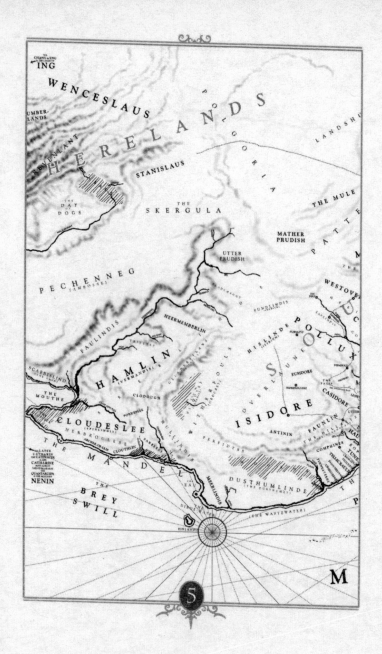

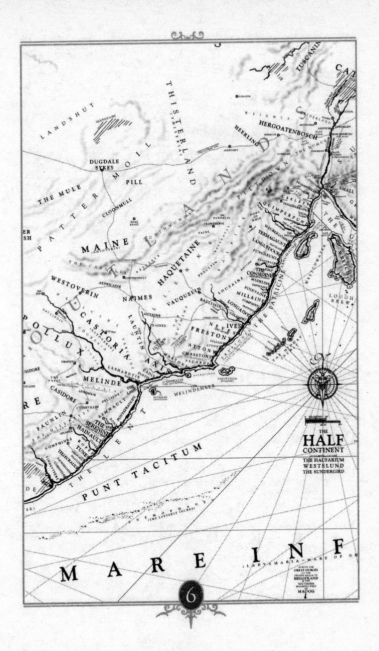

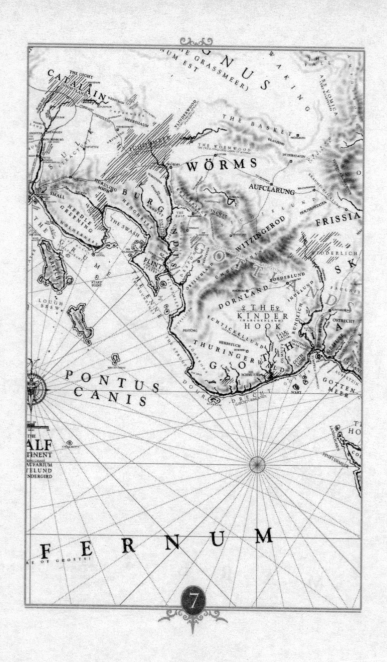

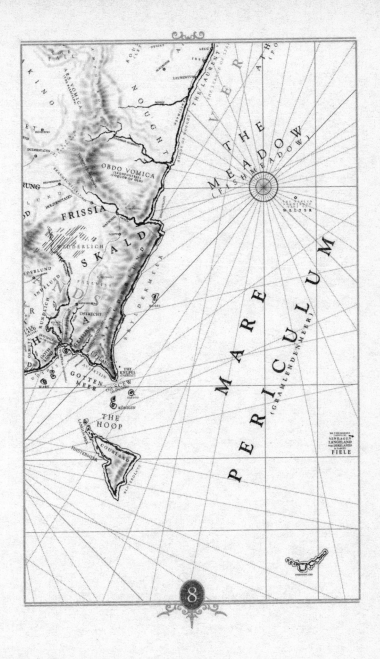